70802
Son of Iniquity

C H A R L I E   T .   S M I T H

PAGE PUBLISHING, INC.
Conneaut Lake, PA

First originally published by Page Publishing 2020

ISBN 978-1-6624-1135-9 (pbk)
ISBN 978-1-6624-1136-6 (digital)

Printed in the United States of America

Part One

"It's a gawd-damn shame wat they done to dat child," someone said. Whether or not the two people that spoke were conversing directly with each other was unknown to Li'l One Gone—he had his head hung low as he made his way through the wall of bodies—but an immediate response was heard when another female solemnly cried out, "Yeah, dis shit is get'n sick-a-ning!" A few other people in the crowd "Amened" in agreement.

Big Happy, being ever so jubilant, excitedly nudged his buddy in the side, attempting to speak lowly so that his words didn't reach anyone else's ears, but loud enough so the person his words were directed to could hear him clearly. His timing was off, seconds before the noise of the gathering crowd would have aided in further concealing his words, for as soon as he began to speak, as if on que, the crowd fell deafly quiet. The silence of the crowd carried his voice. "Man, look at tha pussy on dat bitch! It looks like she got two hound dog ears between her legs!"

Some in the crowd gasped, others giggled at his words, and briefly the tension in the parking lot of the Bricks was lifted as the look-a-whoers set in on Big Happy.

Li'l One Gone's mama had stopped abruptly, her sudden halt causing him to bump into her. The impact of their collision almost knocked Li'l One Gone off his feet. Up until then, Li'l One Gone had never looked up from the ground or backward; his only concern was trying to put as much distance as possible between him and the lifeless body lying on the filthy concrete.

"Nigga, you some silly'!' and "Disrespectful!" someone else said, burglarizing his mama's sentence.

"Dat woman dead as a muthafucka, and you worried 'bout what betwixt her legs?" she said, shaking her head. "A nigga ain't shit," his mama stated. Embarrassment was written all over Big Happy's face. He looked like a teenager that got caught by his mom jacking off. People in the crowd added their two cents to what Li'l One Gone's mama dished out. In shame, he briskly walked away from the crowd, his buddy trailing behind him at a safe distance.

Reality had left Li'l One Gone. Physically he was present, but consciously, well, that goes without saying, for only the Omnipotent One, and he alone knew exactly where his mind was.

The pantomime of human frailty was exulted throughout the crowd. Everyone his mama and he approached as they traversed past the ever-growing crowd bore it. Words were unnecessary; people nodded and shook their heads. Tragedy had connected everyone out there telepathically.

Running was the coward's way out; pride was the only thing that held him in check. Deep down inside, what Li'l One Gone wanted more than anything else was to be anywhere other than where he was. Though moving rapidly, his mama wasn't moving fast away from the scene to his liking.

Every sad face his eyes rested on was like another nail through the heart. Overwhelmingly, holding back the tears didn't help any; the more he fought them back, the more they adamantly escaped his eyes. Fighting them just blurred his blurry vision more so.

Well away from the crowd, he broke down, letting out body-racking sobs. Li'l One Gone's mama grabbed him and held him tight to her person like she used to in times past, when the days were less colder. Even in his darkest hour, through all the mixed emotions, saving face was priority. Once hard, always hard. Big boys don't cry. At least that was one of the many sayings of the streets. Looking around to see if anyone was paying attention to this affectionate moment between mother and son. Satisfied, without wiping the eye water from his cheeks, he dug deeper into the comfortable embrace of his last love, yet neither the heat of her flesh nor his tears could reach the depths of his being and warm his soul.

"What happened ova there?" someone asked over the blaring of sirens and roaring of engines of the emergency response units.

"A girl got shot over in dem projects!" Li'l One Gone's mama yelled over the surrounding noise. All the while, Li'l One Gone kept the side of his face buried into her chest.

"I hope she's gonna be okay." Genuine concern could be felt through the inquirer's voice.

There wasn't a cloud visible for miles before the shooting, or during it, but without warning, the sky opened up and released a light shower. No one had time to react, and the rain vanished as quickly as it had appeared, the great ball of fire above planet Earth shining with such an intense force that the rays that engulfed the area were too bright for the naked eye to view without squinting the eyelids.

The light penetrated the atmosphere like gamma rays instead of sunrays, and with the same sudden flash from a camera, the rays came then ascended. If the light had been prolonged any longer than it was, everyone in the area would have suffered from scorched retinas.

His mama hugged Li'l One Gone tighter, as if to shield him from the revelation of her reply. "She jus' gave up her spirit. God done called her home." Letting out an audible sigh, she continued, "Yeah, when ya dat close to do doe, all yah can do is close ya eyes an' let go." She looked down, gazing into his teary eyes. "If yah wanna go home, go on 'head there. I'ma hang 'round a li'l bit," she stated to Li'l One Gone, gently pushing him away from her, as if to say, "Go on."

Reluctantly he posted up on the sidewalk. At that point, being alone in the house, just him and his thoughts, didn't seem like such a good idea. As usual, when a nefarious act got pulled off, people of all ages flocked into the streets; no sane person would ever volunteer themselves to the business end of a pistol, but many would wade through water to view the aftermath of the release of hot lead. Today was no exception. Some individuals didn't take the time or the liberty to look presentable before they left their home, coming out as is to see the carnage that the coward who pulled the trigger had left behind.

This level of violence was new to most, yet old to some. Everyone wanted to get a look at the empty vessel that once contained a beautiful living soul. Word of T'Sharon's sudden demise had spread through the neighborhood and beyond the tracks like the floodwaters of a levee breach. Those who had chosen to remain in the comfort of their homes knew just as much about who it was and how it happened as those on the streets knew dusk had fallen. It was a very sad day across the tracks. The community had lost a daughter.

Folks who didn't know her personally or anything about her felt the same degree of pain and anger as those who had the privilege of being in her company the instant they looked upon her lifeless angelic face. Although neither of them expressed their true thoughts on feelings in front of the crowd, most of the men took it the hardest. A great injustice had been done. Any crime against a woman or child would rub any man with or without salt in their veins the wrong way. Along with anger, many felt cheated looking at such a fine young specimen lying murdered in the streets.

Besides her immediate family and closest friends, no one else could measure the pain her death had inflicted upon the chubby kid that walked with a limp.

Death wasn't a stranger to him, nor was the concept of life. Death was supposed to be a merciless foe that struck down the elderly and the sick, not those full of life—at least that was the perception Li'l One Gone had about the matter when Grandma Mama, his grandmother, passed away. T'Sharon helped him find solace after her departure, though. Dramatic as it was, she took some sting out of it; her mellifluous voice and the way she put her words together could convince a person engulfed in flames that everything was going to be just fine. Who was going to comfort him now? T'Sharon was now a lifeless body.

Li'l One Gone now stood alone, head hanging low, feeling low, with no one to comfort him, yards away from the one who cared for him when no one else truly did, yards away from the one that was always there when he needed someone, but this time she could be of no assistance, but not because she didn't have the desire to. Truth be told, she cared about Li'l One Gone as much as he cared about her, maybe even more. Her not caring wasn't the reason; she couldn't come to his rescue because she had crossed over into the realm of the unseen.

Days came and went, and visions of T'Sharon lying dormant on the pavement still filled his mind (when he did roam the streets, his eyes were glued to the pavement). The pressure from the ice-cold hand that gripped his heart did not loosen. Weeks went by. Nothing succeeded at lightening his very lugubrious expression.

It was said that what didn't break a man made a man. God created man from dust, and the hood was now polishing the stone it was turning him into.

The Life is only for those who can stand the pain and keep it pushing. Not yet out of grammar school and already experiencing the pain of loss to the streets, also facing the task of rising above it all alone, yet desperately fighting against the sleight of hand of the odds. The test had been administered, a test where there wasn't any correct answer. It was not designed to pass or fail anyone, only for conditioning the mind of the dreadful ones that aspired to live the life or play the game. Many would enter the game, but only few would survive, and even fewer would make it in the game.

Overcoming the pain of someone close being murdered in the streets is a challenge for an adult that ends two ways: a heart of compassion for mankind or no love whatsoever. For an adolescent, it's even more challenging. Oftentimes, the child may withdraw from society, shelling up their feelings, or they tend to exhibit poor impulse control, striking out verbally and physically repeatedly even if what they're striking out against doesn't pose any real danger. The latter was the case for Li'l One Gone.

Juvenile rattlesnakes are deadlier than adult ones because they haven't learned how to regulate their venom. Similar to them is a child whose memories are filled with visions of evil, and a heart filled with tragedy in a society where violence is presumably the only resolution to all situations that may arise, where one finds it hard to direct their feelings accordingly. Such was the case for Li'l One Gone and countless other juveniles in the society whose lives are forged by acts of violence.

Conditioning defines character. Once faced with a traumatic event, one can either fold and choose a new direction or stand firm, planting their feet deep in the dirt. Either way, living must go on. No one should have to confront a tragic death at such a young age, but that has been and will always be the norm when living across the tracks in old Southside Baton Rouge, better known as the Bottom. A place where the unlucky can't buy luck and the hopeless view prison as God's answer to their prayer for subsistence.

Living did continue on for Li'l One Gone, but with a slanted twist. It wasn't the same as it was before T'Sharon's demise, unbeknownst to him at that time, nor would it ever be the same. Even the snacks that she often shared with him, which he delightfully enjoyed, no longer produced the same effect they once did. Consuming them alone caused a strange taste to rise up into his mouth. Not only were his taste buds in disarray; they also wreaked havoc on his digestive system while he ate them. Every aspect of his existence had been thrown off its course by the loss of his friend, his caregiver, his loved one.

Li'l One Gone had begun to slip, and eventually, he had fallen into an emotional dark spot. Memories of her ran rampantly through his mind often after the incident had happened. A strong feeling of emptiness overcame him. When he was out chilling in the park or strolling through the Bricks, his eyes would automatically fall upon the spot where T'Sharon was slain. He would hold his eyes shut for several moments, hoping that when he reopened them, she would be there, standing, waiting for his approach, just like on numerous other occasions. But the only thing that awaited him when he reopened his eyes were tears of anger mixed with a touch of sorrow.

For a while thereafter, life seemed as if it no longer had any other purpose but to somehow, someway fill that void in his life that prevailed over everyday living. Nothing he did eradicated the debilitating, soul-sickening feelings he harbored. Everywhere he went, whatever he was engaged in, whether it was to be fun, a learning experience, or even something as simple as brushing his teeth, visions of T'Sharon, without effort, would approach the forefront of his mind.

Although the overwhelming shock of her life being stolen away would eventually, but also slowly, diminish as the ticks rotated and rerotated around the clock, the stain from the pain on his soul would always remain.

Lost love changes most people, albeit in different ways. Li'l One Gone had been rocked to his core when his first true, tangible object of affection had been removed from his life violently, though in his absence, yet right before him. When things got tricky for him or un-understandable, as things always did in the neighborhood, the very one that helped make sense out of that which made no sense was now removed from the land of the living, completely out of his life, never to be returned, by the senseless act of a coward, without any retribution. She was known and loved by many, including those who were capable of seeking vengeance; but no one did, nor did they even mention retaliation when the subject of their conversations became the murder of the sister, mother, and daughter of the neighborhood.

Acceptance is always easier said than done.

As with all of them, the awakening was a sad occasion. Wails of deep sorrow and sniffling filled the church. Li'l One Gone sat numbly, slouched down in a pew several rows back from the front of the church, where the once-significant person in his life lay in a gold-trimmed white casket, surrounded by an array of lovely flowers. The people in the row directly ahead of him had slid over to allow another mourner to sit down in the packed church. He was glad that the couple in front of him had shifted over to where they obscured his line of sight of the front of the church; otherwise, he wouldn't have been able, on his own, to peel his eyes away from the empty vessel called a body that formerly contained a vibrant life.

At the cemetery, after the last words of her funeral service had been spoken, and as the container that contained T'Sharon's remains was being lowered into the earth, Li'l One Gone stood there staring into the hole, speechless. Wiping away the water that flowed from his eyes was useless, for as quickly as and the more he wiped the wetness off his cheeks, the more rampant his eyes produced the cause of the wetness. Everyone who was mentally stable enough gathered themselves and proceeded to leave the burial site. Some who were too emotionally shattered by the funeral ceremony left with the aid of others.

While the gravediggers were performing the final deposition of her remains, Li'l One Gone watched, paralyzed with emotions, as the soil that was being shoveled into the rectangular opening of the earth began to bury T'Sharon's casket, which now lay within the opening. The sound of someone calling out to him from the direction of the ones who had departed from the burial site reached his ears; he tried to reply, but no words would come out of him, only whimpers escaping his lips. As he turned toward the direction of the voice calling out to him, all of a sudden, out of nowhere, the cemetery faded into a solemn, deep darkness. Minutes later, Li'l One Gone awakened in the back seat of a moving vehicle to a set of unfamiliar yet compassionate eyes staring down at him. Dazed and confused, he closed his eyes, settled his head back down onto the softness and warmth of the lady's thighs, and embraced the comfort she provided.

T'Sharon had been locked in a casket, laid beneath the soil, and entombed for many moons now. But Li'l One Gone still hadn't shaken off the thoughts that produced the feelings of depression; running a head game on himself proved to be futile. As he coached himself not to cry, the eye water forcibly disobeyed him, forming and falling out of his eyes uncontrollably, while body-racking sobs escaped his lips, breaking the quiet of the night as he stared at the walls.

A recovering addict is advised to stay away from other addicts and familiar places because they increase the chances of relapsing. When in the company of an aggravating or an uncomfortable situation, one can remove themselves from it. If there is a known location where there is danger or a high risk for potential danger, the location can be avoided. Even if a person saturates their bloodstream with liquor or contaminates the oxygen carried by the blood to the brain with weed smoke, it's still not a refuge from the self; there's no place to go to escape unwanted thoughts. At least there wasn't a place for Li'l One Gone.

Inadvertently, constantly going through the pain from some form of loss or another ill-feeling-producing event helped him develop a keen know-how to overcome adversity and sidestep opposition. A feat that had been a vital tool to sustain his minor role in the game or while attempting to be a part of the life that most people in the street lived. In 20 percent of the time, his method proved to be successful; the other 80 percent could be credited to the favor of which he had been bestowed by the thug gods. Losing what had started out as a secret crush that evolved into a friendship—perhaps a friendship that ultimately one day could have become a sexual relationship once Li'l One Gone had become a fully developed adult—proved to be a two-punch adversary to reckon with.

Growing up in an environment where violence lurked in the nooks and crannies, waiting to jump out at the sound of the bell to show its ugly face, Li'l One Gone, over time, was forced to develop a propensity to brutality. Emotionally wrecked, unlearned in positive ways to suppress or overcome his personal uneasiness, he turned to a self-destructive behavior, one that T'Sharon had attempted to coach him away from with tender loving care, as a means to get over his feelings.

Fistfights became his way of coping with his issues. Yet still after the excitement of the backyard scuffles and street brawls, the physical pain he endured only was a temporary fix toward repairing or fixing his mental health.

Nothing he had done thus far seemed to fully remove the numb, hollow feeling that had not only invaded but also totally infected his heart like hepatitis eventually does the liver.

Excessive alone time was thought of as being the best road to travel for recouping from the tragedy, so he did so, but isolation only added more pressure on his head. Withdrawal from human contact and outside influences didn't help his situation; it only succeeded in multiplying the anguish, putting a tremendous strain on his mental health.

Not only that, his state of solitude gave an opportunity for the voice to increase its presence, thus exercising a strong influence on his fragile mental state. Every moment alone sucked the seams out of his already-broken soul and, with the aid of the voice, added a small dose of rage to his mentality.

No matter how hard he fought to get past the imposing thoughts of death, it still lingered on in his head. When he slept, dreams of family members or what were once his associates being unresponsive to the call or touch recurred. Some mornings and nights, images of bloody murders, accompanied by the voice instigating, were so debilitating that all he wanted to do was lie stationarily, with the covers over his head, and descend to a place where his thoughts were no longer haunting, vexing him to pieces.

Li'l One Gone was on the verge of unraveling in the worst way. Life as he knew it was at a complete standstill. He stopped attending school regularly, and he only played sometimes. Getting loaded, mobbing around the neighborhood in a stupor became routine. The majority of his time was spent sitting on the railroad tracks, staring at nothing; although everything outside his mind was moving rapidly, everything inside was stuck in the neutral position.

T'Sharon's demise hit him harder than anyone expected. Reaching out was useless. Everyone he tried to strike up a conversation with about what happened or about death in general avoided the topic completely. If they did engage in the confab, they quickly proceeded to shy away from the topic of conversation, like speaking about it was a way of contracting it. Those who did give insight about it, the information given wasn't to his liking, nor were their solutions to overcoming the grief that death caused to the survivors the solutions that Li'l One Gone fancied.

Relief from his great state of depression came about gradually. The source was always available. Li'l One Gone carried it with him everywhere he went; all he had to do was look within himself. Time and distraction were also a part of the remedy to end his depression.

After spending plenty of time meditating and wearing himself out to no purpose, he eventually got tired of carrying around that unwanted weight of grief and soon just let it go. Somehow, purpose and meaning were forged from the stress, chaos, and pain that consumed his life. The pull of the game and the life gave Li'l One Gone a sense of belonging that, in turn, filled some of the emptiness in his life.

Rule of thumb in the streets: whoever's administration a child fall under contributes to that child's character, attitude, mannerism, and ultimately, personality. Therefore, if a dope fiend takes that lost soul under their wing, that lost soul will become a dope fiend. If a hustler takes the kid that's reaching out for direction, that kid will eventually become a hustler also.

With no influence, the unsteady, lost soul on the streets is tossed to and fro. Reverting to his behavior pre-T'Sharon was like placing an ice cube on the hood of a car on a steamy, hot South Louisiana summer day and trying to prevent it from melting. She was the thread that held the materials that fashioned Li'l One Gone's idle mind and contumacious heart together.

Inevitably, another piece of personality had been designed by life out of malice for him. Along with the other derivatives of malice that had been woven in him already through force of circumstance, malice had been cut out from the fashioner's design, then added to the collective pattern of materials from which Li'l One Gone's personality was being made of.

Progressing in life then regressing successively over and over would cause the average person to become volatile in some way, restraining oneself, becoming harder and harder. *Kill* was a recurring thought that frequented his mind; choosing a suitable victim was his only problem.

The Good Book says, "When an unclean spirit goes out of a man, he goes through dry places, seeking rest, and find none. Then he says, 'I will return to my house [heart] from which I came.' And when he comes he finds it empty, swept, and put in order. Then he goes and takes with him seven other spirits more wicked than himself, and they enter and dwell there; and the last state of that man is worse than the first."

He was already born with the spirit of an old Vic in him, and T'Sharon quelled the beast within him by putting him on a path that would lead him toward becoming a righteous man in the eyes of society, mainly the one outside the society from which they lived.

He chose to make a U-turn and travel a road he thought he was familiar with. Lost and not knowing, in the process of recouping from the pain, Li'l One Gone invited something sinister into his life, blind to the fact that when one sells their soul, they're bound to pay something.

All the hope that he had possessed had been voided and replaced with something that eventually would be detrimental to himself and others.

Besides every cell in his body being engrossed with making money, his heart was also bifurcated, one part malicious toward humanity, by dealing death; the other a strong desire to be nefarious, because of the pain he felt.

Overcoming the pain and staying on top of it by any means was priority. Vengeance became a mission, love turned to hate, promise faded into disparity; breaking his promise to Grandma Mama was a catharsis and the answer.

Grandma Mama was absolutely truthful and accurate about everything. She put her two cents in whenever she spoke of things to come. Her words were law way before her beloved grandson came to existence. She had gained a reputation of sagacity and prescience. Like most youngsters, Li'l One Gone didn't realize the value of her wisdom until he ran his head into a wall. She had made Li'l One Gone promise that no matter how many times the voice called out to him or how relentless it was at trying to persuade him, he would ignore it, stay positive, and most of all, never answer. Answering would not only cause the jinx to fall upon him for breaking his vow to an elder, but he would also suffer a premature death.

She had known all the while, even before the words had left her mouth, that he wouldn't expire in a natural state as we know it, but she concealed her knowledge of submitting to the call of the voice in order to protect him, wanting no more than any other grandparent would for their grandchildren an unrestricted opportunity at a prosperous, blissful life.

The entity that lurked in the balance, stalking him, was a principality, a principality that didn't want to end life; instead, it was searching for a vessel to fill and take total control over.

An act once accomplished, a thousand deaths wouldn't be equivalent to what was in store for the victim that it entered. She figured telling him that death would become of him if he gave into the pressure that the force was sure to apply would be enough to frighten even the slightest of curiosity out of him and persuade him to stand fast, resist the temptation to respond, and oppose the urge to bend to its will. A tale of bad luck and death concocted by Grandma Mama for the sole purpose of having a preventable measure to protect the well-being of Li'l One Gone went against what she not only believed but also preached often. Despite her strict policy of honesty, her paternal instinct overrode her moral standards, yet it was all in vain.

Feeling powerless and inadequate, Li'l One Gone felt he had no other choice but to submit. The decision was a no-brainer—he had to do what he had to do. Embrace the pain and do nothing or feel guilty while getting the job done. Regardless, whether it was guilt or pain, the results were going to be the same: he still was going to be feeling some type of way. Although with that in mind, defying Grandma Mama weighing heavily on his mind, he convinced himself that as long as the ends justified the means, his route was the right one.

Now, it wasn't that he was too young or physically incapable to do what his heart propelled him to do. Underage people have been known to have had an impact in their community, even on society as a whole, leaving their marks in more ways than one. Lack of resources proved to be a stumbling block to the progression of his mission, along with not being able to "think past go," to contrive the operation and achieve the end results his heart desired.

What the voice had to offer was the hand he fanned with. Every aspect of the plan the voice formulated coincided with Li'l One Gone's mission and personality. In his mind, there wasn't anything to lose but all to gain; besides, he now had a comforter and a friend.

The voice promised to guide and make everything right in his life; all he had to do was, first and foremost, abide fully, be willing and ready to cause pain or even take a life, without any hesitation, the voice assisting him every step of the way to achieve any and every objective he laid out before him. Simple enough.

17

Truth be told, so many people "point the finger" at their neighborhood, the society, or the company they keep. Some go as far as blaming being born with less for the way that they are. In one formed fashion or another, everyone is a victim of circumstance to a certain degree. Most like to believe that they're in control of their own destiny, captain of their own ship, but the truth of the matter is that much of everyone's lives is dictated by supernatural forces far beyond their comprehension, let alone their control.

Some believe it, others deny the fact outright, some agree but don't act on it, yet others agree with it wholeheartedly and live their lives consciously aware of the fact that their lives are being guided. Regardless if anyone agrees with it, acknowledges it, or even accepts it, humans are puppets with their strings pulled by someone or something greater than themselves.

There's an unseen force that guides humanity toward the divine light of the Creator, and there's also a force that guides mankind toward the darkness of the enemy of the Creator. Blinded by pain, anguish, and overall mental instability, Li'l One Gone made an executive decision and became in tuned with the thing that was encumbered with the task of pulling his strings. What he didn't know was that the one that was now pulling his string was sent with a specific task by one greater than the voice itself.

The body of T'Sharon had been long gone, Mother Nature had done her job removing the bloodstains off the pavement, along with any other trace of a homicide, but the image of T'Sharon lying twisted remained vivid in Li'l One Gone's mind as he walked by, staring at the spot she had lain, slain. Emotions grabbed him. He had come so far and still had much further to go to let feelings get the best of him.

This was the first time he had stepped foot in the Bricks or anywhere near it since his friend's demise, with a totally different state of mind. The period of grief had elapsed, his mind no longer encompassed with sorrow. He now had a mission to accomplish and cause to bring to pass, a cause that his heart was totally fixated on. Retribution and havoc.

Nothing that had been accomplished that day would have come and gone just like the previous ones had come and gone if Li'l One Gone hadn't had the help of the voice pulling him up by his shoulders and making him make the first step toward completing his mission. Human civilization wouldn't have been advanced by the mission he was on, nor would it have been in jeopardy of being extinct, but in the streets his life was about to be advanced and the killers or killer of T'Sharon was about to be extinct.

Who, what, when, where, and how to get it done were the questions. The voice had instructed him to go to West Roosevelt Street, but for what, he did not say. Li'l One Gone was just a flea in the streets among giants, without any means or resources, but a flea that had plans in his mind on causing devastation that could be credited to a giant.

As he wandered around the Bricks aimlessly, doubt started to rise. "What do you want me to do?" he asked the voice. A door slamming in the distance was the only reply he received.

The fire of the mission burning within him started to rapidly fade away. "Fuck," he mumbled to himself. Frustrated, he began to walk back across the courtyard of the Bricks toward the front parking lot. Remembering the words of Monk, instead of going the way he came into the Bricks, he cut between two of the project buildings and then circled back around toward the front parking lot.

He did not want to go home, having nowhere else to go, and knowing that there was some impending business that needed to be tended to, he did not want to fold this early in the mission. Stopping, he leaned up against the wall, mystified and confused. "What da fuck?" he asked the voice again. Then it happened.

Having similar effect to water being splashed into the face, NWA, turned up to the max, blasted from the stereo system of one of the cars parked in the parking lot of the Bricks. The sound penetrated his ears, the thump of the bass combined with a strong smell of chronic burning jolting Li'l One Gone's senses, snapping him out of his momentary trance.

All at once, his mechanism of awareness was triggered and his attention was grabbed with an unexplainable force, and the fire of the mission within him was rekindled into an inferno. Oblivious to the sound of music like a police-trained canine, he let his nose guide him directly to where the blunt was being smoked. Standing there in a mock D-Boy stance, doing his best to look the part, Wet Fish acknowledged him with a half-nod and a smile, then proceeded to bob his head to the rhythm of the beat.

Seconds later, after the track ended, he turned the dial, lowering the volume of the radio. "What's da haps, kiddo?" he asked, still standing at attention.

"Even if I had da number, I still can't call it, my nigga," Li'l One Gone replied at ease, now eyeing the blunt, watching the thin stream of smoke rise from it.

Smiling, nodding, Wet Fish replied, "Yeah, I can feel dat, li'l nigga," extending a closed fist. Li'l One Gone did the same. They touched knuckles, which was a physical way of showing love and confirming that both persons agreed to what had just been spoken.

Neither one spoke as they both looked around to make sure that the streets were clear of any unwanted visitors. Wet Fish was sitting inside the car, so that put them at eye level. Standing, he would have towered over Li'l One Gone by many feet. Looking him straight in the eyes, in an authoritative voice, he said, "My nigga, I need a candy stick." Wet Fish did a double take to make sure he hadn't initially misread the seriousness that was written all over Li'l One Gone's face.

The mask of stone he contorted his face into was almost more comical than menacing. Not having been on the streets for a very long time, he hadn't developed that unprovoked hard stare that came with them. Innocence still emanated from his eyes, but his demand was a far cry from an innocent one. His body language reinforced the message his facial expression projected. Each limb was braced and studied for a defensive attack but coiled and ready to explode into an offensive one.

Speaking clearly and precisely, hearing him correctly the first time, Wet Fish still asked, "What?"

"I need a candy stick," Li'l One Gone repeated matter-of-factly, folding his arms.

Plucking the ashes off the killa, he proceeded to take a long drag from it, staring at the marijuana-filled Swisher Sweet cigar like it contained the answer to the situation at hand. After letting out a plume of smoke, he extended the killa to Li'l One Gone. "Hit dis shit an' be cool." When something was on his mind, weed smoke only enhanced the impending thought of getting what needed to be done, making the matter more of an urgent one. Reluctantly, Li'l One Gone accepted the killa and commenced to puffing on it.

After several rounds of the conventional, universally known smoker routine of "puff-puff pass," his mean mug turned into a grin. The killa didn't produce a delayed reaction; it was some high-grade weed, clouding his brain instantaneously.

The ember of the blunt would have caused more than a mere finger stinger if it had touched the skin of his finger. Li'l One Gone had hot-boxed the blunt. Dropping it to the ground, Wet Fish gave him that what-the-fuck-you-doing look, and as he bent over to retrieve it, he bumped his head against the car. His head colliding with the side of the car brought out an outburst of laughter. Wet Fish picked up the killa, shaking his head, as Li'l One Gone stood there, rubbing his cranium, giggling.

"You holla'n 'bout you need a candy stick, you can't bend ova without damn near fall'n on ya face! I know fuck'n well you can't bust no gun straight. Fuck around and hit sumthang you ain't aim'n at! Anyway, what cha need a candy stick fo'?" Before Li'l One Gone could reply, Wet Fish went on, "I know you ain't got dat type of drama goin' on dat cause fo' ya to let da hammer down on a nigga." Then he said, "Oh, I know," as if the answer had suddenly popped up. "You gotta be trip'n on dat bullshit with dat hoe I seen you peek'n ova there when you walked up." The car held him up as he leaned against it. Wet Fish sat with the driver's side of the car door opened, lounging in the driver's seat of the car. They both stared in the direction of what once was T'Sharon's apartment.

A question and a reply formed inside his foggy head simultaneously, much of what Wet Fish was saying fading off into the wind. "Man, fuck, I'm high as a muthafucka!" were the only words that came out from the depths of his soul. He shook his head from side to side like it was going to help reverse the effect of the high, but the only thing that act assisted in was making him a little more unbalanced.

Placing his hand on his shoulder like a coach does a player after he made a bad play, looking him dead in the eyes through his blood-shot ones, Wet Fish said, "Go home, li'l ole nigga. If you feel the same way tomorrow, come holla at me. I got something fo ya."

"Word?" Li'l One Gone replied with childish amusement in his voice.

Wet Fish extended his fist. "Word," he replied, and they touched fists.

Li'l One Gone walked off dazed, confused, excited, and high, but he felt something he hadn't felt in quite a while, *good*.

Subsequently battling the spirit of anxiousness through the night caused him a sleepless night, the morning coming unnoticed. In the custom of being an earlier riser, although Wet Fish hadn't given him a specific time to meet up with him, he knew that when it came down to taking care of business, the earlier, the better; pro-crastinating was a no-no. Thinking that it was later than it actually was, panic-stricken, he hurried dressing himself, putting on the same clothing he had on for the previous two days. He rushed through doing his morning-hygiene ritual.

Unfortunately, but also fortunately, he ran into Li'l Who when he spun the bend. Huffing and puffing, wide-eyed, hair rolled up like little black balls in salami meat. To top it off, he had globs of dried toothpaste on both sides of his mouth. Li'l Who giggled, impeding Li'l One Gone's forward progress. "Dawg, what, ya house on fire or sumthang?" Looking puzzled, Li'l One Gone looked back toward his residence, cocking his head slightly to the left, trying to grasp the meaning of Li'l Who's question. But before he could answer, Li'l Who pointed toward Li'l One Gone's face. "Homie, you got white shit all on da side of ya mouf. Ya gotta get ya shit together." He moved his hand upward. "Eye boogers falling out one of ya eyes, ya hair all nappy." He now swept his hand downward over Li'l One Gone's shabby wardrobe, all the way down to his shoes. "Look like ya slept in ya clothes, half ya shirt tucked in, da otha' out. Ya shoe laces untied, dragging da street."

As Li'l Who studied Li'l One Gone's body language, his ribbing turned into genuine concern spilling out of his voice; it was written all over Li'l Who's face as well as he spoke to Li'l One Gone. While rubbing the corner of his mouth with one hand, Li'l One Gone pulled his shirt completely out with the other. With the same hand he pulled out his shirt with, he felt for the eye boogers underneath his eyes, and after removing them, he bent over and, without attempting to dust them off, tied his strings.

Standing back upright, eyeing Li'l Who, waiting for his approval, which automatically came from his face, Li'l One Gone asked, "I'm good?"

"Yeah, my nigga, ya a'ight. You don't look like straight-up disrespect to da streets no more," Li'l Who said matter-of-factly. "Shied, what ya gonna do bout dat?" Li'l Who asked, pointing to Li'l One Gone's head.

Rubbing his hand across his head, he replied, "Fuck it." They both burst out into laughter.

They dapped each other off, then Li'l Who threw his arm around his chubby friend's shoulder. "Boy, ya kno you's a pure-dee savage. You don't give a fuck. I don't think I ever saw you with ya shit brushed or combed."

Hunching his shoulders, Li'l One Gone mobbed, on proceeding down Illinois Street in the direction of the projects, a route he could take blindfolded.

If not all the time, most of the time, he became lost for words when he was around Li'l Who. Intimidation wasn't the cause, and it was neither shyness nor fear, for he had no reason to fear him—they were friends. Li'l Who was a natural talker, not to be misunderstood as a snitch, but a person who loved to talk; not only did he love it, but he also had a way with words that would make a person stop and listen no matter their age. So usually, just as in any other day, he remained silent, waiting to pick up the new trending adverbs or phrases that he knew were going to roll off Li'l Who's lips, lingo that was guaranteed to initiate a war of words. Never wrong, he smiled to himself, amused by his foresight. Just as the thought was leaving his mind, it happened, coming out in the form of a question.

"Ya hang'n or slang'n? 'Cuz if ya ain't slang'n, a nigga sho don't need cha hang'n, draw'n heat."

Li'l One Gone was preoccupied with thoughts of a more pressing matter as seconds slipped away; too much time had elapsed for him to reply with a witty response to Li'l Who's comment, anyway. So to avoid any unnecessary racking of his brain to come up with something slick to say, plus knowing beforehand that a late comeback automatically constituted a loss of the word battle, to save face, plus not wanting to add another "L" to his résumé, Li'l One Gone asked, "You seen Wet Fish?" smiling inside as he scanned all the faces on the block and in the area.

Before crossing West Roosevelt Street, he looked over at his friend, his posture, along with the expression on his face, confirmation that his question had the internal reaction he sought. In some cases, when challenging his friend at wordplay, dodging the attack resulted in unexpected wins.

"Yeah." Meagerly still unbalanced from Li'l One Gone's verbal sidestep, Li'l Who replied more aggressively, "Yeah, chubby by nature, he told me to tell ya to find some shade till he gets back, and if ya move, ya lose."

Li'l One Gone grinned at the mention of his physical stature. Insults were sure confirmation that he had won the wordplay scrimmage minutes ago and a form of admittance to his victory from Li'l Who. Feeling himself, he said, "You ole two-foot, scorche, grease'e, shine'e black-ass, thumb-head-ass nigga, what else did he say?" With that said, he defended himself but also gave the advantage to his partner by letting him know that he possessed something Li'l One Gone required.

Quick on his feet, he read the play, satisfied with the results and outcome. Fully aware that information was power in the streets and anywhere else, letting anticipation heighten and unhostile tension build, Li'l Who contorted his face, as if he were searching his memory bank. "Nah, dat's all he said, ole fat-ass nigga. What he want wit ya, anyway?" Everyone in the neighborhood, from the BGs to the

YGs to the OGs, knew Wet Fish's position in the game. It wasn't a secret that he was on the fast track to riches. That's how the game goes; one player strikes out, the next one steps up to the plate.

In Wet Fish's case, it was all about being content with warming the bench, being patient, then at the right moment, he positioned himself to be the play caller and player. By fading into the background, he managed to outlast the other hustlers, then when the demand got high, he switched to pitching them run-hards. When the rest of the dope boys were scrambling to catch up, he was cornering the market. Everyone else in it couldn't do anything but tip their hats to him for the power move he made.

They made it to the playground bench. Food wrapping, beer bottles, cold-drink bottles, cigarette butts, empty condom wrappers, and used condoms were thrown on the ground next to the bench. None of it came as a surprise. Everything out there was the usual littering that could be found at that spot.

Every time Li'l One Gone came to the playground, first thing he did was look around to see what was lying around before he took a seat. Someone's stash could be camouflaged among the trash. Sitting down, eye searching through the trash, he was pestered by Li'l Who with a question, "Fo real, what he want with ya?"

Discontinuing his search, Li'l One Gone answered, "Nothing, I don't know, he just told me to get at him." The words rushed out.

Not convinced with the answer, Li'l Who matter-of-factly stated, "Okay, but I'ma hang right 'che till he get back."

Hunching his shoulder in a "So?" manner, Li'l One Gone drifted off.

Suddenly, the thought occurred to Li'l One Gone. "Oh yeah, what about that shit?" he asked sarcastically, changing the tone of his voice, now drawing his words out. "Ya hang'n or slang'n, 'cuz if ya ain't slang'n, a nigga don't need ya hang'n, draw'n heat."

"Fuck you, you got dat!" Smiling, nodding, Li'l Who continued, "Dat was right on time, my nigga." He extended his fist, Li'l One Gone doing the same, and they dapped each other down. They sat silently, waiting for Wet Fish's arrival.

Posted up, peeping the scene like a seasoned veteran in the game, Li'l One Gone could feel sweat rolling down his face. It streamed down to underneath his chin and dripped onto the front of his shirt, which was already soaked from the salty moisture secreted through pores of the skin from the tubular glands beneath it.

He stopped pacing up and down the block every few minutes, taking a seat on the infamous rail that surrounded the playground. Hunching over, he watched the sweat fall to the ground, evaporating as it settled onto the blazing-hot concrete. Wiping his face with the back of his hand didn't do much good; seconds later, the perspiration was flowing as frequently and as freely as before.

Needless to say, out of all days in the year on his first of day of employment, the great ball of fire in the sky rose that day with the sole purpose of punishing Earth's inhabitants.

True, it was hot that day, but no hotter than any other day. The combination of extreme nervousness, a nanogram of fear, and constant pacing was the cause of his profuse sweating. Quitting wasn't encoded in his DNA. The pedigree Li'l One Gone belonged to hadn't been studied or documented yet. He didn't want to be the first to show a sign of weakness, in case someone was peeping out the newest member of "the block."

Five times in the second hour out, walking off crossed his mind. But possessing a shiny regulator kept his feet in place, convincing him to stick to the mission. The .25-caliber semiautomatic candy stick, with thoughts of all that could be done with it, was more than enough motivation to keep him pushing.

The snickering and giggling from the older and more experienced hustlers every time he blew a lic k or lost a play to one of them further cemented his determination to succeed. Albeit saying "Fuck it" was presently in mind, nevertheless, just like a champ, he quickly rejected that thought.

His debut on the front line of the hustle wasn't all he imagined; he was committed now, no turning back. "Nothing on the streets is given. It's either earned or learned and often taken. Game is not free advice. It, too, comes with a price. Regardless if they're old, young, seasoned, or green, if one wants to play, one got to pay."

When Wet Fish laid out his proposition, Li'l One Gone didn't second-guess it, jumping on it without hesitation even before the actual plan or strategy was exposed, which became another lesson learned in life. Making beaucoup money and getting what he had asked for were agreed upon between Wet Fish and him. Nothing more needed to be said; he was completely sold from the get-go of the proposition.

His down-for-whatever personality overruled reason to the point where it didn't register to him what he'd volunteered for until he was in the commission of the act.

As he was posted up directly under the sun, the alluring images of acquiring money and the candy stick were expunged slowly from his mental as another car pulled up then stopped several feet from where he was located. Some type of agreement was made, and moving swiftly, the dude disappeared behind the abandoned house. When he reappeared, his hand went into the car, then pulled back out of car, and the car pulled off. Li'l One Gone watched the same procedure over and over—different hustlers, different automobiles, nothing changing since the moment of his arrival.

He obsequiously hung on to every word as Wet Fish explained how things were going to go on the block and what to look out for and, most importantly, what to avoid at all cost. Li'l One Gone reflected back on the conversation before he departed for the unknown, and as he visualized it beforehand, for some reason things weren't falling into perspective according to what was promised.

It was a simple instruction. All Li'l One Gone had to do was position himself right before the street, cross over the railroad tracks, and when a car approached, throw up both hands, with index finger on one hand pointing at the occupant of the vehicle while the index finger on the other pointed upward.

Whoever was looking would recognize the signal and stop, state what it was they were looking for, then Li'l One Gone was supposed to direct them to the projects, where Wet Fish was. Most importantly, make sure he didn't send an undercover police to him.

Simple enough? Not quite. Phase 1 of the plot went without a hitch, but phase 2 was somewhat evasive to the script. As soon as they pulled off from him, they stopped at the next available person. Sagacious for a li'l person, Li'l One Gone was convinced by instinct that if things weren't going the way they were planned, he had to be doing or saying something wrong.

Blocking out the heat, fighting back down rising frustration, hell-bent on getting it done, he looked within himself to come up with a solution to a problem that shouldn't be a problem at all. As he was picking his brain, someone slowly rolled their car as if they were lost. Seeing the car creeping wasn't what brought him out of his thoughts; it was the sound of worn-down brake pads that alerted him to the approaching vehicle.

Li'l One Gone instantly regretted throwing up his hands after doing so before making eye contact, noting that there were two persons inside the car. But upon further rapid inspection, seeing that both occupants of the vehicle were female—no harm, no foul—he breathed easily.

Stopping directly in front of him, leaning across the driver's side of the car, the passenger, a light-skinned woman, yelled out, "What cha got?"

"Shied, baby, I got what cha like and need. If I don't have it, I kno' where it's at," Li'l One Gone replied. His words not only took them by surprise; he also was taken aback by his own words.

"Ahh, suckie', nah, girl, ya hear dat?" the passenger asked the driver.

"Sho' did," replied the driver emotionlessly.

"I wonda how much dick ya got in them pants, li'l boy?" asked the passenger, looking down at his crotch area, both women erupting with laughter.

The woman's statement caught Li'l One Gone off guard. Avoiding eye contact, he glanced up and down the street, searching for the proper response. "Do you want me to lie to ya or tell you tha truth?" he affirmatively replied.

"Girl, leave dat boy alone an' tell him what you want. I ain't got time fo' dat shit," the driver frankly stated, saving Li'l One Gone from further scrutiny.

Rolling her eyes, the passenger asked, "Look, I need forty tha hard way. Can you handle dat wit'cha cute fat self?"

Not yet fully recouped from what was asked earlier, he was almost knocked off his game again by *cute* and *fat*. He blushed, already sweating from the heat of the sun, his skin all of a sudden getting hotter. A severe case of shyness rushed over him.

He raised his hand to point to where Wet Fish was waiting with the substance. "Catch ya, head nigga. Get in the car," the voice commanded. Aborting his intended gesture, Li'l One Gone, with a fresh breath of confidence, grabbed the handle of the car, letting himself inside. "I got'cha. Drive over into the Bricks. When ya get there, it's on," he cheerfully demanded. Eagerly, without hesitation, the driver pulled off.

Handing Li'l One Gone a stack of napkins, the passenger said, "Wipe some of dat sweat off ya."

Feeling himself, Li'l One Gone replied, "You do it, sweetie," leaning up to the rear of the front seat, resting his chin on it.

"Jennifer, girl, Peaches told me dat them niggaz across these tracks was something," the driver stated.

Wiping Li'l One Gone's face, Jennifer, which was the name of the passenger, replied playfully, "Um, I see."

"Thank you, darling," Li'l One Gone said when she finished wiping him down.

Simultaneously, in a heavily accented, seductive Southern drawl, both women responded to Li'l One Gone's suaveness, "Baa'biie." Those were the last words spoken as they made their short drive to the projects.

Scoping the scene from the set, before the trio in the car could come to a complete stop in the parking lot, Wet Fish was already up off his post on the bench, heading toward them. "He, got ya," Li'l One Gone said, jumping out before she shifted the gear into park.

"Damn," he heard the driver say as his feet hit solid ground.

Wet Fish stood over six feet tall, light-skinned; years of running behind or in front of a football down a football field, depending on how it was thrown, resulted in him being in great shape. His body was lean, ripped, and solid. In contrast to the other hustlers on the street that were thugging and drugging, he took care of himself.

The two gold chains—one a herringbone, the other a rope chain—draped around his neck were glistening; backgrounded by his bare chest, the gold stood out. He had on a snow-white Kangol bucket hat to match his snow-white sneakers. A real D-Boy in full effect.

He motioned for Li'l One Gone to come to him. "Kiddo, I almost gave up on ya. I was jus' finna holla for ya to get off dem streets. It was lookin' like you wasn't ready fo' dem big-boy shoes." Smiling as he spoke to Li'l One Gone, Wet Fish went on, "Go find some shade an' chill out," walking toward the waiting females. "Let me see what these two beautiful ladies want." By then he was speaking in a tone loud enough for the women to hear him also.

Li'l One Gone eyed Wet Fish questioningly.

When he spoke with Li'l One Gone, it was at a volume that ensured no one else could ear-hustle. Turning toward a cluster of trees located in the center of the playground, he spun, looking one last time at Wet Fish and the women before he walked toward the trees, but not before scanning West Roosevelt Street.

Years earlier, Li'l One Gone had posted up in the same vicinity, under a different administrator, playing the same game, though from a different end of it. As he sat on the slide, his eyes never left the streets as he reminisced about the days when he and Monk pushed— well, Monk pushed and he fetched in the park. Some say that life in general is a never-ending cycle, and so is "the life" that some live and "the game" others choose to play. Everything comes 360 degrees.

Wet Fish's role was now the same as Monk's had been before he got pinched. Coincidentally, he also sat in the same exact spot, give or take a few inches to the left or right, Monk did back then. Though both had become major players in the neighborhood, operating out of and controlling a million-dollar piece of real estate, Wet Fish was quite contrary to Monk.

Across the tracks, living according to the regulations that were laid down way back in the G when a select few were paving the way of the game and the life was mandatory. Playing the game any other way than how it was supposed to go wasn't an option; breaking any rules would result in the streets issuing a penalty that would be enforced by the streets.

Monk's record was impeccable, Wet Fish's also; thereby, their contrast lay elsewhere. Through casual contact, one would come to believe that both were just typical hustlers doing what they did best, one no different from the other. With Li'l One Gone having been sponsored by both, obsequiously observing, it wasn't long before he had studied, identified, and isolated their opposing individuality. He had been inquisitive since his days as a toddler in the game but was rudimentarily savvy in knowledge to its true nature; thus, everyone he interacted with daily and every move made around him came under close scrutiny by him.

Unhappiness with the current situation was also a factor that caused for the comparing of the two also by him. But when he and Monk were in business, Monk was always available for him. Whenever he had a question, Monk answered and patiently explained it. They always talked before, during, and after their jugg session; therefore, every play going down was understood by Li'l One Gone.

Sometimes when trafficking was slow, very seldom in the company of others, mostly alone, Monk would call Li'l One Gone over, rub his head, give him five, and ask him if he was straight. Sometimes he even asked him if he wanted to go play or if he was ready to fold for the day. Feeling comfortable, at total ease, and secure as along as Monk was out there, he stayed right there with him until Monk clocked out for the day.

Even running with Uncle Rich had a different feel about it to Li'l One Gone as he looked further back and deeper into his memory. Wet Fish's mentality was, "His money, his dope, his way, fuck what anybody had to say," which sent mixed signals to Li'l One Gone because he didn't know whether or not he fell in the "anybody" category or was an exemption.

Several times situations arose where he needed to discuss a matter. He wanted to but did not know whether to bring it to Wet Fish or let it play out however it was going to go. Then when the very matter went sour, Wet Fish would scold him for not alerting him when the issue was in its infancy. To add insult to injury, he told Li'l One Gone to never talk of their business in front of anyone, which was understandable, but the problem with that was, Wet Fish was never alone.

When they were in grind mode, "If ya ain't slangin', no hangin'" didn't have any referent to Wet Fish's entourage. All the hangers-on did was drink, smoke, and dance to music blasting from a gigantic boom box. If they were not dancing, they were sitting, bobbing their heads, swaying to the rhythm of the music. Wet Fish was right there in the middle of it, enjoying the vibe of the scene. After he left the set, a few stragglers still remained.

Li'l One Gone got up and hit the set before his appointed time in hopes of getting a little alone time with Wet Fish, wanting to clack with him about thoughts that were ping-ponging over his mental. The thoughts that bounced over his mind that he was trying to decipher and put into context weren't things pertaining to the hustle; they were issues that were close to the heart. Having no one else to turn to, he figured he'd run it down to him in the hope of getting a clear perspective from Wet Fish and advice on how to handle the thoughts he had.

No good. When he made it to the playground, Slick was laid on top of the picnic bench, eyes bloodshot, staring into the horizon. He walked past him, determined to talk before he posted up and his workday began; once the grind begun, his head was going to be in the game. Part of his job was to watch and listen. *If you're talking, you ain't listening,* he thought to himself as he limped toward Building D of the Bricks.

Wet Fish's car was parked ace-deuce in the same exact spot as it was when Li'l One Gone retired the night before. He suspected that he had slept by his mama's apartment or somewhere between here and there, so Wet Fish's leaving with someone in their vehicle never crossed his mind. He very seldom left his domain of the pro.

Not knowing which door to knock on, he stopped on the main walkway of the Brick, standing on the walkway hoping, watching, listening, and waiting for a door to open. A baritone sound coming from the back of the building, along with a motor's constant roar interrupted by switching of gears from a passing truck, reached his ears.

The baritone sound was the sound of a voice, a voice that he instantly recognized and was familiar with; it belonged to the person he was intent on chopping it up with. He moved swiftly, the notion that only a mentally unstable person would be speaking to them-selves and that Wet Fish wasn't alone never striking him. When he rounded the corner of the building, a high-pitched yet soft giggle pierced the quiet morning. The laughter bounced off the red bricks and mortar of the projects.

Li'l One Gone's brain received the sight just as the sound of laughter, which was of a female, had registered in his mind. Even if he had the desire to, it was too late for him to walk away. It was impossible for him to unsee what he was seeing. The both of them were too engaged in their sexual act to even notice his presence.

Wet Fish was leaning with his back against the wall, his shirt raised, held in place by his left hand, exposing his stomach. If not for his pants resting around his ankle, he would have been totally nude from the waist down. Kneeling directly in front of him, bare-chested, was Jennifer. The skin of her perfectly round honeydew-melon-size breasts was a few shades lighter than the skin of her face. The are-ola and nipples of her breasts were tan in color. She had her hands around his hips, her face buried between his legs where his groin area was. She was expertly assaulting Wet Fish's meat pistol with her mouth, lips, and tongue.

She alternated between sucking, kissing, and licking every inch of his meat pistol; he had his right hand gripping the back of her head. She looked like she was struggling to get her face from his pubic region. Every time she pulled her head back inches away from him, he would pull her head back into him. As Li'l One Gone stared at Faye's breast, the sight and sounds of the erotic scene sent a shock wave through the area below his waist.

Jennifer seemed to be utterly enjoying performing fellatio on Wet Fish more than he did receiving it. After several minutes of watching Jennifer's head bob back and forward on her shoulders rhythmically while Wet Fish ground her face, Li'l One Gone pushed out, unnoticed, with an image burned into his mind's eye, one of many images that were promised to come as his days passed hustling in the streets.

He never got a chance to speak with Wet Fish about what was vexing him. Eventually, just like everything else, it got lost in the shuffle of information his mind processed.

He gave up on chopping it up with Wet Fish alone. Lack of communication was only part of his grievances. From the jump, Li'l One Gone should've known that things weren't going to go how he pictured them in his mind; instead, he let himself get caught up in a fallacious, childish fantasy while playing a grown man's game. Though the signs were clear enough for a veteran to read it from the back side or upside down, his immaturity caused him to miss the signs all around him.

It was said that a bought education is the best one. Li'l One Gone was going to have to learn the ways of the street quickly or perish in them

At the end of his first week hustling for Wet Fish, he had accumulated eleven promising new clients in vehicles and six on foot. Just like with Jennifer, several of the vehicles contained more than one person looking to cop. He didn't know exactly how much money was made at his expense, but he knew his pockets wouldn't have any complaints; they would be back smiling, like when he pushed packs of products for Monk.

His feet hurt from being on them all day, his stomach finally giving up on growling and aching after hours of no response, yet he was feeling the effects of missing a meal. Last thing he remembered to cross his lips was a blunt he smoked. He was weak from a combination of heat and hunger; not to mention his mouth, tongue, and throat begged for anything wet. Looking down at his feet, he had made his mind up that if the pain didn't subside soon, he was going to need a wheelchair to maneuver up and down the block to reel in customers. When Wet Fish yelled to him to shut down shop for the day until sunrise of the next, he wanted to jump jubilantly, but the pain on his feet made him thought better about doing so. Exhausted from ripping and running up and down the street all day long, Li'l

One Gone lay back on the slide, his arm resting across his forehead. Wet Fish approached him without any small talk or felicitation, getting straight to the point.

"Do you want the candy stick or some money to put in ya pockets?"

Befuddled, thinking he must have heard him wrong, because the deal was that if he did good, he was going to get not only the pistol but also a few dollars, Li'l One Gone didn't answer him off the bat, hesitating, seeking inside for strength or courage to confront the situation at hand, hoping that his ears weren't deceiving him. When he looked into Wet Fish's eyes, the message was visible.

"Money," Li'l One Gone replied.

Wet Fish handed him a few bills folded into a square. When Li'l One Gone unfolded them, he noticed it was three five-dollar bills.

Getting into his car, Wet Fish yelled back to Li'l One Gone, "Come fuck wit me tomorrow!"

Li'l One Gone contemplated giving heed to Wet Fish's command. He pondered, Was it all worth it? as he sat looking at the three five-dollar bills in his hand. With a sigh, he crumpled the money up, then shoved the bills deep into his pockets, along with the memories of the day and the thoughts of the days to come.

The voice had encouraged him to return the next day and the following days, but his own desire was what led him back and held him mentally captive to the thrill of grinding.

Responsibility caused the feeling of ill will toward the game. If a police car rolled up without him announcing, regardless if someone else warned everyone or not, he'd get scolded. If Wet Fish was busy serving someone and another person pulled up, Li'l One Gone's job consisted of getting the money from the customer, bringing it to Wet Fish.

Sometimes Wet Fish retrieved the product and took care of the person himself, or he would give it to Li'l One Gone to take to them, which he hated, because oftentimes that person griped about the piece or run-hard being too small. One guy went as far as accusing Li'l One Gone of breaking off a piece off his run-hard and keeping it for himself.

Besides the things mentioned above and few things not, Wet Fish was too demanding; the more Li'l One Gone put forward, contributing to his making money or to Wet Fish's safety, the more he wanted the same results every day.

Being a child, he wasn't ready to be performing on the same level as grown-ups. He hardly had time to be a kid anymore. Being restricted from engaging in childhood activities bothered him the most.

When he watched other kids run around, playing and having fun, it disturbed him, although before he became Wet Fish's number one man, he didn't really participate in many children's activities anyway; but the fact that someone was now telling him that he couldn't play rubbed him the wrong way. Just like a typical kid, he got in his feelings.

Any other person would have loved to have the privilege in the game that he was blessed with. His childish attitude caused him to overlook and regret at times when he wanted a break from the grind just to chill out and he couldn't get it, or when things didn't go his way, which never did, he got upset.

Majority of the time, it was just him and his thoughts. Though the playground would be packed with people, he was still alone; therefore, not having anyone to stress to, he had to work out every problem and issue he had, in his head, solo. Even though a child's instincts aren't as fine-tuned as a full-grown person's, they still know when something doesn't feel right or, for that matter, when things are not.

His mind often led him astray. There wasn't much the game had to offer that wasn't available to him, yet he still wasn't satisfied and made issues out of nothing. The concept was the same as the days when he and Monk were out there. Money was the mission, and always would be, which he was now getting. What he failed to realize when he asked himself why things weren't going the way they were was that when Monk took him under his wing, he was still virtually a baby.

Monk spoke, thought, and acted for him. Thinking and identifying feelings and emotions were still being developed by him. Now that he was a few years older yet still a child, his mind was beginning to process the environment as taught to him by Monk.

He searched for answers as to why things seemed harsher, why Wet Fish seemed so hard on him. The fact of the matter was, people in the streets were harder than in years past and situations were, in fact, harsher than they used to be. It wasn't just in his head, as he thought it was; in all actuality, it was the reality of the time.

As Li'l One Gone got older, the game got or had gotten colder. There was absolutely no room for any form of weakness. The days of someone holding his hand were over; every soul in the game or those who chose to be about that life had to carry their own weight on their shoulders. Li'l One Gone was no exception to that rule; Wet Fish saw to that personally at all times.

Not only not being excluded, Li'l One Gone was also being schooled the hard way. Another phase in his culturing was in the process. If he had taken time to think of it in that aspect, he would have noticed the way his mama spoke with him had started to change. Every now and again at home, she would speak to him like she was out in public; as of late, little or no euphemism was used. She spoke to him uncensored and uncut, giving it to him raw, the exact way the world had to offer it.

"There's no room for the weak or weary. Stand ya ground, hold ya own when it came down to get'n yours, what's owed to you. Take no shorts or losses. We play for keeps, baby. It's the only way. Ask once, demand thereafter. In this game, if you let it slide, charge it to the game, or whatever you wanna call it, ya progress in the game gonna slow up, and eventually falling off will be the only option. Them streets will eat ya alive if they figga ya a push-ova or weak out'che. You won't be able to shake 'em or the bullshit they gonna throw ya way. Niggas gonna be on ya like a pack of piranhas on a three-legged ox. You not there yet, but you gonna get there," he said.

"All they"—he pointed toward the street—"understand is death and pain. The more pain you inflict on a person, the less frequently you have to. I can't do it for you." He looked at Li'l One Gone directly in the eye. "You gotta lay ya own law down. After that, you gotta keep some A-one, you know, that high-quality shit, then, my li'l souljah, the streets—no, fuck that—the world will be yours. The niggas in tha street gotta respect ya mind and hustle. Anything outside of that, ya chances of sustaining out 'che is the same as a one-legged nigga winning an ass-kicking contest." Wet Fish punctuated his statement with a knowing smile. Li'l One Gone nodded acknowledging that he overstood what he was saying.

So far, Wet Fish's methods of dealing with people had been tested true. He was the one who told him to pick up a stick and hit Boss with it the day they had a little scuffle over a trivial matter. He had long abandoned the carrying of his nigga-beater; if it weren't for him not carrying it anymore, he would have already been strapped with it. The first blow he struck Boss with the stick was across the knee of his right leg. That disabled Boss from flying away from the altercation. Then he proceeded to strike him over the head with it. Li'l One Gone didn't have enough strength in his shoulders to draw blood from Boss, but he did inflict enough pressure with the nigga beater to cause several "ooo-wee" knots to rise over his head.

Li'l One Gone never had any other altercations with Boss after that incident; in fact, they had become friends for the short period Boss lived in the Bricks.

Over a period of time, Wet Fish became more than of sponsor to Li'l One Gone in the streets.

When Li'l One Gone was on the verge of getting put out of school permanently for disrespecting his teacher and a host of other things, Wet Fish brought him to school the very next day, gave him a card to give to his teacher. Just as predicted, when she saw him entering her class, she grabbed him, asking him what he was doing there. Wet Fish had told him, once that happened, he should not say anything, look down at the floor, then hand her the card and wait a moment, allowing her enough time to read it, then hug her tight and tell her that he was sorry for calling her a stupid funky-junky, that he himself was the one that was stupid. After that, he should let her go then turn around and tell the class he was sorry for disrupting them. He played it to the letter, and she told him to take a seat, left class, came back, and told Li'l One Gone he was good, that he wasn't going to be expelled from school. She went to the principal and had the matter swept under the rug.

As time went on, the voice advised Li'l One Gone that it was time for him to arm himself. Once Li'l One Gone turned down the offer for the candy stick the first time, Wet Fish never offered it to him again; he just gave him cash money for the running and pitching that he had done for him.

Every day, after Li'l One Gone shut up shop and the time came for him to get paid for his services, he brought up the subject about the candy stick. Wet Fish ignored his request every time he asked. Nevertheless, Li'l One Gone was persistent in asking for the candy stick.

When Wet Fish finally offered to give him the candy stick that he had worked so hard for, he told Li'l One Gone that it didn't make any sense for him to possess the candy stick; therefore, he should instead just take the money like he usually did. Reason was that if Li'l One Gone's mama caught him with it, she was going to take it from him, then bring that spark to his ass. Li'l One Gone assured Wet Fish that his mama wasn't going to catch him with it or find out where he was going to stash it.

Wet Fish continued to attempt to persuade him into not taking the candy stick. But the more he tried to convince him otherwise, the more Li'l One Gone pleaded his case. Eventually, Wet Fish gave Li'l One Gone the candy stick he had been begging for. He issued it to him with instructions on where to stash it and with a warning. Li'l One Gone accepted the candy stick anyway, despite Wet Fish's warning.

To Li'l One Gone's surprise, the discovery of the candy stick happened just the way Wet Fish called it. The candy stick hadn't been underneath the hood of Grandma Mama's broke-down Impala for no more than eight hours before his mama retrieved it. It happening just the way Wet Fish said it would happen wasn't just a surprise to him; it also increased Wet Fish's image in the eyes of Li'l One Gone.

Shocking to him was the discovery of the location of the candy stick. Grandma Mama's old car had become a habitat for rats, mice, and other crawling creatures; they would run all over the exterior and interior of the car morning, noon, and night. His mama didn't go into the backyard often, and when she did, she definitely didn't go anywhere near the old car for any reason at all. Her opening up the car door, reaching inside, pulling the lever to pop the hood came more as a shock to him than any other aspect of the ordeal. She was terrified of rats; that was the reason he chose the car for a stash spot.

More of a shock to him than the shock of pain that the thin rubbery tree branch she used to whip him with caused. The switch left welting all over the back of his body. The welts ran across his back, over his butt cheeks, down his thighs, then they wrapped around his legs.

He was accustomed to dealing with physical discomfort, though, so while the whipping took place, picturing his mama in his mind's eye ducking, running, and screaming at the sight of the hairy rodents in the car when she went to retrieve the candy stick distracted him from the excruciating, stinging pain of the switch.

A step above a rookie yet far from being a pro at living, he had been around long enough to know that there were repercussions, rewards, and consequences for everything one does, and for every action it's a must that it be followed by an equal reaction or one that surpasses the action.

Fear of the unknown influences some decisions, changing their initial course of action, while others thrive on the thrill of the mystery of the unknown end results that provoke their actions further. Li'l One Gone already knew what he had to do and what must be done. Instinct told him, Uncle Shortman had told him, the voice had told him and continued to tell him. That day, Wet Fish gave him his input and advice laced with street psychology with a touch of philosophy about the situation. As he preached the street gospel to Li'l One Gone, all his tagalongs "Amened" his words.

Double D's fate as a world-class dope fiend had been officially signed, stamped, and sealed. Being able to flip coke, weed, or whatever, making your product do numbers, is only part of the game. Respect plays a major role in the hustle. Surviving, right next to making fetti, luchi, becomes a hustler's main priority. Dead men or locked up ones don't shine. Staying free and alive is the main objective of surviving. But surviving also consists of being able to shake and move without any obstructions. In order for that to occur, the understanding of who is who has to be floating on the streets. Li'l One Gone had the right game, but he hadn't yet developed the right name for himself to maintain further in the game without incident.

The streets test everyone, and Li'l One Gone's time was at hand.

One of Li'l One Gone's numerous jobs was being a bagman and runner for Wet Fish. No one outside his plug and him knew that Li'l One Gone was Wet Fish's bagman.

No one would ever suspect that at any given time, Li'l One Gone's backpack would be loaded with ounces of cocaine or stacks of fetti. Going or coming, depending on which direction he was stopped, one would have found him in possession of Wet Fish's score fetti or the drugs that he had purchased for him.

Before school began or after it was let out was the time he made his move and took care of that part of the business for Wet Fish. Several days at school, he sat in class, afraid to open his book bag because he hadn't made the drop.

Occasionally, when he went by the spot to pick up, which was in a location not far from across the track, the man would give him a tiny package to keep for himself. That usually happened mostly when his backpack became a little heavier with the score fetti than in the previous times he'd visited him. The man always rewarded Li'l One Gone with a small bag of drugs. When Wet Fish had a few microdots of run-hards left in his sack, called shake, he would give that to Li'l One Gone as an incentive for a day of excellent running for him. He would put all the drugs he received from the hook and Wet Fish's together in one bigger bag.

Wet Fish had pulled off from the set, leaving Li'l One Gone out there alone. He wasn't supposed to be hustling or anything; he was on his own time once Wet Fish left the set.

Karonda was the name of the girl playing basketball on the basketball court the day of T'Sharon's demise. He had intentions of shooting his nelson at her but never could find the right time or opportunity to do so. When he came from behind the building from relieving himself of a few ounces of bodily fluids, he noticed her dribbling a basketball on the basketball court. She was playing alone. Li'l One Gone approached her.

She and Li'l One Gone chitchatted a little in between her shooting and his chasing the rebounds. He fed her the ball and gave her her change when she made the shot. Reluctant to shoot the ball, he was satisfied with chasing the basketball for her.

Double D came through, looking for Wet Fish. He had a camcorder he was trying to sell or trade for a piece of run-hard. Li'l One Gone had dealt with Double D on several occasions. He was a regular customer. Therefore, he didn't have any qualms about dealing with him. Li'l One Gone didn't want the camcorder, nor did he have any use for it, but he wanted to make himself look more important and bigger in the game than what he really was in front of Karonda.

Li'l One Gone told him, "Wet Fish don't want dat shit, and I don't either. Dem niggaz ova there on tha block ain't fuck'n wit either. So git tha fuck on wit dat. Come back wit sum fetti. Nothing but money move thangs 'round here on this set."

Double D, being the professional dope fiend he was, seized the opportunity to introduce, at that time, a bumptious, ignorant youngster to the game. "Are you work'n, li'l nigga?" Double D mischievously asked.

"Yeah, I'm straight," Li'l One Gone replied, looking back at Karonda before he headed to Wet Fish's stash spot in the playground. She watched him with an unwavering stare.

Walking cockily and confidently, he returned to where Double D was waiting anxiously and revealed the contents of the baggie. Double D eyed the baggie greedily. "Let me have a ten-cent piece for the camcorda an' I'm gonna help ya slang it fo' ah yard. Plus, I'ma give ya tha ten dollars back fo' the cam-corda. On top of that, I'ma buy tha rest of whatever ya have left in dat bag," Double D spat out. "Tha day still yung. I jus' needs me a li'l eye open'na to start my day. Ya know how I roll. I'm gud fo' at les' two or three yards once I git it pop'n," he added on to his sales pitch.

Li'l One Gone agreed and gave him what he assumed was a ten-dollar piece of run-hard.

About a half-hour later, Double D strolled back up to where Li'l One Gone was posted up at. "Check dis out. Come roll wit me. I got a sale cross da track wait'n on me. He gonna buy sumthang from ya, plus I'ma square up with ya fo' tha piece ya gave me an' take care of dat issue we ran it 'bout," Double D said.

Li'l One Gone didn't want to leave Karonda, because they were having such a good time, so he asked her to accompany them, then told her that he was going to buy her something from the convenience store after he made a hundred dollars for something he just paid a dime piece of run-hard for. She agreed to walk with them.

The trio walked up West Roosevelt, then crossed the railroad tracks together. Karonda and he lagged back a few paces, talking to each other, while Double D led the way. Once they got on Wyoming Street, Double D pointed to a parked car with a white man in it. "Dat's the cat who gonna git tha camcorda off ya hands. Give it to me. I'ma take care of tha biz," he said.

"A'ight," Li'l One Gone replied.

"You an' ya li'l pretty girlfriend chill right che' till I git back," Double D added.

Li'l One Gone gave it to him, and Double D confidently pushed off toward the white man waiting in the car. He swiftly returned to the corner where Karonda and Li'l One Gone waited. Double D handed him a few folded bills and told Li'l One Gone to sell him something for seven dollars. Hesitant, Li'l One Gone looked at the few shams in his hand like Double D was holding his death certificate.

"Look, I'm still gonna pay ya them ten dollars I owe ya once I win off tha cam-corda, plus spend whatever extra I have," Double D said, rushing his words out. Although Li'l One Gone dealt with money daily—in fact, he had been making money before he learned how to count past twenty—receiving money from his first solo orchestrated drug sell had a different feel to it.

Anticipating the rush, he agreed, Double D dropping the money into Li'l One Gone's outstretched hand. He did so a tad slowly, indicating uncertainty. Li'l One Gone missed it. When he pulled out his pack to serve him, with blinding speed, Double D snatched the pack out of Li'l One Gone's hand, turned, then fled. All his actions were performed in one swift, perfect motion.

Li'l One Gone stood mouth agape, watching Double D run off with Wet Fish's product. Before the last syllable of "Stop" left his mouth, his run-hard, the camcorder, along with Double D had spun the bend. Karonda was amused to the point of laughter. Li'l One Gone shared the moment and laughed with her also. Behind the laughter, he knew that he had made a crucial mistake in the game; the joke was on him, but Double D was going to have to pay for his trickery.

As promised, with the seven dollars in hand, he and Karonda mobbed off to the convenience store hand in hand, stopping first at the Laundromat that was located adjacent to the convenience store because Karonda wanted to play the arcade game Ms. Pac-Man. So while she played Ms. Pac-Man, Li'l One Gone played Galaxy Invaders.

His concentration level was shot. The caper Double D had successfully pulled off on him, along with the anticipation of how Wet Fish was going to react to the news of him getting burned for his stash, weighed heavily on his head. As he thought about Wet Fish's reaction to his loss, an image of a not-so-distant past situation involving Wet Fish invaded his mind's eye. Unable to completely focus on the arcade game, after losing his last life, instead of feeding the machine another quarter, Li'l One Gone just gave up making it past the first stage of the game.

He took a few steps over to where Karonda was at. Though his interest lay elsewhere, he stood behind her, looking over her shoulder at the screen of the arcade game. At first, he watched her play Ms. Pac-Man until he had built up enough courage to do what he had intentions of doing, taking his eyes off Ms. Pac-Man, allowing his gaze to roam from the top of Karonda's head, down her back, to his target area. Without any further hesitation, he went with his move, brushing up against her slightly, slick-legging her. At his touch, she turned, looked at him in the eyes, giggled, then went back to playing the game she was intensely focused on.

With expectations of a different response other than the one he got from her for invading her personal space, seeing that his first move went without the resistance or repercussions that he had expected, Li'l One Gone pushed up all the way against her backside. He gently pinned her against the arcade machine with his body, then placed his hands on her hips the same way he saw the older boys did the older girls.

The closeness of her body next to him erased all thoughts of revenge, feelings of anger, uncertainty, and apprehension. At that moment, he didn't have any cares or concerns. The Laundromat could have gone up in a ball of flames all around him and he wouldn't have moved a fraction of an inch from where he was standing. He was lost in the closeness of Karonda.

When she lost her last life on the game, he offered to put another quarter in the machine, but she gratefully declined his offer. She informed him that she was ready to go to the convenience store.

They went next door to the store, Li'l One Gone's mind relinquishing, and his body still feeling the touch of hers against his. His thoughts were also alternating between Karonda, Double D, and Wet Fish. In the process, his mood swung from happiness to anger to worry.

She placed a grape soda, a bag of Lay's plain potato chips, and a five-pack of grape Now and Laters on the counter. Right on the counter were several jars of pickled foods. She let her hands run over the jars, resting them on the jar that contained pickled pig lips. Several ticks of the clock as she searched through the jar with a pair of tongs had elapsed. Finally, she picked the one that she liked. Only after close examination of the pig lips did she take it all the way out of the jar, then place it into the sandwich bag she was holding, laying the pickled pig lip next to the rest of the items.

The man behind the counter rang up her items on the register, looking over at Li'l One Gone standing next to her, clutching the few remaining bills he had. "Are you gonna get you anythang?" she asked him. In the few minutes it took for her to choose what she wanted and place them on the counter, Li'l One Gone's anger had risen to a boiling point.

Blinded by rage and a touch of embarrassment, he didn't have a taste for anything; the taste he did have had left his mouth when the thought of him falling for Double D's Murphy re-entered his dome.

Ignoring her question, he stared at the man Behind the counter menacingly. The man stated the price of Karonda's purchase, which Li'l One Gone couldn't understand because of the man's thick foreign accent. The numbers on the cash register monitor were blurry to his vision. He violently shoved the few shams he had across the counter toward the cashier.

Li'l One Gone stormed off before retrieving his change from the cashier. Luckily for him, Karonda got it for him, or he would have suffered another "L" for the day. Ironically, everyone in the streets except for Li'l One Gone was up on the game that the users of run-hards would do anything to feed the dragon on their back once it started to breathe down their neck. Being a child in a mature person's game made him an easy target for a drug addict to gibe on. He wasn't the first one, nor would he be the last to fall for the wooden nickel. One thing was for certain: he had just bought and paid for his education in the Devil's University. What he did to repair his lack of knowledge of the ways of the moralless addicts and Double D's audacity to play on his top was what was going to determine his longevity in the game.

Outside the store, Karonda grabbed him by the arm, turning him toward her so that they stood face-to-face. Placing the change from the purchase in his hand, she said, "Thanks." Then she kissed him on the cheek, the same way T'Sharon used to do.

The touch of her lips against his flesh momentarily caused to subside the feeling of anger; the thoughts of Double D, the run-hard, how he was going to cop deuces to Wet Fish about disobeying his orders and explain to him about how he got burned and what he had to do to make it right with Wet Fish, or the two dollars and seventy-three cents he had left out of the seven dollars didn't matter.

Like air rushing out of a pin-poked balloon, the anger he felt when her lips touched his cheek disappeared. He became completely deflated when he returned her kiss, only holding his lips to her face a little longer than she did. Everything happened unexpectedly; getting ganked out of Wet Fish's stash and kissing Karonda hadn't been planned. All things being equal, he had to accept the bitter, which was Double D running off with his pack, explaining what happened to Wet Fish, going home pockets light, with the sweet, talking to Karonda, rubbing up against her, getting kissed by her, and spending time with her.

One thing was for certain: it wasn't gonna stop there. Upon his surrendering to the call of the voice, every incident, good or bad, was predestined to bring Li'l One Gone closer to his final destination, the point of no return.

Putting on a cap and gown, walking across the stage, receiving his certificate of completion of elementary school were all on his mind as he waited for the school bus to arrive. Graduation day at Wildwood Elementary was going to be another day he played hooky until a letter arrived at the house inviting his mama to Li'l One Gone's graduation ceremony, which was astonishing, because for the majority of the school year he was absent by force for misbehaving or because he just decided not to attend school that day on account of something he had perceived to be more important than learning educational fundamentals.

Besides exceeding the number of unexcused absent days, when he was present in class, no in-class work got completed; as long as he sat still and quietly, it was fine by the teacher. Homework, Li'l One Gone couldn't even comprehend the meaning of it—homework definitely didn't get done in his household. Passing to the next level in the schooling system couldn't be credited to his doing. Well, not academically.

All his teachers, all but three of them, got together with the principal and other members of the school faculty and held a meeting at the end of the school year. The subject of the meeting was what to do about the student that had bad grades, poor attendance, and a fast-growing savvy of the corrupted life, who always preached the street gospel to the other students. They agreed that it would be in the best interest of Li'l One Gone if he was promoted to the next grade. No one was more elated than his fifth- and sixth-period teacher. She had to deal with him at the end of the day when he became restless. She was more ecstatic about Li'l One Gone moving on to the next grade than his mama or he was.

Li'l One Gone was moving up from grade school to junior high school, a day that would be forever marked on the invisible calendar of his life, then filed away in his mental cabinet in the drawer, marked ACCOMPLISHMENTS.

Only problem was that it is impossible for a human to be physically at two places at one time.

Right about the time the fifth-grade students at Wildwood Elementary School were in the gymnasium, going down memory lane, smiling, laughing, and being merry while preparing to hear their name being called, and going over the planned entertainment performances they were going to perform after everyone received their completion slip to advance to the sixth grade, Li'l One Gone and Li'l Who were sitting right next to each other on a wooden bench. They were handcuffed to a slab of metal with rings on it that were embedded into a stone wall inside the police precinct on Highland Road, waiting for Officer Lic Johnson to get in contact with both of theirs parents.

A couple of hours after the crack of dawn, Li'l One Gone was posted up with the other children, waiting for the school bus to arrive, the ones that were graduating that day excitedly confabbing about the actual ceremony, while the younger children ear-hustled, their eyes glistening, wishing it were them moving up to the next level of the education system.

Elementary grades ranged from kindergarten to fifth grade; therefore, the parents of the youngest of the students waited at the bus stop with their child or children until the bus pulled up. Although the parents chitchatting among themselves, they were also ever so vigilant. Same sight, same theme, all school year. There wasn't anything out of the ordinary about that day. Besides the excitement of the pending graduation, everyone and everything was in its normal state.

The children in the neighborhood that rode the bus to school waited at the same street, just on different blocks, to catch the school bus. The elementary school bus picked up the school's students on the corner of Illinois Street and West Roosevelt, the junior high school bus picked up the school's students on the corner of Indiana Street and West Roosevelt Street, while high school students caught their bus on the corner of West Roosevelt and River Road.

Just like inside the actual school system, where one moved up in the levels of education and changed their school once they completed each level, their bus stop location changed also. Every kid in school in the neighborhood looked forward to moving up the street to the next block. All knew that once they made it to the bus stop on River Road, their obligation to go to school was nearing an end, and once they completed high school, a new leaf in their life was going to be turned over.

Li'l One Gone realized that he didn't put on any deodorant before he left the house; all the extra attention he gave to brushing his hair caused him to forget. Sniffing his hands after running them over his armpits, though he didn't smell of musk, he hurried back home to take care of his hygiene. A few quick steps down Illinois Street and he was turning down West Garfield Street. It didn't take him long to put on deodorant; most of the time spent was running around the house, searching for an unlocked window to go enter the house.

There was only one key to the house; his mama had it, and she didn't come home the night before, so his initial plan was to stay in bed until he got tired of lying down, then hit the streets. But he remembered that he was graduating that day. Sniffing his hand once again after putting on the first deodorant he laid eyes on in the bathroom, and satisfied, he pushed out, but not before he locked the window he came through, and the front door behind him.

Looking at his plastic wristwatch—it was a waterproof Timex, the one equipped with the stop clock and Indiglo light—and noting the time, he said out loud, "Damn." Either he had initially left the house early, time was moving slow, or he had moved extremely fast, he thought to himself. Either way, he had a few minutes to burn before the school bus came.

Instead of going back the way he came to the house from the bus stop, he went on down West Garfield Street to Indiana Street, since he had time, plus there was no way he could miss the bus.

Besides the few extra feet he had to walk to get back to his bus stop not going to hurt, most of all he wanted the middle school kids to rib him and tell him to get back down the street where he belonged so that he could tell them that he had passed to the sixth grade and that he was going to be posted up with them came next school semester.

While he was walking, Li'l Who was coming down Indiana Street from the opposite direction of the bus stop, West McKinley Street's way. They met up at the corner, and after dapping each other down, they proceeded on. Li'l Who was headed to the middle school bus stop to give his brother money for lunch that his mama had given him to bring to him. Strolling by a truck parked on the side of the street, Li'l One Gone glanced into the bed of the truck. There were a few miscellaneous items thrown about—nothing of value or of any use to Li'l One Gone. The only thing of interest to him was an aluminum baseball bat. He took it and picked up a few rocks, throwing them up in the air, swinging at the rocks with the bat as they walked.

They made it to the bus stop, and Li'l Who gave his brother the money. No one said anything to Li'l One Gone, unlike he had expected. Everyone was in their own zone. Some looked at him but said nothing. They had bounced down the street toward their own bus stop when, as Li'l Who counted out his brother's stack of money, Li'l One Gone saw the back of a man dip into the Bricks. The way he leaned back and swung his hand when he walked seemed familiar to Li'l One Gone. He thought he recognized the person; he just couldn't place a name or face with the walk.

Before they made it up the street, the man dipped back out of the Bricks in front of Li'l Who and him; all it took was a fraction of a second for Li'l One Gone to recognize who the man was. It was Double D. After that day Double D had snatched his pack out of his hand, he had only seen him from a distance. Sometimes he would be on foot; other times he was up the block, jumping into cars. Since the day he burned Li'l One Gone, the two of them never were inside the voice's reach of each other. Several times when he made it onto the set and he'd get ribbed, someone would tell him his boy Double-D had just left. Other than that, this was their first encounter in over a month.

"Where my shit at?" Li'l One Gone asked.

"What shit? An' what the fuck ya talk'n 'bout, li'l nigga?" Double D defiantly replied. Genuine confusion was etched into his face as he stared Li'l One Gone down.

Li'l One Gone raised the bat above his head, over his right shoulder. He feinted with the baseball bat. Double D threw his hands up with his arms to protect his face. Li'l One Gone swung the bat, connecting with the outside of Double D's left shin, the sound of metal and flesh colliding sounding off.

Double D didn't make a squeak. The second swing connected in the same spot, bringing out a scream that frightened Li'l One Gone a bit. When Double D reached for his knee, at the same instance, Li'l One Gone, though he was aiming for his head, landed a solid blow to his shoulder. Turning from his attackers, Double D attempted to get away, dragging his leg like it had fallen to sleep. The blows to his knees had impeded his quick getaway.

Chasing him a few feet down the sidewalk, Li'l Who kicked his leg, then forcibly shoved Double D in his back. Double D stumbled a little before he fell to the pavement. Standing over his prone body, Li'l One Gone commenced to wailing at him with the bat. The more he screamed, begged, and pleaded with him to stop, the more hysterical Li'l One Gone became, chopping down with the baseball bat more viciously. Every chop was swung with ill intentions. From the moment of impact, all the anger, rage, pain, rejection, self-pity, self-conviction, fear, and mercy felt over the years were released. Every strike against Double D's flesh, a new person emerged from the depths Li'l One Gone.

By Double D balling up in a fetal position, blocking and kicking out at Li'l One Gone, defending himself, Li'l One Gone wasn't able to land anything that had noticeable results. Frustrated, he passed the baseball bat to Li'l Who. Reaching into his pocket, he pulled out his pocketknife. When he went back for deodorant, he found it lying next to his mama's personal stuff in the bathroom cabinet. She had confiscated it from him.

Double D saw Li'l One Gone pulling the knife out of his pocket and prying the blade loose from the sheath. At the sight of the blade, he made an attempt to lift himself off the ground. Li'l Who hit him with the baseball bat with all his strength. A hollow thud sounded off when the baseball bat connected across the center of his back. The blow flattened Double D out on the pavement.

Giving up on lifting himself off the sidewalk, he remained still. Frozen in place, turning his head to the side, moaning and groaning in pain, he locked eyes with Li'l One Gone. Double D's facial expression pleaded for help, his eyes begging for mercy. Li'l Who stood over him with the baseball bat raised over his head, preparing to come down on him with a fatal blow.

The pending threat of being hit again with the baseball bat, the pain from the previous blows from the baseball bat—or maybe he was preparing himself mentally to get stabbed with the pocket-knife Li'l One Gone brandished—held Double D firmly in place. He didn't bug.

Zeroing in on Double D, Li'l One Gone moved in on him to puncture the part of his body that he had finally made his mind up to poke, which seemed like it took an eternity for him to decide on. He heard someone yell, "Put down the bat!" in a practiced, authoritative tone of voice, one way too authoritative to be coming from a bystander. When he looked back, a man in uniform was snatching the bat out of Li'l Who's hands; he didn't wait for him to comply.

The officer jerked the baseball bat from him, then pushed him closer to Li'l One Gone, pointing his pistol at both of them. "Kiss the ground, dickheads," the officer commanded. Without hesitation, Li'l Who jumped straight down to the ground. Li'l One Gone moved a tad slower getting down than Li'l Who did. It wasn't because he had something other than getting down on the ground on his mental; he was just afraid that he was going to cut or stab himself while doing so.

When he realized that it was a policeman barking at them, he slipped the exposed knife into his pocket. Looking down the barrel the size of a nickel, he lay down. Getting cut, he decided, was far more better than what was coming out the end of that barrel if he didn't comply to the officer's order.

Even a square knew to keep their hands in sight and not make a sudden move when the lawman or outlaw got the drop on them. The police cuffed their hands together behind their backs, then picked them off the filthy sidewalk. Patting Li'l One Gone down, he pulled out the knife, looked at it, then put it in his pocket.

The school buses had pulled up, but the kids were hesitant loading it; they were too busy look-a-whooing, their interest on what was happening with their schoolmates. The ones that were already on it rubbernecked; they had their faces pressed to the window, fogging up the glass as they watched Li'l Who and Li'l One Gone get escorted by the policeman to a waiting patrol unit vehicle, get thrown into the back seat, then hauled off.

From the back seat of the patrol unit, Li'l One Gone stared into the direction where another officer was kneeling over Double D, speaking into an electronic device. As they rolled up West Roosevelt Street, Li'l Who had his eyes closed, his head leaning back against the seat. Another bullet point had been added to Li'l One Gone's résumé. Whether he wanted it or not, Li'l Who's reputation had begun also. The streets had eyes that saw and a mouth that didn't stay shut.

The trip to the Highland Road Precinct was brisk. Inside the precinct station, hostility could be felt, the atmosphere not friendly. It was cold. Li'l Who pulled at his handcuffs, cold steel against his flesh bringing realization of what was going on to the forefront of his consciousness. He shook his head, disgusted at the overall position he was in. "Bruh, fuck, you think they gonna let us roll up outa dis bitch?" he asked, pulling again against his restraints, this time half-heartedly.

"Man, fuck," Li'l Who expressed, this time jerking away from the wall with force the clanking sound of metal against metal blended in with the rest of the noise in the precinct, then faded away.

"My nigga, be easy. We good." Speaking as if his words were absolute, Li'l One Gone spoke more so to ease his own nerves rather than to calm Li'l Who's. He was just as uncertain of the outcome as Li'l Who was; only difference was, he didn't allow his thoughts or feelings to show. Disdain for law enforcement enabled him to keep his emotions bottled up, and his nerves in check. "Jus' chill out, my friend," Li'l One Gone instructed Li'l Who, putting emphasis on the word *friend*, "and stop pulling against them cuffs. Ya wrist gon' give 'fo the wall do."

Looking into his eyes, he saw that they had begun to water up, turning away from him. "Say, look at that nigga over there behind that desk," Li'l One Gone said. Li'l Who raised his head, puzzlement written across his face in contrast to his now-red eyes. Pointing with his free hand, Li'l One Gone added, "Ova there, that nigga got a dome on him. I thought yo' shit was built funny. His shit shaped like a titty on a basketball, a Nerf ball, or some shit. Gawd damn, his head is deflected like a muthafucka."

He chuckled, fixing his lips into a crooked smirk.

"Real shit," Li'l One Gone emphasized, bugging his eyes out as he spoke to add drama to his words. "Real shit, though, my nigga. Dat's how ya shit gonna be when you get older, jus' like dat ole rusty-ass nigga is, all whop—"

Before Li'l One Gone finished getting it out, slicing his words off in midsentence, Li'l Who started to laugh. "Man, fuck you!" he managed to squeeze out in between chuckles.

They both exploded into a boisterous, full-fledged laughter.

"Hey, cut out all that fucking noise out!" yelled someone concealed behind a wall in an adjacent office to where they were hand-cuffed. Li'l Who quieted his down but didn't completely stop. Li'l One Gone stifled his laughter by putting his free arm against his mouth.

"Hey, cut out all that fuck'n noise out!" Li'l Who repeated, mocking the person who yelled at them.

Li'l One Gone doubled over in laughter. Even the officer with the odd-shaped head joined in the laughter, putting his head down to conceal this action.

Li'l One Gone felt relieved that his boy had loosened up. He nodded at his own thoughts and continued to laugh, a laugh that was cut abruptly. If there's a certain profile that fits an officer that spends most of his time shuffling paper, the man that came out of the office was the poster child for that position. He was a short obese man; the buttons on his shirt looked like they were ready to project off his shirt at any given moment from the strain of his bulging belly. The other half of his stomach was tucked inside his khaki slacks, resting on his lap, which was the first thing Li'l One Gone noticed as he loomed over them. The man's chin disappeared inside the roll of fat that surrounded his neck. He had small beady blue eyes centered on his pasty-white face. Salt-and-pepper hair was cropped short around his ears.

"So you two little motherfuckers think something's funny?" he said, waving a fat, stubby finger that resembled a smoked turkey sausage side to side from Li'l Who to Li'l One Gone. "Look at me when I'm talking to you, little shits," the officer demanded. When he talked, he moved his head in a jerky motion, which made the fat around his chin jiggle. Seeing the fat rattle, shake, and roll as he looked up tickled Li'l One Gone awfully; still, he was able to contain his laughter. Looking up at the policeman's face, noticing one of his beady eyes was severely cocked, he no longer was able to control himself—Li'l One Gone exploded into a fit of laughter louder than he initially was intending to.

Out of his periphery he saw Li'l Who shaking his head.

"Funny man, huh? Well, let's see how funny it is when Jimbo has that big, fat, chubby ass of yours jacked up in the air, ripping your asshole to pieces. And you"—he pointed to Li'l Who—"after he finishes ravishing your buddy there." He nodded at Li'l One Gone, who was now looking like he had swallowed an egg, a rotten one at that, a smile still stuck onto his face but his eyes betraying him.

The policeman continued, "When ole Jimbo pulls his thir-teen-foot dick out of his rectum, blood and shit dripping from it, he's going to make your little marble-head-ass clean it off with your mouth. Uh-huh, can you picture it?" Moving close to the both of them, he had his face inches away from theirs. "Can you picture it?" he sternly asked, staring into one set of eyes, then the other's. "Guess what? I made the call. Jimbo is waiting, and you better pray that the guy you assaulted makes it, because if he dies, you two are going to be acquainted with Jimbo a mighty-long time, and that's a promise.

Now laugh at that!" he yelled as he stomped off. The officer behind the desk whistled and shook his head in a manner that stated, "I feel sorry for y'all."

Li'l One Gone's stomach started bubbling, his entire body starting to tremble. Li'l Who went slack; if he weren't sitting down, he would have collapsed to the floor. Neither one of them had any knowledge of the criminal code and procedure, due process of the law, or their constitutional rights, but they both had full knowledge that a dead man equals a very long time locked up behind fences, away from everything and everybody.

Being ten years of age, Li'l Who wasn't going to the East Baton Rouge Parish Juvenile Detention Center; he wasn't old enough, but he was old enough for the foster home until he became old enough to get transferred there. Li'l One Gone was eleven years of age, which made him eligible for the ride to the "baby parish prison." On a previous run-in with the law, his being underaged saved him, and the policeman assured him that if he violated any time after he made eleven years old, off to Ryan's Detention Center he went.

"Fuck!" he said out loud as the thought dawned on him that his eleventh birthday had come and gone since the last time the lawman had him collared. Li'l One Gone's yelling out "Fuck!" didn't help; it only made matters worse. Li'l Who, looking toward him for answers and strength, fell apart when he heard him say "Fuck!" He knew that his homie had crumbled under the pressure. Their situation was a tight one, tighter than a fish pussy. The only way he saw out of the jam was their age, which had just slipped away, he thought to himself as he leaned back against the wall.

Feeling the cold steal, he tried to pull and twist around his wrist. There wasn't enough slack in the handcuffs to move his wrist an inch in either direction. Cutting out of the handcuffs and bolting for the door wasn't going to happen. He glanced over at Li'l Who, whose face was wet with tears, staring wide-eyed at him. He still was looking at Li'l One Gone as if he was searching his face for answers. The sadness scribbled all over Li'l Who's face caused sadness to stir up inside Li'l One Gone. Turning his head, Li'l One Gone closed his eyes, leaned back against the wall, defeated. He remained in that position.

Beating Double D with the bat into a standstill, tears falling down Li'l Who's face, and getting hauled away to a place surrounded by barbed wire, all in that order, flashed across his mind's eyes. Before trepidation set in, he opened his eyes. Since the death of T'Sharon, Li'l One Gone had devised a way to suppress invading unwanted emotions by means of distraction or mentally distancing himself. Distancing was taking him deeply into his feelings; therefore, he turned off distancing and flipped on distraction.

It was his first time inside a police precinct. This was the headquarters of those who had sworn under oath to protect, serve, and enforce the law. From within these walls, he thought as he looked around, is where pain, joy, peace, and misery are dispatched. A call comes in; someone is in distress or has just been victimized. A call goes out across the airwaves; an officer responds to the call, then arrives on the scene, bringing joy and peace for the victim, but misery and mental pain for the perpetrator of the illegal act. Filled with joy of knowing that their protector in blue has arrived, and peace knowing that a resolution to their situation is forthcoming. For the assailant, being persuaded by the hunters of men, having to peek over their shoulders day and night causes misery. After they've been apprehended, forfeiting life and liberty then starting the drawn-out court proceedings, all while in custody, produces a mental pain for the assailant that can't be described.

Scanning around the room, Li'l One Gone noticed that besides him and Li'l Who, there was one other occupant in there with them, an officer sitting behind a desk facing them in the last or first desk, depending on which end of the office one started to count from. The desk was situated in a row of three that ran parallel to another row of three identical desks that were centered to several metal file cabinets matching the color of the desk that lined the left-hand wall or the right-hand wall.

A set of corkboards, with dozens of papers tacked to it, covered half of one of the sidewall; the other half of that wall had white boards with charts, graphs, and sentences written in different colors all over it. The other sidewall was bare. A few of the desks looked like, from Li'l One Gone's angle of view, and had metal chairs with the green cushions behind them, the others having leather office ones behind them. Only one desk in the office didn't have a chair behind it or anything on top of it. The others had several different articles on the surface, each different, but one thing they all had in common, resting in the upper right-hand corner of the desk or the other, was a black dial telephone. The lone officer now whispered through the receiver on the telephone on his desk.

On the back wall, an automobile pinup calendar, with a 1963 Mustang Shelby GTO picture from three angles on it, hung in the middle of the row of desks. The "May 1988" written across the top of the calendar in large bold black letters caught his attention. Succinctly, at the point in his life, days only mattered, not dates. Next to the calendar was a clock; time was ticking away.

It had been a little over an hour since they made it to the precinct. Although the booking process hadn't even begun yet, unsure of what lay ahead, Li'l One Gone put it in his mind that it was what it was. Wherever he was going, he damn sure wasn't going to walk into the motherfucker with tears in his eyes. He was from Southside, across the track, and he was going to represent that to the death of him. Though his eyes were red, the tears had stopped falling from them.

A barrage of phones in the office started ringing off the hook all of a sudden, like they were on a set timer. People in uniform and suits, both male and female, flooded into the office one behind another minutes after the phones broke the peacefulness of the office. All eyes were on them before and after they stationed themselves behind their desk. The female officers' stares lingered a little longer than did their male counterparts'. Some of the ones standing, conversing, would throw glances in their direction here and there more frequently than those sitting behind their desks would.

There wasn't a pair of eyes that entered into the building that hadn't rested on them at some point or another. Manacled to the wall, Li'l One Gone started to feel like a spectacle. He twisted his face into the meanest mug he could muster, which only caused some of the officers of the law to shoot challenging stares back at him. Those who didn't have that look plastered on their faces that said that they weren't going to stand for any bullshit had a sly grin under their noses.

Under all the different masks of the officers, he held his ground as long as he could, becoming very uncomfortable under the constant stares and glares. For the first time since he had been in there, Li'l One Gone bowed his head, the three stripes on his tennis shoes suddenly becoming more interesting to him than anything else he had seen before. All the fight evaporated out of him. Head down, he realized that he was truly restrained on enemy turf. He was now a captive in their world. Hard or slick didn't count for shit; only thing that counted behind those walls was what was written in the Louisiana Revised Statute Code and Procedure, the law he had willfully violated. Freedom was more of a privilege than God-given right.

All the lively chatter, desk drawers shrieking as they were being opened then banged shut, the sound of paper being shuffled, doors slamming shut, and phones ringing chased out the silence of an empty building, and along with the aroma of freshly brewed coffee floating in the air, it made it seem like an ordinary place of work on the surface. Underneath the surface, though, it was a place where hopes, dreams, and all good things became instantly shattered for those who found themselves in the position Li'l Who and Li'l One Gone were now in, on a metal bench, handcuffed to the wall.

"Which one of you's Damon Hutch again?" Officer Lic Johnson asked.

"Me," Li'l Who replied wearily.

"Okay." He pulled out a set of keys, and with the key, he leaned over then uncuffed Li'l Who's wrist, leaving the other ring of the handcuff fastened to the wall. Rubbing his wrist as if to rub away the memory of the handcuff, Li'l Who meekly stared at the officer. "Get up and come with me this way," Officer Johnson commanded Li'l Who. Still rubbing his wrist, he looked over at Li'l One Gone as he stood to his feet.

"Where ya taking my boy?" Li'l One Gone asked. His voice was low and trembling, but he held his composure like a baby OG.

"To the penitentiary. Don't worry, you're coming too," Officer Lic Johnson said, then throw his head back, laughing as he walked off. He grabbed Li'l Who by the arms as he dragged him through a set of windowless swinging doors. Li'l One Gone's eyes followed Li'l Who as he was being led away. He looked back once before the doors closed shut behind the officer and him.

Li'l Who's face mirrored Li'l One Gone's; he looked scared, like a woman cornered in an alley, with no place to run, with a stranger standing in front of her with his meat pistol in one hand, solidly erect, and a .38 special in the other. Just like Double D's fate had been sealed, theirs had just been stamped, signed, and sealed by Officer Lic Johnson. Li'l One Gone looked once more toward the doors his friend had disappeared through, saying out loud, "Fuck."

The handcuffs felt like they were burning his wrist, as his skin became flushed. He tried to stop his hands from trembling, but they only trembled more. His knees started to bounce up and down, the vibration from them bouncing pushing his heart into his throat. He jumped up to his feet shakily. Suddenly, he found it hard to breathe, then all the lights in the office went out.

When the lights come back on, he was lying in a cold cement floor inside a cell.

A female officer had his wrist in her hand, squeezing it with her fingers while she looked at a watch on hers. She noticed that Li'l One Gone had awakened, so she dropped his hand. "How do you feel?" she asked. After writing on a clipboard, she put it down and pulled a stethoscope out of a bag. Conscious but a bit foggy, he tried to rise, though not forcibly, but she held him in place while she listened to his insides. Puzzled, he lay there, inventorying the contents of the cell. A bench the same as the one out in the office, but longer, lined both sides of the wall. In the back of the cell, there was a wall four feet in length that stood waist-high.

Satisfied, she took the stethoscope out of her ear. "So how do you feel, child? Besides the bruises and abrasions around your wrist, you're gonna be okay," she stated, but it came out more like a question. Li'l One Gone didn't reply. Once she gathered up all her equipment, she winked at Li'l One Gone, then walked out, slamming the bars shut behind her. Full of grime and grit, he dusted the grit off each of his bare arms after he picked himself off the floor.

The smell of stale urine assaulted his nostrils, but it had an overwhelming smell of vomit mixed with it also. Walking to the waist-high wall, peering off it, he saw there was dried vomit all over a stainless steel toilet, also a large pile of it directly in front of it. It looked like someone missed the hole of the toilet or hit their intended mark.

Pacing back and forward, Li'l One Gone gave up on wearing down the soles of his tennis shoes. He plopped down on one of the benches and lay on his back, with his right knee propped up against the wall, one hand behind his head and the other one over his eyes, blocking out the bright light that hung above his head.

"You 'sleep, nigga?" Li'l Who, standing over him with a somber face, asked.

Sitting up, Li'l One Gone realized he had dozed off. He didn't hear the bars open, close, or Li'l Who come into the cell. He wouldn't have heard him ask if he was sleep either if Li'l Who hadn't slapped his foot when he asked him. When he did hear him, that was the third time he had called out to him. Shocked to see his friend, he stared at him a while before he spoke or moved. "Man, where you been?" Li'l One Gone asked after he had shaken off the slumber and overcome the shock of seeing Li'l Who.

"Dog, this ole pussy-ass police had me in a muthafuck'n room, askin' me all types of dumb shit, like why I attacked the nigga, what's his name, how long I've been knowing you. I told the nigga I don't know shit and I ain't done shit," Li'l Who stated, then he went deadly quiet.

Li'l One Gone suspiciously looked up at Li'l Who, instantly noticing the change. He stood up. "What happened, dog? What da fuck else happened?" He'd been around Li'l Who so long he knew when he was holding back on something. He moved closer to him. "My nigga, now ain't da time fo' no games. What happened?" he asked, struggling to keep the whine out of his voice.

"A'ight," Li'l Who stated, then paused, looked around. "Dude, the police…um…before he started asking me them dumbass questions"—he was now talking with his hands also—"he was on some shit, like ya boy had already told him how da shit went down, so don't come in there lying. What up with that?" Li'l Who threw both hands up, his tone accusing as he asked. Li'l One Gone stood there with his hands on his hips, dumbfounded. "Yeah, Wet Fish got mad and left out and left Jennifer, and Sassy was in there when the police had said that shit 'bout you."

Li'l One Gone stood silently staring at the wall over Li'l Who's head. Li'l Who then took several steps back and sat down on the bench. "So?" he asked Li'l One Gone.

Mystified, Li'l One Gone had a hard time getting a grip on what was going on. He turned his back to Li'l Who, stretching out a few ticks before he turned back and faced his friend. "You say Wet Fish and them was with you? What they doing here?"

"Wet Fish and Sassy said that they were my mama and daddy and Jennifer is your mama," Li'l Who replied. "Fuck that, though. You told them peoples—"

Before he could finish his sentence, Li'l One Gone was on top of him. For a chubby kid, he moved with the swiftness of a panther. Many boys and the playground and streets had underestimated him because of his size and lazy movements, finding out the hard way that *fat* and *slow* are not always synonymous.

Li'l Who balled up, Li'l One Gone pulling his punches. They were friends, he didn't want to hurt him, but he did want to get an understanding. Li'l Who kicked out, landing a well-placed kick into Li'l One Gone's thigh, forcing him back a few feet; at the same time he jumped to his feet, he threw his set up. A few inches shorter than Li'l One Gone, he advanced forward, swinging upward. Li'l One Gone landed a punch, and Li'l Who did as well. Feeling his instinct kicking into combat mode, Li'l One Gone grabbed Li'l Who. "A'ight, nigga, chill out!" he yelled, holding onto him, letting him go after quite some struggling.

Li'l Who pushed off him once he was released from Li'l One Gone's grip.

Breathing in then out deeply, Li'l One Gone said, "My nigga, that jive-ass police lied to you on me. I haven't talked to nobody since we been up in here. He played yo li'l stupid ass." Li'l One Gone knew the code: if you don't talk, you walk; if you talk, the walk's going to be your home.

"He ain't play shit," Li'l Who shot back, bracing up to Li'l One Gone.

"Man, sit down and be cool before I knock yo li'l ass through that wall," Li'l One Gone said as he moved to the front of the cell, putting both hands through the bars. He leaned his forehead against them. "Dog, real shit, did he say what he was gonna do with us? I need to know. I heard them say when we came back here that he needed to contact our parents or guardians before something," Li'l One Gone expressed.

"I don't know, but when that punk-ass police brought me back here, he…um…told somebody to call up to Ryan's to see if they got a bed open," Li'l Who said, looking at the back of Li'l One Gone's head.

Feeling his eyes on the back of his head, Li'l One Gone turned around, putting his back against the bars, facing Li'l Who. "Oh yeah, shied, well, it is what it is." He already knew that bed had Vietnam G. Franklin written on it.

* * *

"Open up, four!" a voice came floating down the corridor. Footsteps rhythmically slapped the concrete as a turnkey hurried toward their cell, unlocking then swinging open the heavily barred door. "Franklin, step out," an aging black man who looked like he was bored by the routine and would much rather be on a fishing pond than there commanded Li'l One Gone.

As Li'l One Gone stepped out, the old man stepped back, letting him pass. He moved to the side, turned, and looked through the bars at Li'l Who, who was now lying in the same position Li'l One Gone was in before he had come into the cell, disturbing him. He was about to speak, but *wham, click,* the old man slammed and locked the cell back. As he stared down at Li'l One Gone again, words formed in his mouth, but instead he swallowed them back down.

Impatiently, not waiting for him to move on his own, he shoved Li'l One Gone. "This ah way, boy," he said, pointing toward Officer Lic Johnson waiting at the end of the corridor. "All yours," the old man told Officer Lic Johnson when he and Li'l One Gone made it in front of him. He walked off, whistling, twirling a key chain with a largemouth bass jumping over a boat on it.

Passing through a maze of cubicles, down a hallway of offices, Officer Lic Johnson escorted Li'l One Gone into a room that had the word *interview* in gold letters on black background taped to the door. Inside Wet Fish, Jennifer, and Sassy sat back away from a plastic table. At the table was the man with the cockeye. His eyes fell on Wet Fish. There wasn't anything there for Li'l One Gone to read in his eyes, so he returned a blank stare, then turned away from Li'l One Gone. He then searched Jennifer's and Sassy's faces for a clue. They both had concern written across their faces as they held his gaze. From the expression on her face, Jennifer seemed like she was about to explode from the words she was holding in—at least that was the read Li'l One Gone deciphered from her nonverbal communication.

"Have a seat, Mr. Vietnam Franklin."

He was still reading Jennifer's expression, then something on the wall got her attention. No one besides the policeman had said a word so far. Li'l One Gone took a seat between Officer Lic Johnson and the fat white officer. There was a tape recorder and notepad on top of the table. Pushing Play, shoving the tape recorder directly in front of Li'l One Gone, he started. "Today is May 31, 1988. I, Detective Seymore Ballsaks, along with Sergeant Lic Johnson, have with us one Vietnam G. Franklin. The suspect is accompanied by his legal guardian and aunt." Li'l One Gone turned and looked at both of them when the detective said *legal guardian* and *aunt*. They all gave Li'l One Gone the look, "We are here," so he focused on Detective Ballsaks now as he continued, "To investigate an assault on"—he flipped through the papers in front of him—"a victim with a baseball bat in the 1200 block of West Roosevelt Street, here with the parish of East Baton Rouge, at approximately 6:35 a.m. Sergeant Lic Johnson was a witness to the assault and the arresting officer. Therefore, he won't be participating in the interview. He is here for observation purposes only. The time is…is 1:27 p.m. The interview will now begin."

It was 1:27 p.m., so mentally counting back to when the buses started to pull up, six hours had passed since they'd been detained; two hours left and school would be closed for the summer.

"Son, can you state, ah, say your full name and date of birth for the record?" Detective Seymore Ballsaks asked, interrupting Li'l One Gone's thoughts.

Sitting slouched over with his elbows on top of the table, his face resting between his hands, Li'l One Gone rolled his eyes to the ceiling. "Vietnam Franklin, April 17, 1978," he stated in a voice dripping with sarcasm. Showing his contentment, putting his head down on the table, he started humming.

"What did you have for breakfast this morning?" the detective asked.

Surprised by the nature of the question, Li'l One Gone abruptly stopped the humming. He didn't have to ponder on it—he hadn't eaten anything since the day before—but he hesitated answering because the question brought his dearly departed love to his mind. She would ask him that question regardless of the time of day.

"Nothing," he said, almost inaudible. All the sarcasm had vanished from his tone.

"Don't feel bad, sport. I haven't eaten a damn thing so far either. Been too busy. How about after we finish in here, I have Sergeant there get you and your buddy a nice, hot plate with cookies or chocolate cake for dessert? You look like a chocolate-chip-cookie type of guy yourself, am I right?" he stated, more in a declarative form than that of a question. One of the females snickered at his witty comment, and although he didn't pick his head up to see which one, Li'l One Gone was pretty sure it was Jennifer. "So what is it going to be? Are you going to tell me what you did?" the detective asked, wanting to but not adding another witty comment. On the account he didn't want Jennifer to burst into a full-fledged laughter, he wanted the vibe of the room to be a serious one and not to be misconstrued for a joking one.

"Okay," Li'l One Gone said. The ice between them had been broken. He picked his head up. Sergeant Lic Johnson had made him feel uncomfortable with his cold stare from the time Li'l One Gone had entered the room. He sat silently and stone-faced; there wasn't a crease of friendliness or sympathy etched onto his face. He peered at Li'l One Gone's soul, quickly turning, scanning the room. The expression of everyone in the room had softened a bit, and only a bit. Seriousness was still there, written plain as day, over Jennifer's and Sassy's faces, but Wet Fish was beyond serious; his posture had changed. He looked wound tight and ready to spring, death jumping off his face. Sergeant Lic Johnson was the object of his attention. He then zeroed in on Detective Seymore Ballsaks, briefly burning a hole in the side of his face, then turning his attention to Li'l One Gone, holding his glare, his expression unchanged. He nodded once, then returned his focus to Sergeant Lic Johnson.

"I'm not going to go on and on with a line of questions. Nope, that's not how I operate. Some do, but I don't. I'm not like those other dickheads—excuse my language, ladies," he said without looking in their directions, his eyes shifting from side to side, making it hard for Li'l One Gone to concentrate on what was being said. The fat around his neck that looked like it was doing the funky chicken dance every time he moved his head didn't help the situation either.

It was a tough battle, but he managed to suppress the laughter. As a result of him fighting down the overwhelming urge to laugh, some of what Detective Seymore Ballsaks said had escaped his ears. "Straight to the point" was what he heard when he finished his bout with hysterics.

"What?" Li'l One Gone asked, more frankly now.

"You're," he said, pointing his fat, stubby finger at Li'l One Gone, "going to start from the top by telling me exactly what happened out there this morning, and…um"—he pointed to himself—"I'm going to sit here and listen while you talk." He folded his arms across his endless midsection.

The room had become oppressively quiet. Li'l One Gone's heart was pounding so hard he could swear everyone could see it beating against his chest. Transcending to another place and time wasn't going to be sufficient this time; he wasn't going to have the liberty of escaping the situation by ensconcing himself within himself and waiting until everything blew over. He knew he had to man up. Besides, Detective Seymore Ballsaks came across as a man that had just as much patience as he had access weight, which was unlimited.

Feeling the pressure, he looked around. All eyes were on him. Wet Fish, Jennifer, and Sassy were present in the room with him, providing support, though silent, but they were there for him, in his corner, on his side. The thought gave him a little relief, but he never felt so empty and alone as he did then. Quickly running a head game on himself to gather the rapidly fleeing courage, he knew he had to come up with a quick resolution to the problem at hand. His thoughts took him back to square one. Mental departure wasn't going to be adequate. "Fuck," he said within. He knew he had landed in hot water headfirst. If he wasn't sure, the look on everyone's face conveyed the message, yet for some reason the severity of the situation hadn't breached the realm of reality inside him just yet.

It felt like he was now being the recipient of the brunt end of a cruel joke. Albeit there wasn't a smiling face in the room, nor was there a shred of laughter breaching anyone lips. Wishing to be invincible didn't work; it was as futile as someone trying to excavate a tunnel with a plastic spoon. He tried to fade into the chair that he was sitting in, which proved to be useless also. Finally, he admitted to himself that he had allowed himself to be backed into a corner; therefore, whatever happened, he had to take it on the chin like a champ and keep fighting.

This was the price he had to pay for slipping and allowing himself to get busted in the act of committing a felony. Visualizing incidents of the past, he had watched countless cats from the Bricks, up the street, and around the corner get hauled away with their hands cuffed behind their backs, only to return months later, some years later, while others had yet to return. The very building that he now sat inside was where their journey to oblivion had begun.

Li'l One Gone bowed his head, cupped his face in his hands, then rested facedown on the table. The coldness of the table against the flesh of his hands helped soothe him, thus bringing him to another place in time of his short existence living on the footstool of the son of man. Seeds of righteousness had been planted in him at one time. Over time, the seeds of the world, those of the wicked mankind, were planted in the garden of his heart. The seeds of the wicked had outgerminated those of the righteous.

Grandma Mama's words sprung to the foremost layers of his subconscious. She used to always preach, "No matter what, always tell da truth and shame da devil. Da truth sometimes downright hurts, but it makes da good Lord smile on you, baby." Her voice was so vividly clear and present in his memory that it sounded like she was in the room, speaking to him.

"I'm waiting, son," the detective said.

Li'l One Gone picked his head halfway off the table, then he paused for a second. He picked it up again, looking dead into Detectives Ballsaks's eyes. "Okay, mister, is like dis," he succinctly said, hesitating. "I mean, my name is Vietnam G Didn't-See-Shit-or-Did-Shit Franklin."

"Huh? Say what?" Sassy blurted out, and simultaneously Jennifer gasped out loud.

Sergeant Lic Johnson leaned forward toward Li'l One Gone, then eased back, his face contorting then going back to stone. His transformation happened so quickly Li'l One Gone almost missed it. Detective Seymore Ballsaks remained silent, but the skin covering the rolls of blubber on his neck turned a dark shade of red, revealing his emotional state. The changing color around his neck shot upward into his face.

"Don't know shit or don't want to?" he asked through clenched teeth.

"My name is B-ware, and I don't care. They call me Eddie Lee, and I can't see," Li'l One Gone added. He and the detective locked eyes. Like they say, if looks could kill, Li'l One Gone would have been dead ten times over. Although his bad eye wouldn't stay still long enough to get a read on, the good one told the story.

"You have a lot of alias there, Mr. Vi-et-nam," he spit out like it left a nasty taste in his mouth, fake chuckling. "Let the record show.

Anything else you want to add?" he asked Li'l One Gone, speaking into the tape recorder.

In his zone, oblivious to the tape recorder, he now turned his attention to it, speaking into it directly. "Yeah, my name is Ka'lear, I can't hear. I once went by the name Git-chu, you know what that rhyme wit? Fuck you!" Li'l One Gone defiantly expressed. Li'l One Gone burst out laughing at his wittiness, then in a childlike manner, he stuck his tongue out at the detective. The entire room was filled with laughter.

Losing his composure, the detective vehemently spat out, "You little fat dumbass black nigger!" as he propelled himself up from his seat. "I'll teach you about being smart. All you motherfucking people come in here with no regard for the law and act like we are the ones fucking up!" he yelled. Everyone in the interview room had quit laughing right around the time "black ass" left his mouth. His words struck a vein, bringing out some sort of reaction out of everyone except for Sergeant Lic Johnson. A crooked grin formed under his nose and was stuck in place as he slowly nodded. He was almost the spitting image, in physical stature, of Wet Fish, only a few shades darker than him. They both seemed to be in the same range of age. Where Wet Fish didn't have any facial hair, Sergeant Lic Johnson had a mustache and goatee. He had remained expressionless until the detective got riled up; he seemed to be mentally cheering him on. Sassy, Jennifer, and Wet Fish looked at one another in utter disbelief.

Li'l One Gone stood to his feet. "Okay!" he yelled. "I'm sorry, I didn't mean to say 'Fuck you.' What I meant was, muthafuck you!" he yelled. Then pointing to Sergeant Lic Johnson, eyeing him up and down, he added, "Man, you's ah certified house nigga, and fuck that ole fat-ass, crazy, cockeyed crack'a you roll'n wit."

Detective Seymour Ballsaks dived across the table, knocking the tape recorder to the floor with his stomach. He grabbed Li'l One Gone by the front of his shirt, reared his hand back, but just as his hand was coming down to deliver the blow, Sergeant Lic Johnson bumped Li'l One Gone out of the way. He laid his shoulder into him like a cornerback knocking a receiver off his route. One of the women screamed as Li'l One Gone's body slapped the floor. It sounded off when he hit the floor; therefore, it made the impact seem more severe than it actually was.

"Come on, DT, let's go out and get some air," Sergeant Lic Johnson told the detective, grabbing him around the shoulders. "Calm down, let it go," he encouraged him. Sergeant Lic Johnson laughed for the first time, looking down at Li'l One Gone, pushing Detective Seymore Ballsaks to the interview room door. "We'll get him later," he said, cutting off the laughter. He put his game face on as he guided the detective through the door.

All the bravado having left him, Li'l One Gone lay on the floor, frozen. He didn't move an inch; in fact, he had held his breath the entire time the officers were standing over him, staring down at him, blowing like a raging bull.

"I'm a'ight," he said as he climbed to his feet. He was more embarrassed than hurt. "Yep, I'm good," he said, more to convince himself than the others. Wet Fish had stormed out of the room behind the policemen, leaving him and the women alone.

"Baby, you sho' you ain't hurt ya'self when you fell? You hit dat floor some hard," Jennifer asked, rubbing on his back. "Fuck them bastards. You did right to talk to them muthafuckas like dat. He had no right putting his hands on you, though," she said, looking over her shoulder like she was making sure that no one was listening. "One thing I hate is the police. I can't stand none of 'em," she said, disgust written all over her face. Reaching for the door, Jennifer held him back, Sassy standing in front of it. She hadn't said anything so far. Then she found her voice.

"Oh no, baby, you can't leave outa this room. They'll throw all our ass in jail. Come, let's sit down till they get back," Sassy gently said. Li'l One Gone picked up the chair he was sitting in and moved it next to the one Jennifer was sitting in.

Jennifer sat next to him, leaned over, and kissed him on the cheek, the same way she had been doing since the day after they met. Exhausted, he leaned over, putting his elbows on his thighs, with his head hung to his knees. He reflected on the day's past events as Jennifer caressed his back as he thought, a sour sensation filling his stomach, emitting a foul taste in his mouth. His tears stung his cheeks, and he let out body-racking sobs. At that, moment he didn't give a damn who heard or saw him cry. All the hardness drifted out of his soul. Locked inside the interview room of the precinct, he had reverted back to his original nature, a child, a weak and hurt one.

Later, sitting in the parking lot of Burger King on Scenic Highway, Li'l One Gone stared out of the window of the car, watching a lady kind of on the heavy side bend over, her tight-fitting dress rolling high up her thigh as she searched for whatever it was she was looking for on back seat of her car. "After we drop them hoes off, we gon' hit a few corners," Wet Fish, turning around, said.

Li'l One Gone looked away from the woman. "Cool," he replied, still a tad bit shaken. His voice still had the tone of a person that had lost their confidence and was on the verge of building it back up. When he turned to gaze back out of the window, the woman had stood upright and was tugging at her dress, pulling it back into its proper place. Damn, how lucky they were, he thought as he watched a girl around his age walk into John's Seafood behind the lady with the tight dress.

When Detective Ballsaks came back into the room with a tall silver-haired white man and stiff-backed retired-commando-looking fellow and told him that he was free to go, that there had been a big misunderstanding, he really couldn't believe it, thinking that his ears were lying to him. He sat paralyzed, mouth agape, twisting his head from Jennifer's face to Sassy's until the man yelled, "Come on, let's move it!" He got up and walked out. Detective Seymore Ballsaks didn't like what was going on. Disapproval was evident all over his face.

Staring at his face reflected off the car window, Li'l One Gone thought back to the previous moments.

Detective Seymore Ballsaks followed Li'l One Gone all the way to the exit door before Li'l One Gone could clear the door. He grabbed him, peering down at him. Not only did he see the rage and anger in him; he felt it also. Squeezing Li'l One Gone's shoulder, he said, "Mr. Funny Man, somebody who sits high gave you a pass. You can thank him tonight while you are on your knees. I can't go against the call, but I'm gonna say this: if you come back in here for anything—and I mean *anything*—I will be the one that nails your ass to the cross." Then he slapped Li'l One Gone in the back of the head, followed by a kick to his backside.

Touching the spot where Detective Seymore Ballsaks's meaty hand had connected with his head, he rubbed it gently. Was it the silver-haired man, the one that sat high and looked low, or one of the thug gods that spared him and Li'l Who? he asked himself. Li'l Who was sitting silently next to him in the back seat of Wet Fish's car. He looked straight ahead, his forehead wrinkled up, deep in thought. It had to be God, he thought, settling on the answer as he ran back what Wet Fish had told him through his mind.

Detective Seymore Ballsaks was waiting for two things to happen before he began to process Li'l Who and Li'l One Gone into the system for attempted second-degree murder, assault with a deadly weapon, and possession of a concealed weapon. Although, they sold the exact pocketknife the police took off Li'l One Gone in drugstores, hardware stores, and any retail store in America, the fact that it wasn't folded close in his pocket made the pocketknife a concealed weapon. The detective was waiting for someone at the district attorney's office to approve the said charges and also for the warden at the juvenile detention center to inform him when a bed became available.

Meanwhile, another faction was busy while their life at the precinct was in limbo. Double D was all the way street; if he saw it, he had to get it. "Spare none, let nothing slide" was his motto. He was the type that would never cease or turn from his devilish ways on the way to his execution; instead of repenting, he'd be trying to go with his next move. He was a crook through and through; not a single cell of honesty resided within him.

The EMS arrived and transported him to the hospital for a further examination. On the scene, as far as they could tell, he had only suffered a few bumps and bruises, but per procedure, they had to take him to the hospital for observation and x-ray. Somewhere en route to the Baton Rouge General Hospital, or upon arrival, his junky ass picked the pocket of one of the emergency responders. He hit him for forty-three dollars cash and a couple of credit cards, family photos, and a few business cards the EMS worker had in his wallet. While he was in the room, waiting for the RN to bring him to the x-ray room, he swiped a box of syringes, poured them out onto the hospital gown he was supposed to have on, and rolled them up in it, concealing them.

From the moment they rolled him into the hospital, he had started to bellyache about how bad he was hurting. Inside the room, a nurse gave ear to his cry and gave him some medicine for the pain he was experiencing. She got a page over the PA system; it must have been an emergency somewhere, because she jetted out of the room and ran out so fast she forgot to put the bottle of pain medication back into her scrub pockets. Instead, she left it on top of the counter in the room, right next to a clipboard. That was like waving a color-ful toy that played music in front of a toddler. Double D, true to his nature, just had to snatch it. When she returned after backtracking to Double D's room, he and the bottle of pills were already gone.

But the pills or the few dollars weren't enough for him. An old lady had parked in the visitor's section of the hospital located a few feet over a hundred from the emergency entrance of the hospital, which was also the main entrance of the hospital. A street ran between the parking lot and the hospital, and as she walked up the street toward the entrance, Double D walked her way. She had her car keys in one hand and her purse in the other, and as she strolled up the street, Double D took off limping down the street, bumped the lady, and snatched her purse as she fell to the ground. Purse-snatching is usu-ally a clean, smooth motion. Snatch, then run. Simple. Sometimes the straps on some purses don't snap as easily as do others; therefore, some purse snatchers use a knife or box cutter to cut the straps when they grab it. The downside of that is, sometimes the purse snatchers cause unintended harm to their victims. Not only do they slice the strap of the woman's purse, but in the process, they also end up slic-ing the woman with the knife as well.

Most of the purse snatchers switch to the bump-and-run. Bumping causes the woman to fall, the force of her fall plus the momentum of the snatch causing the straps on the purse to give and break loose from the pressure. The bump-snatch-and-get-away usually goes how it's supposed to, although no victim is ever the right victim. Double D definitely chose the wrong victim. Turned out that the elderly Caucasian lady was the eighty-one-year-old mother of the chief of the Baton Rouge Police Department. She was on her way to visit her granddaughter, who had just had a daughter at the hospital. The chief was on his way to the hospital also. When he got there, he was met by a nurse telling him that his mama had just been admitted. She had been mugged and robbed, and as a result, her hip was broken and she had a mild heart attack.

Word got around the hospital about what had happened right outside to the chief's mama. The nurse and the EMS came forward with their story. Double D's description went out. He had given them an alias name, but once the investigation had begun, it led back to the man that had gotten assaulted on West Roosevelt Street. Which resulted in the apprehension of Li'l Who and Li'l One Gone. Sassy, at that time, didn't know what Double D had done. The police asked her if she knew the name of the man that was assaulted, and thinking nothing of it or that any harm could come from her telling the officer his name, she told them. The all-points bulletin went out on Double D, and a call came in to let the two boys that beat the shit out of him go.

When Wet Fish gave him the rundown, he thought he had to be playing with him. Wet Fish was known to fix things for him. He thought it was just another one of his fixes. He still couldn't believe he knew he was free; there was no doubt about that. "Square biz, it gotta be him," he mumbled to himself.

Jennifer and Sassy returned to the car with an armful of bags and cups. Li'l One Gone got out of the car and opened the passenger door for Jennifer. "Thank you, my love," she said as she got in.

They lived not too far from the Burger King in the Northdale neighborhood, so it didn't take long to make it to Jennifer's house. Jennifer lived on North Eighteenth Street, while Sassy lived on North Fifteenth Street in a neighborhood called Northdale. Li'l One Gone and his partner was quiet as they rode next to each other. Sassy had one door seat; Li'l One Gone had the other. Jennifer got out of the car when they pulled up to Sassy's house. "Here you go, and here you go," she said, handing Li'l Who and Li'l One Gone both a hamburger, an order of french fries, and a cold drink. "And yours right there, Daddy," she said, fingering a bag on the seat. "Now, what you got fo' me?" she asked, batting the long lashes on her eyes.

"I'ma see you later?" Wet Fish asked, dropping a pack in her outstretched hand.

"You would want to," she replied.

Li'l One Gone thought that was some kind of secret code, because every time Wet Fish would ask her that, she would reply the same way.

"Get up front, Vee," Wet Fish told Li'l One Gone.

"What time is it?" Li'l Who asked.

"Three fifteen," Li'l One Gone answered, looking at his wrist, which was now happy (it was lonely in the police station). They had taken his watch, belt, and shoelaces.

Concerned, Li'l Who said, concerned, "My mama—"

But he was cut off short. "Don't trip, Li'l G. I got ya. I'ma holla at ya mama fo' ya. Ask Vee. Tell 'em, Vee. I'ma straighten it out. He ain't got to worry about nothing," Wet Fish stated.

"Yeah, dog, don't worry. My man here can take care of everything. Remember?"

Wet Fish gave him that look.

"Yeah, he got you, my nigga."

Li'l Who picked up on the change but didn't question it. He knew Wet Fish by reputation and from seeing him in the neighborhood, but not as well as Li'l One Gone did. "Okay," he said.

They drove off. Wet Fish waited until he finished his food before he started to talk. Li'l One Gone had already gobbled his food down. He was so hungry he chewed once, then swallowed. "Roll this." Wet Fish handed Li'l One Gone a bag of killa and a Swisher Sweet cigar. He put in a cassette tape some cats from the East Coast had dropped. The origin of the track was easily recognizable because the highs of the beat were hitting harder than the bass.

"You know you my nigga. I got you right here in my heart," Wet Fish stated to Li'l One Gone.

"You my nigga too."

Wet Fish turned around in his seat, speaking. "And, Li'l Who," he said matter-of-factly, "check this out. Every time we rap, it's straight low on some up-and-up shit." A hint of a person that had schooling could be heard when he talked. Wet Fish, just like many other young black cats growing up in America, at one point stood around hopelessly with their hands shoved deep down in their empty pants pockets after graduating high school. The lure of the game was strong; slinging dope was more appealing than manually laboring for low wages. Besides, when it came to deciding to jump in the game, there wasn't any filling out applications, going to interviews, or waiting for someone to call with an offer of a job opportunity, all the while listening to one's stomach complain from the lack of food. All one had to do was come up with a few shams to make a purchase or know someone that was already in the game that was willing to put them on.

Hustling wasn't his first option. He would rather go to college, in fact had gotten into it as a means to get by until something better came through. The vacuum of the streets is sometimes stronger than will. Now he was ten toes deep in the game.

"Already," Li'l One Gone replied.

"You ain't finished pimping that bitch yet?" Wet Fish asked, looking over at Li'l One Gone making the final roll of the blunt.

"Got it!" Li'l One Gone expressed happily.

Wet Fish didn't have to tell him to reach into the console and pull out a book of matches—Li'l One Gone was already searching them. The killa hanging from his mouth, he struck the match. "Man, you smoke?" Li'l Who asked, amazed as he watched Li'l One Gone bring the flame to the killa. He inhaled once, blew it out, then smiled at Li'l Who. That was his answer.

"Come with that. I've been waiting all day to spark one. If it wasn't for you, I would have been blowed at least two or three by now. You and your man's back there wanna lay the low down early this morning." Looking through the rearview mirror, Wet Fish asked after he took several tokes of the killa, "Say, G, you want to hit this?"

Li'l Who turned it down. Wet Fish passed it to Li'l One Gone, who greedily puffed on it.

"Dog, I was scared to death today," Wet Fish spat out. Li'l One Gone had never heard or thought of Wet Fish becoming afraid of anything. Wet Fish had his undivided attention now. "Shit, yea, I thought I was 'bout to lose you to the system." Switching gears, he added, "Vee, you've been on these streets since you started walking. Remember when you used to sit under the tree with them old niggas?" Wet Fish paused, rolled down the window, and plucked the ashes off the killa. Li'l One Gone leaned against his seat belt and reminiscence as Wet Fish talked.

"That was a sight to see, four old niggas, I mean, supa-dirt old niggas and baby sit'n around a burning barrel, sip'n wine. One night, I had dipped through 'bout three o'clock in the morning, creep'n from dis li'l broad house. The fire had burnt out da barrel. All ya coulda saw was a glow. Mr. Harry head was sitting in his chest. Old man Clyde was leaned back on his car, trying to hold himself up. Them other two antique niggas was laying on their backs, stretched out on the ground, and you was stretched out, feet to the barrel, mouth wide open, knocked da fuck out, gripping a bottle of dat ole Thunderbird, looking like a professional wino. I picked you and da bottle up and carried you to ya mama. Them old niggas loved you, bruh." He nudged Li'l One Gone. "Nigga, I know you ain't sleep. What I told you 'bout dat shit? You can't be fall'n to sleep if you gon' smoke with me."

He opened the glove compartment, reached in, dug around. "Here, twist dis one," Wet Fish said, pulling out another cigar. "Winbourne and Thirty-Eighth Street," read the sign high up on the post as they cruised up the street. He thought about where he was. He didn't know, nor did it matter; he was riding, cruising through the city, something he rarely did. And it was all that mattered. Glancing over at Wet Fish, Li'l One Gone smiled. The weed had him feeling lovely, and added with the joy of riding, amusement filled his heart.

Splitting the cigar, he dumped the tobacco into the Burger King bag, dropping the few remaining buds out of the sandwich bag into the cigar wrapper. "You know you gotta break them buds fo' you twist it," Wet Fish jokingly barked at Li'l One Gone.

"I got dis here. Jus' keep them eyes of yours on the road," Li'l One Gone retorted.

Wet Fish allowed Li'l One Gone to learn as he go. Very seldom did he sit down and run the game to him. Recidivism wasn't a part of his profile. Every blue moon the teaching spell fell upon him, the weed helping bring out the professor in him. Li'l One Gone already knew that they were going to be taking a long ride once his mouth started to move. It was as if everything he had been holding in had to come out before he closed it. Then it would be many more moons before he conversed to that degree.

Li'l One Gone glanced at his watch. *It's gonna be a long ride,* he thought to himself.

He lit the killa, glancing back to check on Li'l Who, who was sitting on the edge of his seat like an attentive pupil, waiting for Wet Fish to start up again. Li'l One Gone extended his closed fist. "You good?" he asked Li'l Who. Li'l Who dapped him down. Li'l One Gone turned around.

"Yeah, that's you nigga fo' real, Vee!" Wet Fish exclaimed, extending his hand to Li'l Who for dap also. "What the fuck was I talking 'bout? Ah, yeah, back to you. I was tryin' to say," he said, then paused, puffing on the killa. "This some good shit. I got too catch up with dat nigga. Anyway, you been out here a while now, kiddo, but times are changing. The crazy part is, this shit seem like it flipped overnight. That nigga Rich showed you a level of the game, one that was fitting to you at the time. He taught you how to survive. You was a li'l roguish muthafucka. Don't get me wrong, Rich a straight gangsta. He gonna get down for his crown, but he be on some other shit at times. I can't dirty his name. Believe me, niggas gonna be talking 'bout him after he dead and rotting. That's how much street cred he got out here. Damn, nigga, you go' let that die out?" he said.

Li'l One Gone puffed the killa, bringing the dying ember on the hemp back to life.

"He put you on some shit that was going to get you fucked up out here. It is what it is now. I feel him, though. You had to sample the game out at one level or another." Looking over at Li'l One Gone,

Wet Fish stated, "I know you still be on that sticky finga' shit. Just don't steal from a nigga on the streets. Ya feel me?"

Li'l One Gone nodded.

"If you do, you better have a pistol in your hand. No, fuck dat shit. Get ya own. Don't fuck with a nigga shit. See, Monk saved you 'round that time." Wet Fish paused, peeping over his shoulder at Li'l Who. "You sure that's your nigga?" he asked Li'l One Gone. He nodded. Right about that time, Li'l One Gone was finding it difficult to keep his eyes open, his eyelids feeling like midgets were sitting on them. Generally, talking about business or personal stuff, Wet Fish was always reluctant to do so in front of people. Speaking specific, detailed business or personal issues within ear range of anyone not involved—meaning him and whoever he was talking with—was rare. Li'l Who was Li'l One Gone's fall partner now; he was an exception, so Wet Fish went on.

"Monk pulled you under his wing at the right time. Ya mama was running hard. It wasn't gonna be long before she hit rock bottom. I don't know what happened. She used to dibble here, dabble there, then she was off to the races. She ain't never let her appearance go like some of them dope fiends. She took good care of that body. I ain't gon' lie, ya mama fine as a frog hair, nigga!" Wet Fish said excitedly.

Hearing how fine his mama was used to bother Li'l One Gone, but after he had heard men talk about her so much, it didn't affect him anymore. Li'l One Gone started using that to his advantage. Whenever one of the men brought up his mama, he would lie and tell him that she said that he should have been his daddy or that she had almost chosen him. Then he would wait a minute, then ask for some pocket change.

Wet Fish went on, "Yeah, everybody in the hood knew what was going on with her. That's why them old ladies made sure you had a meal to eat. When word got out what you and ole Rich was up to, they cut that short. They got to thinking that Rich was going to have you stealing from them. Everybody was talking, but didn't nobody offer a hand to you. They left you out in the cold." He shook his head at the thought of the hand life had dealt Li'l One Gone. "At tha time,

I was on my dick. Dawg, I couldn't help my own damn self. Rich went to jail. Shit really got rough. You was scrambling your ass off. The shit Rich showed you was what kept you afloat. At one time, I thought the state was gonna come snatch ya up, especially that night when you caught that hot one and got cracked by dat car. My nigga," he said excitedly. "You is da only nigga I know that got ran ova an' shot at the same time. After ya got back on ya feet, walk'n, ya mama had went AWOL. That's when Monk step'd to the street and tuck'd you next to his rib."

He continued, "That nigga love you to death, man. I ain't lying. All he use to talk about was, 'Li'l One Gone did this, Li'l One Gone did that.' He started everyone call'n you Li'l One Gone. When you left the scene, sumbody shit was leaving with you. You was hit'n them niggaz stash so much they couldn't shake back or move forward. Niggas was drop'n off tha block left and right. People still think that's your real pops. Square biz, kiddo, the shit Monk imbibe into you is something that nobody can take away from you. On top of that, you got a spirit of a G in you. Dog, for what it's worth, you gifted. You da only little nigga pick up on the game like dat." He snapped his fingers. "Nobody have to run it to you play by play like you do a lame." Grinning, he exclaimed, "My li'l podna!" placing his hand on Li'l One Gone's head affectionately. "You got a heart of a hustler, as the say. The game gonna be good to you. All you got to do is stay away from bitches, not all of 'em, just them bullshit-ass ones and them bo-jangle-ass niggas that only exist to bring another nigga down. You manage to avoid them, you gonna be a'ight," he said, pausing.

"This is the thing that fuck with me. There's a new breed of hustlers and new breed of dopeheads out here with 'em. That crack shit is a moneymaker, but it brings the beast outa the smokers and niggas that's slangin' it. The only way to stay planted is to become a beast also, kiddo. Monk a superb hustler, but he's a beast too. Your uncle Shortman, that nigga a good nigga, but once he get started, da muthafucking devil be scared to be in the same room with him. Ole Rich got a graveyard under his belt too. All of them are violent niggas. That's fine to be thataway. You can't go wrong. Ya follow me?" he asked. Wet Fish rolled the window of the driver's side of the car halfway down. He took a long drag of the killa, looked at it, then tossed the finger stinger of the blunt out of the partially open window.

"East Washington Street," the sign facing him read. Almost home, he thought as the light turned green. Wet Fish rolled up the window, and the car jerked forward as he pressed his foot on the gas pedal. "Here's where it get kinda crazy. No man gonna let another man fuck over him. You gotta handle your biz if you wanna stay relevant out 'che. The trip part, them white folks built a place called Angola and other camps for niggas that take care of their biz on the streets. So you damned in the game if you don't and damned if you do."

Li'l One Gone was hanging on to every word that came out of his big homie's mouth. But he found it hard to concentrate and grasp the meaning; the weed had his head cloudy, plus his bowels were on the rim, threating to slip out on their own. The closer they got to their neighborhood, the slower Wet Fish drove.

"Today you handle yours like you supposed to. I ain't mad at cha' fo' dat. Da streets gonna tip its hat to you and your li'l partner. Don't let that go to your head, Vee. Don't get thirsty for blood. Once that lust to cause another nigga pain fill your heart, you gonna pay hell tryna get it outa you. Ya every thought will be to fuck sumbody up. In the end, that way of thinking is going to lead to self-destruction. You reap what you sow. That's how it goes," Wet Fish said, nodding.

Li'l One Gone didn't wait until they made it to their final destination; he unbuckled his seat belt as soon as the car's front bumper broke the plane of the railroad tracks. His bowels had developed a mind of their own, or eyes, because for a minute they had settled down, but when they passed over Nicholson Drive, they reactivated furiously. Li'l One Gone was in fear that he wasn't going to be able to hold it.

"You want to burn another one?" Wet Fish asked.

Squeezing his buttocks tightly, with a frown on his face, Li'l One Gone grunted, "Unh-unh."

"What's the matter with you?" Wet Fish concerningly inquired.

"Man, can you *please* hurry up? I gotta shit like a muthafucka."

Li'l Who slung himself against the seat, cracking up laughing. Wet Fish pressed down on the gas pedal with a sense of urgency. It had suddenly dawned on him what Li'l One Gone had said, and he cracked up laughing.

Weeks following the assault on Double D, the streets were still buzzing. Though they were the subject of conversation, Double D's beating wasn't the topic. Wet Fish, Li'l One Gone, and Li'l Who became an inseparable trio. They were the Three Amigos, without the comedy. If an enterprise could consist of three, they were it. With Wet Fish's guidance, Li'l One Gone's sharpness, along with Li'l Who's eagerness, they brought the game to another level, setting a bar unprecedented by anyone on their side of the railroad tracks.

Since Li'l One Gone had been in the game under Wet Fish's administration longer than Li'l Who, he had a choice. Every day they came out of what part of the hustling assembly line he wanted to be on. *Assembly line* being an accurate term used to describe their program because the operation could've been compared to one. From point A to C, each person's play was a step to producing an end result, a dollar, and to make sure the stash, but most importantly themselves, was secured at all times. Their operation kept the would-be jackers scratching their heads and the police restrategizing every time they hit and missed.

Li'l Who was swifter on his feet than Li'l One Gone was; therefore, he was the stash retriever. Also, anytime a quick getaway was needed, he was the designated sprinter. Li'l One Gone was primarily a solicitor, directing the potential customers to where Wet Fish was posted up. Wet Fish was the salesman. After Li'l One Gone reeled in the potential customers, he would negotiate the deal. Once the customers informed him of their intended purchase, Wet Fish would give the signal to Li'l Who. The signal to Li'l Who by Wet Fish was a few unsophisticated gestures. He would slap his hand against his thigh if the customer was spending ten dollars, wipe his face if it was twenty dollars being spent, rub his stomach if it was a thirty-dollar sale, and clap his hands if it was a forty-dollar piece being bought. Anything more than a forty-dollar purchase, Wet Fish would serve the customer himself. Upon receiving the signal, Li'l Who would run to the stash spot, retrieve the product, then hand it over to Wet Fish, which in turn would give the customers their equal monetary value in product. If anything didn't feel right, Li'l One Gone's job was to retrieve the stash and relocate it to a spot away from the location where they were pitching at and dispose the money that the suspected customer spent.

Some days, Li'l One Gone served while Li'l Who solicited, all under the watchful eye Wet Fish did. The goal was to keep everyone outside the circle thrown for a loop. None of that guessing would have been effective if one of them had served an undercover cop or confidential informant. Nothing is 100 percent foolproof when it comes down to the life or the game, but the percentage can be tipped to increase the probability of staying ahead. To eliminate getting busted, whoever between Li'l One Gone and Li'l Who was assigned the job for the day to work the street, any new face that crossed the railroad tracks, looking to score a hit of run-hard, regardless if they were spending ten thousand dollars, was directed to cats that were posted up on the block, pushing.

Wet Fish controlled the projects pumping out of the adjacent playground; therefore, the new customer was to cop on the block, which was the corner of West Roosevelt and Illinois Street, which lowered the risk of making the playground hot if the new customer was on the side of the law or working with them to cause their shortfall in the game. Once that person panned out, Wet Fish kept a batch of raw to give to them free of charge if they agreed to deal with him. Sometimes they stayed loyal to the person they first copped from initially, but most of the time they made their way to the playground. All three of them, in short-spaced intervals, glanced around, watching for the bust. The chance of an unmarked or marked car rolling up on them was few and far between.

They had their game tight; the jackers couldn't make a move because the drugs or the money never meet. If someone did attempt to go with their move before they opened up shop or after they had closed it down, they had too many units in the projects to choose from, or the person designated to hold it didn't know until the last minute, a person had to be desperate to catch one of them going to the stash during the commission of a sale and go with their move. Whenever they were serving, it was done out in the open. An outsider wouldn't have made it back across the railroad tracks alive if they would pull an armed caper off on anybody on the block or in the Bricks. The ones living in the neighborhood were the ones Wet Fish worried about the most. That was way he moved the way he did. Li'l One Gone and Li'l Who were the only ones that knew how he shook and moved. Only thing he kept from them was the formula to turn powder cocaine into run-hard.

Most of the notoriety they gained was from the ones that were in their late teens and in adulthood. They were the ones that ignited their buzz. Toward the end of the summer, Li'l One Gone had noticed a change in Li'l Who. Their friendship never wavered; they were thick as beeswax. Both talked about the position they wanted in the game. Li'l One Gone was gaining the knowledge he needed to maintain, plus acquiring the things it took to advance. Li'l One Gone was putting money to the side to buy his own drugs to sell. Wet Fish had told him and the man told him anytime he was ready to purchase his own, they were kosher with that. Wet Fish told him that if he did buy from him, he had to pump out of the playground or make his own block. He couldn't hustle on the same set as the competition.

The man informed Li'l One Gone that if he did buy directly from him for his own purpose, he was going to have to come from under Wet Fish's administration and that Wet Fish had the choice to continue sponsoring him or not. He was too fresh in the game to freelance without a sponsor; he was fair game on the streets. Li'l One Gone had the smarts to trap, but he lacked the real estate to open up shop in. Plus, he hadn't developed the resource needed to make certain things happen in his favor. Both were vital assets to surviving in the game.

Li'l One Gone was in the process of making preparation to drop his nuts and go with his move and do his own thing. Around that time, he picked up on the change in his main man. Instead of moving in the same direction as him, Li'l Who had seemed to be distancing himself from the game and avidly avoided the conversation about moving up in the game when they were out on the grind. Li'l One Gone didn't mind talking about sports and music; he enjoyed the company Li'l Who provided him. He remembered the lonely days sitting in the playground, wishing he had someone his age getting it like him to kick it with. So if his friend wanted to talk about beans and corn bread, that was all right by him. It was when Li'l Who downplayed the game and criticized the way of the streets that messed with his mental.

At first, he chalked it up to his friend just having one of those days. Everyone has a day when they're not into or having second thoughts about what they're doing. So he wrote it off. But the following days, it was the same song and dance. He still took care of his business, never missing a beat when he was working, but he didn't perform with the same eagerness he did in the beginning. He moved like a burnout.

When Li'l One Gone brought up anything besides sports and music, his shoulders would slump. To keep from seeing Li'l Who unhappy, Li'l One Gone stopped talking about the streets altogether; he'd just sit and listen to him rant on and on. When he would quote the lyrics from the latest album that his favorite artist dropped, or the lyrics from an old one, his eyes would light up. Not only that, he had always mimicked a move he had seen one of the pros do in one of their televised basketball games. When he did it, it was done with enthusiasm, with an effort to perfect the move. His heart was into music and sports. Trying not to sever their relationship, Li'l One Gone took up collecting sports cards along with Li'l Who. For every one pack he paid for, he would back-door and steal five. The stats on the cards didn't excite him; getting away with the ones in his pocket did. The cards couldn't be smoked, eaten, or drunk, so why buy them? he told himself to justify his action. They say when you enter the game, leave your feeling at home.

School was starting back in a few weeks. The final weeks of summer were rolling out. Li'l One Gone had played tug-of-war with Li'l Who's mind for the better part of the last days of the break in order to keep him stationed in the game with him. Eventually, he wore himself out, and instead of convincing Li'l Who to stay planted, he almost uprooted himself. Li'l Who enjoyed hearing the sound of his own voice. Li'l One Gone pretended to be interested in what Li'l Who was saying, but after pretending so long, he really became interested in spitting a few bars on a track. He started hearing the words of a song instead of just listening to it. Li'l Who was an avid fan of that cat that got drafted from North Carolina to the Chicago Bulls. Besides that sister who set the record in the one hundred meters on the track field, the only other sports icon Li'l One Gone showed any interest in was that cat from New York who was knocking out his opponent in spectacular fashion. Some of his opponents succumbed to his powerful punches, resulting in them hitting the canvas in the opening round of the fight.

Talking with Li'l Who, he was ready for basketball season to jump off. He went as far as reading the back of the cards he had so he could argue stats with his friend. Li'l One Gone almost converted and committed himself to chasing the American dream from another angle. Anger and the feeling of betrayal diminished all thoughts of anything other than the game. Hustling, hanging with his partner, and learning new things, good and bad, Li'l One Gone was in hog heaven. For learning new things in the game, even hustling he could have missed a day of. Hanging with Li'l Who made his day; it had been a while since he had a constant companion his age.

Li'l One Gone went to Mrs. Carry's house, which acted as the neighborhood sweetshop, and bought a few popcorn balls, pecan candy, and frozen cups. Mrs. Carry had been pushing treats out of her house since the late fifties. Everything she sold was an original family recipe. The end product of the family recipe, she shared with the community at a fair price. Karonda had gone across the tracks with her mama, and she told Li'l One Gone when she got back that she was going to chill with him. Wet Fish had walked to the stash house to do his thing in the kitchen. That day was a first in many that was its booming. A day hardly even went by when the dope ran out before they closed down shop. He sat on the slide, eating his popcorn ball, waiting for Karonda to cross the track. He had seen Li'l Who come through the projects and cut to the back of the playground. He didn't pay him any mind because that was his routine every time he arrived on the set. Digging in his bag, pulling out a popcorn ball and pecan candy and handing them to Li'l Who, he said, "Here you go. I bought you a frozen cup too, my nigga. Shied, you made it just in time before these bitches turned to Kool-Aid. Karonda better hurry up before her shit melt!"

Li'l Who took the snacks and sat down next to him. "Where Wet Fish at? Ain't nothing in da spot to count," he said dryly. Already expecting him to come on the set like he was on the rag, when Li'l One Gone picked up the dullness in his voice, he didn't comment or check him about it. He figured, just like every other day, in a few ticks he'd be back to his jovial self. He was going to complain about this and that, then he was going to start talking about music, Li'l One Gone thought to himself.

"Vietnam," he said, addressing him by his government name.

"Not Hamburger Joe, Heavy-Duty Overweight Hustler, or no shit like that?" Li'l One Gone jokingly asked.

"Nah, Vee, smoke dis over, my nigga. This not me," Li'l Who stated.

Li'l One Gone did a double take. He wanted to blast him. "What you mean?" he asked instead.

"You my friend. I like kicking it with you. I'll hang out here all day with you. But dis street stuff ain't me, dog. I'm not trying to get killed or go to jail forever behind a few crumbs."

Stunned, Li'l One Gone couldn't reply.

"I'm better than this. My mama say I can be the next MJ or Doug E. Fresh. That's what I want to do." Excitement filled his voice as he talked.

Li'l One Gone sat there, wondering if he was really hearing Li'l Who correctly. It sounded like he was about to lose his friend to basketball or music. Staring at the popcorn ball, he could feel the last bite tasted kind of funny, or was he tripping?

"This what I'm going to do: I'm gonna save all my money from now on so when I finish high school, I'm going to move to North Carolina and go to college. Once I finish college, if I don't make it to the NBA, I'm gonna move to New York City and do my rap thing," Li'l Who said proudly.

Li'l One Gone was so engulfed in what Li'l Who was saying and deep in thought he must have had his eyes closed, because he neither saw or heard Karonda walk up. "That's for me?" she asked.

Jumping to his feet, he yelled out, "What da fuck do you mean?"

"Huh?" asked Karonda.

"I'm not talking to you, I'm talking to my friend," he said, emphasizing on *friend*. "He spitting some shit at me 'bout he don't wanna go to jail, he don't wanna get killed out here. He got some bullshit in his head he going to the NBA or make a tape or some shit," Li'l One Gone emotionally stated.

"Man, fuck, what you talk'n 'bout? I'm going to the NBA or be a rapper!" Li'l Who exclaimed.

"Dog, you ain't MJ, and yo rap is whack. Yo ain't going to NBA!" Li'l One Gone spit out like the words left a bad taste in his mouth.

"Babe, you can't knock that man because he don't want to be sitting on these corners like you and the rest of these dumbass niggas," said Karonda.

"So I'm dumb now? Fuck both of y'all! Y'all ain't with me," he said, slapping the frozen cup on the ground, stomping it. It left a colorful mud puddle in the sand. He then grabbed the bag containing the popcorn ball and pecan candy, tossing it over his shoulder.

"You too stupid! I can't be fucking with you!" Karonda said as she marched off.

Wet Fish had walked up. He stood back and didn't interfere; he had caught bits of the conversation.

"Ya may as well kick rocks now, nigga. Beat ya feet. I ain't goin' nowheres. I'ma be right here," Li'l One Gone said, slapping the slide he was sitting on. "To I *die*, nigga!" Li'l One Gone yelled.

"I didn't say we wasn't friends. All I'm saying, this not me. I like rapping and basketball," Li'l Who said.

"Fuck ya with a big old dick," Li'l One Gone mumbled as he stormed off in the same direction as Karonda.

Mosquitos buzzed around his ears, so he moved a few feet up the bank, but before he got comfortable, the bloodsuckers located him again, swarming all around him. The more he swatted at them, the angrier they became—they went from a harassing campaign to an all-out assault upon his flesh in all of 0.2 seconds. Watching the sun leave its footprint across the sky as it led darkness in calmed his nerves. Rising waves pushing foamy waters upon the riverbank as tugboats hauling barges cut through the mighty Mississippi had a soothing effect on Li'l One Gone. As ripple after ripple drifted in, so did one thought after another out into the horizon, relinquishing all ill feelings. The sun setting in all its glory did the trick; that was his first time really watching the other source besides water that was substantial for life-forms on earth fade into the night. Caught up in the moment of enjoying the sight, he forgot about his troubles.

When he made it back to the community, Karonda was lounging on a worn-out sofa that rested on three legs and a telephone book in the center of the porch of the house where she lived. Its dark forest-green upholstery complemented the egg white color of the house as it leaned against it. In turn, it framed Karonda's petite brown body for an excellent background to a perfect picture. "What? I do not wanna talk to you," she expressed. She then bolted off the sofa, went inside the house, and violently slammed the door behind her. Li'l One Gone stood there with words stuck in his mouth fighting to come out. Swallowing hard once, he then slowly mobbed off, heading back to the direction of the Mississippi River.

Karonda lived on Indiana Street, so he didn't have far to go to get to River Road, the street that ran parallel with the levy that acted as a barrier between the Mississippi River and the city of Baton Rouge. Consciously, he quickened his step. The slower he walked, the more profound his limp was. On one side of the levy lay a community, on the other a wilderness that lay between it and the Mississippi River. Though part of the community, the vast majority of the inhabitants never ventured to the other side of it; many walked and jogged on top of the levy but never went down to or through the tree line.

Everyone had their reasons that they didn't explore beyond the dense trees. Some were afraid of the wildlife, insects, and creatures that claimed that real estate for their residency, while others were not comfortable with the aloneness the wilderness provided. Li'l One Gone loved it back there. Back when he was younger and the kids didn't want to play with him, that was when he first discovered the wonders of nature, along with the peace and serenity that came with it. Behind the levy not only acted as a place to hide himself from the endless ribbing and teasing from kids but also was a place to hide things before the river rose to its crest. On top of that, it was a place for him to swim in the hot summer days. On the other side of the levy was his paradise in the neighborhood. Posted up on top of it, staring at the many lights of the neighborhood. Although he was at ease, he didn't feel like he was receiving paradise.

"O'nah, Vee!" Wet Fish yelled out.

Li'l One Gone heard him. Looking in the direction the yell came from, scanning the area, he couldn't locate him. Rescanning, he would've missed him again if Wet Fish hadn't opened his car door, letting the dome light illuminate the otherwise-dark parking lot. Dragging his feet, he made it to Wet Fish. "Get in. Let's rap a tad slime," he told Li'l One Gone, who went over to the passenger side, opening the door. "Hold up. What da fuck, you been sitting in mud or something? You got that shit all over ya pants!" Wet Fish stated. Li'l One Gone scoped himself out. It was well into darkness when he emerged from the thickets; there was no way he would have noticed the dirt along with dried leaves and other particles he picked up behind the levy. Li'l One Gone slapped at his pants, trying to clean himself off.

"Don't worry about it. We'll sit on the curb," Wet Fish told him. He raised the tail of his shirt before he sat down on top of a paper bag he placed on the curb. Li'l One Gone just flopped on down next to him. Wet Fish passed him a stick of killa that was already three-fourths smoked up. Li'l One Gone puffed on the killa hungrily, the amber glowing brightly in the darkness. "Goddamn, son, I'm glad we ain't hiding. A nigga could spot dat flame a mile away. You had dat bitch glo'n!" Wet Fish said, chuckling. Li'l One Gone, embarrassed, laughed also. He needed something to take the edge off but wasn't quite sure what the remedy was going to be until the killa entered his bloodstream. Instantly he knew what his body was missing. Instead of long, deep drags, he took a few short tokes after he got ribbed about his Hoover lungs.

"I had heard what went down with you and your podna and that ho'—I mean *girl*—earlier," Wet Fish started off. Li'l One Gone was gazing straight ahead over the project building at the stars in the sky. "Ya heard me?" Wet Fish asked. He heard him clear as day; he didn't acknowledge him because he made up his mind fuck Li'l Who and muthafuck Karonda; therefore, he didn't want to conversate about them.

"Yeah," he forced out, the scorn evident within the sound of the four-letter word he had spat out.

"Dog on some real G shit. You tripping," Wet Fish said.

Li'l One Gone looked up at him with a mask of contentment.

"That's right, nigga, you tripping. Pass dat, please," Wet Fish demanded, pointing to the blunt. "Peep game, check play, my nigga. I'ma tell you this, and I'm through with it, this'll be the last time we converse 'bout this. I'm gon' say what I gotta say. You can either take heed to it or let it go in one ear and pop outa the other one." He took a toke of the killa slowly, pushing the smoke out of his nostrils.

He continued, "Nah, you fell out with Li'l Who. Dat's the wrong nigga to have bad blood toward. Real shit, kid, that's your only friend out here."

Li'l One Gone's head snapped up.

"Me too, I'm your friend to the very end. We fam, cuz, all day. Word." He extended his hand.

"Word," Li'l One Gone said, dapping him off.

"Anyway, the li'l nigga loyal. He got mad love for you. He solid, plus he smart. Both of y'all have the same qualities, my nigga. I see the same thing in you that I see in him. It's the same shit I feel inside of me. Wanna hit this before I throw it?" he asked Li'l One Gone as he took one last drag of the killa. Li'l One Gone received it, puffed on it until the amber stung his fingertips, then tossed it behind them. "Both of y'all gone leave y'all mark somewhere, whether it's together or solo. Dude wanna do it the hard way, the right way. He a down li'l nigga, but he ain't built for this. I mean, anybody can get out 'che and run the streets, but it take a special type of nigga to chase a dream that seem like it run faster and further away from a nigga the closer a nigga get to it," Wet Fish said with a far-out look; he looked like he was looking backward or into the future.

"It's like this: I wish that you'll do something different with your life, but you was born with a soul that long for the streets. Everybody got their calling in life, my nigga. The streets called you, me, and the rest of them cats you see out here. The NBA or music world is calling ya boy. Just like ya girl said, you can't knock him for wanting the same shit you want, jus' getting at it a different way. Real nigga shit, ya boy the reason why dat detective didn't press you as hard as he coulda. He went in there talk'n with sense. He didn't rat or confess. He smooth-talked him and won him over. Him and that good, stickey-finga-ass nigga saved you. Other than that, ya ignorant ass had talked yourself into a ride to the bing. Bottom line, you take this for what it is worth. Don't end ya friendship over bullshit. You do you, let him do him. Y'all come together." He slammed his palms together. "Have fun and learn from each other," Wet Fish said. "Go look in the glove box and see if there's anything else to smoke," he told Li'l One Gone.

He stood up dazed from the killa, but more from the fat that had just been put on his brain about Li'l Who. True, he didn't want to stop being friends with him. Even when everybody called him fat and chubby, Li'l Who would defend him by ribbing whoever it was that had targeted him. On the basketball court or baseball field, everyone was falling over one another to be on Li'l Who's team, but he would always pick Li'l One Gone first. Thinking back brought a smile to his face, but he started to feel bad for the way he handled him and Karonda. He urgently searched the glove box, and coming up empty, hurriedly and anxiously he moved back to the curb where Wet Fish was waiting. He, too, was in deep thought. He had a date with Jennifer.

"Say, what you think about Karonda?" Li'l One Gone asked Wet Fish.

Shrugging his shoulder, he responded, "I don't know. I see her around. I just found out her name the other day. Ya know dat's a baby to me, not to you, though. She might be a good girl."

"Like Jennifer," Li'l One Gone blurted out.

"You like Jennifer?" Wet Fish asked, smiling.

Li'l One Gone didn't respond verbally, but his body said it all. He smiled and searched for something that hadn't been lost on the ground in the dark. He shuffled from one foot to the other.

"Yeah, you like her, nigga. You can't have my women, but she got a li'l sis 'round ya age you can have. I done already closed down shop. I been was 'pose to be out. I was waiting on you to dip back through before I pushed out. Dirk out through da short cut, go change pants, 'cause you ain't fucking my seats up. I'ma pick you up, then we gon' roll by Jennifer. I'ma turn you on to her li'l sister. I wanna see how much game you got, anyway," Wet Fish said, grinning. "Hurry up, fat boy, beat your feet," he added.

A combination of skipping, running, walking, and jogging got him through the shortcut and to the house in no time. Changing clothes, he thought about what Wet Fish had said about wanting to see how much game he had. "Nigga, I got all the game, baby," he repeated what he had overheard someone say into the mirror as he brushed his hair. The fact was, Karonda was the only girl he conversed with on that level; grown women, he flirted with, shooting his stick every chance he got, but when it came down to girls his age, he was downright shy in their presence. He was solid, but when he became the center of their attention, a bad case of goofiness came over him. Gibberish came out of his mouth, and sometimes beads of sweat intruded his forehead. If anyone had seen him preparing himself to meet Jennifer's little sister, one would have thought Li'l One Gone was Don Juan, or maybe Casanova.

"Who you baby'n in there?" his mama asked through the closed bathroom door.

"No, ah, nobody," he shamefully replied.

"Come on outa there, play'n 'round. I gotsa use it!" his mama yelled back.

One last glance at himself in the mirror and he opened the door, his mama standing there with her hands stuck to her hips. "Ump, smelling good. All nice and clean, and you combed ya hair," she said.

Li'l One Gone's skin burned with embarrassment. He stood there peeking at the door. "Wait till I come out fo' ya. Dot my doe."

Li'l One Gone tried desperately to think about what it was he had done wrong in the past days. There wasn't anything significant that stood out. So what did she want? He wracked his brain as he stood at the front door, waiting for his mama to come out of the bathroom. Hearing a car pull up, he peeked out of the window. It wasn't Wet Fish; it was the next neighbor parking their car. Face twisted up, he pondered hard what she could possibly want. He thought, whatever it was, he didn't have time to find out. Opening the door, he walked out soon as he heard music pumping through car speakers beating up the block. From the song blaring out of the car, he knew who it was coming down the street with the bass rattling the windowpanes of the house. He was already on the sidewalk when Wet Fish stopped. Out of respect for the code of the streets, he lowered the volume of his car stereo. As long as a person was mobile, one could blast their music as loud as they pleased, but whenever one stopped in front of any one residence other than theirs, it was common courtesy to the owner of the residence and their neighbors for the person to lower their music.

At the time he was walking up the driveway, his mama screamed, "Goddammit, didn't I tell yo ass to wait?"

"What!" Li'l One Gone screamed back.

"Don't fuck'n what me! Since ya ass don't wanna listen and be smart by the mouth, don't leave my damn house," she said.

"But, Ma, I didn't do nut'n," Li'l One Gone cried out.

"That's ya problem. Ya ass do too much," she replied.

"Get in the car," the voice whispered.

Mumbling to himself, Li'l One Gone jumped into Wet Fish's car. "Man, fuck her. Let's ride."

Shaking his head, Wet Fish responded, "Nah, homie, I'm rid-ing, you stay'n."

Li'l One Gone felt like he had been hit with a bag of bricks. "Why, bro?" he asked in a whining voice.

"Dog, I can't go against ya mama," Wet Fish said, looking over at his mama posted on the sidewalk, glaring down at them. "Listen to her. When no one else there, ya mama always gon be there. Real Gs respect they mama. Besides, nigga, you ain't grown. You still gotta abide by her law," Wet Fish said, as if he had just remembered Li'l One Gone's age. "Get out. I got pussy wait'n on me," Wet Fish said, extending his hand. "Word," he added. Li'l One Gone got out without responding or dapping him off. "Oh, nigga, it's like dat? Ya gonna front like dat?" Wet Fish yelled behind him.

He turned around, shoulders slumped with the weight of disappointment, and said, "Word," dapping him off weakly.

Wet Fish winked at his mama, who smiled and waved at him. Reaching for the volume knob, he turned up his favorite song. "Tha girls are freaks 'cause da crack rocks rolling!" it screamed out of the car speakers before he pulled off. Li'l One Gone listened and watched until the glow of taillights spun the bend.

"Fuck, you trip'n like you need a bump or sump'n," he told his mama. The sound of his voice hadn't left his ears before his mama backhanded him in the mouth. She didn't draw any blood, but she got his attention. "You's a child, and you gon' stay in a child's place. A fuck'n bump? Bitch, you da one need ah bump. Every time I see ya fat ass, you either staggling or can't keep ya goddamn eyes open!" his mama spit venomously at Li'l One Gone. He was still stunned by the blow to the mouth, afraid to invoke her other hand, he stood stiff as steel and silent as a corpse in a casket. He wasn't sure that the words that came out of his mouth were going to be appropriate, so he did the wisest thing possible, stay silent.

"Get flip by tha mouf again and watch I knock ya teeth down ya throat," she threatened, walking off. There was plenty of space between them, but she shoved him out of the way before she walked back into the house. Whatever the reason she wanted Li'l One Gone to wait for her, she never told him, nor did he ask.

On the other side of the town, events were taking place that would forever change his attitude toward life and the way he felt about his mama. Boiling with rage, he sat in the night air, listening to the crickets laugh at him.

As Li'l One Gone stretched and eased pressure off his stiffened muscles and tendons, opening then quickly closing his eyes shut from the onslaught of sunlight delivered blinding pain. He eased his eyes open slowly so they could adjust themselves to the brightness of the new day. An overwhelming itchy sensation overrode all his senses before the realization of where he had fallen asleep struck him, hence why he was itching. Every inch of his skin was covered with ooo-wee bumps, evidence of the late-night feeding frenzy by a swarm of hungry mosquitoes. Due to a marijuana-induced slumber, he arose a few milliliters short of hemoglobin. The killa had his entire body so desensitized that anything could have occurred to him in his sleep and he wouldn't have been aware of it. Pushing himself up out of the chair, he let the remaining blood in his body flow to his lower extremities before he took a step.

Breath stinking, desperately in need of some rubbing alcohol to sooth the numerous bumps that the mosquitoes left, added with severe thirst for a flavored drink, he crept to the side of the house and retrieved a ten-dollar bill out of his earnings from the day before, the one that had just passed. Usually, he kept all his earnings in one location. Behind the chest of drawers in his room, there was a hole in the wall with strips of tape concealing it. Inside of the hole, a piece of string wrapped and tied to the nail hung in the hollow of the wall. At the end of the string, there was a sock inside of a brown paper bag containing different denominations of folded bills. The insect repellent he sprayed on the outside of the bag and sock kept the rodents from being nosy. When he came home, his mama was there, so instead of running the risk of unintentionally revealing his stash spot, he put what money he had in a Dorito bag and placed it between the wall and the pipes on the gas meter on side of the house.

He wasn't worried about anyone "accidentally" finding it, because he didn't plan on leaving it there too long; plus, he had told his mama that he had seen a big black snake on that side of the house. His mama might buck a pack of rats, but she damn sure wasn't courageous enough to risk the chance of running up on a snake in high grass. On his way to the store, he noticed that the usually energized and vibrant atmosphere of the neighborhood wasn't present. Paying it mind for a split second, he thought no more of it and continued on. There were a few people mingling around in the park. He didn't see Wet Fish in the crowd, so he searched the parking lot for his car, but it, too, was gone. He didn't have his watch on, yet he put a little more pep in his step, hoping that Wet Fish didn't beat him to the spot.

To make his walk shorter to Northgate Seafood, he went down the railroad track instead of crossing over it, taking Wyoming Street. The store sat right at the north gate entrance to Louisiana State University. The owner of the store named it Northgate Seafood.

Exxon, turned Chevron, banned him from their store when they caught him lifting sports cards. They locked him in the store, demanded the cards back, telling him that if he even came back into their store, he was going to jail. A week before, he was in 7-Eleven with his baby sister when a guy bumped into her, knocking her Slurpee out of her hand. The man apologized for doing it, but Li'l One Gone wanted him to buy her another one. The man told him that he only had enough money on him to buy himself a cold one. Li'l One Gone told the man to give him the money, but the man just looked. "What!" he asked, shocked. He didn't believe what he was hearing.

"Go stand by the Laundromat. I'ma get you another one," he told his sister. The pulling out his box cutter, holding it to his side, he asked, "Give me ya money."

"Huh? Nigga, please," the man said, reaching for the door.

Li'l One Gone ran the box cutter across the man's arm as he was in midmotion of opening the door. Before the first slice started to spread open from a pinstripe to a crimson gash, Li'l One Gone struck him again.

Ali, the cashier, rushed out. "Stop!" he yelled, shoving the man into the store. He grabbed Li'l One Gone and screamed for someone to call the police. Transfixed, Li'l One Gone didn't realize that he was being held. Hearing the word *police* brought him back to reality. He shoved the point of the blade into Ali's thigh, then ran the blade upward. Ali freed him of his grasp, and Li'l One Gone got light. "Go, go, go!" he hollered at his baby sister. They both fled up West Roosevelt Street then disappeared across the railroad tracks.

Li'l One Gone looked at his arm, thinking back on last week's episode. All the blood, he thought. Regretfully, he tipped on down the tracks. Every time he stepped on a train track rock, it hurt the bottom of his foot or scuffed up his snow-white shell-toe Adidas he wished he hadn't got caught stealing from the Chevron gas station, therefore, he wouldn't have had such a long walk to the store. As it stood, Northgate Seafood was the only store on Nicholson Drive he wasn't banned from for some reason or another.

Like a cold hand on his shoulder in a pitch-black, dark room, the startling realization that a fresh yellow ribbon was tied around the railroad signal pole struck him. He almost tripped as he reviewed the yellow ribbon in his mind's eye. He missed the crosstie directly in front of him sticking out higher than the rest. Paying more attention to his step, he forced the ribbon out of his mind, but not the troubling feeling he had that he couldn't shake. Good thing he put the five-dollar bill back, because he ended up buying boiled potatoes and corn along with the other items he went to the store for. Most Louisianans loved boiled crawfish, crabs, and shrimps. He was more fond of the potatoes and corn they boiled together with the seafood. Leaving the set early the day before, he bought enough food to save for later on. He planned on staying put, putting in overtime.

There wasn't any music blasting from the boom box; the only thing he heard was the sound of passing cars. They, too, seemed like they were trying not to disturb the deadly silence as he strolled to the set. As he stepped up onto the scene, the look on everyone's face wiped the smile completely off his face and soul also. Their mugs matched the somber feeling in the air around them. Grief was so thick it hovered above the crowd like a blanket of fog. Li'l One Gone's stomach knotted up, his breathing becoming rapid as he glanced off at the parking lot then back at Slick. Slick shook his head, dropping it, then shaking it again as he bowed pitifully. Pantomimically, though no one had spoken, it was evident tragedy had struck. Bracing himself for what his gut was telling him, Li'l One Gone placed his bag down. It had started to feel like a hundred pounds of weight. Not only that, he wanted his hands free to catch his fall because his legs buckled from the heaviness of the anticipation that had landed on his shoulders. Other than sniffles from one of the females out there, not a humanly sound had been made since Li'l One Gone arrived.

Impatiently, with his curiosity getting the best of him, he asked to no one in particular, "What up?"

"Ole faggot-ass police did my nigga wrong," Slick said, grief-stricken.

"Bitch-ass nigga stole Wet Fish like dat. He gone, man. Fuck!" Tara grievingly expressed. Tears falling from her eyes, she looked as if she had more to say but thought better of it. She sighed, then stared straight ahead. Wet Fish had his bread up, so it wasn't going to be a problem for him to post bail, Li'l One Gone thought. As long as he didn't kill anyone, he was good. A minor sense of relief overcame him momentarily. It wasn't as bad as he expected. Maybe all the long faces were because Wet Fish was the life of the party, he internally thought to himself.

Those words were dismissed immediately when Slick tipped his bottle. "Fo' my muthafucka nigga dat's no longer with us." Filled with despair, rage, and sadness, he then slammed the almost-full body of liquor on the concrete. The intense irrational reality of what Slick had done and said invaded Li'l One Gone's mental. The newly placed ribbon on the pole was for Wet Fish.

"Damn," Li'l One Gone said. Nothing else needed to be said. Every soul was bonded together by the feeling of sadness, everyone thought about the ordeal with Wet Fish in congruence with one another. Lightheaded, painfully devastated, he took a seat next to the rest of the grief-stricken congregation of mourners. Quietly he sat. If he wanted to speak, he couldn't have because he was at a loss for words. T'Sharon, and now Wet Fish, he thought. His heart no longer could identify sorrow; he regulated that after T'Sharon's death. Hate and anger, with a whole lot of other feelings that unbelief produces, were what he felt. Tears were shed for T'Sharon. Blood had to be shed for Wet Fish. Inside of the police precinct, he left the last tears he would ever allow his eyes to produce. As he looked over to where T'Sharon lay breathless, the notion struck him: he was sitting in that exact spot before he ran to his mama. Was death following him, or was he following death?

Leading up to the day that was scheduled for the wake and funeral of Wet Fish, Li'l One Gone became reticent, just as he did when he was younger. His words were few. His mind stayed on mayhem; mentally killing everyone who ever wronged him was how he spent most of his days. The voice in his ear was encouraging him to kill. Drunk with revenge, on some days he tried to numb the feeling with weed and drown his thoughts with cheap liquor. That didn't help. People came over to check up on him because they knew how close he and Wet Fish were. He would smile and tell them that he was all right, but little did they know the boy had become severely mentally disturbed. He just hid it well from everyone.

The delirium tremors that had begun to control Li'l One Gone had subsided the day of the funeral. Dressed fresh as a pack of Camel nonfiltered cigarettes, Li'l One Gone posted up across the street from the church on the corner of West Grant and River Road. His family chose to have the service right in the neighborhood; plus, it enabled those without transportation to come and pay their respect. Standing outside the church, Li'l One Gone was on the verge of becoming dizzy from all the attention he received. "Stay strong, li'l nigga. Keep ya head up. If you need something, holla" was what was said in the midst of all the handshakes and daps. Li'l One Gone had never seen Wet Fish sleep before, but seeing him laid in his ebony casket trimmed with gold, he imagined that was how he would have looked asleep in a king-size bed. He could've stayed inside the church, but watching how hard Wet Fish's brother Ace and his mama were taking it, he posted up outside with the pimps, players, hustlers, and gangsters along with the skinny boppers out of the hood.

Upon viewing Wet Fish's body, they all hung outside. Their places weren't inside of the church; it was the place of family, friends, and loved ones to grieve the dead. The streets were supposed to mourn through honor; any fallen soldier of the streets got sent away the G way. West Grant Street had never seen so much activity as it did that day. Cars were lined up from corner to corner. Men, women, and children were posted up as far as the eyes could see up the block. The ones that didn't even know were in the midst of those who knew and loved him. Sticks of killa were being passed around; bottles of liquor were being tipped, their contents splashed all over the sidewalk and street.

Li'l One Gone was leaning against a car when Karonda walked up; he didn't even see her approach. Without a word, she grabbed him, hugging him tightly. Li'l Who followed her, searching for words, and confused about what to do, he stood for a few seconds before he extended his hand. Dapping each other off, they both glared strangely at each other because it had been a while since they had acknowledged each other. "We good," Li'l One Gone said.

Karonda on one side, Li'l Who on the other, given the circumstances, Li'l One Gone didn't feel too bad. One would have thought that a party was going on instead of a wake. People smiled, some cried, but the mood was festive. It was a party, just the way Wet Fish would have wanted it to be. He, after all, lived every day like it was a party, so he was going to be sent away in a partying fashion. The streets erupted into a celebrative environment when the doors of the church swung open. Prearranged and okayed by his mama, some cranked up the music in their cars. Instead of silence, everyone would clap, wave, scream, or do whatever they felt. The volume of the radios would peak as the pallbearers carried Wet Fish's body. Once it made it to the hearse, before his body was placed in, everyone maxed out their stereos, blasting the lyrics of his favorite song, "Da girls are freaks because the crack rock rolling, o' yeah." The ones who weren't privy to what was going on were startled. Everyone started yelling, waving, and jumping all around. Those with amplified subwoofers let them bang. For a second, it turned to a crank-it-up contest. When the guys took off for their cars, a woman standing in front with her kids snatched up her baby and was about to run. She panicked, thinking some "drama" was about to kick off. Li'l One Gone stopped her and explained what was going on. He didn't want her to leave; he liked the view.

People bobbed their heads, the song rising higher and higher. From where he stood, he couldn't see the casket when they came down the steps of the church, but he knew when Wet Fish's body had been placed in the hearse. The music had stopped escalating. It was so loud out there that all the sounds were like one. His mama, brother, and a few other relatives hopped in the family car; all other cars filing in behind. "I'ma have something cooked fo' ya when you get home," his mama told Li'l One Gone before he, Karonda, and Li'l Who jumped in the car with Sassy and Jennifer.

It was a lovely sight. All types of make and model cars were in the procession. Most had candy paint sprayed on their rides, with gold- or silver-spoked rims. If it weren't for the motorcycle cops leading and the hearse right behind, it would have looked more like an entourage following a celebrity than a funeral. No one really forced conversation. Everyone in the car was deep inside their own head. It had only been nine days since Wet Fish's death, and two weeks since Li'l One Gone had seen Jennifer, but she looked ten years older than her nineteen years of age. Her once-joyful face had turned to stone. She had a distant look. She could no longer hold eye contact with anyone, turning her head quickly or not looking up at all when someone spoke to her. She acted like her eyes might replay and reveal to whoever peered into them the horror her mind had recorded.

Officer Dicken DaBeaudé of the Baton Rouge Police Department had aspirations of being a professional football player. According to some, he was the best in the school, best in the city; some even went as far as saying that he was the best in the state. High school football was blessed to have him as a receiver, high school football fanatics would often say when they watched him on the football field. There was another player on the field with the same aspiration as Officer Dicken DaBeaudé that went by a funny name.

"Let nothing stand in your way" was one of the mottos he lived by; therefore, he devised a plan to get his shine blocker out of his way. A quarter-ounce of weed and a cornerback tired of being burned by Officer Dicken DaBeaudé to get the job done. Both he and Wet Fish were on the offense. Wet Fish mostly ran options; therefore, he never got to show his full potential on game day. He and two defensive players conspired to put an end to Officer Dicken DaBeaudé's potential football career. They waited until the coach called for an in route across the middle of the field. Officer Dicken DaBeaudé caught the football, but the cat playing the cornerback position grabbed him. He held him up while the other defensive player pretended to block Wet Fish from helping Officer Dicken DaBeaudé break his tackle, but he actually shoved Wet Fish directly into Officer Dicken DaBeaudé. Wet

Fish then dived right on the outside of Officer Dicken DaBeaudé's knee while he was being held up. His knee went out, and so did his chances of being an NFL star. To add insult to his injury, Wet Fish started going out with Officer Dicken DaBeaudé's high school sweetheart. He blamed Wet Fish for corrupting her. Thus, a deep seed of hatred was planted in the broken heart of Officer Dicken DaBeaudé for Wet Fish.

Their worlds collided on that faithful night for the second time since they both graduated from high school. The first time was at a picture show. His heart filled with bitterness toward Wet Fish, he couldn't suppress his feelings, so he confronted Wet Fish. A fight ensued. Wet Fish flexed him like Sugar Ray Leonard did ole boy. Then he slapped Officer Dicken DaBeaudé's date on the backside while he lay on the floor, trying to figure out how he got there in the first place. That seed in his heart then blossomed to a towering tree of hatred.

Wet Fish and Jennifer were sitting in front of her house on North Fifteenth Street. Officer Dicken DaBeaudé pulled up right next to Wet Fish, looked over at him, then pulled off. Streetwise, he felt that something was afoot. "Looka here, sweetness, I'm fixing to shake da spot. I'm dirty. I'm kinda fucked up. I don't wanna give that ole pussy-ass nigga no reason to run me in," he told Jennifer.

"You just got here. It's still early," she complained, poking out her chest seductively. She was a pro at seducing, although they were past that point in their relationship. She cocked her head to the side slightly, batted her eyes, and ran her tongue slowly across her lips.

"I never said I'm 'bout to call it a night. I meant that I'm 'bout to get the fuck outa Northdale."

She brightened up, then eased her expression. "You forgot I got my fast-ass li'l sister here," she said.

"I wonda where she picked that up from," Wet Fish said.

"What?" she asked, puzzled.

"Fast," Wet Fish replied.

She smiled and stuck her tongue out at him.

They never discussed it, but they both felt in their hearts that they were going to be a part of each other's lives for a while. Wet Fish had been racking his head on ways to get her off them run-hards. She wasn't a full-fledged junky for the drug yet, but he knew the longer she dibbled and dabbled with the run-hard, the more she was going to eventually turn into one.

They gazed into each other's eyes, heat rising in their young bodies. "Check this," Wet Fish said, pulling at the lace in front of her shirt. "Go, get in there, an' grab ya sister. We going back across the tracks. I told my li'l nigga dat I was gonna put him on Trina. I woulda bought him, but he punished. His mama got his ass on lock. I bet 'cha sweet ass he 'bout still posted up in his yard," Wet Fish said.

Jennifer got out of the car, and she came back out with Trina, her little sister.

They pulled off, and before they made it to Chestnut Street, Officer Dicken DaBeaudé got behind him then hit the blue lights on top of his police unit. He had his car backed into the dead end of Mulberry Street with the car lights off, waiting for Wet Fish to pass by him.

Wet Fish pulled over to the curb of the street, spotting him in the dead end before he pulled off behind him. He eased his quarter-ounce of redhead into his seat. It was too late for him to hide it properly. "Damn, Daddy, you should've left that at my house," Jennifer said when he dropped the pistol into the door compartment.

Taking long strides, the policeman was at the driver's-side window in no time. Wet Fish's car window was already down. "Get da fuck out of the car," Officer Dicken DaBeaudé demanded, pulling on the door handle. Wet Fish slammed it back and held it with his hand across his body. Trina and Jennifer were paralyzed with fear as they watched Wet Fish and the policeman battle over control of the door.

Wet Fish shoved open the door just as Officer Dicken DaBeaudé was pulling. Off-balance, Officer Dicken DaBeaudé hit the ground. Wet Fish was stunned motionless by the realization of what he had done. By law, that was assault on an officer. Wet Fish was closing the door just as the policeman was picking himself off the ground. As he came up, he drew and fired in one quick motion. Wet Fish threw his hand up, the lead death enforcer tearing through it, taking his pinky finger with it. The lead death enforcer flew past Jennifer's face, then exited out of the passenger-side window. Officer Dicken DaBeaudé looked at his service weapon in awe. Trina yelled and lay down on the back seat floor, covering her eyes. Jennifer was yelling hysterically as the smell of cordite assaulted her nostrils. Wet Fish's blood had splattered over her face, his finger landing on her lap.

Wet Fish hit the gas hard. Nothing happened. While he was reaching with his good hand to switch gear into drive, Officer Dicken DaBeaudé was positioning himself to the front of the car, but not directly in front of it. Wet Fish got the car in gear then hit the gas. Officer Dicken DaBeaudé opened fired again, the lead death enforcer speeding through the corner of the windshield, hitting Wet fish in the shoulder, slamming him back against the seat. The flame continued to jump out of the candy stick as he pulled the trigger, the windshield shattering but holding in place. Wet Fish's body jerked from the impact of the death enforcers slamming into him.

Jennifer went berserk. Eerie screams left her throat as she reached for the handle to open her door. Shots continued to ring out, the lead death enforcers hammering Wet Fish's upper chest this time. The glass shattering made Jennifer abandon her instinct to jump out—she ducked down. Wet Fish leaned over to shield her from the barrage of lead death enforcers, then another one of the lead death enforcers slammed into Wet Fish, this one entering right behind his right ear, exiting at the base of his skull, a fatal shot.

Jennifer thought Wet Fish was still alive when the other three shots were fired. The impact of the lead death enforcers hitting his body had rocked him every time one touched him. The car rolled a few yards before crashing into a parked car. Jennifer, wide-eyed, shaking and screaming, was pinned underneath Wet Fish's lifeless body, his blood drenching her. The smell of burning flesh filling her nostrils, she struggled to get from under him. She stopped scream-ing. She didn't move, her warm tears mixing with the warm blood of Wet fish shining in the darkness on her face. The last thing Jennifer remembered was Trina's scream and the flashing red lights, then everything went peaceful and quiet.

The officer claimed that Wet Fish tried to run over him and that was why he used deadly force. A quarter-ounce of high-grade marijuana, thirty-one grams of crack cocaine, a 9-millimeter pistol were found after the shooting. The mayor of Baton Rouge awarded Officer Dicken DaBeaudé with a plaque and medal for bravery and removing drugs and a pistol off the streets while in no regards of his own safety.

Li'l One Gone's day was going good until he stared into Jennifer's face. Her face stayed expressionless, her eyes looking like the light behind them had been turned out. Combing a hand through her hair, she uttered, "Is my hair pretty?" followed by a childish giggle. His heart bled for her and for revenge.

Li'l One Gone didn't become lugubrious after Wet Fish's demise, but he wasn't quite himself, never much of a talker; he had almost completely become mute. When spoken to, he'd either make a grunting noise to reply or gaze into their face like they were speaking a language he didn't understand. If anyone made any loud noise in his presence, he would attack them. In the heat of battle, he would stop punching and laugh while he was still getting pounding on. His mama took him to Margaret Dumas Mental Institute to get checked. They weren't able to properly diagnose him because his mama could only explain his behavior; they needed to know what his thoughts and patterns were in order to diagnose and recommend a treatment.

Psychoanalyzing was inadequate. Li'l One Gone wouldn't answer any of the doctor's questions verbally or physically. He just stared, nonblinking, when rapport was attempted to be established. So the psychiatrist scheduled regular appointment visits in order to mark his progress or decline in mental health. She told his mama to keep an eye on him and inform her if there were any change in his behavior, good or bad. Everyone thought that Li'l One Gone had lost his marbles. That wasn't the case. He had a movie playing in his head that never ended, because every time someone struck up a conversation with him, the movie would stop and replay. In order to get to the end, he had to withdraw from doing anything—even he, too, would cause it to stop, rewind, and replay. The film that played was a movie about him, everything he'd experienced at birth, and it ended with him draped in gold, with nude women catering to him, while everyone he ever perceived wronged him lying in a casket.

His mama was surprised to hear Li'l One Gone laughing. It was a strange sound to her ears. She eased into his room to see if he had cracked up or was laughing with whatever it was that used to haunt him in that room. She was relieved when she saw that he had headphones on his ears, an empty cassette container with Richard Pryor on the cover beside him. He was showing signs of recovery, yet she still guarded him. Although he didn't spend most of his time inside of his head anymore, she was still concerned because when she gazed into his eyes, she didn't see him; she saw something that disturbed her. An old soul looked out at her. Pain, both physical and mental, he learned to overcome.

Suffering and misery were what he started to embrace. Hardship became his escalator, the feeling of loneness and despair his friends. Anger and rage produced a profound hell that he used for motivation. Training was over; a street soldier was born. His mama had put Li'l One Gone's life in a vise grip; he couldn't make a move without her consent. He didn't mind being under her shadow. For the last few years of his life, she was an absentee, and when she was present, they were at odds with each other. He cherished every tick of the clock with her; it was his loss of freedom to roam freely that he despised. He was now under the same restraints and conditions he was under when the people from child services were on his mama's back. It wasn't them that made her put a lock on him; it was his own doings. She didn't want to lose her only male child to the streets or to the system. No matter how in tune a kid may be with the streets and the evil deeds that men do, the streets still ain't a place for a child to run alone. Especially not one that seems to have a death wish or is campaigning for permanent incarceration.

Summer vacation was right on the heels of a new semester. School was about to begin shortly, and his mama planned to keep Li'l One Gone under her administration just till school started back. She didn't fancy her baby being up under her every time she made a move, but she loved him more than life. She knew that she couldn't change him, but she intended on slowing him down before he was stopped.

Li'l One Gone went through his spurts of violence just like the other boys in the neighborhood, but he had become increasingly violent that, it appeared to her, it seemed like he enjoyed it a little too much. When he'd explain to her the details of how the fight went, he never had an answer to why he was fighting, his face stone with joy, his voice brimming with excitement as he repeated the tale of violence. The words were written on the wall where he was heading. Whoever came in contact with him and became the focus of his raw emotions was going to endure excruciating pain or even death. His mama had been around the block enough times to read the signs. Plus, he was flesh of her flesh; therefore, he inherited a part of her. If anyone knew what he was capable of doing, it was her.

His action had become unruly without a cause. A new jack to the game could predict Li'l One Gone's future. In order to do her job as a mother and protect him from himself, she had to step in, putting her feet down. His mama overlooked what he had done most of the time, but the same occurrence had begun to be too frequent for her comfort. Every time Li'l One Gone left her presence, trouble seemed to find him; he'd return wide-eyed, breathless, grass and other particles stuck to his person, his clothing disheveled, along with his face littered with bruises and scratches. One day he returned home collared by a parent fuming hot, with a bloodied nose. Supposedly, he had viciously attacked her poor babies, not emphasizing the fact that it was two against one and Li'l One Gone was sandwiched in between a barrage of punches, fighting for survival. Nor did she confess her atrocity. It was all Li'l One Gone's fault, as far as she was concerned. Just like if a cookie comes up missing in a room full of children, blame it on the fat kid, so it was with every altercation that Li'l One Gone got the blame of being the aggressor, initiating the scuffle.

His mama couldn't care less about who started what, nor did she give a damn about Li'l One Gone fighting. She felt that boys were supposed to fight; it was Li'l One Gone's inclination to using weapons that caused her to be concerned. In order to keep the white folks out of their mix, he remained with her to cure his loneliness. She became his friend and confidant. She allowed him to smoke his weed and cigarettes at the house; he had to support his own habit, though, which was kind of hard if he couldn't leave the house. Overall, a loving relationship was forged out of tragedy. Team mother and son, a bond that only death could part.

Though his mama was fighting her own demons, she made sure that she never presented herself to him at her lowest point or in her worldly state. The image she portrayed was always one of a person that was 100 percent absolutely sure about themselves. The mask she wore when she hit the streets said, "Fuck what you're saying. I'm in charge." Never did she once degrade herself around him. Some of her associates were proletariats, not just in status, but in deeds also. Some of the things he witnessed hanging out with his mama would make a grown man cringe and puke. All the things he saw further informed him of the ways of mankind.

But it wasn't the horrific acts of violence he saw on his journeys with his mama that were stuck in his head; it was the humiliating levels to which adult men and women lowered themselves in order to obtain a substance that dissolved in water under the heat of fire. Pathetically, some would beg, almost to the point of tears, when their server would refuse them service for being short on their funds or for having no funds at all, coming to him looking for credit. Each and every time he saw one of the users plead with the server, that was one of the most hilarious sight to him. Li'l One Gone would burst out laughing openly, not even trying to hide his source of amusement. His mama warned him, advising him not to find humor in another person's misery, to resist the temptation to laugh at the dramatic spectacle the user put on and see it for what it was.

Yet still after his mama shunned him for giggling at the jonesing people and schooled him on the reason for their conduct, witnessing the pitiful folks beg on a regular still tickled him like it was his first time witnessing the pleas of a broken man. Until it struck him close to his heart.

He was strolling through the neighborhood with his mama, she on a mission to score a bump. Under the large pecan tree on Illinois Street was where the ex-convicts that went straight and the regular jobholders of the neighborhood congregated. They ran past episodes of their lives while sipping on brewskis and hard liquor. As they passed by them, someone yelled out teasingly in hopes of getting some alone time in with hs mama. "I see you got your bodyguard with ya!"

His mama's lips spread into a big, wide grin. Without looking to see who it was speaking or altering the upbeat rhythm of her flip-flops slapping the pavement, she replied, "Yeah, that nigga think he my ole man." Like the statement directed to her from the group of men had suddenly rubbed her wrong, the smile vanished. "Boy, boy, boy, he just won't give up. He'll never smell this pussy. He ain't got enuff of, not a thing fo' me," she spat out. Li'l One Gone was too pre-occupied with thoughts of what mischievous deeds he could get into once they returned from her mission. He had become her road dog; he accompanied her every time she went on her mission. Whatever he devised had to be done with the gypsiness of a professional tiptoe bandit, because he knew that his mama wasn't going to let him out of her sight for long.

It had only been a few days, truth be told, since he was eased off away from her and pulled off a minor caper. In his elementary mind, it might as well have been an eternity. The appetite for destruction and the game, in some form or another, never outgrew his body; he had to be doing something. Mesmerized, as they walked up the street, he became fascinated with how the shadow worked, taking on different shapes but the body that cast it didn't.

Though he was jovial on the surface, subconsciously a serious matter was brewing "money." He realized that after Wet Fish had died, he had made a lot of beefs in the neighborhood but not a dollar. As he thought about the fact, he missed a couple of beats in his mobbing. He stumbled a little; his feet couldn't synchronize with his thoughts, his mind outpacing the movement of his feet. When they reached their destination—initially, when he began going over there with his mama, the spot would be usually dead—there was very little traffic, helping to enforce the discreetness of the score spot. Once word got out where the good stuff was at, it was hard to hide the fact that there was dope being sold in that spot. All that secrecy had diminished.

There was a single-file line of bodies, all with the same demeanor, waiting impatiently to approach the car with that "Stay out of my business" sign plastered over every window. If the line of sprung-out-looking people wasn't a dead giveaway to what was jumping off, Popeye's a punk and Bluto's a bitch. His mama didn't pretend that it wasn't what it was; she accredited him with as much savvy as he possessed. Automatically, he assumed his position well from the action. He had laughed his privilege away from going directly to the score spot with his mama.

She issued precise instructions to wait there on the corner for her return. His mama had much respect for herself and Li'l One Gone, and in fear of leaving him solo, she was left with no choice but to bring him with her on her score mission. Embarrassment touched her eyes for a fraction of a second, then she quickly caught her head. But Li'l One Gone had already seen it. Only the strength of Jesus Christ breaks the bonds of the world or prevents one from falling victim to the perils of the ways of the world. She didn't have any reason to be ashamed; in the heart of her son, she was above all, regarded in high standards. Regardless of the level of the game his mama chose to play, there wasn't any love lost from Li'l One Gone.

For whatever reason, she abandoned her previous banishment on Li'l One Gone. Cars were bumper to bumper on Nicholson Drove. A solitary game of bingo was being played in his head. Bingo was a children's game. Whoever spotted a materialistic item that person wished to have, that person would yell out, "Bingo!" in hopes of acquiring that item one day. Plus, yelling out bingo stopped anyone else from claiming the desired item.

"Vietnam!" his mama yelled out from her position in line. He turned to acknowledge his mama, who was beckoning for him to come to her. He turned back toward the highway, then "Bingoed!" one more time before he pushed out toward his mama. It was a Z-28 Camaro. It had been a minute since he had his mind on anything else besides danger. Li'l One Gone felt light as he closed the distance between his mama and himself. Several people floated by him, closely examining their package while he was examining them.

Some faces were sated, some not, but all had despair engraved on their mugs. All was too familiar. He'd been viewing the faces of the desperate since he was knocked off the porch as a baby. A woman approached. Aghast, she let out a loud sigh. Steeling himself, he moved farther away from her, giving her plenty of room to pass. Feebly he spoke to her to ease the tension he felt. The way she contorted her features, there was nothing but contempt in her eyes, and along with the lesions on her arms, it sent a bolt of something through Li'l One Gone. She would have made a stone-cold serial rapist, thought not twice but thrice about violating her. Slightly taken aback but not frightened, he put several more feet as they passed another, cutting a wide tract to let her pass. He never averted his gaze. A chill ran through his body. She stopped, and he picked up his pace.

Standing in front of his mama, he noticed a person behind the house. The person would come into view, then duck back behind the house. As they neared the car, the line formation of the addicts was more laxed; their state of mind was also. The ones behind him and his mama were still in single file, and they were highly agitated. With every step closer they took toward the man serving the addicts, his imagination swelled. What was going on behind the house really had him doing mental gymnastics. Images of when he walked up on a couple kissing when he was living in Frog E. Moe projects surfaced along with Wet Fish's episode with Jennifer behind the project building.

Buzzing on the playground were the subjects of females, sports, and music. Females intrigued him the most out of all three. Several of the boys in his age group claimed to have touched a female's breast and seen the most desired part of their anatomy by straight males and some bi females. One even claimed to have touched it. Sex was a hot topic. His curination became unbearable.

"Ma, I got to pee," he lied.

"Go head behind the house," his mama replied.

As he passed by the open car door, glancing inside, his attention was sideswiped by the pile of money spread over the man serving out of the car lap. A dollar usually was his motive. Curiosity had a death grip on him, propelling him forward. He wanted to see if they were behind the house, engaged in coitus. He pictured it in his mind the way it was described to him, hoping that he made it in the heat of the moment and wasn't late. He quickened his step.

What he saw would be forever filed in his brain. Unblinkingly staring, he was hypnotized by what was taking place right there behind the house. Intuition didn't lead him astray. There was a male and a female back there. Suddenly realizing that they were not alone anymore, instead of being startled by Li'l One Gone's presence—he had become their lone audience—with the methodical movements of a seasoned, veteran, career dope fiend, the man performed, going through the motions of mainlining her in the groin. When he pulled out the rig, the blood ran from the prick of the rig, and instead of using his hand or anything else to clean it up, he used his tongue. He licked the blood running down her thigh.

Oblivious to the third party because she had her eyes closed, creeping up to get a closer examination, she opened her eyes. "What?" she asked, surprised.

"Nothing." The man shrugged his shoulders.

With the waist of her pants around her knees, she quickly got to her feet. Her equilibrium off, along with the effect of the drugs racing through her bloodstream, she stumbled backward. Though the house held her up from falling on her uncovered butt cheeks, the man grabbed her. "I got 'cha," he said, ushering her to sit back down. Glancing at Li'l One Gone through glossy eyes, she clung to the man, like the sight of him had frightened her. Closing her eyes, she returned to the world behind her eyelids from which she came when Li'l One Gone intruded in them. What he saw wasn't what he wanted to stumble upon, yet it was another scene to add to the book of sights located inside his cranium.

Wisdom is a key to survival in the game or in life. It usually comes with age, and in certain instances, it comes before one is old enough to understand the true power of wisdom. Visions, sights, and sounds are the way humans learn. Learning and retaining what is learned can be called knowledge. Knowledge gives one an upper hand in the race of life, if applied right; if used wrong, straight to the lower echelons of society one goes.

Seeing the behavior the addicts displayed, Li'l One Gone made up his mind that he'd never be a victim to the hard narcotics. Cocaine, heroin, or any opiate-based pharmaceuticals—those were some opponents that one had to battle with to the death of the user. Banging it, plucking it, or smoking it, no way of consuming the drugs was a lesser opposition to fight with than the other. Li'l One Gone didn't have the heart or the muscle to pick a fight with the products. Some got paid pitching it, and others ended up in the poor house or on skid row, using it.

Leaving them alone to tend to their business, heading back to the front of the house, Li'l One Gone left from back there, way ahead of the game. Once again, rolling with his mama proved to be another one of those pros-and-cons situation. Being viewed as a mama's boy was the only thing he dreaded. Other than that, tagging along with her was more educational than any school had to offer. With her, he witnessed game, crime, and life in 3D. Also, his mama was a hustler of hustlers. Turning nothing into something was her forte. Her mouthpiece and her body were methods of gain. Game spilled out of the sway of her hips, the foddering of her eyelids, the seductive way she cocked her head, making the average man bend to her will. Not every time did her mouthpiece work, yet it was still a learning lesson and amusement for Li'l One Gone when she was in action.

His mama was still posted in line, her hand on her hips. She was a few people closer to the car than she was when he left her side. Stepping to the side, she gestured to the person behind her. "Go 'head," she told the man. The man moved ahead of her in line. Being next to approach the car, he happily traded places with his mama. The move by his mama had Li'l One Gone scratching his head, and he questionably gazed into her face. "Just stand here," she said, reading him. Glancing down the line, he noticed several other people had that confused look on their faces also. Edging, Li'l One Gone got closer to the car, and stopping, she pulled him closer to her. Feeling the softness and warmth of her body was strange, but not unsettling, for it was rarely did she express loving emotions or displayed that type of affection.

As he craned his neck, looking up, his mama smiled a smile that didn't reach her eyes at him. Relishing the moment, he returned the smile. With her hand on his shoulder, they looked like they were posing for a photograph. "You got tha paperwork ya owe me?" the server pitching out of the car asked with tightened features.

"No, but—"

"Well, what tha fuck do you want 'round here?" he asked gravely, slicing mama's words off.

Both of their smiles faded away. Anger was storming inside of Li'l One Gone. He wanted badly to say what was on his mind, but his mama had already drilled him to only speak when spoken to and to stay out of grown folks' conversations. Multiple muscles constricted on his face as he looked through the man, waiting for his mama to reply with a defensive response.

For the first time in his short life, he heard uncertainty in her voice when his mama spoke. "I got some money," she said, pulling out a few folded bills out of her brassiere. "Today's my boy's birthday. I had bought him a few thangs. Yeah, my baby get'n on up there," she said continuously, hugging Li'l One Gone tightly. Li'l One Gone was too angry to confirm or protest his mama's statement. He stared frozen, watching the man count the money his mama gave him.

Disgusted, the man blurted out, "What tha fuck can I do with six dollars, bitch?"

"That's—"

That was the only word his mama got out. "Ole pussy-ass nigga, don't be talk'n to my mama like that!" Li'l One Gone screamed, charging forward, his mama snatching him back roughly.

Rising to his feet, the server was a below-average-size man in height, his weight covering where he lacked in height. Li'l One Gone contained too much rage and violence inside of him to be intimidated. His mama sighed and drew back a step, drawing Li'l One Gone backward with her, thus further stopping his forward advance.

Chest swelling, Li'l One Gone braced himself for combat. He was wound tight and ready to strike.

"Now, jus' what in tha fuck you gonna do, li'l fat-ass nigga? I'll dust you and that raggedy dopehead-ass bitch off!" the server barked. A few gasps, grunts, and "Oohs" came out of the line of waiting addicts. His mama had placed her arm across Li'l One Gone's windpipe, holding him back. The more he struggled, the more his oxygen got cut off.

"Can I jus' get sumthang fo' my money and go?" his mama asked pleadingly.

"Fuck no! You gets nothing," the server spat out, throwing the six dollars at his mama's face. "Git tha fuck on from 'round here. Ya fetti ain't no good on this here set till ya come correct and make damn well sure you have the change ya already owe me," the server sternly stated. The bills he threw at his mama didn't strike her; they sailed past her.

Li'l One Gone watched the money as they landed onto the ground. Looking back at the server, he said, "Muthafucka!" fighting to get free of his mama's grip.

Squeezing him, his mama forcibly commanded him, "Stop."

Li'l One Gone paused.

"Thank you," his mama said to the man politely, smiling.

Defiantly the server said, "Thank ya ass from 'round here and don't come back till you ready to square up and have ya money straight." He and his mama glanced at the two bills on the ground.

"Get tha fuck on," he said angrily, flinging his arm like he was swatting at an invisible fly. If he were large enough, the ground would have shaken from the vibration of his body. It wasn't fear that made Li'l One Gone tremble; it was rage ready to erupt. They walked off, his mama shoulders sagging, but she wasn't looking at the ground. Her face was toward the shy. Li'l One Gone peered at the line of addicts waiting to be served. Most avoided eye contact with him. Only one woman met his gaze, sympathy glaring out at him. There wasn't going to be any support from the waiting addicts if the server attacked the mother and child. No one wanted to or had the courage to run afoul with their drug supplier.

Li'l One Gone went to pick up the money. "Leave it," his mama said, calmly pulling Li'l One Gone back. Anguish was there when Li'l One Gone looked up at her. "It's over with, baby," his mama added, holding back tears, nodding. She then smiled, saying, "I love you." Joy leaped into the place of anger and anguish that was there. Wary of the sudden change, Li'l One Gone peeked over his shoulder at the server. He was back on his grind. He wasn't paying them any mind as they walked off. If he had not been so preoccupied with exchanging his product for the addicts' currency, he would have seen his future in Li'l One Gone's eyes. It was said that two mountains will never meet, but two men will meet again.

Karonda had warned him that if he had gotten into any more trouble, she was going to break up with him. Li'l One Gone spotted the car as soon as it pulled into North Gate's parking lot. They were arriving at the same time. He pulled up short. "What?" Karonda asked when Li'l One Gone abruptly stopped walking.

"Let that nigga in that car go first," he said, pointing.

Anxious to enter the store, she blurted out, "Why?"

"Just cause. Now wait." His tone of voice steeled with his mask.

Being street, she read the severity of his features and sudden change of demeanor. Usually feisty and outspoken, Karonda submitted. "Okay," she replied meekly, staring at the direction of Li'l One Gone's menacing stare. When the man got out of his car, turning, before he revealed his face completely, Karonda said excitedly, "I know him, I know him!"

Zeroing in on him, Li'l One Gone watched his every move, noticing instantly the man wasn't up to par to say he lived off the streets. He didn't have that survival instinct. Not once did he glance over at Li'l One Gone or any other direction when he stepped out of his car, he looked one way, straight ahead. "Oh yeah, fuck him," replied Li'l One Gone.

"No, boy, I didn't mean it like that. I don't know him *know* him. You remember when that woman got shot in the projects?" she asked.

Transfixed on her, and she him, Li'l One Gone turned his gaze. "Yeah, T'Sharon," he answered.

"That's the nigga who shot her," Karonda said matter-of-factly.

Li'l One Gone's heart pounded. "You fo' sho?" he asked, barely able to contain himself. He pulled her to the side of the store.

"You damn skippy I'm fo' sho. Do you remember I was on the basketball court the day that lady got killed? I remember see'n you," she stated, smiling. "This my first time see'n him since then, but I'll neva fo'git his ugly-ass face," she stated.

Digging into his pocket, Li'l One Gone pulled out a few shams. "Here, git what you want outa there. I'ma git at you later," he told her, slamming the money into her hand. "Don't say shit to that nigga. As a matter of fact, don't even look at him," Li'l One Gone commanded her. Before she responded, he marched off.

The flame inside of him from when Big Ed had blatantly disrespected his mama had never died out. The newfound revelation about him being responsible for the death of T'Sharon was a stick of gasoline-soaked dynamite added to the flames burning inside of Li'l One Gone's soul. Why didn't matter. Upon further question of Karonda, Li'l One Gone had gotten the entire story from start to finish. With the exception of a few gangster-turned-drug-dealer, most drug dealers are not confrontational; they hide behind their money. At that point, a newcomer to the neighborhood going by the moniker Big Ed had just entered the game; therefore, being fresh in the game, he didn't have any money to spread around in order to get work done for him. So he took it upon himself to put in his own work. Li'l One Gone found out later in life the way it happened. According to the streets, Mark introduced him to the game by sticking him up. He humiliated him by making him run down the street buck naked after he relieved him of his drugs, his money, and the few pieces of jewelry he was sporting.

Though the wages of sin is death, T'Sharon wasn't the intended victim. Karonda said she had seen the man pacing on the side of the building out of the view of anyone else besides her. He then vanished to the back of the projects. Thinking back as she spoke, Li'l One Gone recalled seeing his car parked in the back of the Bricks when he came through to confront Floyd. Not able to address the static he had with Floyd, he ended up chilling in front of T'Sharon's

118

apartment with her and a few other cats before his mama summoned him to come stroll with her to the store. Apparently, Big Ed's coat had been pulled to who had stuck him up and where he hung out. He vanished out of sight, and when he reappeared, he was jogging around the side of the building, coming off West Roosevelt Street. Like a true coward, instead of him walking up to his target, he accelerated his jogging pace into a run, shooting from the hip as he passed in front of where the group was standing, striking T'Sharon and the brick wall behind her. None of the death enforcers he squeezed out of his candy stick hit his intended target.

Closing arguments were heard. The jury left the courtroom to deliberate, then in one minute and nine seconds, the jury reached a verdict. Guilty. The sentencing was eternal sleep by way of an overdose of sleeping pills, then hot lead ones. Li'l One Gone volunteered for the job to carry out the sentence of the condemned coward, knowing exactly what job needed to be done, how it was to be done, and the deadline for the contract to be fulfilled had been sorted out. Acquiring the tool to get the job done was the last part of the plot to be sorted out. In most cases, the tools are already on deck way before a mission is planned or a job comes up. This was going to be Li'l One Gone's first time taking on the role as executioner; he was unprepared for the job.

As he brainstormed on whom or where he could get a candy stick from, the voice whispered in Li'l One Gone's ear, "In the room." There was only one room in the house that he hadn't been in in many moons. Uncle Shortman's room. His room was off-limits. He had told Li'l One Gone's mama to keep an eye on his stuff, meaning not to let anyone go into his room while he was gone. Li'l One Gone's mama honored his wishes and kept her word to him. She even changed the locks to his room's door; only she held the knowledge to where the key was. Uncle Shortman had fallen victim to the penal system a little while after Monk and Uncle Rich did. Up to date, all the figures in Li'l One Gone's life were on lock, either in the casket or in prison.

Uncle Shortman was a gambling man; craps, pool, and betting on sports were how he made his extra money. He had placed the bets by sticking to his guns. Going with the odds was his game plan, and it had paid off. He often told Li'l One Gone, when gambling on sports, bet with knowledge and not with feelings for a certain sports team. The year previously was his off year. He placed his entire check on the LA Lakers to win. The Boston Celtics upset the Lakers, and Uncle Shortman also. Two weeks of hard work's pay was gone, right along with the Lakers' hopes of being the NBA champions for that season. The following season, Uncle Shortman placed the same bet with the same person; this time, the Lakers were victorious.

Some folks can't greet failure in their lives the same as they greet triumph, which was the case with Frank, Uncle Shortman's coworker. At the end of their shift, they clocked out, went to the bank. Frank cashed his check and handed it over, every cent of it, to Uncle Shortman, the same way Uncle Shortman coughed his up to him when the Lakers lost. They departed, going their separate ways. All went well. For the last thirty years, Friday night was prime time on East Boulevard, with Johnny's Liquor Store as its main attraction. This particular night wasn't an exception; the strip was live and getting livelier by the minute. It seemed like everyone was out and in a merry mood. Especially those who took the odds on the Lakers or had bets straight up. A few people out were sour about their loss but pretended everything was all right, inwardly feeling the lost. Then there was Frank, who visibly wore his emotions.

Uncle Shortman slipped into Johnny's a little after nine o'clock. He planned on staying long enough to feel the effects of the few drinks he was going to have. He liked to drink in public, but he got sloppy drunk in the privacy of his own residence. Elbowing his way up to the bar, he went into his pocket to retrieve the few dollars he had put to the side for his drinks. They had a woman next to him, separating him from Frank, who was there nursing a drink with his head down.

"Look what the cat done drag in," Frank mumbled, voice dripping with venom.

The woman heard him, glancing over toward Frank. Whatever she saw in his face, she didn't want any part of it—she quickly emptied her seat.

"What up, my boy?" Uncle Shortman shouted over the music when he spotted Frank bellied up to the bar.

"Fuck you," Frank mumbled, tossing his drink back then slamming his glass down on the counter aggressively.

Uncle Shortman peeked over his shoulder before he pulled out his wad of US currency. Cash in hand, he peeled two one-dollar bills off his bankroll. "A shot for me and one for that woman that just walked off!" he yelled to the bartender.

"Nigga, you done won all my muthafucking money. Throw another one of them up there fo' me a drink too," Frank demanded menacingly.

"No can do, my nigga. You bet, you lost, take it like a man," Uncle Shortman said, then laughed.

"Fuck you!" said Frank, leaning over and snatching up the money Uncle Shortman had laid in front of him for his drinks. "Right here, babycakes!" Frank yelled to the bartender, waving Uncle Shortman's money. "I got the money. The drink is mine," he spat out matter-of-factly to the bartender, who was staring mystified at Uncle Shortman and Frank.

"Put my money back down," Uncle Shortman stated calmly.

"No can do, fuck you!" Frank spat out.

The bartender stood there confused. She knew that Uncle Shortman had initially ordered the drinks, but Frank held out the money. Placing the drinks down in front of Frank, she took the money out of his extended hands. "Tha" of the word *thanks* was the only thing he got out; Uncle Shortman drew, aimed, and fired in one swift motion. The sound of the candy stick was deafening; even over the chatter and music inside of the liquor store, it rang out loudly. A .44 bulldog slug slammed into the side of Frank's face, knocking out teeth, flesh, and bone as it exited the other side of his face then lodged itself right through the neck of a Budweiser bottle on a poster on the wall. The impact of the slug jerked his head to the side, then his body followed. Frank toppled to the side. He then collapsed to the liquor store's filthy floor. He lay on the grimy floor, holding his face, trying to push the blood back in as it gushed through his fingers, squealing like a pig.

"Get up, nigga," Uncle Shortman demanded. With the business end of the candy stick trained on Frank, Uncle Shortman roughly snatched him off the floor. Frank stood on spaghetti legs, cupping his face, blood spilling through his fingers on both sides of his face. The side the bullet exited had a golf-ball-size hole in it. Uncle Shortman propped Frank up against the bar. "There go your drink, nigga," Uncle Shortman said. With the barrel of the candy stick, he pushed the shot glass in front of Frank while he held him up with his other hand and shoulder against the bar. "This how this here gonna go," he said calmly, pausing. All the chatter in the liquor store had ceased when the .44 barked. Frank's moans of agony joined the sweet melody of the music playing in the background. Uncle Shortman placed the barrel of the candy stick to Frank's head, violently pressing the barrel into his temple. "You wanted a drink, now you got it. There it is. You gon' swallow every bit of that shot too, nigga. If a drop of it roll off ya lips, I'm gon' blow ya shit off," Uncle Shortman stressed, pushing the barrel harder into Frank's head to emphasize his message. Frank's body started shaking uncontrollably. Uncle Shortman had to hold him to keep him from falling. Fear poured out of his pores right along with the blood that streamed down his face. Frank grunted and gurgled. When he removed his hand from his face, where the bullet entered, there was a nickel-size bloody hole sitting on top of a large contusion.

Shaking, he reached for the glass, then cringed with pain when he attempted to glance over at Uncle Shortman. With glass in hand, he hesitated, "Go 'head, sip, nigga. If not, die. Either way it's fine with me," Uncle Shortman stated, his finger resting on the trigger. Frank picked up the glass and threw it back, pouring the contents into his slackened mouth. The liquor spilled down his chin, mixing in with the blood that was running down his neck. Throwing up his hand, mainly to ward off the suspecting bullet, Frank cried out in a combination of grunts, groans, and squeals, his chest heaving as the fiery liquid burned the inside of his mouth. The liquor had rolled out of the sides of his face in a crimson stream. Still gripping the shot glass of the fiery spirit, Frank collapsed to the floor. Uncle Shortman laughed and strolled out of Johnny's Liquor Store, clutching his candy stick. The few remaining patrons rushed out of Jonny's Liquor Store behind Uncle Shortman. They didn't want to be the ones that were stuck with the task of explaining to the lawman what happened to Frank.

Uncle Shortman was now a few years into his ten-year prison sentence when Li'l One Gone eased into his room after he spent a half-hour trying to pry open the door with a pair of scissors. The room had a stale smell floating in the stuffy air. Searching wasn't necessary; a well-oiled .410 shotgun rested in the corner of the dimly lit room. It radiated beautifully. If it weren't his purpose for entering the room in the first place, the splendor of the shotgun would have drawn him to it. No experience or training with firearms, he toyed with the shotgun until he discovered the release mechanism. When he cracked open the breach, there was a brand-new shell in it waiting to cause havoc. The shotgun was a single-shot model.

He scanned the room. Next to an LA Lakers cap, behind an alligator clock on the nightstand, was a box with *Winchester* written on it. With the shotgun and box of shells in hand, Li'l One Gone could feel a surge of empowerment run through his body. His emotions ran so rampantly through him that they exuded from his body. His feelings could have been felt by the touch of the hand as he exited the tranquil room.

Li'l One Gone's entire being changed the second he had laid eyes on the shotgun. His walk had a longer stride, with a bounce to it as he roamed the neighborhood. He stayed keyed up, on the defensive side more than he usually did. He started to place himself in predicaments to where there wasn't a way to avoid the altercations. Mean-mugging had become his fixed look. All transpired within thirty-six hours after he came to possess the .410. He felt powerful, yet he still couldn't bring himself to the point of killing. With his cousin's pellet gun, he had shot plenty of birds, plucking them off powerlines, trees, on top of fences, or wherever the unlucky fowls landed. He couldn't understand why he couldn't bring himself to dropping the hammer on the neighbor's German shepherd.

He patted him on the head with one hand while he held the trigger of the shotgun that lay an inch away from the dog's nose. The dog was standing on his hind legs, with his front paws leaning on the fence, wagging his tail, oblivious to the present danger. Gazing into the dog's exciting pupils, Li'l One Gone eased his finger off the trigger, releasing the tension. Applying it would have delivered a definite kill shot. The dog had been his only friend during his time of trouble. When he sat alone in the backyard, the dog would stand next to the fence where he was sitting and nudge and paw at him through the fence. When the dog sensed that Li'l One Gone didn't want to be bothered and that he was in a foul mood, he would just lie next to the fence and will Li'l One Gone to cheer up with his eyes.

There was a herd of cows on the levy that belonged to the Louisiana State University School of Veterinary Medicine. Passing them up, Li'l One Gone went into the woods, firing into the trees. A few birds fell. He was getting familiar with the feel of the shotgun. That day in the woods was the first time he had pulled the trigger with a round in it. Instantly he fell in love with the way the shotgun responded. On his way out of the woods, the cows had moved closer to the edge of the woods, grazing. Raising the shotgun to his shoulder, he leveled it to the cow nearest him in the herd. He didn't have to aim at it. A target that big, missing it with a shotgun was nearly impossible. As he steadied himself, the cow raised his head, grass hanging out of its mouth while it chomped and ground down on it. Li'l One Gone's heart filled with sympathy for the big friendly animal; he couldn't inflict pain on it. Lowering the barrel, he mobbed on.

Li'l One Gone gave up. He found out that he wasn't a killer. He'd try again later, he decided as he walked into the neighborhood with his head down, heart heavy with disappointment. Someone or something bigger than a bird had to die so that he could get the feel of the kill, he thought to himself. He knew that people carried guns and that they weren't afraid to use them. When the time came, he wanted to have enough experience to get it gone, not hesitating to squeeze off a shot, resulting in him getting himself hurt or even put up by his intended victim if they were armed also.

Coming through the door, then stopping, he stared at his mama lying peacefully asleep on the couch. He clutched the shotgun and watched her chest rise up and down, looking back outside, making sure no unexpected company approached the house. Satisfied, he turned, staring into his mama's face. He froze in his tracks, making sure not to let the floorboards creek as he walked up across the living room. He eased the shotgun from out of his pants. Desperately he tried to keep the fabric from rustling and the shotgun from snagging his pants leg or his waist while he maneuvered it out of the place he concealed it. It cleared without a hitch. Looking at his mama one final time, he swung the barrel forward, then proceeded up the hall to his room. Initially when he entered the house, he was going to head straight to his bedroom. The shotgun acted like a brace against his leg, enabling him to bend it when he walked. Dragging his legs across the loose wood tiles would have awakened his mama from her rest, something he honestly didn't want to happen.

"It's time!" the voice screamed in Li'l One Gone's ear. Unloading the .410, snapping it back close, he shoved the barrel down his pants leg, the stock lying against his rib cage. It felt like it belonged there. In a state of tunnel vision, he crept up the street, his focus on making it to the spot, getting into position, and accomplishing the job without any form of hindrance. It had been four days since he planned, strategized, and plotted against the man that disrespected his mama and who was the reason for T'Sharon's early departure from earth, death. All the necessities to succeed had been assessed, then reassessed, and finally approved by him. It was simple; all he had to do was get there, point the shotgun at him, then pull the trigger. The vision of the proposed act replayed in his mind as he swiftly moved up the street. Mentally, he was overprepared. There wasn't anything he wanted more in life than vengeance. Ever particle of him was consumed by it; to do it was the only source of relief, the thought of murder having become a thorn in his side that had to be removed. The moment was near.

A stray potlicker hopped up the street on three legs—that was the only breathing organism that stirred since he had posted up. Li'l One Gone waited on the side of the house, out of view from anyone passing down the street or anyone approaching the house. The house was the last one on the dead end of West Grant Street. On the other side of the track from where he lived, there wasn't a chance of anyone coming up the street spotting him because the ditch on the side of the tracks was overflowing with rainwater. Only way that his position could have been compromised, foiling his plan, was if someone walked directly up on him. Other than that, phase 1 of the plan was good. Now, all he had to do was lie and wait for the dude to pull up. He didn't know if the guy lived at the house or what time he would be arriving. Intuition was strong inside of him; therefore, he wasn't worried about failing to complete his mission. Besides, how could he? The voice was on his side also. Back against the outer wall of the house, Li'l One Gone yelled, "What the fuck!" Panic rose up from the location where he felt the tug. A hand snaked from underneath the house and pulled at his pants leg again. Jerking his leg free, he stammered, "Who dat?"

A child poked his head out, sliding partially from underneath the house. Lying on his back, he stared up at Li'l One Gone, eyes resting on the shotgun. "Man, you tryna stick Big Ed too? Fuck dat! I've been scoping out this nigga fo' da longest, plus I've been under here, waiting fo' a minute now," he stressed.

Li'l One Gone stood there speechless. "Check game. We gon' hit 'em together, split everythang fifty-fifty. Cool?"

"Cool," Li'l One Gone said surprisingly. He knew the child from seeing him in the neighborhood, but he didn't know him on a personal level; they had never had words before.

"C'mon," the child said, sliding back underneath the house. Li'l One Gone got down on his knees, still puzzled by the turn of events. He peeked under the house. "C'mon, nigga," the child urgently commanded.

Sighing, Li'l One Gone said, "Okay." He crawled underneath first, then he pulled the shotgun under. The dampness of the ground, along with the tight space, had heightened his senses.

"What up, kid? They call me Magic," the kid said, introducing himself, his fist extended.

Dapping him down, Li'l One Gone replied, "Vee is what they call me."

Awkwardly he looked at Magic, then peered out toward the street. From their point of view, his feet and up to his knee were all they were going to see of Big Ed. "Dog, how is we gon' pull this off from under here? I can't see shit!" Li'l One Gone asked. He wasn't interested in small talk. That won Magic over. He came for business also; he didn't want a stickman; that was why he came alone in the first place. He wasn't sure what Li'l One Gone's purpose was for being there, or who he was, for that matter. When he saw the stock of the shotgun on the ground between Li'l One Gone's leg when he squatted down, he took a chance of revealing himself. But only after he had studied Li'l One Gone a few more minutes.

"Just follow my lead. I got dis," Magic stated surely.

Li'l One Gone did not foresee the current situation when he was going over the list of the dos in his mind. A mild feeling of uncertainty overcame him while he lay there, pondering, but there was one thing he did know for sure, that there was no turning back, that the job had to be done.

Magic didn't have any inclination of his true intentions; therefore, he wasn't going to cause any interference. When to shoot was the only thing he had to work out quickly. Robbing him had never occurred to him; he had planned and come strictly for murder. Smiling inside, he thought to himself, *Money is always the mission.*

"What?" Li'l One Gone asked, catching Magic peeking over at the .410 for the third time.

"Man, where you got dat ole bitch there from? I ain't never seen a nigga stick a nigga with a rifle. You gon' fuck 'round and blow your mission with that bitch. A nigga gon' already be up on game when he spot you with dat," Magic said, expertly speaking.

A little embarrassed, Li'l One Gone stated, "Shit, this all I got."

"You cool, Vee. I'ma lace you with something sweet as soon as we pull this here off. Be quiet now, tho," he stated, like he had just recalled that they were on a mission.

Li'l One Gone studied him for a few seconds. He pulled the shotgun closer to him, making sure that he had clear access to the target. He then focused on the front of the house with Magic. Being in the company of a new person always made Li'l One Gone uncomfortable. Every male he met was a potential enemy in his head until they proved otherwise. Especially those who initiated contact with him first. Even when their intentions proved to be genuine, he was still leery about extending his hand to friendship. He didn't feel that way about Magic as they both lay in wait of their chosen prey. Seriousness, no bullshit exerted from him as he stalked the street, his head never moving, but Li'l One Gone got the impression that he was watching everything that moved.

Li'l One Gone knew without a shadow of a doubt that Magic was prepared and ready for action; what he didn't know was how he was going to react when he went with his move. Hoping otherwise, what Li'l One Gone suddenly regretted was not bringing extra shells for his shotty.

"Suit up, kid. There he go," Magic said, yanking the bandanna around his neck right up below his eyes. Volts of adrenaline raced through his veins when he saw the Oldsmobile glide down the street. Impatiently he began to twist his body around into position to crawl from underneath the house. Grabbing his shirt, Magic asked, his voice muffled, "What, you go'n naked face him?"

Li'l One Gone was lost to the terminology of this part of the game, confusion displayed across his features.

"You ain't bought shit to cover ya face," Magic stated.

"Nah," Li'l One Gone replied stupidly.

Magic shook his head. "We gon wait till he get to the back of the house befo' we stick 'em. I'ma go out dis way, you come out on yo side. After he run everything he got, we gon make 'em smash out toward da track. You got me?" Magic asked. "Get ready," he said before Li'l One Gone responded.

Big Ed pulled across his yard, parking parallel to the street.

He didn't jump right out of the car when he turned off the car's engine; he sat a few minutes before the driver's-side door came ajar. He still didn't exit his vehicle; he swung a leg out and sat a while longer. From beneath the house, they couldn't see exactly what it was that he was doing inside of his car; only thing visible to them was from ground up to his knee. It took every gram of fight within Li'l One Gone to stop himself from crawling underneath the house, running up, and blasting Big Ed. He had deviated from the plan he envisioned repeatedly, something he had never done, and it caused second thoughts to cross his mind. A part of him told him to abort the mission, but glancing over at Magic, he was steeled. Readily lying on his stomach, he looked like a commando stalking the enemy. Quickly suppressing the thought of walking away, he, too, assumed the same position as his new stickman.

When Big Ed first rolled up, he was antsy with excitement, ready to get the job done, then he was slightly stricken with doubt for a spell. Now he watched Big Ed's feet with the calmness of a viper ready to strike. Tunnel vision set back in, and the world seemed to slow down a bit. He couldn't hear anything, not even the rushing, roaring sound of the blood passing behind his eardrums as he got lost in his thoughts. Watching Big Ed approach the house, he glanced over at Magic. His feet were the only part of his body underneath the house. When Magic climbed to his feet, that was when Li'l One Gone made his move to come from underneath the house also. Big Ed walked toward the back of the house on the side Li'l One Gone was on; therefore, he had to wait until he had cleared the area before he broke the plain of the house's outer wall.

Moving too quickly would have revealed his hidden location, exposing himself. Though he had the element of surprise on his side, Big Ed was standing upright. Li'l One Gone would have been lying down, giving Big Ed the advantage of an attack. Quietly sliding over the damp grass, he kept constant eye in the location he wanted. Making it completely from underneath the house, he reached back and pulled the .410 next to him. He looked across to see that Magic was still hidden on the other side of the house. In a flash, he was up on his feet, shotgun in hand, crouching low. He moved with certainty along the side of the house. Tunnel vision had faded away when he snaked his way from underneath the house. Open-minded and alert, he let his ears precede the rest of him around the house. Big Ed was just in the motion of turning when he spotted Li'l One Gone out of his periphery. He jerked his head around to face Li'l One Gone, but before his head completed the turn, Magic thrust forward, candy stick in hand, aimed directly at Big Ed.

"Touch da sun, bitch!" he barked out.

Without hesitation, Big Ed's hands shot straight up in the air.

Li'l One Gone raised the .410 shotty, leveling it right at his mouth. Hands in the air, he glanced down Li'l One Gone's barrel, then at Magic's barrel. As he stared menacing at Li'l One Gone's face, recognition flashed over his pupils. Encouraging him to speak before, then he was scared silent.

"Dis what it is, li'l nigga," Big Ed spit out. Li'l One Gone couldn't speak; his mouth had become glued shut, his feet feeling like he was standing in cement. All the while his finger lay over the trigger. He had thought about pulling the trigger, but Magic was on the other side of the fire, too green to move around to get a clear shot. He just stood there motionless.

"Come out ya pockets with everything, nigga," Magic commanded.

Slowly lowering his hands down, he winked at Li'l One Gone before he turned and faced Magic. "I got a li'l sumthang on me, a stash ova behind da tree and the rest in the glove box," Big Ed said.

"Run it, nigga. Hurry up," Magic barked, one of his hands extended palm up. "Get dat from behind the tree, G," he told Li'l One Gone, watching Big Ed's every move as he spoke.

"It's in tha Burger King wrapper inside tha plastic shopping bag," Big Ed said.

Li'l One Gone hurriedly retrieved the package, shoving it into his pocket without examining it. He pointed the shotgun back at Big Ed as he closed the distance.

"That's all I own, yungin, you got it all," Big Ed cried.

Magic held out the bankroll, showing it to Li'l One Gone, then quickly ran it into his pocket. Big Ed stared at Magic like he was trying to place his voice or remove the bandanna off his face with his eyes. "Strip down to ya birthday suit," Magic demanded, pushing the pistol out angrily in his direction.

Big Ed snatched his shirt apart, popping the buttons off it as he did so. Mumbling, he proceeded to unbuckle his belt, pulling it loose. A flower with "Mom" written on it on his chest became a target for Li'l One Gone; he had positioned himself right next to Magic. Big

Ed was no longer a human being in Li'l One Gone's mind. He had transformed into an object that needed to be destroyed. He peered at Big Ed. He was fumbling with the zipper on his pants when Li'l One Gone pulled the trigger back. *Kaboom!* The blast broke the silence of the afternoon, the heat from the fire that leaped from the end of the barrel felt behind it.

Li'l One Gone was standing so close to him that it seemed like the force from the sound of the blast from the shotty had knocked Big Ed backward. A fine crimson mist and particles of flesh flew into Li'l One Gone's face as Big Ed's chest blew apart. It happened so quickly the flame coming out of the end of the barrel was still visible when his chest exploded. Falling to his final resting place, face twisted in agony, Big Ed flopped like a fish out of water. His body vigorously gyrated on the well-kept Bermuda grass. An eerie gurgling sound escaped his throat as he struggled to fill his lungs with oxygen. The gyration of his body suddenly began to subside. Then all movement by him ceased completely. Li'l One Gone stood over him, watching his eyes plead for help, then they turned to absolute disbelief before they clouded over. He momentarily stared into the horizon before they shut permanently.

Wiping Big Ed's blood off his face, Li'l One Gone felt nothing as he spun away from Big Ed's dead body on the back lawn. Magic glared at him. He noticed that although it wasn't trained on him, he had a tighter grip on his candy stick than he did when he was relieving Big Ed of his property. He had moved back away from Big Ed's body before it lay motionless. They were posted up shoulder to shoulder before Li'l One Gone let the hammer of his shotty drop. Walking off, Magic took a side step, giving him ample space to pass by him. He paused. Magic shook his head disapprovingly, glancing over at Big Ed, then back at Li'l One Gone. Li'l One Gone let his gaze fall down on Magic's pistol. Quiet was as thick as the fading smell of cordite and fresh blood in the air as they faced each other off. Making the V shape with his index and pointer finger, he tapped the sign two times over his heart. Magic, easing the grip on the pistol, nodded in acknowledgment of the gesture.

"Damn," Magic said, then sighed, watching Li'l One Gone limp away with a murder weapon stuffed down his trousers.

One gone, one more to go, he thought, peeping around the house. Nobody. Adjusting the shotgun, Li'l One Gone strolled up the street. A weight had been lifted off his mind. The sky seemed bluer, and a warm sensation raced through his body. He was already lapsing into a mild state of euphoria as he walked away from his first official kill, the voice's felicitations in his ear increasing his emotions, pushing him deep into ecstasy.

In the presence of true pimps, players, gangsters, and hustlers, also being a product of hopelessness, being smack-dab in the mix of the action of the struggle touched Li'l One Gone in a special way, producing a feeling only the experienced could describe. Putting someone up, delivering death, devitalizing a human being of its privilege of life was a catharsis that initiated a new desire (or beginning).

Later that night, safe and secure in the comfort of his home, he lay in bed in his favorite position, staring at the ceiling, recurring vivid thoughts stimulating his being, arousing him. His hand fell on the newly found swelling of his manhood. Caressing it, rubbing it, he released it from the confines of his boxers. As he squeezed tightly, rapidly stroking his meat pistol up and down, the scene from earlier played out across the back of his eyelids. As the drama unfolded in his mind's eye, the orgasm gathered at the base of his erect meat pistol. Every stroke increased sexual pleasure, driving him closer to climaxing. The .410 bucked in his hands, his body shuddered, and light from the barrel flashed in his eyes. Big Ed staggered backward, and warm liquid erupted out of his meat pistol, oozing over his hand just as Big Ed's blood oozed from the gaping hole in his chest. The warm liquid rested on his hand, the vision of his victim's lifeless form settled on the green grass of his backyard fleeing his mind just as his meat pistol began to lose its stiffness.

Sixth grade at Kenilworth Middle School proved to be intellectually challenging, as well as sociably, for Li'l One Gone. On the streets his comprehension and understanding of the game exceeded his preteen life, and he was steadily gaining knowledge. Cognitively, in the aspect of existence, he was ahead of his age bracket and some above it. Scholastically, his education didn't advance in grade with him; it had fallen off somewhere between the third and fourth grade. It wasn't that he wasn't capable of obtaining the necessary level of education to maintain in middle school; he just didn't have the desire. His interest lay elsewhere.

He and Karonda shared first-period prealgebra together. She was his only motivation to attend school. Li'l Who was in his seventh-period English class. He was his source of strength to see the entire day through. In between he sat in the back of the class with his heavily tinted sunglasses, called Locs, on, mouth closed, eyes roaming. Magic went there also. He was in the eighth grade. During lunch period, they would meet up in the restroom, get faded off a joint or two, then attack the lunch counter. DARE and the Say No to Drugs campaign had been and still was effective with the square kids. Once word got out that Li'l One Gone and a few of the eighth-grade boys were smoking killa; they shied away from him like he had tuberculosis or a contagious fungus on him.

The student body automatically segregated themselves by social status and interests, but mostly neighborhoods. Every neighborhood had their designated sitting area in the gymnasium and lunchroom. Southside held down the best spot, the big-dog spot. Big dogs did big things; therefore, every other neighborhood that fell in the school district was gunning for the big-dog title. The Southside neighborhood of Baton Rouge held the title of big-dog status down for years and didn't plan on handing it over, whether it be in the face of force or intimidation. Regardless if Li'l One Gone was down for the cause or not, he was from across the track, a section of the Southside; therefore, it was mandatorily represented for those who were there presently and those who had come and gone and for those who were sure to follow.

The first two weeks of school went by uneventfully. Those days were used for the feeling-out process. Girls were choosing the boys they wanted undercover, while the boys were choosing the girls they wanted openly. New friendship was incubating among the masses of children. Potential enemies were secretly sizing up their soon-to-be opponents, while the teachers were mentally separating the real troublemakers and the wannabes from those who were there for the sole purpose of getting their education. Those whose wardrobes were up to par or beyond, as well as those whose wardrobes were below average, got stares and glares from the students. Only difference was, one group got looks of approval, admiration, and the other got looks of disdain, disgust from the unofficial fashion policies. Well-dressed students made friends easier than those whose clothing showed that they were born with less and were still in the same conditions. Students flocked to the well-dressed kids like they were celebrities, with the exception Li'l One Gone. For some reason, they avoided him

Li'l One Gone's gear was in tune with the lasted D-Boy fashion and those hopping cats. He got his style particularly from the streets, the rest of his fashion style poured on him from cousin Mimi, the daughter of his uncle Shortman. Raised in the same household, she viewed Li'l One Gone as her little brother. Though she had left the household years before their grandmother had passed away and started her own family, she still found time to return home to spend time with Li'l One Gone. Mimi stayed up-to-date with what the entertainers had worn or were wearing. She knew what styles were in, on the way out, and predicted the ones that were going to spread like wildfire. In his heart, Li'l One Gone didn't give a damn about his appearance to others; he was what he was. So his style was that of the streets. Mimi insisted on adding another arsenal to his wardrobe because some people deem a person's character by the way they dress. When it came time for him to purchase school clothes and supplies, Mimi volunteered to take him shopping. Li'l One Gone slipped up and revealed the count of his bankroll, so she passed up his usual shopping spot at Wieners and shot straight to Cortana Mall. Of the twenty-seven hundred dollars he had saved, he was left with twelve hundred in cash, the rest in merchandise. She made sure Li'l One Gone was dressed to the nines. The third week of school had rolled in, and he still had several outfits he hadn't worn hanging in his closet, waiting to be picked. If being dressed freshly was a subject in school, with the help of Mimi, Li'l One Gone could have been the professor of that class. Yet he still didn't have any kids lined up, trying to become a friend of his.

He couldn't relate or communicate with the majority of his classmates. They didn't speak gangsterism, the only language he understood. He gravitated toward the eighth graders. Magic's crew became his. He started being the first one to the smoke-a-thon and the last one to leave. A couple of the guys dabbled with heavier drugs, using their nose to consume. Li'l One Gone was hip to it; he had seen grown men and women treat their noses, but it amazed him to see kids a little older than him indulge in the act. With them, he felt like he belonged, like he had found a place, but sometimes after the pleasure of belonging, there is pain.

Toward the end of the third week of the start of school, the bottom finally fell out from the weight of the animosity the neighborhoods carried toward one another. Southside, Baton Rouge, was a large neighborhood. The neighborhood was divided into subsections that quarreled with one another but joined forces to oppose any advisory to the Southside in general. From Highland Road on back to across the track fell in the Kenilworth School District. Across the tracks, a.k.a. Da Tracklife, was its own neighborhood apart from the section called the Bottom, but a part of it that often claimed the Bottom at times. Mayfair Mafia had joined forces with the G-lane Gorillas, plotting to dethrone the Southside Kings; the Bottom Boys were representing the entire Southside at Kenilworth.

There weren't any cats from across the tracks left at Kenilworth that were about that life. Majority of the kids that were in the sixth grade that claimed that track life were focused on education and preparing themselves to become productive citizens within the established system. The bus from the Bottom usually made it to school before the one that transported the students from across the track did. This particular day, they pulled up to the school within seconds of one another. All the students waited in the gymnasium until the first-period bell rang. That was the only time that all students from sixth to eighth grade from every neighborhood were at the same place on the school campus at the same time. The place and time had been picked, and all hell broke loose. As soon as the first person from the

Southside stepped into the gym, the cats from Mayfair and Gardere Lane were in full force, waiting.

They had formed two rows of Soul Train lines, with all their hard hitters on the front row. Theodore was a nerd; he didn't know how to spell *trouble*. Blindly he rushed through the door, running dead into a straight right from one angle and left hook from another. He dropped to the floor like a fruit falling from a tree. For those who were in the blind as to what was happening, when Theodore hit the deck, their senses were jarred. Everyone fell into battle formation. The two forces collided, and no one had time to pick an opponent. They attacked whoever was standing in front of them. The Southside was outnumbered three to one, so there was a shortage of persons for the oppositions to assault.

Li'l One Gone shoved his way forward, pushing Karonda out of the way. He fought the boy she had tangled up with. These cats had instructed all that were falling with them in combat to spare none; boy, girl, geek, or gangster, if they were from the Southside, they were fair game. That was exactly what went on. It took the staff all of forty-five minutes to retain order. Like the referees do in hockey when a fight breaks out, they waited until a person fell or separated themselves before they stepped in and separated the two "scufflers." Several of the teachers got rocked trying to intervene in the many ongoing scuffles. Eventually, they just stood back, blocking the way for any fresh bodies to join the fight, while the ones engaged tired out. Once they fell out of a clinch, the staff stepped in.

East Baton Rouge sheriff deputies had been called in to assist, though late as usual. By the time they made it to the school, there wasn't an all-out gang fight in process; it had died down to a few isolated bouts. The ones whose blood had boiled a little hotter than the others', the ones that were too caught up into the moment, and those who enjoyed the act of violence were the ones still engaged in hand-to-hand battle when the lawmen burst through the gym doors. Li'l One Gone snapped a quick jab, following it with an explosive, high right hook, both punches landing on target, the face of a supposedly hard hitter from Mayfair. The cat dropped his head and swung a blind overhand right at Li'l One Gone. Foreseeing the thrown punch, Li'l One Gone took a half-step to the left; in the process of counterpunching with a guaranteed knockout uppercut, he was met with a face full of pepper spray. The smell cut his breath before the sting of the liquid overtook him.

"Get down!" someone commanded.

No longer fist-fighting, Li'l One Gone was now fighting to gather his breath, and fighting to open his eyes without the excruciating pain that thwarted his attempt to open them. His pupils were on fire. The entire globular organ and everything associated with the eye burned when he squeezed them tightly shut, then burned more so when he opened them. All over his face felt like a million ants with their feet aflame were marching across, biting his flesh as they mobbed on. In the midst of that, he was fighting to register in his mind what was happening to him.

"Get down now!" someone yelled again.

Unbeknownst to him, the sheriff deputy was cocked and ready to hit him with another blast of liquid heat if he didn't promptly comply. Li'l One Gone was trying to gather his bearing, trying to contrive a way to drop down without hurting or removing his hands from his face. Before he could come up with a solution, he felt himself get lifted off his feet, going airborne for a split second, then all of a sudden, the gymnasium floor rose up and met his body. While he was on the floor, the deputy sprayed him again; this time he held down the trigger of the pepper spray canister for several seconds, drenching Li'l One Gone with the debilitating liquid heat. On the floor, gasping for air, he cried out in between breaths, "Shit, shit, fuck!" Frantically wiping at his face with the front of his red-and-white-striped Ralph Lauren polo shirt, Li'l One Gone kicked out like a spoiled child throwing a temper tantrum.

Surprisingly, no one got seriously hurt or arrested, though a few students got lengthy suspensions. Li'l One Gone experienced his first gang fight and his first bout with pepper spray. Later that day, once everything had quieted down, after the who was who, who fought on what side, and whatnot got sorted out, Li'l One Gone was allowed to leave the school early. As they had no telephone service at home for them to reach his mama, they let him catch the city bus home.

He threw on his Locs and hurriedly mobbed to the city bus stop. He didn't have the sunglasses on to look cool or to block the sun out; he put them on to keep people from staring in awe at the swollen slab of meat that covered both of his eyes. He never figured out if the ole boy he fought closed his eyes up with his fist or if the pepper spray did it. One thing was for sure: his pride and his face hurt as he strolled through the Kenilworth subdivision. The day of the fight was the last day he attended middle school.

Outside influences can only tap into and bring forward the sins of a man that already lie dormant, restrained in the confines of one's soul, waiting to be unleashed. Environmental circumstances cultivate the actions of some, while their peers help fine-tune their acts. When worse and worst collaborate, there are no boundaries to their iniquities. One not giving a fuck about anything, the other in the process of not giving a fuck, made matters so dire. Neither of them was old enough to understand the meaning of life.

The weather seemed to have changed with Li'l One Gone's mood. When he left the house, the sky was bright and cloudless, and he was in high spirits. Minus the dark half-circles beneath both of his peepers, evidence of the gang fight he was involved was still slightly visible. At the end of the bedlam, he had sustained more injuries than the swollen eyes. The inside of his lip had a quarter-inch gash across it from where ole boy's fist smashed it against his teeth. Several inflamed contusions had grown over his head. He didn't realize they were there until the night of the fight. When he lay down to sleep, as soon as the cotton pillow touched the raised contusion, they pulsated with pain. That night was a restless night for Li'l One Gone; the pain kept him tossing and turning, trying to find a spot where there wasn't any pressure being applied to his head. Every which way he turned, he was meet with pain. His right hand was also swollen. All the reminiscences of the battle had faded from his mental. A new leaf in his life was about to be turned over.

A touch of loneliness gripped him as he sat on the slide in the playground, looking over the horizon. He had hidden behind the project building until all the buses had pulled off. The street was clear; there wasn't a soul in sight. The lack of human activity in the area only added to the dreariness. Being alone wasn't what activated the feeling of loneliness. The only time he missed the ones that were no longer available to be a part of his life was when he was still. As long as he had a cause to contemplate or he was moving around, thoughts of Wet Fish or T'Sharon didn't creep into his mind. Posted up, he glanced over at the bench where Wet Fish and Monk before him pitched from sunup to sunrise, then over at where T'Sharon once lived, the stinging sensation of tears starting to form, jumping from one eye to the other. Li'l One Gone looked around once and wiped his eyes with the back of his hand. He pushed the eye water back into its well, but he couldn't shake the empty feeling.

A smile crept underneath his nose as he visualized T'Sharon in her glory, but the pain still ran deep. Most people who used drugs had a telltale sign they gave off when the drug had taken its effect on them. Li'l One Gone became deadly silent when the THC soaked his brain. T'Sharon would put her head down and swing it from side to side. Sometimes she'd swirl around in circles a few times. Reminiscing, Li'l One Gone realized the coup de grâce to his soul was, after she finished rattling her brain, she'd look right into Li'l One Gone's eyes and start singing to him. No one could tell her she wasn't Whitney Houston. She had the most beautiful smile, the softest eyes.

Approaching footsteps broke him out of his daydream. Even in death, T'Sharon had influence over his feelings. Li'l One Gone didn't turn to see who it was approaching. Friend or foe, it didn't matter; he was past the stage of worrying about anything or anyone anymore.

Looking up, he noticed the sky had turned gray and cloudy. Right along with his mood.

"What's up, my nig?" Magic yelled a few feet away from him.

"It look like it's about to pour," Li'l One Gone said.

There wasn't a plan behind the act of playing hooky from school when Li'l One Gone left the house. He didn't take into consideration that he was going to be on the streets for eight hours. He had a few shams in his pocket; he had thought that far, so food was covered. Sitting idly for eight hours wasn't something he had done since his body cast was removed. He figured he could handle that. He failed to equate the possibility of precipitation in the formula. Ducking school and avoiding his mama were his main concerns. The playground wouldn't be exactly the best place to hide from his mama, or anyone, for that matter, for it sat right in front of the street. Yet the playground was the only place he had to go, another error in his nonplan.

No effort on his part, avoiding his mama was one phase of his nonplan that was covered. Lately, she had been bedridden. As far as she went was to the bathroom and the kitchen. Therefore, he wasn't worried about her dipping down on him. A couple of mornings past, Li'l One Gone had awakened to the moans of a person in agony. He and his mama lived alone, so there was no question of who it was. Concerned, he ran into her room. Right around that time, she was groaning and calling out for the Lord Jesus. The covers of her bed were thrown all over it, hanging partially on the bed, dragging on the floor. His mama was lying in the middle of the bed on bare mattress, balled up into a fetal position, shivering and crying. Her face was glistening with sweat, her nightgown, paper-thin from numerous washes, sticking to her drenched body. It was so wet it looked like she had jogged sixteen miles then boxed twelve rounds. She was soaked. Highly concerned about her welfare, Li'l One Gone asked her what was wrong. His mama being mama, never wanting to come off as weak, said, "Ah, nothing, jus' muscle aches, stomach cramps, and feel'n a little woozy." She managed to get that out in between grimacing from the pain, with clenched teeth. She said it had to take its course and after that she'd be fine and fixed. She balled back up tighter after she finished talking. When Li'l One Gone left out of her room, she was shivering and shaking. An hour later, when he went back to check on her, she was still fighting off the dragon that was riding the hell out of her.

"It'll probably go. Do a li'l something, not too much," Magic replied.

The air-conditioned schoolhouse didn't seem like the right place to ditch, Li'l One Gone thought as he gazed into the threatening sky. Returning home before school let out wasn't even a consideration. "Fuck," he said under his breath. "What up with you, my nigga? Don't you 'pose to be in school?" Li'l One Gone asked jokingly. Though they hung out at school for the short time they were attending it, he really didn't want any company behind the levee that was his Elysium. The playground was his office. But the change in weather forced him to change his mind. Not only that, but he had also figured Magic was cool. The police hadn't come knocking; that meant he was solid.

"Shied, nigga, I'm olda than you. Don't you 'pose to be in school?" Magic replied.

"Muthafuck school!" Li'l One Gone said with a faraway look in his eyes, his words spoken unconvincingly, his body saying something else.

"Word," Magic said, extending his fist.

Snapping back to the present, Li'l One Gone replied, "Word," dapping him down.

"You gonna sit here all day, ah ya gonna shake da spot with me?" Magic asked.

Dampness of the impending rain touched his skin. Li'l One Gone searched the sky, Magic leaning against the slide with his arms folded, waiting impatiently for an answer. He didn't come across as nervous, but he was fidgeting around like he was pressed for time. Magic had crossed his mind a few times after the incident with Big Ed. Li'l One Gone wondered what type of person he was. The OG said, "If you feel that you can rob a bank or go to war with a nigga, roll wit 'em." Reading him now, Li'l One Gone didn't receive a bad vibe from him.

He looked up once more at the rolling clouds. Without asking where to, jumping off the slide, Li'l One Gone said, "Let's dip."

Magic sighed, releasing his breath. He had hoped he didn't turn him down. "We gonna go by my crib, wait 'n see what da rain gon' do, then we go take care of a li'l something I got lined up," he said excitedly. Li'l One Gone nodded once. "What, ya down, huh?" Magic asked, uncertainty dripping from his voice. His posture slacked up, he took the single nod as a sign of reluctance.

Realizing that Magic was reading him also, Li'l One Gone shot back, "Down, nigga. I'm up, down, all around. You can't miss me straight like dat." He stood in his version of the B-Boy stance, face emotionless. The streets had aged him, so much so that he looked the part of a seasoned villain.

Magic soldiered back up. "C'mon, G," he said with authority. He led, and Li'l One Gone followed.

There were only a few kids in or around his age bracket that he click-clacked with, and Magic was an exception. Li'l One Gone cottoned to him off the bat. When they were hiding in the boys' bathroom, getting high, he felt a connection. He chalked it up to the weed causing him to feel that way. He was intrigued by Magic, and also curious. He didn't want to come across as a super-all-right, double-okay, friendly-ass nigga, so he never approached him on any other level besides the one they were already on. That level was until the killa was finished smoked. Once the drugs were gone, all the thugs went their separate ways.

Li'l One Gone would occasionally scope him out from afar, studying him, often coming to the conclusion that there was some-thing about Magic, something more than met the eye. He wasn't any different from the rest of the cats that were street, so that couldn't be what illuminated off him when they crossed paths. Then one day they were in the bathroom, smoking on some redhead sess. It hit what exactly it was about Magic that stood out to him. Just as the killa was doing its due, it struck Li'l One Gone like an uppercut to the solar plexus. Strangely, when he looked at Magic through the haze of weed, he saw himself, more in mannerism than features. Still, that didn't quite satisfy his questionable reason for the inclination he had to the gravitational pull toward Magic that had ignited within him. Eventually, Li'l One Gone gave up on trying to figure out Magic or why he cottoned to him so much. He ruled it as another part of human nature to be interested in a person one had been bonded by blood with.

As with other aspects of life, the answers to all his inquiries on his mind about Magic arrived readily and unexpectedly to Li'l One Gone. There was a weird feeling that came over him when he walked into Magic's house. It felt like he had been there before and just now returning. The house was asleep. He and Magic were the only ones there, their sole job to attend school. Everyone else was gone or in their bed, unconscious. "Sit there," Magic whispered, pointing to an overstuffed chair, "until I get back." Then he added as he walked away, "And be quiet." Li'l One Gone complied without speaking, afraid that he might speak too loudly. He nodded instead. Sitting, he looked around, taking inventory of Magic's home. The furniture wasn't considered to be cheap, but inexpensive. Family portraits were displayed all over the living room. Photographs of smiling faces covered the walls, coffee table, and end tables. From what Li'l One Gone deduced from the photographs, Magic was part of a family of eleven—his mama and daddy, four sisters, four brothers, and he being the youngest of the family. One of the photos was all the boys and girls, all of walking and talking age, except one baby boy cradled in the arms of one of the girls. From the design of the house from the outside and the size, one could conclude that it was a modest three-bedroom home. A comfortable, cozy, but lively one. The love and excitement were felt the moment Li'l One Gone entered it.

It was fine with him if they posted there all day, he thought to himself as the energy of the house flew over him. He settled back into the chair, scanning the faces on the wall grinning out at him. One in particular grabbed his attention. The fact that it was an old-time red-dish-color photograph caused his gaze to stop on it, but the content of it was what had drawn him to it. In disbelief, he sprung up out of the chair, mouth wide open. He crept over to the wall where the picture hung. Having twenty-twenty vision, he saw things clearly. From the distance he sat from where the picture was, there was no way he could have mistakenly identified the woman that was posing on the photo. Closer now, he stared at the woman in disbelief, wonder, and awe. The lady looked exactly like his daddy's mama.

Spinning away from the wall, excitedly, he was about to yell for Magic. But remembering that he had told him to remain quiet and to sit still until he returned, he flopped back into the chair, staring at the lady, a strange surge zooming through his body. On the edge of his mind, racing as he waited for Magic, one question lay heavily. Sitting there, he felt like he was going to explode from suspense if he didn't get an answer soon. Several times he almost bolted into the direction Magic had ventured. But with unfamiliarity of the house secondly, and not wanting to disrespect Magic's home first and foremost, he kept his butt cheeks glued to the chair.

Magic said, "Look—"

Before he could finish, shockingly, his words were cut short when Li'l One Gone rocketed out of the chair. "Who dat right here?" he asked, walking and pointing to the photograph.

Hesitantly, he positioned himself to get a better look at all the familiar faces that lined the wall. In the process, he quickly wondered which one of his sisters Li'l One Gone had got big-eyed over. It never failed; whoever he invited to the house took an interest in one of his sisters, Magic thought to himself. When he eased back into the room the first time, he spotted Li'l One Gone through the mirror that hung on the opposite wall staring at the photographs. He was going to interrupt him before the smile of one of his sisters enchanted him, but he fell back a few more minutes to make sure Li'l One Gone wasn't weak for females. He heard that Li'l One Gone was schooled by straight Gs; they chased paper, not pudendum.

"Fuck," Magic said to himself as he realized the reason for Li'l One Gone's sudden outburst and action. Li'l One Gone was standing directly in front of the photograph that captured the images of his sisters. A touch of disappointment came over him as he looked up into Li'l One Gone's face, his eyes sparkling. Magic almost walked past him without acknowledging him, throwing the book bag over his shoulders.

"Who her?" he asked, following Li'l One Gone's finger. "Yeah, that's my grandma," Magic said, looking at Li'l One Gone questionably.

"Her name Sara?" Li'l One Gone asked.

"No, Mary. My great-auntie named Sara, her twin sister."

"Her twin sister?" Li'l One Gone excitedly yelled out.

"Ssh, man, be quiet," Magic said, grabbing, shoving him toward the door.

Li'l One Gone and Magic's great-grandparents had twelve children. Mary and Sara were their only set of twins born into the Franklin clan. Most of the women married off, changing their surnames. Grandma Sara kept hers, while T-Mary took her husband's name. Magic's mama was given her mother's maiden name, then she took her husband's last name; therefore, the last name Franklin had gotten abandoned after the first generations. Regardless of his last name, Magic was a true member of the extended Franklin clan that flooded every hood in Baton Rouge. His grandparents settled in the Lakeside neighborhood of Baton Rouge, but his mama and daddy returned to South Baton Rouge. He got game from the cats off the Lakeside, and wisdom from the Gs from the Southside, making him a young OG.

Everything had suddenly come to the light. Magic and Li'l One Gone had the same mixture of blood pumping through their veins. He no longer had to question the messages his radar picked up from Magic or why he intrigued him so much. It was now evident why the spirit of the originators of their bloodline had unwittingly magnetized them, inducing their unholy union. If the revelation of their kinship had any impact on Magic, he didn't show it externally; he kept his game face on. Contrary to Li'l One Gone, whose face showed exactly how he felt, elated. Surprisingly, the boy he pulled his first documented caper with happened to be family, he thought to himself. He had found a distant but not-so-distant cousin. For their entire life, they lived within walking distance from each other.

"I told ya I'll look out fo' ya," the voice said in his ear as they mobbed up the street. Glancing over at Magic, he half-smiled, shaking his head, amazed at how things had fallen in place. "Word," he mumbled to himself in agreement to his thoughts and the voice.

Magic swiftly navigated his way through the neighborhood, and though on the verge of breathlessness, Li'l One Gone matched his stride step for step as they cut through alleys and pathways, through worn-out lawns of abandoned houses. Burning calves from pumping his chubby legs up the inclined streets had his legs wobbly as they stood at the back of the house across the street from the one they were scoping out for the hit. Li'l One Gone caressed his legs and thighs, the feeling reminding him of the days he pounded his feet up and down the basketball court. Though he'd never admit it, he was corpulent and dangerously out of shape; the killa and Camel unfiltered cigarettes he smoked daily didn't help his health at all.

"You all right, kid?" Magic asked, concerned.

Li'l One Gone was sweating profusely, bent over at the waist, one hand on his knee, the other rubbing his chest, breathing like an asthmatic having a heart attack. "I'm good, G," he pushed out in between breaths.

"You sho? I don't need you crooking like a old man on me," Magic stated, scanning the street as he spoke to Li'l One Gone.

"Nigga, I said I'm good. I jus' need to catch my breff. It's been a while since I hiked this far," Li'l One Gone spat out, looking up at him.

Removing the book bag from his back, squatting down, Magic placed it on the ground between his feet. He was a naturally muscled kid; his traps looked like they were resting on the sides on his neck. As he bent over, digging into the book bag, Li'l One Gone noticed that his upper back muscles strained against his T-shirt. In another life, Magic must have been a career running back—he had the physical stature of one, Li'l One Gone thought as he watched him rummage through the book bag. Concentrating on Magic's every move, he forgot about his throbbing legs, nor did he realize that his breathing was returning back to normal.

Li'l One Gone was openly staring at Magic as he removed the contents from the bag. It was a known fact that he was only fourteen years of age, but he moved like a person who'd been around awhile and had the pose of a veteran in the game.

"Here," Magic said, handing Li'l One Gone a bundle. Unwrapping the shirt, he noticed there was a skullcap, a bandanna, and a black semiautomatic handgun concealed within it. His attitude changed as soon as the weight of the cold steel rested in his palm. Magic didn't have to tell him to force everything else out of his head; it was game time. He turned off the lights on his conscience and turned on the lights on the blank space in his mind, inside of which anything went. Tucking the candy stick, in his zone, he stood at attention, waiting for Magic's instruction, amped up and ready for action. The feel of the candy stick against his skin sent power surges through his being, visions of the past corpus delicti, along with the faceless soon-to-be ones, zooming across his mind's eye.

"What?" he asked foolishly when he noticed Magic eyeing him conservatively.

"Nuttin', my nigga, nothing at all," Magic replied dryly. When he walked back from retrieving Big Ed's stash, Magic had seen a change in Li'l One Gone. It was like another person gazed out at him; whoever, whatever it was was looking at him through Li'l One Gone's peepers now. "Look, bruh," Magic said, thinking better of what he wanted to say. He wanted to tell Li'l One Gone not to wig out in there, but not wanting to sound lame, he held his tongue. "Look, bruh, peep game." Magic was at a loss for words. Li'l One Gone's devilish grin shifted his train of thoughts.

Selling drugs side by side on the corner with another person is dangerous. The potential of someone getting jealous and bracing to move on the one they're jealous of is always an ever-so-present danger. Any level of the game is risky when money and drugs are involved, but pulling a kicked door with another person is extremely dangerous, the assessment of risk off the charts. When two people with firearms staring at riches in front of them, in the blink of an eye, one can decide he would much rather have the whole bag than half, then turn his gun on his stickup partner, leaving him with his brains hanging out of his head onto the floor while he makes the dash with the drugs and money.

The game was crazy. Magic was street. He knew there were warehouses full of case files where friends turned to foes in the midst of making ends meet. Li'l One Gone didn't give off the impression that he was cutthroat; he wasn't concerned about him putting a bullet in him after they pulled off the armed robbery, but that crooked smile that hung on his face and old-man eyes staring out of Li'l One Gone's baby face put him on the alarm.

"Take that shirt off you. Go on and put that one on," he said, nodding at the shirt in Li'l One Gone's hand. Tying the bandanna around his neck, Li'l One Gone copied Magic's move. "Leave ya short here when we get 'cross da street, then we gon' put da caps on," Magic said.

"Dig," Li'l One Gone replied, dropping the shirt on top of Magic's book bag. "Dis ain't gonna be like dat there on Grant Street. It's another ball game once we hit that doe."

Li'l One Gone looked at the door.

"Shit gonna be crazy. Whoever in there gonna be in panic mode. Thangs gon move fast. If they on top of their game, they already ready fo' us. If not, dat's better fo' us. One thang you gotta keep in mind is, they don't know if we come to rape, rob, murda, or all of the above. So any chance they git catching us slipping, they gon knock our dick in the dirt." Magic paused to let his words sink into Li'l One Gone.

He knew that he was down; that was why he chose him. But he also knew that it was a possibility that Li'l One Gone might be green to this level of the game. Their lives were going to be in each other's hands once the home invasion was in progress. Regardless if he wasn't familiar with the process of the hustle or not, it was his duty to school him to the concept and plan at hand. "Soon as we get in there, the first thang we got to do is gain control over everybody. They gotta lay down. Anybody stand'n is a threat. They got da 'vantage over us because they know da lay of da house. So when we hit da doe, whoever we see got to get down. Make sure they stay quiet. Then I'ma search every room, bring out whoever else in there. We gonna put them all in the same room. After we make them know who got da power, we gon' make 'em give up da shit. There 'pose to be only two women in at dis time, but you never know. All them niggaz might be in there too. You ready fo' dat?" Magic asked. Li'l One Gone had digested every word that he had fed him. He was running it play by play through his head. Instead of speaking, he did his usual thing, nodding. Then he glanced back at the door he'd been trying to see through since Magic pointed it out to him.

Planning an armed robbery is similar to composing a fight. Fundamentally, they're basic but complex also. A fighter develops technique and skills to put down their opponent while protecting themselves the entire time. No matter how well they may know their opponent, they can't accurately predict his moves inside of the ring; therefore, even with all the preparation for one style of fighting, the fighter has to be ready to adjust in the heat of the battle. If he doesn't, it's lights-out. With armed robberies, everyone knows it's taking anything of value from another while armed with a dangerous weapon; that's the elementary part of the plan. Emotions are high, victims fearful for their lives, looking down a stranger's pistol, not knowing what's on their assailant's mind. Wondering if that person is going to get what they've come for and go or if that person wants more has them on the edge the entire time. Some become courageous; others refuse to heed to the sticker's demands. The preparation for a smooth stick-and-move goes south, and now the stickers have to adjust, using whatever tactic it takes to get what they've come for and contain the situation. If the sticker loses control of the situation, then the sticker may become the victim. Depending on the would-be victim, it won't be lights-out or count time for the sticker-turned-victim; it's going to be curtains.

Li'l One Gone had many conversations about this level of the game he was now involved in. He knew enough to get by. If anything went wrong, he was certain that he and Magic were going to be the only ones walking out of there. In a strange way, he kind of hoped something would go wrong. Anxiously he waited for Magic to give the green light on the mission. Excitement pumped through his veins vigorously when Magic marched off. No words needed to be said. Li'l One Gone was on his heels. Magic slipped the skullcap over his head, then raised the bandanna up, stopping it right underneath his eyes. Li'l One Gone followed suit. Feet away from the door, he pulled out his matching black semiautomatic handgun. Quickening his step with a burst of acceleration, Magic glided through the air, his foot colliding with the waiting door. It flew open on contact. Before it came fully ajar, he was inside of the house, moving like a running back through a wall of defenders. His uncanny movements didn't fit him. Once he hit the door, it was like Magic transformed into someone else. Li'l One Gone kept a few paces in between them, candy sticks in hand as they jetted five steps up the hallway into the living room. A woman was sitting up on a sofa, paralyzed with fear.

The banging open of the door must have jarred her all the way out of her sleep. When they ran into the living room, she was looking at their direction like she was expecting someone other than them. She opened her mouth to scream, so Magic rushed over and grabbed her by the throat squeezing slightly, preventing sound from coming out. Candy stick inches from her face, he said menacingly, "Shut up, bitch. You bet' not scream. Hear me?" Then he asked, "Who else here? How many?" releasing his grip slightly.

"Jus' me and Kenya," she replied, frightened.

Li'l One Gone stood next to him, with the candy stick lined up with her mouth. "Get down on da flo', bitch," Magic demanded. "You got dis, kid?" he asked Li'l One Gone.

"Got it," he replied.

While she was going through the motion of getting down, she moved the cover back. She had red polka dot bikinis on. "You good, huh, bruh?" Magic asked Li'l One Gone.

"Good," he replied without looking away from the lady, the bikinis wedged between her buttocks, exposing two perfectly round smooth-skinned butt cheeks. Lying facedown on her stomach, she dug the bikinis from its hideaway, snapping it as she released it.

"At ease, nigga, it's me!" Magic yelled down the hallway.

Another woman, thick in the waist, appeared first. Magic escorted her with his candy stick, drawing a bead on the back of her head as he pushed her forward. "Get down over there by her," he commanded her. She walked past Li'l One Gone, mean-mugging him, the lay next to the other woman, pouting and complaining.

"Say, you already know what we come fo'. Where da shit at?" Magic said.

"What shit?" the thick woman asked defiantly. "Man, ya'll tripping with this bullshit here," she said, smacking her lips.

"I'm gon asked ya no mo'. Tell me where da stash and money at, bitch," Magic spat out.

"We ain't got shit," the thick woman mumbled out loudly.

Magic jacked a hollowed-tipped death enforcer into the chamber of the candy stick. The eerie sound of metal on metal echoed through the house, and both women stiffened at the sound. Li'l One Gone looked at his candy stick, then at Magic. He shook his head and mouthed "No" at Li'l One Gone. "Turn da fuck over, both of y'all, and strip. Since y'all don't know what we come fo', you ain't got this, you ain't got dat, well, we ain't leaving dis muthafucka without nothing," Magic barked out with venom. Red Polka Dot Bikini Girl had flipped over onto her back with practiced precision, her shirt coming off. Magic hadn't finished speaking yet. Arching her back, gripping the sides, wiggling a little, she pulled the thin fabric over her head.

Li'l One Gone walked around her, moving from his position over her head. Standing now at her feet, he watched her every move. Focused only on her body and movements, lost in the moment, Li'l One Gone failed to read the entire scenario properly. Seductively she stared into his eyes, holding contact as she teasingly rolled her bikini bottoms down her thighs, then past her legs. He leered at her smooth body. She had skin the color of butterscotch, and as she breathed heavily, her C-cup breasts, centered on her chest, rose up and settled slowly. There was a half-inch strip of hair on her pubic mound. Fascinated by the sight, he couldn't divert his attention from the divided, inflated flaps of skin that resembled a pair of lips turned vertical that the hair pointed to. *Finally*, Li'l One Gone thought to himself.

Though standing directly over both of the women, Li'l One Gone had become oblivious to the thick woman lying next to the now-nude Polka Dot Bikini Girl. Facing her, she wasn't naked yet, defiant as ever. On her face was a frown throwing daggers at Magic. She lay on her back with her arms folded snuggly over extralarge breasts that were threatening to burst out of her one-size-too-small brassiere. Roughly nudging her with the toe of his shoe, Magic said, groping himself, "C'mon, bitch, birthday suit. This ain't no game. Since you wanna bullshit us, we leaving this bitch with a case. Me and my li'l nigga gonna find out is that thang of yours really is more precious than gold."

"No, please." The thick woman whimpered and gripped herself tighter. Fiercely she faced off with Magic.

He ferociously kicked her on the side of her head. "Bitch, take that shit off or I'm gonna stomp ya fucking brains out." Polka Dot Bikini grimaced when the blow landed. She searched Li'l One Gone's face, but he just stared blankly. Anticipating his next peep show, he turned back to the thick woman. Holding her head, whining, she snatched down her brassiere, releasing her breast. Though her move had a hint of feistiness in it, her hand trembled slightly, revealing the fear she held in check.

Sniffling, she pleaded, "Bruh, you ain't got to do this to us."

"Shut tha fuck up!" Magic yelled, moving now to the side of her.

Fear had replaced the frown she was wearing, her entire body now shaking. The beige-colored brassiere hugged her body right below her breasts. Li'l One Gone examined them; they jiggled with the tremors of her body, even harder, with the body-racking sobs that escaped her lips. The jiggling was what stroked his curiosity. Her skin complexion was dark brown, but her breasts were a couple of shades lighter than the rest of her body. A few strands of hair poked out of the areola around her nipples, which had the same complexion as her body. Confused by the sight, deep in thought, unconsciously he groped himself. Polka Dot wiggled and giggled. She hadn't said a word either in protest or otherwise. The sound of her giggle captivated Li'l One Gone for a second.

"So what's it gon be?" Magic asked.

"Okay, okay," she said, her voice cracking. "It's all in da room. Er'thang under da pillow, an' I got a few dolla's in my purse side da bed," the thick woman cried out submissively. "Take it all, jus don't..." Tears rolled down her cheeks as she shook her head from side to side. "I mean, please don't do us nuttin', baby." The volume of her voice decreased as she spoke. Fright oozed from her pores, her expression portraying the thoughts she pictured in her mind. Closing her eyes, she shook her head from side to side, stopping in the direction of the wall, inhaling and exhaling heavily. "God, dis shit can't be happening," she cried out softly.

Polka Dot Bikini seemed indifferent both as to whatever was said and what was happening. Nonchalantly, she never removed Li'l One Gone from her line of vision. Magic rushed back to the room he kidnapped Thick Woman out of. Li'l One Gone stood in between a partially nude woman facing away from him, eyes lightly closed, attempting to shut out the world, and a totally nude woman whose empty constant stare was starting to make him sweat. She came across like she'd been in this same situation before. The only time she showed any sign of emotion other than what she was exhibiting now as Li'l One Gone looked down at her was when they first entered the house. The thick woman's attitude went from fight in the beginning to now dreadfully wishing she had an avenue to fight. Polka Dot Bikini expressed shock, but only briefly, then every other proceeding motion, gesture, and face expression were those of a woman inviting a lover to share her world.

Bursting under the pressure of her stare, out of all the things that could have been spoken out, Li'l One Gone asked, smiling, "What up?" Polka Dot Bikini did the same, but hers didn't reach her eyes.

Running her fingers through her hair, spreading her legs wider, she let her hand drop between her legs, landing over her private area. She patted her vagina once, shrugging her shoulders. "Don't know. You tell me," she replied in a husky voice, her pointer finger on her lip. Her light-brown eyes sparkled. She was attractive, though not beautiful; her body didn't have a flaw or blemish on it as far as Li'l One Gone could see. Although the sight of not one but two naked women was breathtaking, this wasn't how he pictured his first encounter with a naked female to be; he wasn't mentally prepared for what was happening. The power he felt before the door of the house went crashing in had diminished as he returned from the blank place in his mind to the present reality.

Li'l One Gone looked around the living room, then down at the woman. He looked at her like it was his first time seeing her. Contemplating, he bleeped to a spot in his mind that he had never been to before. As he lowered the pistol to his side, Polka Dot Bikini propped up on her elbows, lips perked out, and with her finger she motioned for Li'l One Gone to come to her, spreading her legs wider. He took a step closer to her, then she eased down, lying flat on her back. Li'l One Gone walked in between her legs and stopped at her knees, one foot in between her knees, the other one on the outside of it. The palm of her hand was pressed down on her pubic mound, her finger moving around playfully. Li'l One Gone knelt down, the odor of her femininity racing up his nostril. The smell unbalanced him, and when his legs bushed against her, the feel of the softness of her thighs made all his blood rush to the area below his waist. He leaned over on all fours, the pistol flat on the floor, with his hand on top of it. Polka Dot Bikini smiled, the she perked out her lips for a kiss. Without hesitating, he started to stretch himself out over her, his body barely touching hers, his eyes on her lips as he made his way up to her face.

"Put it down right now, bitch!" Magic yelled from the entrance of the living room.

Startled, Li'l One Gone looked over at Thick Woman; he had forgotten that she was in the room with them. She hadn't budged a centimeter since the last time he peeked over at her. Confused, feeling the pistol under his hand, he looked up at Magic, who was standing over them with his pistol aimed at Polka Dot Bikini's nose. "My nigga, get da fuck up," he told Li'l One Gone disgustedly. Rising up, he then noticed that the hand that was once planted on top her womanhood, with its finger moving around it tantalizingly, now held a straight razor blade in between those same teasing fingers. Focused on her nice, full lips, Li'l One Gone never noticed when her hand snaked out of sight, or the sudden change of the light behind her peepers.

"You deaf bitch, I said put it down," Magic said sternly. She let the razor slide from her grasp. Jerking her hand away from it, she winked at Li'l One Gone, then locked her fingers over her belly button. Astounded by the girl's bravery and his own naivety, he stood motionless, staring at the razor. "C'mon, get that," Magic said. His voice snapped him out of his momentary trance. "Ah, ah, dis ain't sleeping time," Magic said as he nudged the thick woman with his foot. He had moved over to the other woman, proceeding with the mission. Li'l One Gone was still stuck on the razor blade.

"What? Damn, jus' leave us alone, please," she stressed, twisting her head around to face Magic.

"That can't be everythang. I know y'all got more in here. That nigga of yours roll'n. My people already laced me up on him. Let's get it. I ain't leave'n till I got every crumb of dope outa this bitch!" Magic spat out.

Covering her face with her hands, she said, "Ole my God, Tiff, tell dis nigga ain't nothing but that li'l shit Danny left us to push us all in here. Man, you got da money and whatever dope left. Nobody lying to you, dude," Thick Girl cried out.

"That's it, bruh," Tiff said, confirming Thick Girl's statement nonchalantly.

"Fuck all dat, bitch. Why don't you take them fucking drawers off? You playing with me," Magic said aggressively.

"I can't, I can't, no, I can't!" Thick Girl yelled out, pouting. She rolled her head from side to side. Magic raised his pistol up.

"Kenya, girl, please do what he say so we can get dis over with," Tiff begged her. She looked at her friend, and Tiff nodded weakly.

"This what you want?" she stated angrily, yanking her panties down, kicking them off. Still wondering where Tiff had the razor blade concealed when Kenya raised her legs for her panties to fall off, Li'l One Gone saw a flash of white hanging out of her vagina. On the street, he'd seen female hustlers stash their dope inside of the pants when they saw the police rolling up. Some of them posted up with the dope stashed there, pulling it out when a sale rolled up, then going back under with it when they finished serving out their package. Hoping to redeem himself from his earlier mishap, he knew absolutely nothing about the width and depth of the female sex organ. In the split second he saw the flash of white between her legs, he imagined ounces of dope or a big bankroll of money stashed inside of her.

To add to his speculation, Kenya lay there with her thighs jammed together. Magic was moving around to her feet. Feeling that his chance for getting the credit for spotting the stash was about to slip away, he hurriedly said, "What dat white thang is 'tween ya pussy?"

"She hiding something. I saw it when she took her drawers off," Li'l One Gone confidently said.

Kenya looked at the both of them, bewildered, her mouth agape. "Man, you gotta be trippin'," she stated, looking at Li'l One Gone questioningly, then at Tiff. Tiff had a sly grin on her face.

"Open ya leg. Let me see," Magic demanded. He pointed the candy stick at her vagina like he expected something to jump out of it. Defiantly she raised her legs up, spreading them apart. A little string stuck out of her.

"See? Nothing," she said, then flopped her legs down.

"Shied, bitch, what dat tiny piece of rope is? What's that tied to?" Magic asked.

"It's nothing," Kenya said sarcastically.

Tiff laughed out. The vibe in the room changed suddenly.

"Give it up. Pull whatever it is you got hidden in ya pussy out. Let me have it," Magic demanded.

Li'l One Gone moved closer to get a better look at Kenya. Unlike Tiff, Kenya had a baby afro for pubic hair. "Give it to him," Tiff encouraged her.

Kenya reluctantly complied, scornfully staring at Magic through hate-filled eyes. There was a hint of amusement in her eyes also. Lifting her legs, she reached underneath them, then feeling for the string, she got ahold of it, paused briefly, then peeked over at Tiff. Tiff nodded at her, a broad grin plastered across her face. She slowly commenced to pulling the string. Several tenths of an inch of white string slid out, then it suddenly turned red. Kenya then jerked the remainder of it out of her. At the end of the string, there was a blood-soaked ball of cotton. When she jerked it out, a light stream of blood rolled out behind it, rolling down between her butt cheeks. "Here you go," she said, holding it out toward Magic. The bloody cotton ball dangled at the end of the string, rotating in the air like a bright rouge Christmas ornament on a Christmas tree.

"Man, what da fuck is dat?" Li'l One Gone yelled out in disgust.

Tiff held her stomach, rolling from side to side, laughing uncontrollably. Magic's face would have been pasty if he had been of the white race. Li'l One Gone's eyes were wide in shock. *There goes the big bankroll of money and ounces of dope,* he thought to himself, watching the blood-soaked object spin.

Kenya said, "I told ya. Nah, this one on you. Here."

"I don't want that shit!" Magic barked out, stepping away from her outstretched hand. "Let's be out," he said, moving toward the door, avoiding the bloody cotton ball as he maneuvered his way around Kenya.

"Uuuah," said Li'l One Gone as he darted past Kenya, pulling his arms closer to his body when she pushed it out to him like a vampire hunter crosses over at vampires. She laughed when Li'l One Gone bumped into the doorframe on his way out, his body moving forward while his head was turned backward. When he accelerated, his foot clipped the frame of the door. Stumbling, he collected himself before falling. Booking out, he looked more like a circus clown running, pretending to be frightened, than a stickup kid fleeing the scene of a heist. Laughter, followed by the sound of a door being slammed shut, was the last sound he heard as he jetted slowly across the street.

"Hurry up and change ya shirt an' let's get da fuck away from here," Magic said, hurriedly stuffing the loot, gun, and his disguise into the backpack. He looked around nervously as he held the backpack out to Li'l One Gone so that he could follow suit. New jack to the stickup level of the game, high on the thrill of the hustle, gloating in the joy of seeing two women nude, their labia majora and labia minora, the most sought-after thing, next to currency, right there on display inches away from him, along with the share of money that he had coming to him from the caper, plus whatever else Magic had come across, Li'l One Gone couldn't help being swollen with delight. His high suddenly came crashing down, elation quickly deflating, and a brush of fright struck across his being when he noticed that the usually cool, calm, and collective Magic now moved with terror and stricken urgency.

"What's wrong?" Li'l One Gone asked, concerned.

"My nigga, it's called stick-an'-move. We got to put distance 'tween us an' them. If they call them peoples and them white folks catch us on da spot, our ass is grass," Magic stated, seriousness scrawled all over his face. "Since we on Tennessee Street, we gon' shot down to Georgia Street, see if we can catch Duce slip'n. After we light'n up his load, we gon' head back to my house," Magic said, walking off. He had his shirt tucked into his pants, and the backpack was thrown over his shoulder. Magic looked like a schoolkid on his way to school. Li'l One Gone tucked his shirt in under his belly. He was stretching his legs to the fullest extent, but almost to a slow jog was the only way for him to maintain Magic's stride as they maneuvered through the obstacles and navigated the route from which they came, with the exception of one turn; they ended directly behind Duce's house. In his backyard, there were four pit bulls chained at all four corners of the yard. The chains were distant out so that the dogs had enough length to protect the property, but not enough chain on their length to attack one another. Surveying the yards, Li'l One Gone wondered how they were going to pull the caper off. The element of surprise by lying and waiting had been compromised by the dogs barking, growling, and running around hysterically, which would soon alert the occupant of the residence to their presence. The thought had just run across his mind.

"C'mon," Magic commanded Li'l One Gone before he had time to react to his mental assessment.

The dogs didn't stop barking until they were several seconds out of their view. All the chaos increased the chance of someone other than their intended victim coming out to investigate the source of the commotion, causing them to become suspicious of the two of them lurking at an hour when most burglaries were committed. The farther they got away from Duce's house, the more Li'l One Gone's inclination of being busted before the hit faded. Truth be told, Li'l One Gone wasn't too enthused about pulling off another robbery; he nervously looked around as approaching sirens blared in the distance, knowing that in a matter of minutes the police presence was going to be beyond notable in the area. Although they couldn't be positively identified by the victim, Li'l One Gone's knowledge of his guilt and participation in the crime had him edgy. He would much rather be anywhere else on earth. He could foresee his own arrest in his mind, and as he walked up the street, every step he took felt like it was one step closer to his doom. Magic jumped a fence that led to the back of an abandoned house. He was so concerned about being busted that he never realized that everything the law needed to nail them to the crime, followed by the cross, was in Magic's backpack. His face was in Magic's butt crawling through the only window of the house that was boarded up. The sirens ceased. It didn't seem like a good idea now, Li'l One Gone thought as he scanned the sunlit room of the vacant house.

Magic peeked out of the window. "We good for now," he said. "For now" had a certain ring to it, Li'l One Gone surmised, overthinking the situation now.

"Goddamn, them people's everywhere," Li'l One Gone protested, his breath shallow when the face of Detective Seymore Ballsaks popped up in his head. Bracing himself, steadying his breath, he looked over at Magic, hoping that he hadn't witnessed his near panic attack. With much false bravado, he said aloud, "It is what it is."

"Be easy, my nigga. It's too late in the game for you to trip out. We already wrestled the meat from the bear. All we gotta do now is make it outa the cave, baby. I gotcha, homie," Magic said, smiling. After removing the disguise, he went into one of the other rooms with them, returning without them. "If we do so happen to get jammed, all I have is money, dope, and a pistol on me. That's everyday gear for a street nigga. That won't be enough to tie us to the caper," Magic informed him. "Let's wait a few minutes before we bust out," he suggested.

Li'l One Gone agreed by nodding. He trusted Magic. A sixth sense told him that Magic had been in this predicament before and knew the way out of it. Li'l One Gone lowered his head out of habit. "Dude, I was scared as a muthafucka." He raised his head up, looked at Magic questionably.

"When I went to the back of the house, I thought you was gonna kill one of them hoes. I was rushing, searching for the shit. I was tryna get back up there to you in a jiffy," Magic stated.

"Nah, I wasn't gonna shot no woman," Li'l One Gone shot back.

"Naw, I know you shot ole boy. I thought you was one of them niggas that get off on killing people," Magic said jokingly, but serious about his assertion.

It didn't matter to Magic what Li'l One Gone's reason might have been that compelled him to pull the trigger. Magic was intrigued with Li'l One Gone, just as much as he was intrigued by him. Also, he was certain that if it came down to it, Li'l One Gone wouldn't hesitate to drop a body. What better partner in grind to have?

"I'm not like that. That nigga had it come'n. I delivered," Li'l One Gone spat out. A flash of anger crossed his eyes, followed by satisfaction as he thought about Big Ed's final moment.

"Okay," Magic replied. "Here," he said, handing him one of the candy sticks. "Dog, you owe me one fo' real," Magic stated, pausing, letting the words sink in. Li'l One Gone's expression didn't waver. "Yeah, I saved your life. That broad was 'bout to slice your ass to pieces. What was you doing on top of her, anyway?" Magic inquired, asking the question that had haunted him since he walked up on him on top of Tiff.

"Man, she asked me for a kiss and told me to come to her," Li'l One Gone replied frankly.

"Ya sho' you didn't jump on her on ya own?" Magic asked, looking at him accusingly.

"Shit no! Why would I do that?" Li'l One Gone retorted.

"You like pussy, don't you?" Magic challenged.

Silence answered for him.

"You ain't neva had no pussy!" Magic shouted, surprised, shaking his head.

Li'l One Gone's interest fell on the cold steal in his hand, examining it. He waited for Magic to rib him the way he had seen other cats get ribbed when their friends found out that they'd never experienced the warm wetness of a woman's hidden treasure. Li'l One Gone had been on the streets so long that he often forgot that he was technically still a baby; therefore, he wasn't held to the same standards in certain aspects in life or the game as the mature individuals were. No one expected him to have had enjoyed the wonderful sensation of a woman's hot box, but at times when the topic of sex got tossed around, he beat himself down a little for not having indulged in the sweet gift God gave man. Under Magic's glare, Li'l One Gone started to become warm under the collar from embarrassment.

It's human nature to feel some type of way when someone whose opinion and thoughts matter discovers a hidden secret. Although his body was occupied by several souls of gangsters of the past, he still was a preteen child.

"Even doe you ain't neva had pussy, you still cool with me, G. I only got some one time. My big bro had a girl over. He let me do it to her. It's all right," Magic said, peeping out of the window once more. "I liked it. You might like it too, but I like hustlin' mo' better. Money is always da mission. Ya feel me?" Magic solemnly said, turning toward Li'l One Gone, extending his hand.

"Word," Li'l One Gone said, dapping him off.

Magic and Li'l One Gone were the same height with different body masses. They stood chest to chest, eyeball to eyeball. The gesture wasn't an aggressive move or a crowding of one's personal space to provoke one or the other to violence, nor was it a challenging act of intimidation. A man will protect the three feet of circumference around their person with their life to the bloody end. Giving up personal space by stepping to a friend of the same gender, grabbing him behind the neck, bumping each other's head together slightly, is the universal sign of masculine endearment. When Magic gripped the back of Li'l One Gone's neck, then touched his head with his, pride knocked the air out of his lungs. He had witnessed the act many a times before; he knew that from that day forward, Magic was bound by the code to be his brother-in-arms, connected for life. A smile spread over his face, he stood amazed.

"As long as you don't turn into no ole maggot-ass, slimeball, pussy-snatching, ass niggaz, you gon' always be my little bro. I don't have to tell ya to stay real. That run in our blood. Ya feel me?"

"I will always," Magic continued, slapping his chest, "keep ya laced with game and be down wit'cha no matter what. Whatever I give ya, I expect da same from you, homie. You dig, homie?" Magic gripped his neck tighter.

"I dig ya, homie," Li'l One Gone replied proudly.

It was happening, but Li'l One Gone couldn't really believe it. Wet Fish said that the day was coming when he was going to find his thug brother. Even after death, his prophecies were being fulfilled, he thought, standing next to Magic at the window, watching a cop car roll by. Magic ejected the magazine out of the 9-millimeter semiautomatic handgun, shucking off five death enforcers out into the palm of his hand. "There, put one in ya clip," Magic commanded. Not quite grasping the concept of what was taking place, Li'l One Gone accepted the single death enforcer, puzzled. "What, you don't know how to load a tool?" Magic asked.

"It's not that. What I need mo' bullets for?" Li'l One Gone asked, examining both pistol and bullet.

"Check this, bro. Ain't no heart stoppers in dat tool. Yo' shit is empty," Magic said in a subdued voice.

"What?" Li'l One Gone yelled, stunned. "If my shit—wait a minute, boy, you're a slick nigga," he concluded, grinning. He shook his head at the profound revelation of what had transpired.

Magic smiled back at him knowingly. In the game, placing a loaded firearm into the hand of a person a trust hadn't been established with is the same as signing one's own death certificate before reading it; the act is twice as vital when anything of value is involved. Giving credit where credit is due, Magic as well as he knew that rule to the game. For a split second, he thought that was the reason his war weapon was empty, but the epiphany of the real reason hit him hard. Li'l One Gone couldn't do anything but respect Magic.

"C'mon, let's push out. We'll rap 'bout dat later. You ain't that green. You already know why," Magic pointed out, sensing a question or statement was forming within Li'l One Gone.

"Yeah, I got'cha, my nigga," Li'l One Gone stated, impressed.

Every time the sun rises, even when it sets, class is in session, and if one is lame, the lesson will be missed.

Crawling out of the house, as the old outlaws would say, Li'l One Gone was ready to ride the river with Magic. Monk, Rich, and Wet Fish had seniority over him; they entered the game and lived the life before him. They fed him, providing him with the essential substances that it required to stay alive. In the process, when the opportunity presented itself, he sometimes took the fork they provided, shoved it into the plate, and ate on his own. But overall, they sponsored him. They were responsible for him; there was no equality with either of them with Magic. Though they were playing on Magic's field, the same rules applied. Everything he was to eat henceforth, he had to gather, prepare, and feed himself. There wasn't going to be any more free meals or a nibble here and there off anyone else's plate. He was now officially a part of a team. Knowledge of what to eat, how to preserve, or how not to taste at all had been imbibed in him. To eat on the streets means to get money, but to one that's deeply rooted into the streets, it not only means to eat but is also a way of life that consists of rules to live by (preserve) and things no standup guy should ever engage or indulge in (not taste). Magic was street, taught by another breed of hustlers other than the ones that schooled Li'l One Gone.

Li'l One Gone knew things about the street and ways to make things happen that Magic didn't, and vice versa. When one joins a team, the other players expect one not to know the plays of their playbook but have general knowledge of the game. The false promise of having fun while working was evident. Li'l One Gone knew he had a lot to learn about the stick-and-move part of the game, but he was ready to learn and also prove his worth. Just like with Li'l Who, where every smart remark was made by a counterremark that tested, revealed, and eventually sharpened each other's ribbing skills and honed wit, it was the same now with Magic. But instead of words, it was actions that were designed to build up their relationship, keep each other thinking at all times, and test each other's knowledge of the game. Why he now gave him the bullets was understood; the reason it was empty in the first place was no longer a relevant issue to reflect upon or ponder. Li'l One Gone knew that Magic didn't give him the ammo to shoot out with the police; only other reason should be was that whatever the next mission was, they were heading to a dangerous one. He allowed himself to think in between rubbernecking on the lookout for the police. He was very much aware that determination pays the bills but stupidity gets one caught. Magic didn't seem stupid, looking over at him as they moved quickly up the street. Li'l One Gone couldn't help but admire him.

The area was hotter than the block in Dallas on November 22, 1963, and they were strolling with two loaded pistols, drugs, money—not to mention they were truants. Magic didn't show a sign of concern about the possibility of them being harassed by the police; he moved with a stealth determination. Li'l One Gone gained confidence from walking with him, mentally preparing himself for whatever it was Magic was leading him to.

"Say, we not gonna lurk around for dat nigga Duce. Right around the bend, two houses down, is where the nigga push from. We might get lucky and catch him getting out of his car or posted up on side of the house," Magic said, looking over at Li'l One Gone to make sure that he was paying attention to him while rubbernecking also. Seriousness was the order for the moment; it was written all over Magic, all business. "I hate to do it like this, but this one we gon' have to bare face it, throw from the hip if he's by his car. If he on side of the house, go with it. However, be ready for everything. The nigga game, so see with your eyes, then look at two steps ahead in your mind. Them white folks rolling, and we hotter than a nigga with a fur coat and turtleneck sweater on in July," Magic stated. "You ready for that, kiddo?" he asked.

"Tha mo' danger, tha mo' betta," Li'l One Gone replied. He appreciated Magic informing him of the pros and cons of the next mission, but he preferred silence. The quiet before the storm. Things were transpiring so rapidly he didn't have much time to gather his thoughts then sort them out. Thinking on one's feet with the added pressure of the police presence in the area, along with the prospect of what couldn't and could happen, was a task for even the best of the best of hustlers. Transitioning from sitting down, waiting for things to happen, to being on the move, making things happen, wasn't going to be done with the same comfortability, but damn, Li'l One Gone thought, who knew it was going to be like this? Fear, anticipation, excitement, joy, and anxiousness all came together to heighten his sense of awareness. The rush was off the chart; it felt the same as when he made his first official dope sale, but more intense. He was feeling the satisfaction of a completed caper. That was evidence of his confidence in getting the job done, but it was too early to feel that way because that type of confidence could be blinding, giving into deception rather than the true reality of the matter.

"Steel yourself, focus, come off that high horse. You slip, one of you is going to die!" the voice screamed in his ear.

Li'l One Gone's body and mind contained a host of emotions and thoughts that were clashing and conflicting with one another to surface. Neither thought nor feeling was the one needed for the task at hand. He was frenziedly excited about the new hustle, like a child who has won a game the very first time ever playing it and now about to play it again, this time for higher stakes. The words of the voice produced results instantaneously, like a dose of heroin used intravenously, calming him. Preserving, then detaching himself from his feelings after an additional two-second bout of self-check, he dropped his feelings off on the corner of East Grant Street as he turned onto Georgia Street. Emotions or feelings, no matter what end of the scale they lie, are liabilities in the preparation stage or in the commission of any act of business, whether it be legal or otherwise. Though stick-and-move is a sport to some and strictly business to others, Li'l One Gone was a greenhorn to the craft. He hadn't pulled off enough capers to develop an opinion; therefore, it was imperative that remain poised, clear minded, and on point.

Indurated, he clutched the candy stick stuck to his hip, glanced over at his comrade, gave him a nod, then started gangster-strolling, penitentiary-style. Magic observed him going through his mental transfiguration without letting on. A dab of pride touched him when he saw how smoothly Li'l One Gone had gathered himself, going from one psychological state to another in the blink of an eye. The words of the wise ones crossed his mind. It is said that "a man can be and most of the time will be judged by the company he keeps." Magic smiled at that thought, looking over at Li'l One Gone. He had no doubt about his capabilities, but he was ready to see exactly what type of material his new stickman was cut from.

"Ther' he go. Dat's him," Magic mumbled.

There was only one man on the street. From his posture, it could be concluded that he was a dope boy—his wardrobe spoke it. Li'l One Gone's expression remained the same. Inside he felt the way a killer does when he spots a mortal enemy. Unconsciously, his mob quickened and hardened.

"Slow ya roll, walk normal," Magic cautioned, throwing his arm around Li'l One Gone. His words and gesture threw Li'l One Gone for a loop. He slowed his pace almost to a complete stop. Confused, he gazed at Magic. Silent. His faced asked the question. "Dude, tha way you walk'n, anybody with a li'l bit of gameness about them can tell that you pack'n heat," Magic said. "Don't do dat," he added through clenched teeth. Li'l One Gone's hand had jerked toward his hip. Removing his arm from around Li'l One Gone's shoulder, Magic ran his hand into his pocket, coming out with a few shams. He pretended to count them. "Peep this. Da nigga on us. Pull out ya money," Magic requested. Li'l One Gone complied. "Peel off a few bills and reach 'em to me," Magic said, looking up the street at Duce. "Say, you gon' have to be da one that up on him. I'ma act like I'm tryna cop sumthang. You got it?" Magic asked. The distance between them and their chosen victim was steadily shrinking.

Swallowing hard, Li'l One Gone replied, "Um, yeah, sure." Hearing about it but never actually living it. He knew that the game sometimes moved unbelievably fast, realizing that the second hand was near the minute of the showdown. If he wasn't prepared, he didn't have a slight margin to get prepared; they were feet from being on top of Duce.

Like it was said, if one stays strapped up and ready for war, one never has to get ready. *Shit moving too fast. No wonder so many hustlers stumble and fall by the wayside,* Li'l One Gone thought. Then quickly he expelled the thought. The thought very likely could lead to disaster. Superstition ran rampant in Louisiana. Crossing himself to keep the jinx, regretting it as soon as he did it, he sighed, "Good." Duce wasn't looking at them. There wasn't any more time to feel, think, or question. The ball had started to roll. "Calm and steady," the voice whispered in Li'l One Gone's ear.

"What's good money? Ya working?" Magic asked Duce, who was eyeing the both of them suspiciously but scanning the cash in Magic's grip greedily.

"Everythang is everythang, baby," he replied. The thought of who had directed them to his cut, or the fact that Magic and Li'l One Gone looked every bit of the schoolkids that they were, never dawned on him. The only thing that sat on his mind was the amount of money they had come to drop on him, and serving them before another police could spin the bend. "Look here, youngsta, lower that there money some. Them white folks been block'n like E'muthafucka. A nigga musta got they ass splattered up da way. Say, y'all ain't seen 'em on y'all way ova here?" Duce asked.

"Nah, just one," Magic replied, counting the money, looking over his shoulder. "I got two-sixty. Do me something right fo' dat," Magic expressed diligently.

"Two-sixty," Duce repeated excitedly. "Where you li'l niggaz get that kinda bread from? What, y'all robbed the milkman or some shit?" he asked jokingly, folding his arms as if he were waiting for a reply.

"Nah, it ain't like that," Magic replied.

Out of the corner of his eye, Duce caught a swift motion. His mind was a few clicks slow registering the movement. He was so focused contemplating how to relieve Magic of his funds without giving him the proper amount of product his money covered that he had forgotten that Li'l One Gone was standing there. He was too preoccupied to notice the space that was between them. Though side by side, they had positioned themselves to where neither was in his direct line of vision. Duce would have had to turn his head away from one to speak to the other.

"Nah, but we robbing you, ole nigga," Li'l One Gone said calmly. There wasn't a trace of menace in his voice; though precise and steady, he didn't sound convincing.

"C'mon, let's get it. Run that shit. We want everything," Magic commanded. He had quickly replaced the bills that were in the palm of his hand with his matching 9-millimeter semiautomatic.

Duce glanced around in disbelief. "A'ight, jus' chill that shit out," he said pleadingly. The sound of the whining in his voice must have struck a chord within him. "Y'all know who da fuck I am?" he said, speaking more aggressively now.

"No, and we don't give a fuck," Li'l One Gone stated matter-of-factly.

"Fuck all that. Empty your pockets," Magic commanded, extending his free hand palm up.

"A'ight, fuck," Duce said, surrendering. He slowly fumbled around in his pocket. Li'l One Gone had drawn his gun hand back down to his hip; that way, anyone dipping up the block wouldn't have noticed that there was an armed robbery in progress. Magic had done the same also.

"This shit real. It ain't no drill," Li'l One Gone stated to break the silence.

Duce knew all too well that this wasn't a game. He handed Magic all the cash he had in his pocket, along with his wallet, watch, and chain. They all came and went. As he fumbled with his earring, Magic spat out, "You can keep that shit there." He paused. "Good, good," he then stated, looking at his booty.

Duce stretched out his arms as if to say, "That's everything."

"Nah, nigga, where da dope at? Don't play us for dumb," Magic said, bursting his bubble.

Duce had figured that once they had the fat bankroll and the jewelry in their mitts, the robbery would be over with. He had calculated the value of the gold along with the money mentally. No loss, big or small, is ever good, but with the amount of drugs in his stash, it was enough, once sold, to cover his loss, purchase more drugs, and still have a substantial profit. He had no qualms about kicking out his dough. When Magic asked where the drug was, that struck him with the same effect as a doctor telling a person that had sex only once that they were HIV positive. "Fuck, fuck, fuck," he said attempting to stall.

"Fuck nothing! Let's get it!" Magic screamed.

"C'mon, it's in the back. I'll get it," Duce said, taking a step forward.

"Don't move," Magic commanded, raising up his candy sick. "Stay there. Tell me where it's at. I'll go git it," Magic stated.

Duce had concocted a plan. He knew that only commandos could buck two people with pistols trained on them and come out unharmed. What he had hoped for was that on his way to the back of the house, he would have just enough lead way to break, running away as fast as possible from the baby jackers. That went south as soon as he planned it. "Back there under the blue tarp, there's a paint can. The work in there. That's everything, my nigga. That's all I got," he cried out. Which was true. Besides his own drug habit, he had a woman habit. In turn, that woman had a gambling habit he supported, causing him to hustle hard to break even.

Magic moved out to retrieve the stash, leaving Li'l One Gone in control. Duce viewed Li'l One Gone as the less threatening of the duo. His round chubby face had a friendly glow about it. Opening his mouth to say something, he snapped it shut. Staring down the barrel of a gun being held by a young villain, he knew that his next breath could very well be his last one. To a youngster in the game, life existed from one thought to the other; the next man's life didn't fit in between them. That wasn't what sent chills through him. Sizing up Li'l One Gone, he braced himself to move on him. Even though Li'l One Gone had the drop on him, he still felt he had a chance. Distracting was going to give him the window of opportunity he needed, or so he thought. His glance met Li'l One Gone. The words were on the tip of his tongue, but he swallowed them hard. Li'l One Gone looked different than he did seconds prior, Duce shockingly observed. Staring into his eyes, he was visibly shaken by what he was seeing. What he was looking at weren't the eyes of a child. They were blank, dark, and cold as death. *Death,* he thought. He went with his move, drawing his gun from the back of him. Li'l One Gone was already two beats ahead of him, waiting until the pistol was in plain sight. *Blucka!* He fired, shooting from the hip. The bullet struck true, shattering Duce's wrist, entering then exiting.

A dose of horror mixed with extreme agony jumped onto Duce's face when he raised up his mangled wrist. He let out a shrill of terror that could've raised the dead. Holding his arm, he glanced at Li'l One Gone questionably. *Blucka!* The second slug hit him in the side inches above his waistline. Magic grabbed Li'l One Gone, knocking his gun hand off target, away from Duce. *Blucka!* The third bullet went whistling by his ear. "No, G, don't," Magic protested. "Let's get ghost, kiddo. Fuck!" He added hysterically. Duce stayed curled up against his car, clutching his stomach, blood spilling out between his fingers as he attempted to push the warm blood that was running like a running back back into his body. As he stared wide-eyed at Li'l One Gone, the nerves in his left hand twisted one last time. The bullet splintered a wrist bone, which in turn shredded the main nerve to the wrist, thus rendering everything below it useless. Gravity pulled on him, and he slid down the side of the car.

"Ah, man, fuck," Duce cried out weakly before his head rested next to the fourteen-inch triple-gold Dayton rim on Vogue tires. He begin to convulse, violently rocking back and forth on the ground in agony.

Magic gazed into Li'l One Gone's face in shocked disappointment, the noises of a wounded man splitting the silence between them. Breaking his stare, Magic turned to Duce, who was kicking out, dragging his foot across the ground, digging a shallow trench. The pain he was suffering was evident on his mug; he was beyond either of their help. They caused pain, not relieved it.

Magic looked down at Duce, not with sympathy or compassion, but with regret. He didn't want it to end with him bleeding, but his perspective changed when his attention fell upon the pistol lying beside Duce's leg on the ground. A sour sensation welled up in his stomach, reaching the back of his throat. Approaching the pistol cautiously like it was a venomous reptile, he glanced back over his shoulder at Li'l One Gone differently. Now he knew very well that it wasn't an attempted thrill-killing on his part. If it had gone the other way, the coroner would have been zipping him or Li'l One Gone up in a black bags. Magic had slipped, the thought of his neglect reactivating the sickening feeling inside of him that he had fought back down. Scooping up the pistol, he almost lost it when his fingers touched the weapon that could have led to his demise. Negligence on his part would have been the blame.

Cardinal law: when one runs up on a potential victim of a jacking, the first order of business is to search and contain, then get the prize. Magic had slipped.

In the middle of a long, drawn-out moan from Duce, Magic turned then snatched Li'l One Gone by the arm, almost dragging him forcibly, urging him to follow. Chaotically, sirens blaring filled the air from rapidly approaching emergency responders and police units. Li'l One Gone glanced back again once more at his work before he and Magic bailed out in the opposite direction of the coming heat already patrolling the area in search of the suspects from the earlier home invasion and alleged sexual assault. Cops arrived on the scene in a matter of minutes. If the description of the clothing the suspects of the shooting assault had on went over the air seven seconds before the first officer to arrive on the scene hopped out of his unit, he would have chased down the two young black males he glimpsed zooming around the corner through the gathering crowd. Ms. Daisy, the old lady who lived next to the house where Duce lived, usually minded her business. She knew what went on daily at the house, besides the few dollars Duce laid on weekly. Ms. Daisy was one of the ones that understood the struggle. She felt that every individual was entitled to make their living however they so choose to. When she saw Li'l One Gone and Magic approach Duce, she couldn't believe what she was seeing. She knew Duce didn't have any kids; therefore, the two boys weren't his. She was curious to see what business that two little boys had over there. Though she'd never seen either of their faces, their stature along, with the fact that Magic had a book bag, led her to believe that they were kids. They were too young; they couldn't be buying drugs, she thought to herself.

She told the officer taking her statement that she had watched them. From her angle, she saw that all their attention was on whatever it was in the hand of one of the boys, then suddenly Duce's expression changed. After a few more words were exchanged, the boy that had the money went around to the back of the house. She walked into the kitchen to turn the fire down underneath her pots. That was when she heard the most awful wail she had ever heard in her life. She told the officer, rushing back to the window when she peeked through, that was when she saw Duce in agony, holding a limp, bleeding hand. She turned to grab the phone to call for help, and that was when she heard a gunshot. On the phone with 911, she heard another gunshot ring out, and that was when she ran to the back of the house. She told the officer that she was afraid they might have seen her and was going to shoot her. When asked if she saw a pistol in the boy's hand, she said no. She added that the short chubby kid was the one in front of Duce; the other one was the one that walked off.

Li'l One Gone's share of both robberies, after taxes for the one that put Magic on the hits, was put to the side. Before Magic divided up the loot, it came up to twenty-seven hundred and forty dollars in cash, nine ounces of cocaine, fifteen bundles of heroin, and a .22-caliber semiautomatic handgun. The weight of the sack that held his portion of the spoils of the last heist filled him with joy from excitement of the successful completion of his new hustle. The dust hadn't settled yet, but Li'l One Gone was ready for the next mission. There was no greater thrill than crossing deep into felony territory. He decided that he was going to savor the moment and relive it as often as possible. Professional stickup kid was going to be his occupation, he thought, admiring the cash and stash of drugs that were now his. He asked Magic where the next one crossed his mind. While he reflected back and pondered the near future, a homicide detective had found one single witness to the murder of Big Ed. The witness didn't see the actual crime, but she heard the shotgun blast and saw two young black males leave the area. One was short and chubby and walked funny, the other around the same stature but was of a stocky, muscular build.

The lead detective on the homicide case was the husband of the detective from the sex crime unit assigned to the case of the alleged sexual assault of Kenya. Both he and she and one of his junior homicide detectives that had the shooting assault case of Duce were now racing to put a face to the description of their suspects. The case against Li'l One Gone and Magic started to take shape. Even though they all were on the same team, playing for one common goal, a wager had been placed among them of who was going to be the one to arrest them. Neither one of them wanted to lose. The countdown to destruction had begun. Atonement to every evil deed is always near, whether the offender knows it or not.

Back at the police precinct, Detective Seymore Ballsaks overheard the confab the detectives were having about the new case they had gotten assigned to. Each detective had gotten the same description from the victims and witnesses. The description of the chubby kid that walked funny rang a bell, but the other kid's description didn't match that of the other one that had slipped out of his hand a while back. He wanted to voice his opinion on their case, thinking it could be his boys. Robbery, shooting, and sexual assault were a far jump from beating a piece of shit with a bat. So he left it for the other detectives to sort it out.

Proud and elated, Li'l One Gone was told that every new trick learned in the hustle trade is another tool added to the survival belt of life. What he wasn't told was that every new scheme learned in the game was another drip of corruption that would be added to an already-poisoned soul. He had every right to be happy. Money wasn't going to be an issue for a while. If he did run low on cash, he knew a quick way to get it. In his heart, his future seemed a lot brighter. He proudly told himself that from here on out, his pockets were never going to suffer from a malnutrition. In his mind and through a few acts, Li'l One Gone had made a big leap from the days of pitching for a few shams in the playground, moving up in class. Sad to say, though, there wasn't going to be any breach of contract by quitting the team he willingly signed up for. He was now officially the newest member of the league of gentlemen destined for jail or a lifetime of posting up on a burnt block in hell.

"Dog, before I split, I just wanna tell you, good look'n. You was on point with that. I just thought you had wigged out and blasted fool, until I seen the tool," Magic said, felicitating Li'l One Gone for his role in the caper.

"If I did so good, why you ain't let me put 'em up?" Li'l One Gone asked.

"G, you can't just go around kill'n everybody. Dude was connected. Bad enough you burned him. Alive, he gotta handle his own. Dead, all his Gs gon' ride. We want money, not war," Magic explained. Just like a naive child, he didn't weigh the consequence of his action before he acted, nor did he consider them now. Magic's words were precise and direct, foretelling of things that might come. He might as well have been speaking pig Latin to Li'l One Gone. He looked at him like he didn't understand a word he said. Fact of the matter was, he understood him well; he just didn't care about what could be, and he couldn't grasp why Magic cared either.

Death or pain was a way to subdue the weak and used as pressure to break the faint at heart. "Death before dishonor mean real Gs die fighting instead of running," Monk's words echoed through him from the audio file in his memory. "You scared to die?" Li'l One Gone asked.

The question caught Magic off guard, jarring him slightly. Collecting himself, Magic answered with little assertiveness, "Nah." He paused. "Everythang alive owe a debt to death sooner or later he coming to collect, right? Shied, we all gotta die. Everythang must die, me, you, cats, dogs. Nut'n lives fo'ever," Magic stated matter-of-factly, stating the obvious. His words were true, but they lacked conviction. Magic understood that there wasn't glory in death for the deceased. Dead was dead, life ceased to exist, and the person was no longer active or functioning. Game over. No more money was going to get made, no skinny boppers were gonna get laid, no more getting high, and no more anything going to take place. Once the lid on the casket closed, that was going to be the last time anyone would see the deceased person's face in the flesh again.

Magic really considered explaining death that way to his little down-ass homie but thought better of it. At the tender age of eleven years, he, too, thought the way he was taught to think and felt in his heart that however the male influence in his life said he should feel, that was how he was supposed to feel. Magic had become wise enough to decide the good of his own. His thoughts and feelings on life and the game had shifted in a different direction than what was taught.

Li'l One Gone would deprogram on his own. He was sure of it. He could have initiated the process of deprogramming within him, but seeing the admiration in Li'l One Gone's eyes that he had for him, Magic couldn't present himself no less than G status to him. Sometimes it's hard for youngsters to accept the things that are not as their minds infer to be.

"It's still early. What we gon' do next?" Li'l One Gone furtively asked, toying with the candy stick. A mischievous grin spread across his face, and taking aim at an invisible target, he let out, "Bang."

"So what's da biz?" Li'l One Gone asked playfully, but the seriousness behind the question and his gesture was evident as the night is dark. Magic smiled to himself, knowing firsthand how his li'l stickman felt. The anxiousness couldn't be missed; it pounded out of him like a teenage boy losing his virginity. As gung ho as he was for his next feel of the inside warmth of the female body, so was Li'l One Gone for the next caper.

The pleasure from the hustle could be more habit-forming than any substance, causing an addiction to it stronger than the likes of cocaine or heroin. Just as with the addiction to drugs, unchecked, the stickup addict is in for a helluva ride.

Li'l One Gone had the same energy radiating off him Magic did when he and his big brother returned from his first caper; even his demeanor and posture had been copied, Magic thought, examining him standing at attention like a good soldier waiting for a command. Ready, his being filled with desire and fire, zealous to engage in the sins of the world. Magic knew, with or without him, his little homie was going to go with his move. "Look, I got something in the making. Once I pay our taxes, ole boy gonna put me on another mission. It might be soon, could be later. Whenever, believe, my nigga, I'm gonna lace ya up," Magic stated, hoping to stall the inevitable.

"Word," Li'l One Gone retorted excitedly.

"Word," Magic replied, extending his fist. They touched knuckles. "Let me ask you something, Vee," Magic said calmly. "How you like hitting licks?"

"It's a'ight."

"A'ight, huh?" Magic repeated.

Li'l One Gone nodded in response. With the change in Magic's attitude, he didn't know what to make of the question. "Why you ask?" Li'l One Gone inquired.

Magic let the suspense build a few seconds.

"Why you asked me dat shit bro?" he barked out impatiently.

"Street law, rule number 7 says that a nigga has the right to do whatever it takes to get by as long as it doesn't go against the code. Ya feel me? Taking a nigga shit mean whatever, right? But stickup kids are the most hated of all the hustlers. Ain't nut'n fuck'n with a nigga that rob but a hitman he at da top. The dope slanga don't like a stick-and-move artist because he know he could be looking down their barrel any day, and the folks in the other world would feel a lot more comfortable knowing that a nigga making a living taking people shit at gunpoint is locked up for a long time," Magic lectured. "We enemies of society, G. You feeling that?" he added, hoping to douse the fire that was burning inside of Li'l One Gone. He watered the robbery game down a little. Magic was thrown into this way of life by his big brother. Initially, his modus operandi was stealing car music systems, purse snatching, and burglarizing homes.

One night out, lurking for something to pilfer, he stumbled upon a robbery in progress. It was his brother holding the candy stick on the victims. His brother had upped on a group of three guys mingling around in the parking lot of the apartment complex that Magic got most of his best merchandise from. Upon hearing his brother's voice, he scanned the area, located him, then ran to his side, not knowing what was taking place. Fortunate for his big brother, he arrived right at the nick of time because the situation was beginning to spiral out of control. In that instant, Magic became his trusted accomplice. "Anyone of these niggaz move before I say so, down him," he instructed Magic, handing him his candy stick. He then commenced to viciously beat the arrogant, unruly, unwilling participant of the armed robbery into submission. Henceforth, they were brothers in crime, until his brother stuck up and shot an undercover policeman posing as a drug dealer looking to buy a large quantity of high-quality heroin.

His brother's due process by law wasn't favorable for him from the go. His bail was set a five million dollars. All the motions filed by his attorney before his trial were denied. The evidence that was presented by the state was weak against him. The evidence presented at his trial was mostly circumstantial. The testimonies against him were done by the lying tongue of a cat in lockup with him looking to get a deal from the state on the simple theft-of-goods charge he was fighting, and a female he promised to spend forever with but left after he sexed her. Both of them testified that Magic's brother admitted to them that he was the one that went with his move on the undercover agent. During that time, his brother used to rock a trapper hat on his head, with the flaps of the hat fastened underneath his chin, with dark sunglasses on. He was wearing that the day the policeman got stuck up. Despite the fact the injured officer couldn't positively identify the person that stuck him up and burned him with that heat, and his brother didn't get apprehended on the scene or in the area of the crime scene, he blew trial. A jury of his so-called peers found him guilty of armed robbery and attempted first-degree murder of a police officer. As a result, he would have to spend the next 169 years of his life in prison. A sentence that the judge said was reasonable and appropriate due to the nature of his crimes.

The same brother that turned him on to the stick-and-move game now was the same one that was writing him letters and calling from the Louisiana State Penitentiary in Angola, Louisiana, to persuade Magic to do something meaningful in God's sight with his life. Although Magic had lost the passion for robberies that Li'l One Gone now displayed, he couldn't quit. The thought of getting murdered by a would-be victim or ending up like his big brother was always present at the forefront of his mind, but the crusade of accumulating enough funds to help pay for his brother's appeal lawyer and to have the simple material luxuries in life was his motivation to keep pulling of stick-and-moves. The pros and cons of what to expect as a stickup kid Magic revealed to him appealed to Li'l One Gone. Magic's words plucked a chord within him, but not the one he had intended.

"Say, you know all the rules to the game?" Li'l One Gone inquired. Magic's admonishing of the inevitable future of an armed robber hit him squarely, the warning anchored only momentarily to Li'l One Gone's conscience before his interest into furthering his knowledge of the game, the streets, which they called life, overrode the affect.

Besides, none of that mattered. In his heart he already felt that anyone not living the way he inspired to live was against him. Not only that, but on his way to Magic's spot, he had already decided that he was going to be a professional armed robber.

"Yeah, bruh, I do," Magic replied reluctantly, realizing that he might as well have been pratting; it was obvious that the rules of the game were more preponderate than knowing the breaks of the stick-and-move hustle. Speechless, he thought, *A man can lead a horse to water but can't make the horse drink the water he leads him to. But when the horse is thirsty, it would lead the man to the water, and there won't be a damn thing man can do other than kill the horse to stop it from drinking the water.* He thought about what his brother had written on one of his numerous letter to him.

"So what, you gonna lace me up?" Li'l One Gone asked for the second time.

"You want me to tell you all of 'em right now?" Magic asked, smiling, changing tactics, persuasion through friendship. The closer he got to Li'l One Gone, the more influence he was going to have. The battle wasn't over, he reasoned. Far from innocent, he knew his sins were plenty and there was going to be more to come until he reached his goal. Li'l One Gone had a streak of pure evil in him; the only bright spot was that he was young. He could either grow more nefarious or he will grow out of it. Either way, Magic had made his mind up also. He was going to ride with Li'l One Gone until the wheels fell off. It was bittersweet. He wanted a straight-up-game stickman on his team, but he didn't wanted to see his comrade fall victim to the virus that led its victims to the brig or underneath a pile of dirt.

"Let's blow dis good killa I got," Magic said, walking out of the house. Li'l One Gone followed. There was a portable toolshed in the back of the house. He and his brothers had christened it as their man cave. Magic lit up a piece of a blunt he had from the night before. He had followed his big brother's advice about staying clearheaded and focused when pulling off capers, so the desire to smoke had been present all day. There was no need to fight the urge now. His strong want for the high showed the way he pulled on the killa. He puffed on it like a junkie taking their last hit before entering rehab.

Passing the killa to Li'l One Gone, Magic asked, "You know where the rules to the streets started at?" Li'l One Gone shook his head no. "How many of 'em you know, then?" Magic asked.

"Um, um…ah," Li'l One Gone stammered.

"Don't worry about it," Magic retorted, hitting it, exhaling. "See, this shit goes way, way back"—he waved his arm—"to the slavery days, you now, when niggaz was in chains, working from sunrise to sunset." Magic punctuated his words. He had Li'l One Gone's undivided attention. Sitting on the edge of his seat, he wasn't trying to miss a word of what Magic had to say. "So many people speak of the street law, rules to the game, and so on, but few know all of them or where they actually originated from. It was every OG duty to inform anyone that they sponsored into the game the SEC, street ethic codes, also known as the rules of the game, or more simply, the law. Somewhere along the line, the practice was abandoned, then when it resurfaced before falling off again, amendments had been added to the original set of laws."

"The most important one, keep ya mouth shut. Never tell on self or friends. Should be rule number 1, and at one point in the game, it was, but it got bumped down to number 3," Magic said in disgust. "Everybody think eat'n cheese came along when people started call'n niggaz that snitch rats, but it started early in the slavery days. Matter o' fact, G, 'stay silent' was one of tha first law passed by the slaves. The field slaves use to say they would rather take the whip on their back than taste master cheese. See, cheese was like steak is now. It was expensive. The shit came from cows, but it took a lot to make it. The slave master use to give the slaves that worked in the house tha cheese right before it went all the way bad for do'n a good job, basically being a good nigga. But he use to give him a fresh piece of cheese and a warm slice of bread when he revealed some secrets about what was going down on the plantation. The house slaves couldn't eat at the same table as the white folks, so he had to sit on the back porch and eat his bread and cheese. After a while, everybody became hip to the act. The field niggaz knew that every time they saw tha house nigga eat'n fresh cheese, sumthing got told. That's where calling a person that tells a cheese eater come from," Magic explained.

Li'l One Gone's fondness of Magic shot up a few more notches. Listening to him talk, he sat mouth agape, mesmerized by the jewels that were being handed down to him.

"There really were rules niggaz had to follow by when out in public. Back then, when they were slaves, a black man couldn't look a white man in the eyes. A nigga couldn't look at a white woman at all. They called that shit reckless eyeballing. If a white man was walking down a sidewalk, the black man had to get off the sidewalk and let him pass. A nigga wasn't supposed to speak unless spoken to. When they did talk, it had to be 'Yes, sir,' 'Yes, ma'am,' shit like that. If a nigga broke any of the rules, they whipped tha skin off his ass!" Magic exclaimed.

Li'l One Gone chuckled.

"Real shit, that was during slavery, when they whipped niggaz for that type of bullshit. See, after slavery ended, if a black did anything on the street other than what the white man felt a nigga should do, even for tha same shit that use to get them beat, the white man straight lynched niggaz. If a nigga violated, he found his ass hanging from a muthafuck'n tree. Them crackers wasn't showing a nigga no love or mercy. A nigga best bet was to 'bide by every law the white man had laid down for them to live by. You feel me?" Magic asked, though not looking for a reply.

Li'l One Gone was afraid to answer, because he was afraid Magic was going to end his lecture. Hungry for more, he looked confused, pretending not to understand.

"There always been gangsta-ass niggaz that didn't give a fuck and bucked tha system. All da G's got together back then and came up with their own rules to how niggaz should carry themselves out in public on them white folk street. Most of 'em talked that shit 'bout fuck da white man law, but none of them niggaz wanted to be da first one to go by the black man new laws of conduct on tha streets. So one afternoon, in a small town in Alabama, 'bout fifteen niggaz got together and strolled up the main strip. They mean-mugged every passing white man. They refused to get off the sidewalk to let a white couple pass. No one said a word. They all walked in silence, head held up high, eyes roaming the streets. You already know them crackers wasn't going for that. They ambushed them niggaz, hitting them with bricks, bottles, bats, boards, and whatever else they could get their hands on. Them niggaz fought back. It was an all-out warfare. They got their ass handed to them, but they stood together as they fought and fell for what they believed in. Word spread 'round the world 'bout the black men in Alabama that tore it down with them white folks. When asked what the cause was, one of the men told them that they had come up with their own rules that a black man should follow on the street. Instead of breaking their own law, every one of 'em stuck to the rules, even under pressure. Then he was asked, Was there anything that could make him change the set of rules? He said that there wasn't anything that could. He lived by and died by them. Them cats was looked up to by many."

"Everybody wanted to know what their rules were. Their rules to the street turned into gangsta street ethic codes, which then later on turned into the rules of the game. A lot of shit get reworded and more shit got added, but overall, my nigga, we gotta stick to the code just like they did, no matter if they the original ones or the ones that we got laced up with," Magic told Li'l One Gone, finishing the history of the rules of the game.

"Name da rules," Li'l One Gone requested.

"Rule number 1, always stay true to self and real with ya homies. Want for your homie what you want for self." Magic went on all the way to rule number 10, giving him all the rules to the game in order. Then he even told him the ten minor rules, called codes. All the time Li'l One Gone spent on the streets, in the company of Gs and major players, the day he ran it with Magic had been the most educational one by far. That day was one of the few that could be credited to his becoming. He left out of that rusty old toolshed light-years ahead of the rest; there was only a handful of cats living the life or in the game that knew the history of or all the rules to the game. He was now one of them. He vowed to never reveal the knowledge to anyone that he didn't deem worthy of it.

* * *

"When I wanted to go out party'n an' do my thang, I ran across money out tha ass to fuck up. Now that I'm tryna do tha right thang, I can't squeeze a goddamn nickel outa a dime," Li'l One Gone's mama cried out to Janice, one of her few known friends. Janice was the only person she started out by saying "my friend" when referring to.

"Girl, I know exactly what ya mean. Shit been extratight on my end too. I damn near thought about selling tickets to niggaz to let 'em dig in this gold mine I'm sit'n on," Janice said, smiling embarrassingly when she looked up and saw Li'l One Gone standing in the hallway.

"What up, Ms. Janice?" Li'l One Gone asked.

"Nut'n but the bills, baby," she replied.

Li'l One Gone came out of his room when he heard his mama's voice. He stopped dead in his tracks, hoping to ease out of the house undetected. Hearing Janice's voice, he continued on, relieved. He knew that when his mama had company, she paid no attention to him unless he drew attention to himself. He leaned over and hugged his mama. "Hey, Mama," he said, feigning excitement.

"Boy, get ya ass off me," his mama said, shrugging her shoulders. Li'l One Gone held on to her longer. "Girl, please close ya legs so Vietnam can stop looking at ya snatch. Nigga thank he slick. I know'd it was a catch to him grabbing on me like dat. He was getting him a better look."

Janice looked down between her legs, giggled, then crossed them. His mama joined her in laughter. Li'l One Gone blushed, grinning from ear to ear like a Cheshire cheetah.

"Where ya going?" his mama asked. Surprisingly, it had been months since his mama showed any interest in Li'l One Gone's comings or going.

"Ah, to da sto." He spat out the first thing that came to his mind after he recovered from the shock of her question.

"You got money? 'Cause if ya do, you need to give Mama some," she stated.

"And me too," Janice added.

"I got a li'l something. I got'cha when I get back," Li'l One Gone promised.

"Boy, get ya ass out of here with that. Thank you, but no, thank ya. Keep ya li'l bubble gum money. I need me some big money," his mama shot back, smiling. She shoved Li'l One Gone slightly, walking off. His mama and Janice had engaged back in their conversation before he had taken two steps. He hit the door, leaving the women to their lively chatter.

There was minimal activity on the block, which was unusual for late afternoon on a Saturday. There wasn't any woman out in their skimpy outfits, hustler-shopping. Not even a dope fiend or con man was on the scene, trying to run a Murphy on a dealer. Strangely, there wasn't a dealer in sight. Dooley and Double D were the only ones posted up on the block.

"I say, what it do, Vietnam, a.k.a. da Kid Vicious, a.k.a. Fat Bastard, a.k.a. Li'l One Gone?" Dooley said.

"Dis dick. Fat bastard that nigga," Li'l One Gone replied.

Dooley threw his guard up, then approached him, hitting him with a quick one-two to his chest. Li'l One Gone returned the punches, lacking the same speed but with more intensity. "Say, homie, ya strapped?" Dooley asked.

"Why you say that?" Li'l One Gone replied.

"I watched you comin' up tha street. Tha way you was walk'n was like a nigga clutch'n a rod," Dooley explained.

Pulling out the pistol from his waist, Li'l One Gone said, "Yeah, I got my candy stick on me," proudly holding it up.

"Look, you get that off ya. Them people been roll'n hard. Duck it off under tha step wit my shit," Dooley advised him.

Hurriedly he stashed it, returning.

"You li'l niggaz growing up too fast. Real talk, dat's a nice li'l tool. That bitch fit'cha," Dooley said.

"Wet Fish taught him well," Double D added.

Face screwed into what he felt was a frown, Li'l One Gone asked Double D, "We good?" Retaliation is always a breath away in the streets.

"Good as a fat-bitch pussy," Double D retorted. Dooley laughed at his reply.

"You still owe me," Li'l One Gone said sternly, his face still fixed in a frown.

"I got'cha, baby, soon as I shake a leaf off da tree. I ain't forgot dat ass-whoopin' or dat good dope I got my ass whooped fo," Double D spat out. "I sho' miss dat nigga Wet Fish. He stayed with some good shit!" he exclaimed.

"I know this bitch used to roll like a set of Vogue tires when that nigga was alive," Dooley said in amen. Both looked over at Li'l One Gone.

His features had softened. "Yeah, I miss him too," he said, gazing off, envisioning Wet Fish's face in the clouds. "Check this out, Doo," Li'l One Gone commanded, walking through the cut, peeking out toward the street. "What can I get for this?" he asked, dropping three packs with a black cobra stamped on it and a nice size of white powder into Dooley's hand.

"You got coke and heroin, Vee. Where ya get dis shit from?" Dooley asked.

Li'l One Gone hesitated. "Don't worry 'bout it. Fuck where it come from. You got a couple hun—"

Cutting his words off, Dooley informed him, "A few dollars here."

"Say, how 'bout you sell it and share the money with me?" Li'l One Gone suggested.

Dooley eyed him curiously. "Word," he let out.

"Word, nigga," Li'l One Gone confirmed.

"Fuckin' right I got'cha," Dooley said happily, smiling. "Man, this li'l nigga Vee fucking me up. I 'pose to be pop'n him off, an' he pop'n me off," Dooley mumbled to himself, looking at the drugs in his hand, shaking his head in disbelief. "I know you gotta be in da six or seven grade. You got packs of boy, a knot of girl, and you strapped down with a tooley." He nodded. "O yeah, you a product of them

184

tracks, straight up gangsta," he said, extending his fist for dap. They touched hands. "Soon as I get off dis shit, I'm coming break you off," Dooley promised, rushing out the cut, back to the corner.

Li'l One Gone stood, watching him walk off, wondering what he'd just done and, most of all, why he did it. "It is what it is," he answered himself.

Early Sunday morning, Dooley banged on the door. *Boom boom boom.* His excitement made his hand heavy. "Goddamit, I'm coming!" Li'l One Gone's mama yelled out, following another round of knocks. Li'l One Gone stuck his head out of his room curiously. "Fuck dat is beating on my door like they fucking crazy?" his mama grumbled, yanking the door open. "What?" she asked angrily.

"Um, my bad, I didn't mean to wake ya, but I need to holla at Li'l One, Vietnam," Dooley stammered.

Li'l One Gone headed toward the door, hearing Dooley's voice. His mama glanced back, blocking him. "What'cha want with my boy dis early in da morn'n?" she inquired.

"He did something for me. I brought his money. I wanna see if he wanna make a few more shams," Dooley responded in his best salesman's pitch. His mama lightened up. "Ya lucky it's 'bout money. I was fix'n to cuss ya ass out like a dog, come'n here this early," his mama informed Dooley, moving out his way. Li'l One Gone approached the door cautiously, gazing up at his mama.

"Dog, them junkies running like a baby with a cold nose for that shit you gave me," Dooley blurted out ecstatically.

Glancing back, Li'l One Gone noticed his mama was feet away from him, standing with her hands on her hips. Having not yet exited the house, pushing Dooley backward, coming from underneath the ceiling, he attempted to close the door. "Don't shut my damn door. You don't pay no bills here!" his mama shouted.

Dooley, either oblivious or not concerned, with his mama, said, "Just like I told ya, I'm a nigga of my word. Here's your cut." He handed Li'l One Gone a small wad of bills folded up. Without counting it, he hurriedly shoved them deep into his socks; the shorts he slept in didn't have pockets.

"That was all of dat shit you gave me or you got more?" Dooley asked, hope filled.

"More of what?" Li'l One Gone quizzed him.

"Either or both," Dooley replied.

"Wait here," he commanded. Entering into the house, he was relieved that his mama had gone back into her room. But what he didn't know was that she was at her window, ear-hustling. As always, when he go to his stash spot, he moved swiftly, placing everything back in order. Then he returned to Dooley, who was comfortably sitting on the porch, waiting patiently. "Here, my nigga," he said, dropping three more packs of heroin and another ball of cocaine on his lap.

Dooley picked the packages up, examining them. "Hold up, Vee. This not tha same. Tha coke good, but this not tha same dope you gave me last time," he stated, handing the packs out.

Instantly he realized his mistake. All the heroin he had was wrapped identically in wax paper; the difference was, one was stamped with a black cobra—that was Big Ed's mark—and the other one had a red heart with cupid's arrow through it. They were the ones he stuck Kenya for. Rushing, he had grabbed the wrong ones. Now he was faced with a catch-22. If he went back into the house and replaced the packs Dooley held, not only did he run the risk of letting Dooley know that there was a high probability that he had a lot more of drugs in his possession but also there was a strong possibility that his mama might get curious as to why he kept going back and forth to his room, then investigate, resulting in him unintentionally exposing his stash spot along with his contents, the latter more a concern to him than the former.

"I can't do nothing with this," Dooley conned. He knew very well that drugs sell itself; the thing was, he knew how potent the packs with the black cobra stamped on it were. He was sure to find out, but at the moment, the others were a mystery to him.

Against better judgment, Li'l One Gone relented. He jetted up the hallway, speedily uncovered his hiding spot, removed three packs with the black cobra stamped on them, placed everything back in order, then burst out of the room. He ran straight into his mama. "Let me have that," his mama demanded. Without arguing or without resistance, he silently placed the packs into his mama's outstretched waiting hand. Arching her brow, staring at the packs, a hint of recognition crossing her face, she peered at Li'l One Gone through prowling-for-an-answer eyes. She spun with elegance on her heels, gliding toward the door. Li'l One Gone followed. "Give me the others Vietnam gave you," she demanded politely. Her tone of voice alarmed Li'l One Gone. Dooley complied, and his mama handed him the ones she confiscated from Li'l One Gone. "Look, baby, that's the last of da last. I'ma hold on to these here. Do what you got to do to flip and get on. Whenever you get right, come back and give my baby his share of the money for that powder and them there packs, okay?" his mama stated sternly.

"Bet," Dooley replied, then mobbed out of the yard.

"I'm so mad at you! I don't know what to do—my pressure sky-high!" his mama fussed, slamming the door. A gangster in the street, he was a child at home, nothing more. A child that learned early in life not to disrespect his mama by talking back whenever she lit in on him. He could never get used to it; there wasn't any way to condition himself to his mama's tongue-lashing whenever she scolded him. It touched him deeply, sadness to the brink of tears. Head hung, mouth shut, biting his bottom lip, he braced himself for the lashing that was coming,

"I know you got more. Go get it," she said, fishing. There was no way for her to have known. Surprisingly, his mama didn't trail him into his room when he went to retrieve the cache of drugs. He handed her the remainder of the cocaine in the sandwich bag he dug in to give to Dooley, along with another ball of cocaine. Each of the nine individual sandwich bags contained an ounce of cocaine. Also, he gave her five bundles of heroin, three black cobras, and two of the red-heart-stamped ones, each bundle containing ten packs. His mama's eye bugged at the amount of drugs he had placed in her hand. It was obvious by her expression she didn't expect him to have had that much drugs.

"You didn't give that boy this much, did you?" his mama asked.

"No," he answered dryly.

"You ain't tell 'em how much you had?" she inquired.

"No!" Li'l One Gone raised his voice a decibel.

"Good, all right, okay," his mama ranted, lost for words "You sho nobody know you got this shit?" she questioned.

"Yeah, somebody know I got this. Me and my friend split when we found it," he explained, biting the truth about how they obtained it.

His mama was streetwise. "Bullshit! You ain't find shit. Nobody slang two different marked packs of dope. I don't know where this one with the heart shit on it, but these here with the damn snake..." She cringed, contorting her features, showing her disgust at the snake and at the thought of the man that pushed the packs with the snake stamps. "Only one nigga I know have these," his mama said, falling silent, bucking her eyes at him.

Trying to hold his ground, Li'l One Gone crumbled under the weight of his mama's accusing stare. His knowledge of his own guilt caused him to avert his gaze to the floor, shuffling his feet.

"Stop dat! Stand still and pick ya damn head up. Look me in the eyes. What I told you 'bout that shit?" his mama barked. He raised his head up, and he didn't have far to look up. His mama was only a few feet taller than he. "I'm gonna ask you one time, and you betta not lie to me. How did you get a dead man dope?" his mama quizzed him.

"He gave it to me," Li'l One Gone stated.

"Muthafucka, you must think I'm crazy!" his mama snapped.

"Fo' real, Mama, I'm not lying. He gave it to me," he repeated.

His mama examined him. By some kind of sixth sense, parents know when their child is telling the truth or not. Reading his body language, she comprehended there was some truth to his word. But instinct told her that there was more to what he was saying. "Okay, if he did give it to you, why would a grown man give an eleven-year-old child this much dope? Big Ed don't sell coke, so where you get that?" she pressed. Li'l One Gone knew his mama was like a bloodhound on a runaway slave's scent, relentless. She wasn't going to give up until she was satisfied with the information she got from him.

"A'ight, fuck, I'ma tell ya!" Li'l One Gone yelled out.

His mama was about to scold him for the use of profanity in her presence, but she didn't yet. "Go 'head, tell me," she said calmly.

"Me and my friend rob 'em. I went over there to shoot him 'cause I didn't like how he had talked to you that day, and he splattered T' Sharon. When I got there, my friend was waiting to rob him. I waited too. He gave it up, then I shot him. That's how I got it. You happy now?" Li'l One Gone shouted out after he gave her the short version.

Stunned at the news, keeping her composure, his mama searched his face for a few seconds. "What gun you used?" she asked, shaking, hoping that what she just heard was just a tale from a boy with a wild imagination.

"Uncle Shortman shotgun," he said regretfully.

"Go get it," she whispered, breathless.

When he came back with the gun, she jerked the .410 out of his grasp before he made a move to hand it to her. She snapped the breach up, the spent shell jumping out of it. Mama stared at the empty plastic-and-copper shell, horrified, in shock, hyperventilating. "You stupid muthafucka, go to your room," she managed to squeeze out between breaths. Almost in a full run, he pushed out to his room. "Oh god, my child," he heard her say as he closed the door to his room behind him. His mama stumbled to the couch in a daze.

Sitting, she rocked like she was rocking a baby to sleep, tears rolling down her cheeks. From the lone witness, word on the street was that from the sound of the gunshot, Big Ed must have been killed with a shotgun, and a chubby short person walking funny was one of those seen leaving the scene. His mama knew that her boy was responsible for the death of a human. The tears didn't fall for Big Ed; they fell for Li'l One Gone. They fell because she felt that she had let all her children down as a parent, especially her boy, whom the streets had chosen for its own. Only God could save him now. She did something she hadn't done in years. She said a prayer, dried her eyes, got up, then marched into Li'l One Gone's room. It was empty. He had jumped through the window and blazed out while his mama was collecting her thoughts. He was already halfway around the corner.

Whatever his mama had to say, she was going to have to say it later. For now there was more serious business needed tending to.

Taking the few dollars out of his socks Dooley gave him, counting it, he discovered that the money was kinda funny. He recalled Dooley stating that the drugs, once sold, were going to be a couple hundred dollars before he bit off his sentence. If so, the seventy-five dollars that he received wasn't anyway close to a shore of a couple hundred. "Grab ya gun. Go get what's yours," the voice said into his ear. Mobbing up the street with a grudge and a loaded semi-automatic hand pistol, Li'l One Gone could feel his blood boiling hot at the fact that Dooley had shortchanged him. Added with the perceivable wrong to him by his mama, this was one of the times that weed wasn't going to calm him. Someone had to feel his anger. "Causing pain to another is the only way to alleviate the rage," the voice encouraged him as he scanned the block for his intended victim, who was nowhere in sight.

Thankfully, Dooley was MIA (missing in action) and no one came along, rubbing Li'l One Gone the wrong way. He waited on the block with evil on his mental. Eventually, after repeatedly inhaling a stick of genie, too high to function, he floated home to an angry awaiting mama. Unexpectedly, his mama stayed calm, delivering what he would have bet his last penny on that would-be fiery speech. Surprisingly, everything that came out of her mouth was loaded with tender love, her words heart-filled, striking home. If he hadn't become so hardened, he would have joined her in tears, cut deeply by her display of emotion. Misty-eyed, he refused to let the tears fall; instead, he buried his face in her bosom, holding her tight, pupils burning from the sting of the eye water that welled in the ducts of his lids. "Sorry," he said, the words muffled by her breast, but understandable.

His mama pushed his head away from her gently. "No, baby, I'm sorry, and I love you," she replied, with every single word dripping with genuine sincerity. Just like a square, the notorious Vietnam "Li'l One Gone" Franklin melted in his mama's arms.

They say that even sinister villains have a soft side, and his mama touched his. Alone, still under the influence of that pressure he consumed earlier, he reviewed bits of the conversation his mama had with him. She said that she wished he would do the things normal boys his age did. He cried out, brokenhearted, "I wasn't normal when I was pretending to eat out of the garbage can as a hustle or, before then, when people found out I was stealing food. I wasn't normal when the old lady 'round the corner fed me hot meals. Was I normal when I was fending for Grandma Mama when you were gone?" His body trembled from the outburst of suppressed emotions. Fighting back tears, he continued, "How 'bout when I sat on that slide in the park all day, pumping for Monk and Wet Fish? Then you slide up on me, take most of my fetti and then disappear 'fo ah few days. Huh, Mama, was I normal then? Mama, I'ma do the only thing I ever knew to do; make thangs happen." Realization hit him hard. Believing he had done what his mama called sassing her, he grabbed her to avoid the blow that he expected to come for his sass. He added "Sorry" to deflect it.

The mixture of PCP and weed he smoked had him tripping. Every time the floor creaked, his head popped up like a chicken. His mama's personality and attitude kept him unbalanced. He never knew what to expect from her. She had, in the past, smiled when the situation was a sad occasion, and frowned when the room was full of laughter. Tears were new to him. He believed that his mama had something awful in store for him.

The night came and gone; too frighten to move a muscle, if he would have left his room at any time during the night, he would have found out that he was alone. His mama had hit the streets with a vengeance. Money was the motive. The game owed her, and she had her heart set on collecting her due, and proper, with interest.

Part Two

"How ya livin', thug?" Pimp asked Vietnam, handing him an over-stuffed blunt.

"You already know. Real, stay real, tryna get dis paper," Vietnam replied, eyeing the blunt suspiciously.

"It ain't dirty or dip'd. It's too early in da day to get max'd," Pimp assured him.

"On some, G. Shit, li'l homie, them people been hitting these tracks like E' muthafucka, look'n fo' a li'l nigga called Li'l One Gone. Dat ole faggot-ass cop they call Bruh Stupid jus' hemmed me up, talk'n 'bout where my buddy at with that good dope that like toting pistols. I'm like, 'Who da fuck you talk'n 'bout?' Da bitch grabbed me like dis." He collared Vietnam. "Li'l One Gone, dat's wo da fuck I'm talking about, motherfucker. I shoulda decked him slap-dab in his fuck'n face!" Pimp vehemently stated. "Ya dig?"

"Right, right," Vietnam agreed. "Check dis out. One of 'em, sumbody musta dropped a dime on me. Them dicks been at my top him for a li'l minute now. When I got a whiff of it, I let everybody know. Don't call me Li'l One Gone no mo'. My name is Vee, or Vietnam. That Li'l One Gone shit is dead." He paused. "Say, did they ask anythang 'bout my mama?" he asked, concerned.

"Nah, she good. I don't know what'cha been doing or how ya been doing it, but ya name rang'n through these streetz like that clock they call Big Ben rang'n through the streetz of London. I can't tell no man how to do what they do. Real talk, you gotta slow ya roll a notch. You making money. Let thar extra shit go," Pimp warned him.

The streets never closed its mouth. The entire neighborhood knew how he was living. Magic had introduced him to more members of the Franklin clan. They had the corner of Polk and Minnesota Street back to Taylor Street on lock. Nothing moved without the say-so of one of the family members. Everywhere they went, they left their mark. Vietnam fell right in, taking his position in the pack on the front line. It wasn't hard to miss a short fat nappy-headed kid that walked with a limp, a three-inch herringbone chain draped around his neck, pants sagging to one side from the weight of a candy stick, that they called Li'l One Gone. At the picture show, the arcade, and the bowling alley, places where people went to enjoy themselves, the Franklin clan kicked up dust, with Vietnam going above and beyond the call of duty. Causing ruckus on the streets, bringing major pain to busters in the name of the Bottom, the neighborhood they loved and claimed, was the secondary jobs of each of them. Some primary job was pushing crack cocaine, some chose to push straight cocaine as their way to make dividends, while others pumped heroin or marijuana on the block. A couple were stickup kids. None of the members in the clique of relatives was over the age of sixteen. No matter how one decided to eat, they all ate together. Vietnam's blood gave him an automatic invite, but his heart and how he shook and moved got him a welcoming stay.

Smoking on the killa, thinking back on his mischievousness, he knew why the heat was on him. Some heat came from the flame of the game. Vietnam was afire. Most of the attention on him from the authorities came as a result of his own doing, the rest derived from guilt by association.

"A'ight, Pimp, I feel ya. I'm 'bout to raise up outa them people's street till tha sun die down. You gotta enuff work?" Vietnam asked, handing him his killa back a few inches shorter. The weed was some good, but he silently wished it were something stronger.

"Yeah, I'm fixed. Ya mama pop'd me off proper like," Pimp replied. "You be easy. Walk light, my nigga," he added.

"Bet," Vietnam shot back, dapping Pimp off. Code number 5: "Stay free, stay alive, get money," he mumbled, walking off, shaking his head, the pressure of the game getting to him. Avoiding being captured by a relentless lawman and staying clear of the sights of a would-be-jacker-turned-killer-gun, all while collecting money, was a far cry from being just a mediocre task. When the reason that Monk and Wet Fish had limited his role in the game under their administration became clear as a glass of vodka to him, he had been living with the reality of it in the forefront of his mental ever since he achieved the renowned level of the game he now played on.

Unintentionally on his part, Vietnam's reputation and status on the streets skyrocketed. Ordinarily, if one stuck to their gun, putting in work on a daily basis, sooner or later, they were going to be playing the game from above the rim. Some even took a fast track to the top. No one with desire in their heart to rise stayed at the bottom of the totem pole forever. Therefore, it didn't come as a surprise that another hustler had raised the bar on the streets in the game. It was highly expected. Everyone knew that was how the game was designed. What surprised everyone out living the life was the age of the one they called Li'l One Gone. Word of the boy from across the track with that A-1 dope moved through the city like a shock wave. From the streets all the way to the cellblocks of Angola, the buzz was about a middle school cat from the Southside getting it jumping. It was said that Vietnam's product was so good it had fiends from Scotlandville walking all the way to the Southside to cop from him if they couldn't bum a ride. With every new tale spun about him, his popularity increased, also raising the interest on him from unwanted attention. Along with everyone else, the buzz about Vietnam had reached the ears of the five-O also. They chased his drugs down too, but for different reasons than the users and pushers did. They couldn't deny it. The pack they had confiscated off a dummy clown was the best they'd seen thus far, at least since the golden days of the game. They wanted to get their hands on the supplier with a passion. Unbeknownst to Vietnam, before he had passed the drugs off to Dooley, the police had put a dent in the game by capping off a vital pipeline of drugs to the street.

Drug trafficking had slowed down until Vietnam rose from the flame like the phoenix with a cache of extragood stuff, resurrecting the drug game across the track. The fruits of Vietnam's labor were throughout the neighborhood. Each bundle of heroin he had taken from Big Ed was potent enough to take a five of a cut to each packet that contained a 225-dollar gram of dope in it. With the cut added, the profit increased. As a result, indirectly or directly, everyone ate. It wasn't outside the norm to find a batch of cocaine that had already been mixed with something before one of the main distributors put it on the street, then the hustler worked their magic with it further. Stretching the product was not rare, but it was almost rare to find a package of drugs that was pure and uncut. So when the cocaine Vietnam hit for touched the streets, the users fought for it and the dealers went into a panic. On the brink of losing their clientele, they searched high and low for a product equal to or better than the quality of cocaine that was being sold down the street around the corner from Louisiana State University.

Magic and Vietnam had stumbled upon eighteen ounces of pure cocaine. If so desired, one could have mixed in a ten or a twenty-eight without a detectable decrease in the potency of the drug, which in turn boosted up the dealers' income by a thousand dollars if they made a hundred dollars off a gram after they broke it down to individual packs. If they didn't want the high profit, they still had a choice to give the user more bang for their buck without feeling it in their pockets. However, it was a win-win either way. West Roosevelt Street was the stage, and Vietnam was front and center on the spotlight. The old-timers say that if one is good to the game, the game will do the same to one in return. It is also said that fortune favors the brave. Vietnam didn't fall under either category; he was extremely apt at positioning himself at the right place, at the perfect time. The chips fell in order for him with little or no effort on his part. With that, it could be deduced that he had much luck, or either the game highly favored him or the streets had a purpose for him. Even without the money, whoever has the connect to a good quality of drugs, at more than reasonable prices, has the power in the game.

Vietnam had been sitting on a pipeline to the connect way before he even became aware of exactly whom it was that he had been dealing with. There wasn't a shortage of drug suppliers in the city, but the person Wet Fish had introduced Vietnam to in the past that he'd dealt with regularly under Wet Fish's administration, the same man that told him that once he lost his sponsor he was on his own, was the one that pushed nothing but the best of the best of both heroin and cocaine. It was unusual to find a man pushing boy and girl; most chose one or the other. But not him. He had a lust for money that was hard to fulfill. Like he told Vietnam, "If you give it to them the way you get it, you'll never be broke." Fond of his young moneymaker, he kept him with uncut drugs. Vietnam made money, and so did he. The constant cash flow from him wasn't the only thing that drew him nearer to him; he admired his heart more so than Vietnam's hustling abilities. Money doesn't impress money; character does. Other than himself, he had never met anyone that had steel ball bearings for testicles. Surprisingly, a child named Vietnam, formerly known as Li'l One Gone, was the one that possessed balls of steel—that or he was too stupid to recognize and be afraid of imminent danger. Either way, the man liked him.

As always, when he was preoccupied with thoughts other than the business at hand, anywhere else, overlooking even the smallest detail would have cost him his life or freedom. First mistake he made was failing to immediately recognize the vehicle parked next to the man's car when he arrived at his house.

"What up, G? When you gon' let me have that big-ass gun?" he jokingly asked, referring to the black TEC-9 submachine gun that hung at the end of the strap off the doorman's broad shoulder. He entered the house.

"When you grow some hair 'round that naked-ass lip of yours, li'l nigga," the doorman retorted playfully. He pushed Vietnam forward by the back of the head. "Go'n in there," he stated. Vietnam turned and eff'd at him. The doorman if'd back. They both chuckled. There was some form of physical contact between the two of them every time he came to the man's spot. The man was standing with his back leaned up against the wall behind the table. He conducted business with a dissatisfied look upon his face. There was another man sitting in the chair before him, fumbling with something on the front of him on top of the table. Moving in closer, he spotted the snow white on the man's arm. Not thinking much of it—it wasn't strange to see someone bandaged up, patched up, or cast up—he quickly disregarded it, redirecting his attention.

"Old faithful one," the man said, excited, his features brightening when he noticed Vietnam's presence in the room. "Come here." He gestured with his hand to Vietnam, who slid the backpack off his back and walked up toward the man. "See this little boy here? He gonna put all of us out of business one of these days," he said to the man at the table, who was busy sorting out stakes of fetti. "Always on time, never a dollar short," he said accusingly. "My main man, what'cha got for me, Li'l One Gone, baby?" the man asked.

With the mention of the name Li'l One Gone, the guy sitting violently twisted his head to the side, zeroing in on Vietnam. "You li'l muthafucka!" he yelled, jumping to his feet. The sudden explosion of his movement grabbed Vietnam's attention. Instantly his words placed him on alert, his hand dropping to his waistband, jerking at it, furthering his alertness to the highest level. For a fraction of a second, time seemed to have frozen. He watched Duce draw, raise, and point his candy stick directly at him.

On point and always ready for the added threat to his way of life, the man had drawn also a hair ahead of Duce. He stood cocked and ready to let hot lead fly. Though armed, with every right to engage into the conflict that was taking shape inside of his shop, the man stayed neutral, curious to find out why Duce drew down on Vietnam. He let things play out so that he could put a hand on the cause. Not only that, but he also didn't want to shoot anyone for real. He was a businessman not a shooter, he had cats on his payroll to do his wetwork, but when it came to his little protégé he was willing to burn any and everything that posed a threat to him. Solely on the strength of the love he had for him. He never let his trigger finger rest, watching the both of them suspiciously.

"Yeah, I know I was gonna run 'cross ya funky fat ass sumwhere," Duce spit out. "I ain't gon' cap ya in my man's spot." Duce knew that it was a sure bet, if anyone did get shot in the Man domain, him and his doorman were going to be the ones doing the shooting and most likely he was going to be the one riddled with hot lead. "C'mon, bring ya pussy ass outside," he said, walking toward the door with his candy stick. "I'ma knock ya shit loose, nigga!" he exclaimed.

When Li'l One Gone entered the game, he knew his fate was going to be the same as Wet Fish's, death, or the same as Monk's, incarceration. There was no way to beat the percentage. It had to happen. Vietnam turned to follow Duce's command. He was prepared to take his medicine like a man. Real gangsters didn't beg for their lives, and neither was he, but he did regret getting caught without his candy stick, looking down the business end of Duce's.

"Hold up, boy, you ain't going no damn where with him!" the man yelled, stopping him. "That boy came to see me, and he gon' leave when we finish our business, and not a minute 'fore then," he continued.

"G, this ain't got nuttin' to do with you," Duce stressed.

"I be damn if it don't. Dis my muthafucking spot!" the man shouted angrily. "Nah, you can tell me what you got 'gainst my boy, and I decide how you deal with it, or there's the door," he stated matter-of-factly. His patience had grown short when Duce called himself, putting him in his place. He had no other choice but to put his foot down.

"Dis muthafucka here and another little bastard was the one that stuck me and try'd to bag me," Duce stated, glaring at Vietnam menacingly.

Vietnam returned the look. "Sho' did. I shoulda killed you too, nigga," Vietnam replied calmly.

Duce's hand tightened around the grip of his candy stick, his breath shallowing and increasing rapidly, his eyes widening. *This is it,* Vietnam thought to himself. He swallowed hard, hoping that neither Duce nor the man had seen his only sign of fear. "Do it," he whispered, breaking the momentary quiet.

"Hell nah! Ain't nobody gonna do shit," the man piped in. Then staring at Vietnam in disbelief, he said, "Enough of that. You"—he aggressively pointed his gun at Duce, who caught the gesture out of his peripheral vision and tensed up slightly—"put that fucking gun up." The man's tone was deadly, his words felt. Duce's expression faded into a saddened, shocked one. Vietnam gazed back emotionless. The man was the only one in the standoff with a glint of excitement in his eyes. He knew he had control of the situation; plus, he had just witnessed an act of bravery on par with none. Duce felt betrayed because the man didn't back his play. On top of that, the moment he had envisioned since the medics sedated him had come and now was sliding out from under his finger. Disappointed, he licked his wounds. Vietnam? Well, to him this was just another part of a tale to tell. He didn't think or feel.

"Ah, man," Duce cried out after he lowered his gun.

"What, goddamit?" the man barked out.

The raised sound of his voice sprung the doorman into action. His heavy footsteps rang out through the house. He burst into the room, gun raised, looking mean. All eyes fell upon him. A surprised look crossed his face before he hesitantly let the submachine gun drop to his side. The man never spoke; a signal of some sort had to have passed between them. His focus wavered a tad bit from the gun in Duce's hand to the man's outstretched pistol as he backed his way out of the room. He nodded, then turned.

"Huh, what?" the man continued to question.

Duce lowered his head like a child that was being scolded.

"You lame-ass piece of shit, don't you ever raise your fuckin' voice or a gun up in here, you got that?" the man voiced. Duce's head sprung up, his face screwed. He wanted to respond, but instead he returned his gaze to the floor. "If you let two young rookies in the game creep up on you, take ya shit, then put a couple of caps in ya ass, you deserved it," the man stated.

"Man, I didn't let—"

"Shut da fuck up! I ain't finished!" the man screamed, cutting Duce's word short, leaving him with his mouth agape, opening and closing like he was a fish out of water trying to catch its breath. "Now, dig this jack. Go ahead and scrape that change up and get the fuck outa my spot. Today is ya lucky day, nigga. I'm not gon' kill you for disrespecting me, but if anything happen to my boy right there, I will

put a price on ya head that will have every nigga in the state lookin'
to collect on. That's if I don't kill ya my fucking self," he threatened.

Duce gathered up his funds, stuffing it into a wrinkled-up paper
bag, then he stared at the man silently.

"Get," the man said, raising up his candy stick but not aiming
it at Duce.

Salty with hate-filled eyes, he turned to Vietnam, made a kissing
gesture, then exited the room. "Fuck you!" Vietnam hollered behind
him before the sound of his footsteps on the wooden floor drifted
out of earshot.

"Sit," the man commanded. Vietnam took the seat Duce was
in when he arrived. Digging into his backpack, he started to pile his
money up on the table. "Put that shit up," the man told him.

"Okay," Vietnam said, shoving the cash back into his backpack.
He looked at the man questioningly. When he put the backpack on
the floor, the man spoke.

"Son, straight up, next time ya go out to rob people, if you
decide to shot, make sure they down for the count. Otherwise, baby
boy, you might get put down. You got me?" the man advised and
chastised him. "That pretty-boy Floyd shit, throw that shit out da
window. You a excellent hustler. You ain't gotta jack for a livin'. Keep
moving that dope tha way you been doing, and 'fore you know it,
you'll be tha man, kiddo," he continued.

"Okay," Vietnam replied with his mouth, though his heart was
dead set on sticking-and-moving in the future one day.

They conducted their usual business. The man looked down
at Vietnam with sheer admiration in his eyes and a proud heart. Li'l
One Gone had his mind fixated on sending Duce to his Maker. He
left with a few extra ounces in his backpack along with a new pistol.
The man gave him his personal gun, warning him to watch his back
at all times.

But he and Duce never crossed paths again; Duce had been
found slain. The news reported it as an drug deal gone bad. Then
after the incident at his spot, the man welcomed Vietnam with open
arms, treating him with the same reverence as a close, beloved rela-
tive. He even revealed and allowed him to address him by his given

name. When Vietnam told him his government name, he said to himself that the first name fit, but the last name explained his character. Vietnam had been derived from a pedigree befitting the likes of kings, warriors, entrepreneurs, and all-around stand-up guys. Part of the reason the drug trade existed in Baton Rouge was that a member of the Franklin clan took the initiative to go outside the system to better his condition. The man predicted that Vietnam was going to be a part of some type of new history in the game, and he planned on being part of the making. With the man, Vietnam didn't find a simple favor within. The favor the man had for him was rooted deeply. Once again, the game blessed him. All he did was be him.

Once all the buzz surrounding him died down, he was firmly standing stronger than ever. His feet were well planted in the game. Vietnam became a household name. Whenever talks in the barbershops, locker rooms, liquor stores, or any street corner arose and the topic of the conversation was about the cats on the streets that were in the spotlight or on their way, his name got thrown around. He had defied the odds. There wasn't a single documented freelancing kid hustling in the city controlling real estate, doing numbers like he was. Money rolled in like army tanks into battle, nonstop and unstoppable. His mama sat at home, jugging, while Vietnam pushed out of the playground. The two of them were officially business partners. Some of the proceeds from the drug sales, his mama invested into turning their house into a cushy home. The rest went to Vietnam to cop more drugs. Therefore, no matter who handed the money that landed across the tracks for drugs, a portion of it ended up in Vietnam's hands.

While other families were forging a bond with their children at festivals and after-school activities, he and his mama bonded at the kitchen table, weighing, packaging up drugs, and putting rubber bands on counted-up stacks of fettiluchi. Their relationship flourished. Vietnam's heart wasn't fully in it. The days he longed for a mother's touch were bygone, not just because his mama's personality was like the weather, ever changing; therefore, he knew he would have been setting himself up for a crash landing if he allowed his feelings to rise to the occasion of their forced arrangement. Enjoying her warmth but expecting a cold breeze was how most of his days with her were spent. His mama, having a dominant personality in the mix of the rest of her difficult ways to deal with, found it hard to adjust to the fact that her son was the go-to guy. She appreciated the package he gave to her free of charge, no doubt—her way of accepting it without a quarrel, in her mind, she viewed it as payment for room and board from him. But once she had sold out and was in desperate need of the high-quality drug to continue her up-and-coming enterprise, initially she had refused to score from Vietnam.

Majority of the money she made off the drugs she used to take care of the household; the rest, instead of returning to the well from whence she came, she went out with her last and scored more drugs from an unknown source. The stuff was so poor it was a gram away from being counterfeit cocaine; all the users complained to one degree or another. Dangling out on a ledge, her career in the drug trade was about to be ending before beginning. Reluctantly, she made a boss decision. Although Vietnam had been her savior twice and her avenue into the drug game—he had blessed her with money for so many years—she still abhorred the fact that he was her beholder. She birthed him into this world, and he gave her life into another level of the game. Awkwardly, together they had the neighborhood sewn up. It was a long time coming, but it happened. Money stopped having meaning to him. The hole in the wall became too small to hold any more money. He had long abandoned the bag on the string; he just dropped the cash in the hole, and once the money piled up to the mouth of the hole in the wall, he started putting his money in another safe, secure, never-would-be-discovered location. After running back to his stash spot increasingly, he got tired. Giving up, he stopped going through the trouble of hiding it—he placed it wherever he felt was suitable inside of the house. His mama was so busy keeping count of her fetti she didn't pose a threat to his. Vietnam didn't spend or lend; all he did was collect.

Double D was the reason his revenue multiplied tenfold. He taught him the art of using a triple beam scale, how to properly package the drugs, and showed him the fault in selling users wholesale, as well as pushers. Double D did something neither Monk nor Wet

Fish ever did: he revealed the true value of the product he was serving. There was twenty-eight grams in an ounce. Wholesale, an ounce of cocaine went for the max twelve hundred dollars. Of each gram in the ounce package, just right around a hundred dollars could be made off. Therefore, it was more profitable to sell a user a half of gram for fifty dollars as opposed to a whole gram at the same price. Forty or fifty dollars per gram was for dealers only. Each tenth of a gram of cocaine was sold at ten dollars a pop to users. Even if they had enough money to buy anything bigger than a gram, they got user's price. He schooled him on how much an eight ball and quarter ounce of cocaine should weigh and how much they sold for. Double D gave him the formula and showed him how to turn cocaine into crack cocaine. Also, everything from the user aspect to the dealer, Double D laced him up on game. The users got heated at the changeup in the way he moved his drugs, but they still shopped with him, simply because he had the best. On the other hand, the dealers were elated. Added with the money his mama made, when it was time to visit the man, he was never short, but he went frequently. Once Double D put him up on game, his visits were less frequent, but with more cash to spend, making the man proud. He was campaigning for more one-hundred-thousand-dollar bet on the rise of Vietnam.

Though knowledgeable about heroin also, he packaged it in grams, selling as is. Therefore, he didn't have to compete with the user to sell to the user. Double D was to Vietnam what Vietnam was to Wet Fish and Monk. When no one else was in the playground, they were there, making money. Vietnam didn't put a whole lot of trust into Double D. His moves were limited. Besides their previous encounter, he didn't show any signs of "sheistiness." It was a rule: Vietnam was the dealer, and Double D was the worker. Their business was on a need-to-know and not a minute before then. Vietnam didn't keep count of his sponsor's money or had total control of their drugs, and neither was Double D going to. That was how it went then. That was how he made sure it went now. Since he began to walk, the park was his favorite destination. He was no stranger to its history or the way it operated. Now he was walking in the footprints left behind by those that came before him and the ones he walked side by side on the grind with—only difference, he never took the liberty of sitting on the bench. He stayed in the spot he started at, on the slide. Others pushed out of the playground alongside of him. He didn't have a problem with any of the other cats working his spot; the drugs they sold came out of his bag. It made it easier for him to move his work. A few of his people off Polk Street would come across the track, kick it with him, make a few plays, and push out, leaving him with an invite on their block. Magic posted up with him to get rid of the drugs he came up on on one of his capers, then he'd push, vamoose, only to be seen again when he needed a place to push from.

Magic invited him a few times to accompany him on a mission. Though he so desired, he stayed true to his word to the man's declaration. He suppressed the very thought of armed robbery out of his mental and stuck to what was fattening his pockets. The thug gods had smiled upon him once more. Miraculously, even when he occasionally squandered his money, lost drugs, or traded his work off for bottles of genie water he came to overly enjoy smoking, at the time to re-up, his money was always true, never short a penny. Falling off in the game was nowhere in his deck of cards. Upward was his destination. Even with the heat of police harassing, shaking every bush in the streets, looking for Li'l One Gone, cops hitting the tracks missed him by the hair on their chin, along with the detectives from robbery/homicide division, sexual assault unit, and narcotics building their cases on the description of a person matching his. His longevity in the game still was promising. Vietnam had taken his rightful place on the throne. The streets undisputedly crowned him prince of the game across the tracks. On West Roosevelt Street and abroad was his kingdom. Inside of his mama's wound, he had been molded by the thug gods. Since the day of his birth, every incident, whether blissful or harsh, endured, and every encounter, ill or favorable, he faced was tailored by the lord of the game in order for him to achieve his predestined status. The streets cultured him every step of the way. Undeniably, his time had arrived. He knew it. People in the game knew it. The ones living the life knew it also.

There was only one thing that could knock him off his high horse or stop his shine. And he plotted Vietnam's destruction while Vietnam fought to hold down his crown.

The playground had become as electrifying with criminal activity as it did a few years back. The new breed of hustlers, like Monk called them, was a rowdy bunch. Everyone out there packed a tool and was anxious to use it. The genie, cocaine, and crack cocaine, smoked mixed with killa, didn't help; it increased the chances of some hothead pulling out their guns, blasting away. It was an active, hostile environment; no one was beefing, but everyone stayed on the alarm, waiting for the jump-off to jump off.

The playground wasn't a place for kids to play; thus, most parents banned their kids from the playground without their supervision. Karonda's mama was one of the mamas that had imposed that rule. Instead of opposing her mother's wishes outright, she skirted on the brink by not crossing the barrier that separated the play area from the projects. Standing on the walkway, she and Vietnam would conversate, hug, kiss, play-fight, exhibit all the actions that young people who had intimate feelings for another displayed, for hours. If it weren't for Double D backing his play once Karonda came into the picture, a dime wouldn't have been made directly by him. They never sat down and came to terms about their relationship. As far as the neighborhood was concerned, they were a cute preteen couple.

Karonda had Vietnam sandwiched between her and the brick wall. They were having one of those one-sided future conversations. Mostly she talked; he just okayed every idea she came up with about his life and hers together. She was right in the middle of a list of things that she was going to purchase with the money he made when Magic dipped down on them.

"Let me holla at 'cha right fast, G," Magic requested, though it sounded more like an order.

"Well, hey, to you too," Karonda snapped playfully.

"Oh, my bad. What's up with ya, Ms. Kay?" Magic half-heartedly responded to her correcting him for being impolite.

Vietnam stood quietly, smiling, watching the exchange between his friends. "A'ight, my G," he piped in, ending any more word passing. "Don't," he mumbled to Karonda to further ice the situation. From her facial expression, it was obvious to all that knew her she was getting ready to get flipped by the mouth. Magic turned, then stepped away from them. Vietnam released Karonda from around her waist. She didn't move, blocking him. "What?" he asked. She gazed into his face goo-goo-eyed, not speaking. "Oh." Realizing what was going on, Vietnam leaned over, then pressed his lips against hers. When he drew his head back, she then cleared out of his path. Lately, anytime he walked off from her, even if it was only a few feet for a brief moment, she wanted a see-you-later kiss, like he was going on a journey. Vietnam looked back. She was posted with her arms wrapped around herself, watching him. He flashed her a smile, then turned.

"I got a nice li'l stick-and-move job lined up," Magic said, bypassing formal thug greetings, getting straight to the business when Vietnam reached him.

Doggedly he turned down every proposition Magic had thrown his way to team up with him on a caper. Though there was a part of him dying for some action, he stood on his word. "Nah, dog, I'm good on that shit there. I'm getting good money," he replied. Every time he turned his friend down, an empty feeling passed through him. It was like a feeling one gets when they self-check after they break a bro code. Averting his gaze, Vietnam said, "I ain't with it no more," more so to convince himself that he was making the right decision, not only for declining Magic's offer, but also for denying himself his own desire.

"I really need ya on this one, my nigga. This the one that we both gonna be straight for life off. C'mon, jus' this one more time," Magic pleaded.

The promise of everlasting money made Vietnam waver on the grounds that he firmly stood on, but the look on Magic's face persuaded him to sidestep it altogether. "Where's at?" he asked. Karonda sighed in the background, a gush of air rushing out of her lungs. She stomped her foot, then smacked her lips. They sounded like a .22-caliber pistol shot ringing out. Magic stepped out of her ear range. Vietnam followed without looking back. He felt her eyes burning a hole in the back of his head.

"It's 'cross town," Magic answered. "I got us a hot one" he added.

"A nigga must be major. You talking 'bout we gon' be set for life. What's it hitting for?" he inquired.

"You remember that big party they had at the Cajun Hall everybody was talkin' 'bout?" Magic asked.

"Yeah, I think I heard somebody say'n some shit 'bout it," Vietnam answered.

"Peep this, the nigga throw a million-dollar bash, celebrating his first million dollars he made in the game. That nigga pumping that dog food heavy on Bogan Walk Street. Ya feel me?" Magic said matter-of-factly.

"And what about it?" Vietnam shot back.

"If ya listen, nigga, I'ma tell ya. Nah, my people's son, the one that be putting me on all of my licks, anyway, he was telling me 'bout how the party was. He was, like, he ain't know that the nigga was clocking paper like that, and I was, like, how ya figure, right? So dude hit me with some shit like he see dude leave his house every other morning, you know. He was, like, his shit didn't look like a nigga with millions house, but he did have some nice rides parked in his yard, though. See, fool work for BFI, bumping cans. One of his routes in Baker. That's where he say tha boy lived at. So I got a rock rental, went, checked it out. Sho' as a snake is slippery an' shit stank, it was what it was, jus' like fool said," Magic finished. "If we push out now, we can hit an' be back in the hood in 'bout a hour," Magic added.

It wasn't out of the ordinary for a dealer to sell from one location and live in another area. The chances were great that the dude kept his money where he slept at; there wasn't a rule that said so, but it was good practice for a true hustler to never let his product and proceeds be at the same spot at the same time. If all failed, Vietnam thought, if they didn't find a million in cash in the house, there was going to be a helluva lot of heroin somewhere in there, which was as good as US currency. "Let's be out, then!" Vietnam exclaimed excitedly. After a split second, his brain sent the signal to his legs to move before they could comply.

Karonda slammed into the back of him, wrapped her arms around his body. "No, don't go," she cried out, hugging him snuggly. Vietnam chuckled. Magic shook his head, speechless by the display.

"Let me go," Vietnam commanded.

"No, nigga, I'm not!" she yelled.

"Girl, stop acting fucking crazy. Let me the fuck go. You trip'n!" Vietnam stated angrily, prying her strong grip from around him loose.

"Go 'head, then. I was gonna give ya stupid ass sum!" she shouted out behind him.

"Man, fuck you, you lying," he said quietly, almost mumbling.

She heard him. Running behind him, she shoved him in the back. "Fuck me, oh, fuck me! Nah, you really ain't gonna get none!" she yelled hysterically.

From the moment they started seriously hanging out with each other, she had promised to give him some, especially right before she asked for a few dollars. Still, he had yet to see the waistband of her underwear. He stared at her. *She just might be serious,* he thought to himself. "Muthafuck her, go get that money!" the voice shouted in his ear. Glancing back at Magic, he patiently waited, his hands in his pockets. He didn't force the issue one way or another, but the look in his face revealed his thoughts.

Standing in the middle of his two friends, Vietnam pushed put without turning back to look at Karonda. "Say, my G. I ain't gonna be able to fade you on this one," Vietnam said, changing his mind.

"It's all love, baby," Magic replied, expressionless.

"Sho?" Vietnam asked curiously.

"Everything made for love with us thug," Magic answered, smiling, extending his fist. They dapped. "I already had my li'l podna on deck to roll with me, but I was hope'n you would laced ya boots up with me. Li'l one ain't never stomped in the mud before," he added.

"I—"

"Don't worry, it's cool. I'm out," Magic interrupted, cutting Vietnam's words short. Abruptly he turned on his heels, throwing up the deuce as he mobbed away, leaving Vietnam lost for words.

Karonda had a big bright smile that spread up to her eyes across her face. Seeing Magic bounce away solo filled her with joy. When Vietnam faced toward her, she hurriedly dropped her head, pretending to have been in a saddened pose all the while. "Stop faking. I seened ya cheering ya ass off!" Vietnam poked at her. They then joined each other in laughter. "Oh yeah, you gonna give me some too, real shit. I ain't going for that 'I'ma get ya right later,'" Vietnam pressed, hoping it would finally happen.

"Boy, I said I gotcha," she replied shyly.

Regretfully, Vietnam glanced back in time to see the back of the four-door Celebrity Magic was driving creep over the tracks, gone. "Fuck, I should have went," he said to himself. A strong feeling of betrayal attacked him, causing his mood to nosedive toward stupor rapidly. Making the situation no better, the voice said mockingly in his ear, "I told you to go." An outburst of a cheerful shriek from Karonda brought him out of his thoughts before he soured completely.

Karonda ran to Sassy, embracing her like they were long-lost sisters reuniting after years of separation. *Girls,* he thought, watching them carry on, cackling. Their feminine sounds lifted his spirits a little. He looked at the tracks once more before he stepped over to join them. Sassy had plenty of hugs to go around in her arms. Her soft breast and the overwhelming fragrance of her perfume smothered Vietnam. She held him a few licks too long against her for a normal greeting, he thought, but he couldn't bring himself to let go of her.

"Hey, my baby, how ya been?" she asked.

"I'm good. Same ole, same ole, honey," Vietnam answered, burying his head into her chest, inhaling deeply.

"Boy, you a hot mess," she said, then giggled when she felt a poke against her thigh. She brushed her hand over his erection before she widened the distance between them. "Anybody doing something over here? What's wrong with you?" she asked. Vietnam had one of the silliest expressions on his face; a seasoned comedian couldn't have topped it. The sensation from her light touch on his penis was still playing over in his head.

Embarrassed, he caught his head. "Um, I'm good," he replied.

Karonda stared at him in wonder. She had missed the incident. Sassy giggled again. "Ol' po' thang!" she exclaimed, then smiled. She knew exactly what was going on. No matter their age, unless homosexual, she had the same effect on males. Unknowingly, if he so desired, he wouldn't have been able to control himself—the perfume she was wearing was especially formulated to increase hormonal activities in the male body. She wore it whenever she went out hustling or to cop drugs. Whoever she came in contact with would be more focused on her than what was going on. Vietnam wasn't her intended target; he just so happened to fall prey.

"Well, like I was saying, sweetie, you know where I can get something at?" she asked, sticking her chest out.

The first time he had met Sassy and Jennifer, Vietnam didn't pay much attention to her then, or afterward. This time, he couldn't concentrate clearly. All his focus was on every detail of her body and face. "No. Shit, I mean yeah. What you tryna get?" he stammered. The lust was so apparent in his features that Karonda got mad and stomped off. Sassy was a woman first, drug addict second. Popping game was bred in her. Instead of running her hand through the collar of her shirt to retrieve the money from out of her bra like most women did, she lifted her shirt up, cocked her head, then ran her hand slowly up her abdomen up to her breast. She pulled down on her bra, relieving one of her light golden-brown breast out of the cup while she searched around it for the crumbled-up bills. Vietnam's brain wave activity increased. His hand readjusted his stiff meat pistol to a more comfortable position. Sassy didn't miss the moment.

"The way she acted, she must be ya li'l girlfriend or something now," Sassy stated. "Last time I seen her, I thought her and ya li'l friend Li'l Who was talking, how close they were sit'n next to each other in the car," she added. Vietnam looked over at Karonda, who was stalking them from afar. "Anyway, she treating that thing right?" she said, staring down at Vietnam's groin area. "That li'l girl don't know what to do with all that meat," she continued, straightening out her money in her hand while she talked. Unconsciously, Vietnam massaged his loin.

"I'll have you not wanting to leave the house for months if I whip this pussy on ya," she stressed.

Hearing her say *pussy* sent a tingle down from his head and up from his feet, meeting in the middle of his body. For once in his life, he wanted something more desperately than money. He wanted to ask her how much, but he was too ashamed to do so. She chuckled. "Let me stop foolin' with you. Boy, you still jailbait. I got seventeen dollars," she informed him. "Stop playing with ya self. You heard I got seventeen," she said, smiling. *If only you were older, I'll have all your dope and money,* she thought to herself. Surprisingly, she had become moist down below.

Vietnam snapped out of his trance. Double D's job was to fetch the product from the stash spot. It was only him and Karonda on deck. There were a couple of other cats out hustling. At first, he was about to send her to one of them because he didn't like going to the stash spot alone, but then he recalled Sassy's DOC (drug of choice) was cocaine. He was the only one that sold both. He went quickly, glancing back at Sassy. Her red hair was like flame around her head. Karonda leaned against the wall, arms folded, throwing daggers at the both of them. Quickly he went to the stash spot, returning.

"Ya girl Jennifer is in the car," Sassy spat out. "C'mon, let's go holla at her," she suggested.

Vietnam dropped the baggie in her hand. Examining it, she hurriedly closed her hand, then placed her arm over his shoulder. Vietnam reached into the bag and pulled out the first pack his fingers touched. It was a half-gram baggie. He was in a rush to get back to the smell of her. When he left her presence, he noticed the change in him instantly. It felt like a foggy high clearing out of his head. Her fragrance, the warmth of her body, and the softness of her skin were intoxicating. They bumped hips a couple of times as they slow-walked to the parked vehicle.

Words were being spoken by her, but Vietnam didn't hear anything that was said; he was in another world. Nor did he see when Karonda pushed herself off the wall right on their trail. Jennifer's condition had worsened. She looked like she had aged twenty years since he last saw her. There were patches of hair missing from her head, a direct result of her continuously running her hand through it and pulling at it the way she did when she was trying to remove Wet Fish's blood and brain matter out of her hair.

"Say hey to Vietnam," Sassy told Jennifer in a childlike voice. Jennifer glared at Vietnam. Sunken in their sockets, her eyes didn't show any sign of recognition of him or a flicker of her former self. Repulsed not by the sight of her—her features still held the shadow of a beautiful woman—but by the condition for which she was in, Vietnam turned his head away. Even though Sassy's body was pressed up against his like they were Siamese twins, joined together at the hips, his erect meat pistol went limp.

"Pussy-ass police," he said angrily.

"I know. Dat was fucked up. I think 'bout dat every time I look at her," she whispered sadly.

Karonda had posted up behind them. "Um, you still live in Northdale?" he asked.

"Why you wanna know where she live at?" Karonda butted in.

They both turned. "'Cause...," he replied with a devilish frown on his face. "Go somewhere till I get with you," he added.

"Ump," Sassy sighed. Reading the hurt and angry scribbled on his face, Karonda complied without retort.

Sensing the change in his mood, Sassy tensed up, loosening her arm from around him. "Yeah, I do. What's up?"

"What made you come way over here to cop? You coulda went holla at Big Ham in CC or them niggaz twin or Li'l Mike. That ole nigga Gregor Boo doing something in your hood too, huh?" Vietnam pressed on the line of questions like he caught her with her skirt up.

"What, you ain't happy to see me?" she shot back.

Vietnam didn't respond, and his silence choked her up a little.

"Yeah, you right, I could've holla at Mike or them niggaz on Mulberry Street or stopped on the Lake and got with Leech ball-head ass, but I didn't want them all in my business. My sugar daddy be trip'n on me get'n high. Word mighta got back to him," she replied convincingly, leaving out the fact that she owed everybody on her side of town. Her reason for choosing to shop with him didn't matter; he asked the question for the benefit of Karonda's ears. He didn't have to peek back over his shoulder to know that she had them under the microscope and was listening to every word that was being spoken also. Sassy had her hands on her hips, posing like a working girl, staring down at him.

"Say, that faggot police officer Dicken DaBeaudé still work in Northdale?" he asked quietly.

She had to strain to hear him. "Yeah, he still got his hoe ass 'round there, tryna fuck everythang with a pussy 'tween their legs," she replied disgustedly in equal volume as Vietnam.

"He tried to get with you?" Vietnam inquired.

"Um-hum," she stated, studying his face. The signs of danger were there.

"That nigga gotta get it," he mumbled out loud to himself. Sassy's stomach did a somersault. "Look, I'ma need you to do something for me."

The sound of footsteps approaching interrupted him. "What da fuck ya'll all hush-hush and shit fo'?" Karonda yelled out.

Sassy didn't pay her any attention; she was fixed on Vietnam, dangling on his words.

"Come back and get with me when the sun go down," Vietnam whispered to Sassy.

"Kay," she replied, checking Karonda before she pushed off.

Karonda let the lack if his attention get the best of her. She flashed out. "You don't have to hurry up and bust out. I like to talk too!" she screamed out behind Sassy, who never acknowledged her. "So now you in the business of giving shit away? You got it like that, huh?" She lit in on Vietnam.

"Fuck you talking 'bout?" he questioned, facing her.

"I didn't see miss thang give you no money for that shit you gave her. Everybody else come through this bitch gotta pay," she spat out, rolling her head, punctuating her sentence. "I heard her say something 'bout some pussy. What she said? She was gonna give you some pussy? That's why she ain't pay ya?" she asked, pouting, her lip poked out.

"Why da fuck you watching me like that?" Vietnam responded, casting doubt, adding fuel to her suspicions by avoiding her question. They'd been down the argument road so many times before he already knew that neither a lie nor the truth was going to satisfy her when she was in that state.

"So she did," she went on.

"Fuck no! She said that she was gonna pay me later," he explained.

"I bet," she retorted.

His temper rose. "You know what? Stay the fuck outa my mix, bitch," he blurted out, regretting it as soon as *bitch* left his lips.

"Bitch, ha? So now I'm a bitch. No, nigga, yousa a bitch. That's why that hoe jacked you ole raggedy ass!" she exploded. Her eyes blinked rapidly, her head rocking from side to side so roughly it looked like she was about to snap her neck when she dressed Vietnam down. "That's why you ain't getting no booty," she added, marching off. This was routine also. If she had promised to let him sow his oats earlier, later she'd build a case on him to renege on her part of the deal. Vietnam was prepared for her predictable tactic.

"Fuck it! Sassy fine ass gonna break me off later. I don't need your cat. I'm gon' get some grown-woman pussy!" he screamed behind her, then he went back into the playground area.

His words caused her to stop. She stiffened up like she had been physically struck. She had a wild look when she spun around after several seconds of stillness. Disregarding the barrier, she stormed straight up to Vietnam. "I'll never give anybody else my stuff but you! That's how you gonna do me. I knew you didn't like me," she expressed, staring him dead in the eyes with her puppy-dog look.

Vietnam couldn't hold up. "I do like you," he assured her.

"What about her?" she meekly asked. He didn't respond readily. "See!" she cried out, her eyes misting up.

Foolishly, Vietnam nervously giggled. The pain that spread through her was obvious. Her shoulders slumped, and her face went slack. "I love you, baby" strangely rolled off his tongue. It didn't dawn on her right off what he had said. When it did, the same eyes that were misty dried, then brightened up. She smiled, then passionately hugged him. "You almost blew it, kid. I took care of it," the voice said into his ears, explaining where "I love you" came from. Holding her once again, he hardened. Puberty was riding him like that dragon on a junkie's back. "Now, ditch the broad. You know what we gotta do," the voice said.

"What the day is?" he asked. His mind had flipped.

"Friday. Why, bae?" she answered.

"No thang. That mean you can stay up late tonight, right? So I'ma buy a few boxes of pizza for everybody, some movies, and I'ma bring my game system over. We gonna hang out. Don't worry, I'ma look out for ya mama too," he informed her. Although she was transitioning into a developing female, she still had that little-girl cuteness on her pretty face.

"Okay, what you want me to do?" she asked in her husky, sweet voice.

"Take these few shams." He pulled out and peeled off a few bills off his bankroll. "Give 'em to ya'll mama and wait at home till I get there," he instructed her.

"What ya fix'n to do?" she shot back.

"It's 'bout to be rush hour," he said, looking at his watch. "I gotta get ready to get dis money for us," he added, lying. He really just wanted her from under him so that he could work out his thoughts. She puckered up, so he kissed her, letting it linger longer than usual. Neither one of them wanted to be the first to break the kiss. Finally, he did. He watched her, amused, as she tried to twist her slim hips as she walked away. If he didn't know better, he would have thought he felt some type of way when she disappeared.

Vietnam posted up, exhausted. Double D didn't show up until dusk; therefore, he had to accommodate all the customers. The stress weed he smoked had gotten ahold of him. It had him feeling sluggish. Taking it in early was a sweet melody playing in his mind. Thoughts of Karonda kept him from dancing his way home. When she left, he wanted to leave right behind her, but his dreaded responsibility to the game prevented him from running behind her like the little lamb did Mary. Impatiently he watched the timepiece on his wrist, waiting for the plan he orchestrated to manifest. Glancing up the block disappointedly, he fired up another unfiltered Camel cigarette.

Thirty more minutes, he thought. Realizing and regrouping when things went left was one of the capabilities that separated the real from the wannabes. Alone time with Karonda would have been perfect. Any time at all with her was good thinking that his scheme had blown up. He suddenly wished he had kept his money in his pocket. Ms. Wendy, Karonda's mama, occasionally enjoyed gambling. Also, she liked to lounge around at the club Chatter Box. With the few extra dollars on deck, Vietnam bet that she was going to be heading out to paint the town rouge. Ms. Wendy always extended a welcome to her home to him with stipulation: Whenever he was in Karonda's room, the door had to remain open at all times. No later than 11:00 p.m., he had to be off her property, which was fine with him. That was before his nature started to get the best of him and before Karonda's and his touchy-feely matches began. Tonight he didn't have a mind to obey her rules. The only way he could get away with it was in her absence. Like the old-timers say, "You live to fight another day."

Tired of waiting for Ms. Wendy to depart, Vietnam said, "Say, D, find us some wheels? I need to run on Government Street to Blockbuster and the pizza joint."

"Man, you shoulda said sumthang early, Vee. I coulda had sumthang lined up. It's gon' be hard to find one nah," Double D cried out.

"I got money, I got dope, make it happen," Vietnam barked menacingly.

"Be easy, baby. You ain't gotta swell all up. You know ole Danny Boy gotcha. If you get mad and shot me and kill me, who gon' find a ride fo' ya?" Double D stated comically.

Vietnam could never stay angry around Double D; he must have come from a heritage of jesters, because he made light of all situations. Finding humor even in the worst of times, Double D turned everything into a form of joke, which was one of the reasons Vietnam allowed him to stay close to him.

"An' don't come out here late again, nigga. If ya do, ya gonna find another gig!" he yelled behind him as he mobbed off into the darkness. His words didn't reach Vietnam's ears clearly, but he knew that it was a wisecrack.

Gathering up the money and remaining drugs he didn't push far from the spot where he had the money and product hidden separately, he returned to an awaiting Sassy and Double D. "I got ya a ride, playa," Double D hollered out cheerfully.

"You ain't got shit, nigga. She was already coming," Vietnam returned, matching his cheerfulness.

Double D's smile was erased quickly when his gaze fell on the bag in Vietnam's hand. "What's up, Vee? It's over so soon?" he asked seriously.

"Shop closed. I'm going in," Vietnam replied, pushing past him to get his candy stick from next to the trash barrel lying under a balled-up, soiled T-shirt. "C'mon let's dip," he told Sassy.

Double D followed them. They got into her car, starting it up. "Why he standing there looking crazy?" she asked.

Vietnam looked over at Double D standing on the curb, looking like a run-hard smoker that got their last push on the pipe. Cracking the window, he yelled, "If ya here when I get back, I gotcha!" Then he told Sassy, "Let's roll. He shouldna came out'che late." She pulled out into traffic, and Vietnam peeked through the back window right when Double D was taking a seat on the walkway of the Bricks.

"Look, baby, I thought about why you wanted me to come back. Effin it's what I think it is, I don't want no part of it," Sassy protested.

"What you think it is?" he asked, groping his crotch, smiling up at her from the passenger seat.

Maintaining control of the vehicle, she didn't see his gesture. "I seen it all up in ya face. You wanna do something to dat police who killed ya friend Wet Fish, baa-biie," she said, stretching the two syllables. "I ain't spending the rest of my life in nobody's jail fo' hurting no policeman," she stated matter-of-factly.

I don't plan on hurting his ass, Vietnam thought. "I don't want you to help me hurt him. I want you to set him up for me to get at him," Vietnam replied.

"Oh my gawd," she sighed, tightened her grip on the steering wheel. "Hell to tha double fuck no, boy!" she exclaimed. "You niggaz from dat Bottom fucked up. Y'all are crazy! No, nothing, zero from me on that. We ain't even gotta discuss that 'cause the answer still gon' be da same," she added.

"I'll give you four thousand dollars if you turn me on to him. You ain't gotta do shit but point me in the right direction," Vietnam proclaimed.

"Nigga, you almost made me wreck my damn car. I almost ran into the back of that car in front me talk'n 'bout four thousand dollars! You ain't got no four thousand to give to yourself," she stressed. Vietnam opened the bag, pouring out the contents on his on his lap. Three knots of cash fell out of it, with a few loose bills spilling out also. Along with the cash was a cache of both cocaine and heroin.

Picking up the fettilouchi, Vietnam spat out, "This what I made today. It should be close to four thousand grand, minus the hundred dollars you eased off without paying me."

"Nah'um, boy, dat wasn't a hundred-dollar shit, more like thirty dollars. Anyways, I'ma let you take that off my fee when you make eighteen," she shot back.

On the way back, they almost passed Double D up until she spotted him running toward the car, waving his hands in the air hysterically. Despite him not earning anything, out of good measure, Vietnam broke him off a few crumbs anyway. He gave him just enough to stop the dragon on his back from getting angry, anyway.

Outside Karonda's house, he squared up with Sassy for the ride to the movie store and pizzeria and added incentive. He pulled out a small pack of powder. "Here," he said, passing it to her when she had her head turned. It fell right on target, between her legs. "My bad," he claimed. Before she could react, he went with his move, ramming his hand after the pack.

"Whoa!" she cried out at, cringing at the sudden invasion of her privacy, then to his surprise, she spread her legs wider so that he could retrieve the pack that had settled right next to her vagina. Seductively, she gazed at him. "You think you slick, huh? You did that on purpose, didn't ya?" she stated.

Vietnam's brain had succinctly short-circuited. Though he heard her, he couldn't respond verbally; he just grinned. Sassy chuckled at his lack of response and the silly look on his face.

"Um-huh, dat's what you get," she joked. "I seen ya looking down there all night. I felt you was gon' try something," she added. "Where we at? You owe me for that touch," she pressed, holding her hand out palms up. The spell had worn off him.

"Add that to my fee when I make eighteen, baby," he retorted.

"Get'cha ass out of my car 'fore I go tell ya pretty li'l girlfriend you in here, feeling me up!" she squealed playfully.

Vietnam picked the stack of pizza boxes off the back floor. He placed them on the porch, then returned for the bag of drinks and the bag of movies he had his property in. With everything in his arms, his gaze dropped between her legs, running his eyes to meet her peepers. "Thank you, baby," he said slyly.

Catching his drift, she replied, smiling, "No, thank yo' ass, baby, an' next time, you gon' pay for touching my pussy." The she added, "Good night, boy." Sassy was a year younger than Jennifer was, and watching her spin the bend, once again he wished he were older than what he was.

Ms. Wendy wasn't there, but Karonda was, babysitting her little brothers and sisters. After they ate, she bathed them. When she finished, she made a pallet on the floor in front of the TV. While she was bathing the kids, Vietnam had sneaked out and taken a few puffs of the wet cigarette he coped on the way over. Zooted was the only way that he was gonna be able to stay still long enough to watch a movie without falling asleep. They sat on the couch, all touchy-feely underneath the blanket Karonda had draped over their shoulders. She played with his chain and neck while he ran his hands down her thighs. He carefreely touched Sassy's vagina. Since forever, he thought about touching Karonda's, and now that the opportunity presented itself, he was dismayed. His heart started to beat its way out of his chest, lungs starting to take air in and rapidly pumping out. His brain projected a preview of his wanting actions. His penis throbbed more, and the palms of his hands started to perspire. He rubbed the moisture off his palms onto his pants leg, then he placed his hands back on her thighs. Lips dry, he licked his lips, inching his hands up toward her heat like a snake creeping up to a campfire. All his senses went into overdrive. When his brain sent out the signal that it was about to go down, Karonda's body went stiff as his hand got closer to her hot box.

"What time is it? I gotta catch the news!" she yelled, jumping up.

Vietnam took a deep breath, then settled back into the couch. "Ah, 9:57," he answered without any enthusiasm.

"What?" she asked, picking up the change in Vietnam. "We gon' finish looking at the movie," she assured him, thinking that was the cause of his attitude change. "I always watch the news," she went on explaining as she pressed the Power button on the VCR. Vietnam couldn't care less about the news; in fact, he couldn't tell you what was the name of the movie they were watching or anything about it.

He was disappointed that he didn't go with his move sooner. The thought was present, but all heart for it had diminished under extreme pressure. Masturbating was heavily on his mind. "I need to use ya bathroom," he said shamefully.

"Go 'head," she said without turning his way.

"Coming up at news at ten, two teens were struck down in an afternoon shooting in Baker. One died at the scene, while the other is being treated for life-threatening injuries and is now listed in critical condition. The police don't have a motive for the crime or a lead on the suspect or suspects as of the moment. If anyone has any information about today's shooting, please call Crimestoppers at 344-STOP. That's 344-STOP. Governor Buddy Romer..."

Though the news was still being broadcast, the volume on the television might as well have been turned down to zero. Nothing else was heard. The room became quiet as a grave as Karonda and Vietnam halted to a complete stop. When "Two teens had been struck down" reached his ears, they stared at each other, frozen, both mentally and emotionally disturbed by the report. Their identities weren't given, but it had the feel of Magic and his stickman to it. Vietnam's legs noodled off, then gave out from underneath him. He fell back onto the sofa, sighing. "Damn!" he yelled out in total disbelief. *Can't be,* he thought to himself. When Vietnam mindfully entered the game, the streets injected him with a vaccine to produce immunity to violence and sob stories, but every so often, his helper T cells slept on the job, allowing some acts of violence to infiltrate, breaking the barriers of protection within him. This was one of those times when violence affected him. The symptoms were disbelief again and remorse. His high receded at mush speed. Thoughts of ejaculating were chased off his mental by visions of his thug brother lying spiritless in a pool of stagnant liquid life.

As he sat, eyes wide open, glancing around the room but not seeing, Karonda moved over to him, comforting him, arms around him, holding him. She whispered, "I'm glad you listened to me," next to his ear. Vietnam was numb to her touch and mute to her consolations as she continued to speak. A breath of warm air stroked his neck with every word she spoke, yet he neither felt her breath or embrace nor heard a word Karonda had said. It wasn't too premature to feel the facts were damn near evident as to who it was. In the footage from the cameraman's angle, a flash of the car Magic was in could be seen in the background, he recalled when his senses returned. But it was too premature for action until he found out who the deceased person was. Until then, all he could do was chill and hope. Enjoying the rest of the night was as dead as the body that was wrapped in a purple Rabenhurst blanket tied down on a stretcher being pushed into the back of the meat wagon the news had cast earlier. For now, he had her, and she had him. He returned her hug, and they remained locked and twisted for several long seconds.

"I be worried about you when you be out in that park," she confessed, breaking the quiet spell that had fallen on the room.

"Don't be. Ain't shit gonna happen to me," he assured her, internally wishing that his words were the gospel truth.

"How you know?" she asked concerningly, her big brown eyes roaming over his face, waiting for a sufficient response.

"'Cause…," he replied. Getting his barrens in line, searching the information in the storage compartment in his brain for a half-perfect explanation, he found what he was looking for. Not the one to give up information freely, he waited for her to ask the question. He knew "'Cause…" was never going to fly with Karonda.

"'Cause what? Why you say that?" she asked, just as he expected, with an also-predicted twirl of her neck.

Vietnam hesitated, pretending to ponder her question.

"Why, bae?" she impatiently picked up.

"It's like this." He started off the same way the person from whom he received the knowledge he was about to reveal to her did. Didactics of life or the game were treasures that didn't get passed to anyone. Karonda, at that moment, was his girl; therefore, she was a part of him. There wasn't any problem giving her the game.

"Although money is the motive, there's a big difference how niggaz in the game get their paper from the niggaz in the life get theirs," he said, gazing at Karonda, who was attentive, like always. She never put on, but she enjoyed hearing him talk. She had her head on his shoulders, like a baby listening to a nighttime story. Wanting to make his point clear and precise, he went back to the beginning of the story, preaching it the way it was given to him. "See, there's gods of the thugs, also known as drug dealers. They are rulers of the games. Then there's the lord of the life. They're the rulers of the niggaz that living the life. Magic live the life, and I'm eight toes deep in the game," he said to make sure she was listening.

"You got eight toes?" she asked in a sleepy voice.

"No," he replied. "Anyway," he continued, "the thug gods appreciate ingenuity of schemes hustlers craft to make money. They smile on the charismatic, they never hold back on blessing those who finesses their contrived paper plans, moving with style and grace play by play. They honor and protect those playing by the rules of the game they officiate. The thug gods were businessmen before they got promoted to join the ranks of the gods. All their business dealings were square business. That's how they found favor." He reached for the cup of Coke on the table, Karonda leaning over and getting it for him.

Sipping on the drink, he continued, "On the other hand, lords of the life are merciless. They have no compassion for the weak or those who are not willing to take. They're blood-crazed villains.

They only appreciate cruel acts of violence in the process of making ends meet. The more heinous the hustle, the more they smile and want more. They're never satisfied. They honor and protect those who inflict pain on another willfully. There's only one rule to the situations they officiate: life for the one that's standing, death to the fallen. The lords of the life spare none. They come to the attention of the regulators of earth through their deed. Thus, getting promoted to the rank of lords of the life. The lords were businessmen also, but all of their dealings were underhanded and shady. They specialize in using the fear of bodily harm to lock people into business arrangements. 'Rob, steal, cause pain, or kill' was their motto. They believed in whatever it took to make it happen, do it." He ran it to her the way it was run down to him. "The thug gods are watching over me. That's how I know I'm gonna be a'ight," he finished. Listening to Karonda breathe heavily, he stopped talking and fell back into his thoughts and feelings. One thing was for sure: if Magic was the one laid up in the hospital, someone must have been praying to the King of the heavens for him. Only the almighty Creator of all can overrule the judgment of the lords of life, he thought to himself as he dozed off, joining Karonda in slumber.

Memories of weeks spent in the hospital raced out of his subconscious to the forefront of his awareness as he sit somberly quiet bedside his fallen comrade. Magic's condition had improved since his incident, but with all the wires and tubes running from machine to his body, it was hard to tell if he was expected to fully recover. One machine monitored his blood pressure and heart rate; another moved up and down, pumping air through a two-inch round tube into the lung a bullet from his would-be executioner's gun had pierced. An IV ran to both arms, administering small drops of some type of substance. A fresh white bandage was wrapped around his head, stopping an inch above his eyebrow line. With all the attachments to his body, laid underneath a fresh sheet, Magic looked more like a scientific experiment of Dr. Create-It than a medical patient. Seven of the death enforcers entered his body, damaging everything in their path. One went into his head. A total of eight shots hit their mark. Magic was lucky to be alive. His stickman succumbed to two gunshot wounds, one of the death enforcers entering right above his right eye, exiting out of the back of his head, killing him instantly. The second one, just for surety that he had ceased to be, struck center of mass on his chest, tearing through his heart, clipping his spinal cord on its way out of his body. Failure to communicate or negligence on either of their parts wasn't the reason for their shortcoming; they were doomed from the onset of the thought of the caper. With any caper for high stakes comes an even greater risk. We all know that the streets don't blink an eye or stops listening. When word of what happened on that dreadful afternoon to Magic and his partner floated across the track, it didn't surprise Vietnam. In fact, he never investigated. He knew sooner or later, someone was going to tell all.

Ole dude they intended to sting started off as a stickup kid himself. He was hitting licks years before it became a fad among the youth; therefore, former-armed-robber-turned-drug-dealer, he took extreme precautions to protect his assets from any would-be regulators of cash and properties. He worried more so about jackers ripping him off than the cops busting him. If Magic had done his homework, he would've known that in all the years in the game, the dude never took a loss by way of stickup, and why. The dude stayed game tight. Both houses adjacent to the one he lived in, in addition to the one across the street from his, were owned by him. The house across from his residence was used as a guard shack. The occupants secretly came and went undetected. When one passed by the house, it seemed like another abandoned structure with a well-kept lawn. Thick sheets of plywood were nailed to the doors. Evenly spaced two-by-fours were nailed across every window. To further enhance the vacant appearance, there was a mailbox on the wall overstuffed with weather-exposed articles of mail. Inside, the house was alive, busting with men paid to protect the dude's property. When Magic parked his mission car in the driveway of the house, unknowingly he became a target in the sights of henchmen that were dying to put in work for their keep. Magic and his stickman had the cats at a loss for a hot second. On account of their youth, the men didn't expect them to be robbers.

Initially, they had them tagged as two teens from the neighborhood stashing a stolen vehicle at a vacant house, until Magic's partner showed way too much interest to their boss's residence. Suspicion heightened in the veteran gunman on lookout when he noticed that Magic's stickman was clutching a gun; in that day and age, petty con thieves didn't pack pistols. He alerted the others and zeroed in on them. Magic doing his usual routine, he ran to the back of the supposed-to-be empty house to gear up for the caper. As soon as they darted around back, the gunmen transformed into high-level security mode. The threat was active, and they were more than willing to respond with lethal force. With their boots laced up, strapped down with heavy metal, ready for combat, they filed out of the door. Magic and his partner were so in tuned on their task that they didn't even see or hear three men in mask creep up behind them. Before they stepped onto the dude's residential property, one of the gunmen shouted out to them. Magic was on point, and his stickman was positioned slightly to the rear flank of him. Spinning around to acknowledge the sudden, unexpected disruption of their mission, he was greeted with two quick shots from two of the gunmen's pistols. *Blucka blucka.* Magic turned, firing from the hip, before his partner's body dropped. His shots went wide right, killing a two-by-four on the house across the street. When he fired, he drew fire from all three of the gunmen.

Bullet riddled, Magic lay on the pavement, unconscious, clinging to what little life he had left while he fought with the grim reaper over his soul. The gunmen were erasing any trace of evidence to Magic's attempted caper and their crime. They went through both of the fallen teens' pockets, taking anything of value. After confiscating their candy sticks, they removed Magic's and his partner's disguises so that their bodies wouldn't bring about excessive heat from detectives to their boss's spot. Their final act was ditching Magic's mission car elsewhere. From the beginning to the end, the gunmen did their job in a professional manner. They prevented Magic and his partner from entering their boss's house, and they had the detectives scrambling to put a case together with little or no evidence. Throughout the neighborhood, gunshots were heard, but no one got a description of the shooters. To top that, cops didn't have a clue as to why two teens from Baton Rouge were gunned down in the late afternoon on a quiet street in Baker.

According to the rules of the game, being that Magic fell in the commission of a jacking, retaliating wasn't a must; it was left up to discretion of the fallen homies. Looking at Magic in his vegetative state, Vietnam was confused. He didn't know what to let his heart feel or what to let his mind think. What he did know for sure was that however the chips might have fallen, if he had gone with Magic, it would not have ended well for him. Either Magic's partner's cards would've been dealt to him and it would've been him lying in the morgue, waiting to be planted next to a bunch of strangers, or Magic's hand would've been his to play. In each case, the dealer had the winning hands. Although it appeared that Magic wasn't in a coma, the doctor had him under heavy sedation to prevent him from moving, also to manage the pain derived from all the holes in his body, the ones from the gunshots and theirs in attempt to save his life.

"Thug again soon, nigga," Vietnam whispered to Magic, then he gave him the gangster's salute before he left his friend's side. Violence was a grim reality. *One day it might be me,* he surmised to himself as the door closed behind him. *Up until then, it's back to business,* he further thought.

Sassy had told him the information he needed. She happily fingered the girl Officer Dicken DaBeaudé was involved with as well as the house she lived in. There were a few more hours until phase 1 of his plan went into play. Badly he wanted to get zooted, but he resisted the temptation. He knew that he had to be sharp every step of the way. Some people can function like a champ under the influence of drugs, but Vietnam wasn't one of them. "Time move slow as E-muthafucka when ya not high," he stressed to Li'l Who, who was anxiously waiting to roll with Vietnam on the mission. "Unh-huh" was his only reply. He was deep in thought, fantasizing about all the money he was about to come up on. Vietnam tried to strike up a conversation to get his mind off his second desire, to no avail. Just like every other dealer in the game, he, too, had another vice besides the passion for money. Realizing that Li'l Who wasn't going to be any use as a distraction to the mental storm that was arising in him, finishing peeping out his surroundings for the umpteenth time, he allowed himself to fall into his thoughts also. An unsettling concept occurred to him. Since way back when, he had already decided to ride for his big homie, but he hadn't planned on pulling it off with anyone else. Li'l Who was a perfect candidate for the ride. Along with his heart to squeeze triggers, to deliver death was in question, but all things considered, he definitely wasn't a snitch, which, above all, was the greatest quality one could possess in a gangster's journey, also called life.

The way Vietnam decided to take Li'l Who along with him on the who-came-about wasn't out of goodwill; his decision bothered him slightly now that the moment of truth was ticks away. It really didn't sit well on his conscience. Not too many moons ago, they were close road dogs. Though neither ever mentioned it, things weren't the same. Time had put a gap in their friendship. Things between them were hanging on by mere threads. At one point or another, they found common ground to meet on as far as conversation went. As of late, Li'l Who had become antagonist. But he wasn't antagonizing Vietnam as a person; it was the game that he represented that Li'l Who opposed. Initially, he had written it off as Li'l Who being Li'l Who, the one that ribbed everyone and stayed with a wisecrack, but then over a period of time, the conversation would turn hostile when the subject about the game got thrown around. Vietnam would be on the defense, defending the game, while Li'l Who vigorously opposed it. On one occasion, in the midst of a heated debate, Li'l Who indirectly, in so many words, proclaimed that people who get theirs out of the mud are third-class citizens that don't deserve to be sharing the same air that hardworking, honest-living folks breathe.

Heart, body, and soul, Vietnam was street. When his friend looked him in the eyes and said what he said about hustlers, there wasn't any other way he could have taken it but as a personal insult. Although they had some fond memories together, loyalty being deeply embedded within him, it was hard, but reluctantly Vietnam had made up his mind to sever all ties with Li'l Who based on that comment that he made and adamantly stood behind. Offensively, the matter in which he voiced his opinion wasn't serious enough to move on him, but it did strike a sensitive chord, causing Vietnam to feel that his transgression against him and the game did warrant the deliverance of a negative response, so he plotted. The act of vengeance had been postponed, then lost in the shuffle of life and plenty of killa and cigarettes dipped in genie water, then totally forgotten. Vietnam didn't give what had taken place between his friend and him any more thought until he came around, reaching out to him for help. Li'l Who wanted to make some quick money. He approached Vietnam, seeking professional assistance, which Vietnam didn't mind. In fact, he was enthused about the prospect of Li'l Who and him back together again, working the playground like groundkeepers. Vietnam proposed that he'd front him want he needed plus allow him to serve his clientele until he got on his feet. Li'l Who turned his offer down—not only did he decline his offer, but he also audaciously stated that he'd never be a low-life dope pusher. Then he specified in dictatorial fashion exactly how he wanted to be helped out of his financial crisis. Vietnam's first impulse was to hit him with a ferocious three-piece combination to his face, then send him on his way with a kick to his backside to finish it off, the way presumptuous dope fiends were being handled. But instead, he agreed to meet his demands.

Vietnam devised a scheme to get even with him. He started beating the bush, searching for the most dangerous capers to pull off in the most hostile environment he could find. The catch was, Li'l Who was going to be laying dealers down with an unloaded pistol. Eventually, he came to realize that the chosen course of action was too cruel and cutthroat. So he abandoned that plan. High as the stars off his favorite potion, considering a just punishment for Li'l Who, he glared at his hands, then his feet, his face. After further examining his person for injuries, he questioned himself, "Why are you heated with Li'l Who?" Then he admitted to himself, "'Cause da nigga touched me." And he further inquired himself, "Where?" As soon as he answered himself, he knew what it was going to be.

Li'l Who had hit him with a mental jab. In order to get even or one-up, he had to counter with a mental jab of his own. He had just the plan to rock and daze him. Coming out of his thought or daydream, he stated, looking over at Li'l Who, "Say, my nigga."

"What?" he angrily answered.

Vietnam stared at him momentarily. *Still on your high horse, looking down your nose at me,* he thought. *Even though the game ain't fair, kid, you still gotta play fair.* "Check this out. My people slang'n pounds of dat good bud for two hundred and fifty dollars. If you cop ten or more, I'll hit ya with twenty-five hundred to get right," he stated, giving him a way out.

The tone of voice Li'l Who had used to answer him or his facial expression had earned him a pardon. If Monk's words hadn't rung in his head, though he intended to, he wouldn't have green-lighted him a way out. With the future in his eye and time on his side, he could always cross him readily, he figured.

Even in a vindictive state, he still remained true to the game first. Square business weighed more heavily on his mind than revenge did. There wasn't anything square about keeping your partner in crime in the blind about a mission. This mission wasn't an ordinary one; it was one that was going to shake up the city, all the way to the state capitol building. It was going to be talked about.

"Dude, I already done told you that me slang'n, it ain't happening. We gon' do this thang you got on deck. After that, I'm going my way and you do what you do," he vehemently replied.

"Look, how much bread ya need?" Vietnam asked. Li'l Who didn't reply. "Anyway, dog, right now you can get off oh pound for six or seven c-notes a pope. After da flip, that's six or seven G's easy. You touch me back with the twenty-five, you still got forty-five notes, then you take twenty-five of them, cop ten more thangs, and still have two Gs to play with. That's love, homie," Vietnam stated convincingly, painting a vivid picture of the cop-and-flip. "Shied, you might can get eight for it," he added to make it sound even sweeter. After he finished throwing his recruiter pitch, he flashed an artificial right smile.

"I'm good, no dice, thug," Li'l Who replied.

"Sho ya right," Vietnam retorted, ending the conversation.

Both watched the tracks quietly, waiting for their getaway vehicle to cross it. Every so often, Vietnam peered at Li'l Who, wondering how he was going to react when the truth came to light about the caper. He chuckled, imagining the priceless look that was going to be on his face. *Joke's on you, nigga,* he thought. Then that was when it occurred to him. Li'l Who's reaction was unpredictable, but the damage from the rounds of the loaded handgun that was going to be in his palms once they started to fly was very much predictable. "Fuck," he mumbled. The wise say, "If one plays with fire, there's a good chance of getting burned." Vietnam intensely stared at his ace boon coon.

Death's going to become someone else, along with Officer Dicken DaBeaudé, and it damn sure won't be me, he thought. All Li'l Who had to do was glance to his left and he would have called the whole ordeal off. The look in Vietnam's eyes was as telling as a codefender turned state evidence. He hadn't become street enough to be savvy with the mischief that awaited him from the cold stare. Fault of his own, he never looked. He presented himself as one that was ready for the life. Before the jump-off jumped off, Li'l Who had made a costly error, one that caused many men to have their name typed on death certificates. He didn't pay any attention to his stickman. According to Magic, there was only one reason not to give your partner a look-over in the game of stick-and-move, the reason being one didn't care about their stickman's condition because he had a different outcome planned once the mission was completed. Vietnam read people like an astronomer read the night sky. Whether what he picked up from Li'l Who's demeanor was in fact his own mind deceiving him or he was accurate was yet to be told. He saw something that had him second-guessing his plot for revenge, not on the account of Li'l Who or his safety, but because the mission could be compromised. There was too much money, thought, and energy put into it to allow that to happen. Li'l Who wasn't fidgeting like a new jack going to hit his first caper; he was calm, like someone that was sure. Vietnam picked up on that as soon as he posted up with him. There wasn't anything disturbing about that, though it didn't go undetected. Some people are natural in everything they do.

Closer to the time to pull out, the red flag came up during their brief politicking. Li'l Who kept his remarks short, and he didn't give Vietnam the usual eye contact when they spoke. Taking that as a sign that something was afoot, Vietnam could sense his nerves shift to another gear. Paranoia got added among the other phycological things that were going on with him. Uncertain, he invoked the voice for guidance. "Ain't no right or wrong when life or death is on the line. It's your call, baby," the voice said in his ear. Vietnam sighed, then went into that empty space in his mind.

"You quiet as death back there," Double D stated, following his statement with a sly snicker the way one would do when they were privy to an inside joke. Vietnam peeked over at Li'l Who to see if he caught the witty remark in what was said before he replied.

"Just drive, nigga, an' don't worry about us," he commanded.

Double D glared through the rearview mirror at Vietnam. A wisecrack had formulated in his mouth, but he held his tongue. Under different circumstances, him complying without a remark would've been an oddity, but things had changed. Double D wasn't anyone's dummy. He knew that Vietnam was armed and deadly; that added with the fact that lately he'd been having a hair-trigger temper, he didn't want to do anything to provoke him. They were certainly on a mission to commit evil; therefore, wickedness was already pumping through his veins. It wouldn't have been nothing for the tides to shift and he found himself taking the brunt of someone else's intended act. Driver or no driver, it was clear to him that he was expendable. He, too, avoided further eye contact with Vietnam.

Vietnam didn't pick up the switch of Double D's attitude; he was busy studying the back of Li'l Who's head, contemplating. Quickly he could lift and fire the candy stick he had been clutching, exposed, cocked, and ready on the side of his leg since he took the beat seat of their mission car. Luckily during the entire ride to their destination, Li'l Who didn't make a sudden turn in his seat. If he had, his brain would have been splattered all over the windshield. Paranoia had settled his brain and was riding him like the dragon he had on his back. It had gotten so bad for a minute that he suspected that Double D was plotting his demise. Relief from his thoughts came when Double D parked the car. It was game time. Vietnam's foot was the first to touch the ground; he jumped out of the car with purpose, hoping that the faster he got out of and away from the enclosure of the vehicle, the faster his paranoia would recede. The paranoia was still underlined, though thoughts of the mission had suppressed it. Kicking into autopilot, he let his legs take the course. Everything that was to happen the second the car came to a halt had been played over in his mind more times than he could count.

Li'l Who and Double D matched his stride. Double D came along as a lookout, and once they were secure in their location, that task ended, then it was on to his next one, as getaway driver. From the observation of a casual observer, they looked like man and children strolling through the neighborhood under the moonlight innocently. What they didn't look like was a group up to no good. That was why Vietnam decided that Double D should walk with them. Two kids mobbing after dark, someone would've had them under microscope. Vietnam crept alongside of the car parked in the yard, then he jetted out between the house into the darkness, Li'l Who right on his trail. Double D posted up on the sidewalk directly in front of the house Officer Dicken DaBeaudé frequented. His instruction was to scan the streets for potential witness, then once the boys were out of sight, he was to head back to the car, keeping it running until they returned. It took less than one minute for them to duck out of sight. Double D marched off while Vietnam and Li'l Who positioned themselves in perfect ambush locations.

Nothing's for certain when evil is involved. Anything can transpire. A million scenarios spun in his mind while he anxiously waited for Officer Dicken DaBeaudé to roll up. As more ticks slowly passed by, the wilder the scenes in his head became. As Vietnam glanced around, lying beneath the house, he realized there wasn't much to be seen in the dark. His eyes fell on the shadowy figure of Li'l Who lying motionless. He was lying on his stomach, arms folded out front, with his head resting on them calmly. Too calm, Vietnam thought. Li'l Who's state of easiness played into the preposterous premonitions that were roaming over his head. Three bodies laid out after the smoke cleared was the vision that replayed over and over in his mind's eyes. Opening his mouth, he abruptly snapped it shut. To talk now would go against his own instruction. Speaking would not only reveal to Li'l Who that he wasn't as disciplined as he put out to be, but any other noise besides the natural sounds of the night would also alert anyone who happened to hear him to their whereabouts, which could be drastic for the plan and fatal for anyone who was brave enough to investigate. Apprehension by the police or injury that could lead to death for him or Li'l Who by the hands of another wasn't going to happen on his watch; that would be considered a failure. Failure isn't in the vocabulary of those who play for keeps. In Vietnam's heart, he was the keeper of the game.

Underneath the house, the temperature was considerably cooler than it was out in the open. Air was freely flowing. The space wasn't tight, yet to Vietnam it was stifling. He was about to reposition himself when the beam of headlights bouncing up the street caught him in the act. He then steeled and readied himself for action. He glanced over at Li'l Who. If he was on point, he didn't give any indication of being so. He was still in the same position when he looked over to him previously.

"Psst," Vietnam let out as quietly as he could without running a risk. Li'l Who didn't respond. "Psssstt!" This time he let it drag out longer. A reaction. Li'l Who moved his head off his folded arms, glanced toward Vietnam, nodded once, then focused in on creeping to the car. From his side of the house, he had a clear view of everything rolling on North Seventeenth Street, turning off Chestnut. On the other hand, Vietnam's view was obscured from Mulberry Street. Vietnam relaxed when the sound of the vehicle engine reached his ears. Officer Dicken DaBeaudé drove a Trans-Am. What he was hearing was the bad roaring of a clunker with a damaged muffler. He loosened his body when the car cruised on past him, but not his grip around the handle of his candy stick. Vietnam never once considered another alternative to settle the beef he had with Officer Dicken DaBeaudé. Verbally he lacked the skills to express anger appropriately—in some cases, talking is always a much better way to resolve an issue with someone than with violence. If someone could've suggested a powwow with the officer, he would've laughed and walked away, then most likely added their name to the list of sworn foes for even advocating on the officer's behalf.

In many cases, the streets teach the participates the finer points of conflict resolution. Officer Dicken DaBeaudé took something valuable from Vietnam, which in turn, unbeknownst to him, initiated a conflict where death was the only resolution. Vietnam's heart was set on applying his learning. Late fall, the nights were quieter and calmer than the preceding season's nights. In the distance, the humming of air-conditioner units still in use could be heard. Every now and then, the whisper of the cool breeze blowing by could be heard when he listened closely. When they first sneaked under the house, the variety of footsteps above and around them had him jumpy. Now they were a part of the rest of the noises he tuned out. Blocking out every peep, even Li'l Who's breathing, he strained his ear to its maximum capacity. The old clunker had been drowned out by the sound of dual pipes from a truck's engine. *Oh, please, God, let dat be him,* he thought. Lights from ultrabeams flooded down Mulberry Street, getting brighter by the second. The lights were broad, but the beam danced closer to the pavement, which meant that the unseen vehicle had to be sitting low. *Rrruummm.* The driver pressed the gas, the sound sending static through him. Though sports cars awed him, the feeling came more from knowing that phase 3 was ticks away from going into effect than fascination of fast cars, adding to the excitement.

It wasn't long before vision confirmed the signal he had heard zip to his brain earlier. Even in darkness, the candy paint on the T-top Trans-Am shone. Glossy, its rims flipped like ninja stars, cutting through the air as the vehicle reared. From his location, it wasn't possible to clearly identify the driver, but the silhouette closely resembled that of Officer Dicken DaBeaudé. That was all it took for Vietnam to spring into action. On his stomach, he rose, propping himself on all fours. The position that he was in made it very uncomfortable to tie the bandanna around his face. Maneuvering in the tight space caused his neck to spasm and cramp when he lowered his head to secure it, then when he made an attempt to crawl from underneath the house, his legs cramped up as well. Good thing the plan wasn't to gun him down while he was still sitting behind the wheel of his car. Although Officer Dicken DaBeaudé hesitated getting down out of his car, time would've still been against them. As most people do when they roll up and park, scanning the area is the first order before exiting their vehicle. Officer Dicken DaBeaudé scanned then rescanned the area. If Vietnam was on his way out, he would have been spotted in between the scan sessions. Slow as he was moving, battling with his lack of sodium or potassium, whichever was the culprit, if the officer was on point, it was certain that a death enforcer might have greeted him on his way out of their hiding spot.

Unaware of the aches Vietnam was going through, Li'l Who eyed him through the dark, ready, waiting for him to make his first move as planned. Before the car had come to a complete stop, he had started to suit up. As a law enforcement agent, Officer Dicken DaBeaudé had sworn to protect and serve the community. No different from a street player, he had a passion for women. Good for the crooks; instead of chasing them, he was out chasing tail. Half-ignoring them, half-relieved from the muscle cramps, Vietnam was set, moving. Officer Dicken DaBeaudé cracked his door ajar. The inside of the car illuminated against the gloom of night, forming him, turning what was a silhouette into a form of flesh. Vietnam's heart started to beat erratically from the hormonal release of a heavy dose of adrenaline pumped into his bloodstream. *Gotcha! It's showtime!* he thought, smiling behind the bandanna. Officer Dicken DaBeaudé was messing with something inside of the vehicle when Vietnam eased closer to the edge of the house. In true ambush style, he was going to let off his first shot from underneath the house, then hop to his feet, running up close, finishing the job.

Li'l Who crept forward also. "Say," he whispered.

Vietnam ignored him. He saw what had frozen Li'l Who also, but he knew beforehand who their target was; therefore, realization didn't stun him. Officer Dicken DaBeaudé was styling and profiling in his personal vehicle, but he was still in a Baton Rouge City Police uniform.

"G," Li'l Who said quietly.

"What?" Vietnam replied in equal tone. He kept his eyes on his prey. The policeman came around the front of the car. Vietnam aimed.

"Man, we gon' jack five-o?" Li'l Who asked a decibel higher than a whisper.

Officer Dicken DaBeaudé moved as if he were late. He snatched the passenger door open.

Still stuck in place, he pleaded, "Is we?" after a stretch of silence from Vietnam, who couldn't answer because he was choking down an outburst of laughter. The fright in Li'l Who's voice was hilarious to him. Another part of his plan had shaped up. "Ha?" for the third time, he pressed for an answer.

Officer Dicken DaBeaudé retrieved a white plastic bag and a six-pack of what looked like wine coolers from within the car. He placed the wine coolers on the roof of the car, frisking himself. After finding whatever it was he was feeling for, he slammed the car door shut. As he spun with the bag in one hand and wine coolers in the other, his unbuttoned uniform shirt flopped open. A bright-yellow jaguar with SU written in block letters over its head in matching colors sat in the middle of his chest, staring out at the world. Unsuspectingly, the policeman took a step forward, merchandise in hand. Vietnam flashed to the empty space in his mind that he would later fill with images of Big Ed and Officer Dicken DaBeaudé as well.

"Nah, I'm 'bout to knock his ass off," Vietnam finally replied.

In a trillion years, Officer Dicken DaBeaudé would not have guessed that his next step was going to be the last one he ever made forward. When his foot kicked out and planted, the yard exploded into light like he had tripped a land mine. The muzzle flash was blindingly bright. The night's quiet fled the area. The candy stick report was amplified by the confines beneath the house. Normally, in close quarters, the blast from a .45 handgun would be deafening. Vietnam was too pumped for the sound to faze him; he fired again, this time bracing himself for the mechanical action and reaction of the firearm. His first bullet made good behind the flash. He didn't see when the impact rocked the policeman. A second shot was fired for safety.

Arms away from his side, head down, Officer Dicken DaBeaudé stared at his midsection. Releasing both items from his hand, the glass bottles bursting on contact with the ground, simultaneously he cried out in agony a nanosecond before the third of the death enforcers went through the jaguar's mouth.

Vietnam crawled all the way from underneath the house. Springing to his feet, arms extended, he moved like a trained assassin toward the wounded man. No mercy in his eyes. The second bullet forced him backward. Still standing, Officer Dicken DaBeaudé frantically reached for his hips, then he ran his hand to his waist front as he watched Vietnam close in on him. When he took off his bulletproof vest and utility belt, he had removed his service pistol as well. They missed it when he tucked it behind his waistband. Vietnam was close enough on him to smell the boiled crawfish that had spilled out of the Tony's Seafood bag. Keeping a jacker's distance away from him, waiting, at first glance, he noticed there was a small circle around the holes in his T-shirt, then the blood began to spread rapidly, covering larger areas. Weakness from the death enforcers that invaded his body, or fear, had caused a minimal task to become a struggle. Every movement he made, the pain registered on his face, then it happened. Vietnam waited until Officer Dicken DaBeaudé armed himself, then he opened fire. Stepping in closer, the barrel of the candy stick a foot away from his chest, he cut loose in rapid session. *Blucka blucka blucka blucka.* With every pull of the trigger, the .45 bucked, jarring his aim. Though off target, they all hit near it.

Officer Dicken DaBeaudé made one fluid movement when death enforcers slammed into him; head, shoulder, body, knees, and toes joined together and did the "murder man" dance when the barrage of bullets struck him. The fine mist of blood from the blowback from the bullets covered Vietnam like fine particles of dust. Officer Dicken DaBeaudé fell on his back pockets, partially jackknifed, feet up on the curb. His head rested against his shiny Trans-Am. The bloody mass of his body slouched in the gap between the car and the curb. Vietnam stood over him. Street justice had been delivered swiftly. Officer Dicken DaBeaudé raised his head up. He stared out, eyes wild in disbelief. Blood spewed from his mouth and dripped on the shoulder of his already-blood-soaked T-shirt. He made a gurgling sound as his lungs filled with blood. The once-boyish face was now twisted into a mask of sheer agonizing horror as he struggled to take in oxygen, his eyes wide with panic, a true sign that he was witnessing the death angel descend on him. The fallen policeman coughed weakly, gasped, then stillness followed. Vietnam's nostrils flared. He smelled a sharp odor. Officer Dicken DaBeaudé's bowels had released, the stench rising over the smell of boiled crawfish and copper. The policeman was dead as dead can get. Head leaning to the side, a string of blood dripping from his agape mouth. Vietnam pressed the barrel in his ear. He pulled the trigger. *Blucka.* The slug to the head snapped his neck, knocking his body over onto his side. Vietnam didn't see the damage the bullet had caused on its way out. One can only imagine the damage a hollow-point .45 would do to a skull and the brain it protects. No time to waste, he scooped up the dead policeman's service gun, tucked it away, still locked and loaded, with his, then he picked up the bag of crawfish. He tucked his candy stick away and pulled the bandanna down to his neck while he walked to his flee-the-scene vehicle. Good thing he never looked back—a nosy neighbor was peeking out of his window when he strode by, swinging the bag of warm boiled crawfish.

Li'l Who booked out as soon as the shooting started; he dashed through the preplanned getaway route in record-breaking speed. The route was simple. Haul ass across the backyard of Officer Dicken DaBeaudé's broad's house, jump the fence between the houses on the next street, then get extralight up the block to where Double D was parked. While the policeman's body was falling, Li'l Who was diving into the back seat of the mission car, yelling hysterically for Double D to put his feet to the gas.

There's no way to predict human actions. Even if the person in question has been known for a lifetime, one can never really say what they may do in situations. A person may have been evil since day 1 and, moments before a situation arises, may be touched by the Lord, causing that person to do the godly thing instead of exhibiting the expected behavior. When planning a caper, foresight is a critical ingredient of the recipe.

Vietnam knew that in order to pull off the near-perfect assassination, nothing could be overlooked or considered as minor. Every little detail had to be viewed seriously and considered. Vietnam instructed Sassy to hang loose on the corner of North Eighteenth and Chestnut Street while Double D waited on North Sixteenth Street. To keep Double D in the blind, despite his loyalty to him, Vietnam instructed him that no matter who made it to the car first, he was to pull off without any hesitation and, by all means, not come searching for the other one, knowing very well he was going to be the missing party. Several reasons being, in case later on, in the investigation of the homicide, when description of the suspects hit the air, if someone so happened to remember seeing them hop out of the ride driven by Double D, no one would be able to testify to seeing Li'l Who and him returning to the waiting vehicle. Neither Li'l Who nor Double D knew it, but Vietnam hadn't planned on rolling back across the track with them unless necessary. Secondly, instead of guessing, leaving which direction the authorities were going to zoom in from to chance, Vietnam strategically had one vehicle waiting a street behind where the hit was taking place, and another a street ahead; both were within quick jogging distance from the scene. The coup de grâce was that if the shots fired would've drawn spectators, they would have witnessed people fleeing in opposite directions from each other, away from the fallen off-duty policeman.

Vietnam placed the bag of crawfish on the floor, adjusting both candy sticks to a less compromising position. He then lowered himself into the car, slamming the door shut, concealing the blaring music that had escaped into the neighborhood back into the vehicle. Sassy questionably stared at him. She had foreknowledge of the hit, but from Vietnam's body language, she couldn't determine if he had completed his mission or not. He felt her peering gaze. Childishly he refused to look at her, believing that his features would be telling. Finding humor in the suspense, he turned right, looked out of the passenger window at a television through the window of the house they were parked in front of. Sassy twisted the dial of the volume button backward. At the lowering of the music, Vietnam faced her, giving her a silly look. She bucked her eyes, rolled her head, crossed her arms; her body posture was as if to ask, "Ha?" Suppressing an abrupt laughter, Vietnam glanced sideways—tires smoking to Chestnut Street was the answer. Sassy's face went slack. Blue lights alternating with red didn't have to speak; the police unit turning off Scenic Highway, gliding between flashes and pulsating burst rapidly, flew through the air toward them.

"Go!" Vietnam yelled.

Sassy exhaled loudly, and with the precision of a professional getaway driver, she eased off the curb, squaring the vehicle slowly. She accelerated up the street. Two more units fishtailed onto Chestnut one after the other. In the distance, the blue lights of more units approaching, filling the air like lightning over a clear horizon.

Stopping at the stop sign, Sassy glanced over at Vietnam. He noticed, even with her features expressionless, she was still beautiful. Her freckles seemed three-dimensional, jumping out of her face. Features of the dashboard and the glowing surrounding lights danced over her face as she pulled into traffic with much tension. She gripped the steering wheel. Vietnam was lusting over her too hard to notice that she choked the steering wheel to hide her nervously shaking hands. In his mind, he was just another youngster putting in work; to her, she was in fact sitting next to a child killer, also an accessory after the fact to the murder of an off-duty police officer. Units urgently shot past them. In the rearview mirror, more units were coming up Scenic Highway. Cops were descending into the neighborhood from every direction, and with every passing roller, she glanced at him. To her disbelief, stunningly, Vietnam was cool as the day before; he didn't show any remorse or concern. He looked like a teenager in the presence of a girl whom he had a crush on. She didn't have to worry about him causing her any harm, but suddenly she became afraid of him. The air in the car became thick. Sassy's feet became heavy, and her hands shook uncontrollably. Deep down in the pit of her gut, something had begun to churn. As they came out of the Lake, entering the Top neighborhood of the Southside, a strong desire to pull over the car, hop out, and run came over her. Only thing that held her back was that in her quest for riches, he greedily accepted an extra five hundred dollars to drop him back in

South Baton Rouge after he did the deed. Easy enough. Not. It took everything in her power to steel herself.

She squirmed in her seat. If it weren't for her two-dollar designer jeans, she would have given up the fight by letting her bladder relax. *Uncomfortable* would be a compliment to how she felt. The more she looked over at Vietnam, the drearier she became. In deep prayer, making vain promise to God to never do anymore wrong, she ran a red light. Vietnam stared at her. *Oh god, get a grip on yourself,* she thought, easing up on the pedal. Afraid to meet his eyes, she focused ahead. He turned, and she stole a peek at him. In that interval, a vehicle had stopped at the four-way stop on East Boulevard and Julia. She slammed on brakes, the car screeching to a halt within inches from kissing its back bumper.

"What da fuck?" Vietnam expressed.

"Please, I'm sorry, baby," she whined, voice trembling, on the verge of tears. "Ugh!" she cried, slamming her head on the steering wheel. Sassy's internal loss of control had surfaced. She rocked back and forth in her seat, tears in her eyes. Vietnam placed his hand on her thigh. She jumped at his touch, cringing away from him, pressing herself against the car door. Wide-eyed, she looked like a terrified child. The vehicle behind them impatiently pulled around them, the driver angrily waving his hand as he passed them. Vietnam glanced around. Though he was no psychologist, it was evident that he witnessed Sassy have a nervous breakdown. Her eyes were closed.

"Sassy, please drive," Vietnam pleaded. "We gotta go."

In the middle of the block, passersby started to stop and stare. Vietnam's thoughts were jumbled as he pondered his next move. Subsequently, the feel of cold steel against his flesh with its weight riding his hip became increasingly noticeable. *Fuck dis,* he thought. He opened the door, and the sudden rush of light into the car did the trick.

Sassy sighed, mumbling something. Vietnam, one foot out of the car, looked back at her. The color that drained from her face was returning, accompanied with a smirk. "You a'ight?" he asked. She nodded slowly, straightened up behind the wheel, then combed her fingers through her hair. She smirked, cautiously gazing at her.

Lifting his foot, he fell back into the seat, closing the door. "You sho' you a'ight, Sassy?" he asked weakly.

"I'm good," she replied, pulling out into the intersection without looking left and right. Good thing that the traffic signal was green, because she didn't give any indication that she was going to yield or stop.

As they turned onto West Roosevelt Street off Thomas H. Delpit Drive, Vietnam's shoulder rammed the door. Sassy didn't drop speed as she turned the sharp corner. When they coasted through a yellow light on Highland Road, a patrol hidden behind a parked car in Quick Sack parking lot fell in behind them. Vietnam saw him when they dipped past him. "Them peoples…" He couldn't get the rest out; he was hot on their tail. His headlights beamed, surrounding them. Sassy didn't flinch; she stayed on course, hands ten and two, back straight, head forward, still smirking. Vietnam was on the edge, mouth stuck closed. Mentally he was trying to will her to hit the gas, shaking the cop, or pull over so that he could jump out and run with the hot candy stick. The cop tailgated for a couple of blocks. So far, he didn't flash his lights. Officially, they were to the good. Vietnam hoped that it stayed that way. Up ahead, the traffic signal light on Nicholson Drive was on red. Nervousness crept through his body. Since her breakdown, none of the traffic laws had been abided by her. Streetwise enough to know to never look back or turn suddenly when five-o was sweating, he rotated his cranium slightly to the left, then glanced out of the corner of his eye at Sassy.

Beautiful without a doubt, but he didn't like what he was seeing. She was rigged stiff, like she was bracing for impact—at least that was how he read it. He braced himself. However it went down, getting caught wasn't a part of his plan. On the slick side, he readjusted the candy stick to where it didn't slide down his pants leg when he jetted out of the car. They were now coming up on Nicholson Drive, and Doc's Laundromat was in sight. Light was still red. *If this bitch run this light, it's curtains,* he thought, hand on the door handle, a lump in his throat, holding his breath. She did it; the car eased to a complete stop. They weren't in the clear yet. The light changed to green, but the car didn't move. Sassy had her arms on the steering wheel, with her face buried on her hands. *Oh fuck,* he thought. "Go, go, go!" he panically yelled out. *Whoop whoop!* the siren wailed, flashing blue lights filling their car along with the ultraviolet rays of the police unit's headlights. "Muthafucka!" Vietnam expressed, pulling the door handle to dash. The car propelling forward stopped him short. Confused, he gazed at her. Smiling, Sassy nodded at him. There wasn't any comfort to the situation to be found in her smile; he was ready to do what all outlaws did when the law was coming down on them and they weren't prepared to hold court or take that ride—that is, take flight.

Surprisingly, the cop pulled around them, killing the emergency flashers. Vietnam stared after the police unit in shock as it vanished over the tracks. Apparently, the officer wanted to be somewhere else but they were in his way.

In many cases, traffic stops turn to busts because the driver panics or the passenger gets nervous and moves bad, causing the officer to investigate more closely. The word about Officer Dicken DaBeaudé lying in the gutter, body punctured with .45 slugs, hadn't reached the Bottom yet. Other than the police casting a dragnet over Northdale for leads, no one was on the radar, but his guilt almost caused him to act erratically. True, he had two burning-hot pistols on him. Ordinarily, if Sassy's credentials, along with the paperwork to the car, were on the up, the officer would have written her a ticket for her infraction, sending her on her way without bothering the passenger. In theory, that was how it would go. But Vietnam, always when in doubt, put the code before logic. The officer's actions couldn't be predicted. Running, ditching the guns was the best option. Crossing the tracks, he was still ready to beat his feet on the concrete. Seeing that the police unit didn't stop in the vicinity, he allowed himself to ease up, though not fully.

All the pressure about anything going sour on his mind left when Sassy stopped in front of Karonda's house. A change came about her. She no longer seemed stressed. She was still squirming in her seat, but her expression was settled. Pushing the door open, Vietnam energetically leaped to the sidewalk. The bag had turned over. As he gathered up the loose crawfish, Sassy noticed them for the first time. "Ooo-wee, them crawfish sell some good!" she cheerfully said. "Where ya git them from?" she asked.

"Ole boy," Vietnam replied.

The glow in her face dimmed. "Ole boy?" she repeated.

"Yeah, um, Officer Dicken DaBeaudé. Want some?" he asked, handing her the bag.

Sassy's hand shot up to her mouth. With her free hand, she swung her door open and leaned out of the car, the liquid bile oozing between her fingers before she could remove her hand. She called Earl, vomit splashing over the street, emptying the contents of her stomach. She slung the bile off her hand, wiping the remainder on her leg. Vietnam stood stiffly at her display of weakness, in shock. "Close my door!" she yelled, dry-heaving when her gaze was fixed on the bag, her hands up, using them to shield it from her sight. When the dome light went out, she peeled off, leaving him planted there with a stuck-on-stupid look on his mug, until her car disappeared out of sight into the night.

Karonda was delighted to receive the bag of crawfish. To express her gratitude, she reciprocated with a tighter-than-usual hug and a juicy, lingering kiss. Her lips were pressed hard against his, causing a feel-good type of pain that eased several minutes after she backed away. Relaxed, lounging on the sofa, puffing on a cigarette, Vietnam watched in amazement as Karonda and her siblings devoured the mudbugs. It was hard for him to fathom how a cuisine could bring so much joy and excitement to a person. They say Louisiana food is for the soul. The boy giggled, fighting with the crawfish like action figures. Her little sister was studying them, trying to figure out a way to peel them without getting her little fingers messy. In the midst of keeping an eye on her baby sister, making sure she didn't get frustrated with the tedious task of deshelling the farmed crustacean then, in turn, start eating them, shell and all, along with feeding herself, she stole a glance at him, smiling bright enough to light a dark room when their peepers meet. With a few of them peeled, she extended her hand, offering them to him. Not a fan of boiled seafood, he declined with a shake of his head. Very assertive, she stood up, stepped over her little brother, who now had his older brother's mud-bug pinned down for the three-count, and walked up to him, and realizing what was going down, knowing that protesting was useless, he parted his lips. Without hesitation, one by one she gently shoved the pile of meaty crawfish tails into his mouth. He chewed. A furnace felt like it had been lit in the inside of him. If someone was to ask, he couldn't explain to them if it was the delicious taste of the food, her hand feeding them to him, or the sparkle in her big eyes, which he held, refusing to look away from, that had him feeling all warm under his skin. The mood surrounding them was light, everyone in high spirits, though Vietnam wasn't as joyous as his girlfriend and her siblings were. Looking around, he had to admit to himself the vibe was right. Tranquil moments in a hustler's life are miles apart. Unfortunately, when they occur, they're never long-lived. Over time he learned to grasp those moments, imprison them in his mind for later enjoyment.

Taking in the scene once again before it took flight, he said to himself, "This is how it is in a perfect world. Everyone jolly, like ole Saint Nick." He averted his gaze to the block. Sadly, even in a so-called perfect world, time had its way of quieting laughter and turning smiles upside down, he thought. As he floated in between emotions and reality, the pull in both directions was strong. Like a G was supposed to do, he managed to remain neutral. His feelings back to reality, he realized no much time had elapsed since he left the other side most likely the crime scene was still active crawling with cops trying to make head out of tails. Streetwise, Vietnam knew he wasn't out of the frying pan until he shed the extra weight he was packing.

"Look, hon, I'm 'bout to blaze," he told Karonda, pushing off the sofa. She jumped to her feet. Feigning sadness, she cried at the mention of news, "Why? It's still early. At least after the news go off."

Officer Dicken DaBeaudé's face popped up. Blinking away the image, Karonda watched him closely, waiting for a reply. He couldn't speak. Suddenly, he was lapsed in his mental function. In the presence of another person wasn't how he wanted to relive the act. That was a private matter. He had never been tested in that area before. Hearing his work be described in detail and seeing the aftermath on television before he did his meditating ritual might cause him to lose self-control. Although staying was a much better action than going, running the risk of slipping in front of Karonda wasn't something he wanted to chance. His hesitation in responding made her examine him. Surely, she was going to pick up on the slightest tick from him.

Finally, after what seemed like forever, he said, "I can't. I gotta handle sumthang 'fore I go in." He stepped the first and third step off her porch. He was on the walkway.

"Wait!" she pleaded.

He spun to face Karonda, who was standing on the second step with her arms stretched out. He walked over to her, and she placed them on his shoulder. "My hands dirty, boy. Hug me," she stated. Vietnam grabbed her around her slim waist, pulling her against him. His face rested in her tender, firm young bosom. Loosening his grip, he sank into her large soft eyes before he released her from his embrace. "Thank you again. See ya later," she said politely. Quickly marching away, afraid that she might see the bulge in the front of his jeans, he yelled, "Bet!" without looking back. As he mobbed down the street, he decided his first order of business was to stash the pistol, followed by an hour of masturbating.

Days following the slaying of Officer Dicken DaBeaudé, grinding and thugging went on as usual. Drugs continued to be flipped without interference, while player moves were being made without interruptions. It was a good time to be in the game. The streets were jumping. Vietnam sat proudly on his throne of painted iron and wood, scanning his kingdom, collecting money. Meanwhile, the cats in Northdale couldn't squeeze a penny out of a nickel. Five-o wasn't letting them breathe without smelling their breath for the right odor. Baton Rouge City Police Officers' presence was highly noted. Every department within the city came together to solve the murder of their brother in blue. Investigators went door-to-door, day and night, asking questions.

Plainclothes officers took over the blocks throughout the neighborhood the dealers had up and running. Some of the blocks had been established through enduring many hardships on the trade, others by lead and blood; however they established their dope spots, they couldn't do anything about the loss of their spot to the police but accept it. Evicting new tenants of their real estate damn sure wasn't going to happen. One had to be a certified madman to confront them about their takeover. One cat passed by the cops and openly expressed his grievance about their presence and got handled badly by the coppers. After they finished with him, he had to have reconstruction surgery. The policemen posted up, lounging in old cars, smoking Joes, talking trash, and stunting; they exhibited the same swagger as the very ones they locked away. When they first hit the block, a lot of the customers were fooled by their behavior and demeanor. Being as much a part of the streets as hustlers were, they knew the lingo as well. By the time the person realized they were trying to score drugs from the police, it was too late. Several of them got canned for various charges and outstanding warrants, others left with warnings. A few dealers got crafty, opening up shop elsewhere, not knowing that the police department had cops hovering the area, on the lookout for such a thing. Their impatience bit them hard, causing more in the end than what the package they sold was worth. Most were lucky to make three sales before their door came flying off the hinges. Whoever was in the house when the tactical team entered, male or female, was brutalized, then tortured to tell before they were hauled off to first district for processing.

The game was on lock. Nothing moved. It was so tight around Northdale not even the prostitutes up and down Scenic Highway were able to sell their goods. Two nights of a full-court press campaign removed the working girls from the area also. Those who withstood the harassment the first night finally folded their hands the second night and pushed out, relocating to Plank Road, where they were met with strong opposition from the transsexual male prostitutes out there selling "shit pussy." By the time the females were forced to move around, everyone in North America that watched the news knew that in Baton Rouge, Louisiana, an off-duty officer in uniform had been murdered, but word of how much heat had come down in Northdale as a result of the killing hadn't traveled the city streets to the Southside neighborhood yet. When the females arrived on Plank Road to twerk their monkey, the trannies thought they were boldly moving in on their turf. Powwowing alone didn't quell their beef; still suspicious, only after they cruised Scenic Highway did they believe the women prostitutes. To their surprise, a bunch of fresh women with that beginner glow about them were working the strip. A second glance at the street walkers revealed the truth about them. Every one of them was workingwomen, but not prostitutes.

The group consisted of female police officers from different precincts of the city. Several were regulars on a beat, while some of the women pushed paper since they joined the law enforcement agency. Now they all were on the front line in a battle to produce a suspect. Impersonating a prostitute was their assignment. Posted up, they had the gap-legged stance perfected. Walking with that hooker dip in their hips, along with the glide in their stride, was on point also. Even their outfits were enticing enough to make a priest want to spend a few dollars with them. They definitely had the appearance, but not the look. Instead of being flirtatious, their eyes were prowling, like that of a predator hunting prey. When cars crept by, they didn't throw themselves at the could-be john when they slowed down in their cars, the way real broads turning tricks did; the impostors displayed many other false advertisements of the hoe game that spelled out *police* to a person that was street. With all the signs there, they still didn't have the shortage of horny men that took the bait. Majority of them were detained until the women's shift ended, then released with a citation to appear in court. Then there was the unfortunate ducks that got sent to the parish prison, awakening the next morning, if they slept at all, to find their name, date of birth, and home address in the crime-and-arrest section of the newspaper for solicitation of prostitutes. The trannies called a truce with the females when they returned from peeping out the scene. Reluctantly, they portioned out a section of Plank Road the females could work from until their strip cooled off.

All the drug dealers that didn't have a nest egg put up or had a partner in another neighborhood that would let them eat alongside them starved. The white folks had declared war on all crimes and criminals in Northdale and weren't going to ease up the pressure until they had the person that executed Officer Dicken DaBeaudé in custody.

The ninth decade in the twentieth century was a pair of moons away from replacing the current one. People all around was already discussing the things in their life that they weren't satisfied with that they wished to commute for something better; also, the habits that they planned to leave behind, not carrying with them into the new decade, were a hot topic being tossed around. Besides those very near and dear personal desires, majority of the population in the neighborhood prayed and hoped for excellent health, peace, prosperity, and all the pleasures life had to offer. Vietnam didn't have space in his skull to envision those types of thoughts, if he tried, or the liberty to indulge in such pleasantries of imagining that wishful thinking came true. The writing was clearly written on the wall. The streets had the crown prince of South Baton Rouge in a two-four twist. Even the best couldn't wiggle their way out of that submission hold. Only hope that was feasible in his predicament was to be able to see the new year free and on solid ground, the two highlights that are always petitioned for in a hustler's prayer. "Boy, if I had your hands, I'll chop mines off and throw 'em away. I wouldn't be worried 'bout a goddamn thang!" people would often excitedly express in their greetings to him. When hearing that, he thought, *If only you knew,* before replying. In fact, it was preposterous for one to think that just because a person had the best illicit drugs on the market that generated endless funds, they didn't have any concerns about their welfare. Vietnam never condemned or corrected them for their lack of wisdom of the heart and soul of a hustler; he just took their comments at face value for what it was, a mere compliment. Now, "Be careful" and "Stay up, G" were the popular phrases expressed to him mostly used by those whom he had grown on over the years. Others didn't give a damn; they sat back, waiting for his sins to catch up with the pressures of life to overthrow him. Desperately, he wanted to holler to someone, "Please take my hands. I want out!" But gangsters don't cry, fold, or beg for mercy. So instead, he just swallowed his tears in anguish, sighed, pushed on, and waited for his number to be called. Life had gotten harsh and hectic. No one, not even Sister Cleo, the future reader, could've predicted that making money or hanging out would be as perilous as it had become in the territory he claimed.

Across the tracks, in a way, had always been a tinderbox that would suddenly explode without warning, simmer down, then lie dormant, giving of the illusion that the flame that ignited the explosion was fully extinguished. Vietnam was on the streets the last time the violence erupted in the neighborhood, but he managed to come out the wild pistol-popping unscathed. Nor did he feel the effect the civil insurrection had on the economy. That was because at the time the battle of Da Block and Da Bricks jumped off, he was a bystander, spectating. There wasn't an obligation for him to be in the hot zone. The coin had flipped since then. His office, warehouse, and distribution point were the designated battleground. At any given moment, business transactions were being interrupted by the sound of gunfire. Even junked-out junkies didn't want to risk getting accidentally dead-ended by a stray bullet, trying to cop hit. As a result, traffic slowed down, money became slack, and cash lines were hard to meet, which caused everyone to compete for the same customers. Some didn't have the skills to play fair. Snaking rose to an all-time high, developing a beef that could've been avoided among the dealers that once cold-feuded but since had settled their differences, quashed their suspicions, and bubbled together. Virtually, there was more firepower in the arena to accommodate those who were willing to stand their ground. Undeterred by the drastic events, Vietnam got up early every morning, posted up in his spot as usual. Swivel-necking, he was on everything that moved. Man, woman, or child—everyone was suspect in the conflict. This was one of the breaks of the life he chose.

He had come to accept the things he had no direct control over, but that didn't mean that he liked the changes that had occurred and were bound to worsen. The easy days were rapidly being replaced with turmoil, with no end in sight. Vietnam hated every aspect of the new wave rolling in, but he couldn't just up and walk away. Bloodshed or the threat of it didn't faze him; it was the feel of uneasiness in the air that came with it he hated. Neighborhood wars are always a thorn in the side of those that strictly hustle. Though he wasn't losing money like the rest, he wasn't turning over packages like he once did. The other pushers contributed his emotionless stare as a result of lost wages—they weren't close to the matter of the issue. He had been taught that war was the thug gods' clever strategy for leveling the society, in which their game was being played by removing those who weren't living by the rules set forth or to eliminate those that had the potential to stray away from the guidelines. That way, the street cleansed itself without the help of authorities. Contrary to what many believed, no one on the streets got eighty-sixed for no reason. Anyone who chooses to live that life is guilty; therefore, they're fair game. It didn't matter to Vietnam who lived, died, or got shot out there. The thing that irritated was the increase of police patrol. When they hit the set, anyone out there got hemmed up, shaken down, then expelled from the set with a stern warning. And because Karonda honored her mama, she stopped coming around. Things in and near the playground had gotten too dangerous. When he went to visit her, her mama ran him off. In her mind she had him pinned as one of the gunslingers. She wasn't rude to him; she just stated that as a mother it was her duty to look out for the safety of her children. Frankly, that she didn't want any of her little ones receiving a bullet that had his name on it was the way she politely laid out her reasons. He couldn't help but respect her mind. That day, he left her house with a vendetta with every cat involved in the madness, those from the block as well as those from the Bricks. Nightly he lay down to sleep with killing all on his mind. It wasn't time, so he chilled.

In order to control himself from wigging out or, around anyone's space, drawing a negative reaction from people, when out hustling, he kept his distance from the rest, with his candy stick on deck. To justify his action, he vowed not to provoke anyone, but he promised that for the slightest disrespect, that person was going to die. Homicide stayed on his mind just as much as his girlfriend did. His pointer finger was itching to be scratched by a trigger, while his body was longing for Karonda's touch. He was alone in the playground the morning after the day of shootings that claimed the life of one and injured six, including a five-year-old girl that had sneaked out of her apartment to play in the playground that was rightfully hers. One of the gunmen got shot. His shooter ran toward the direction the little girl was playing, and falling down, he returned fire, missing his target, striking the baby in the right shoulder. The screams of the little girl's mother alerted the gathering crowd to her condition. She hadn't been noticed until then because her small body had fallen, hidden behind the tire structure she was playing around. Silenced by the excruciating pain from the foreign object in her, she lay there without making a sound. If her mother didn't show up when she did, the little girl would have bled to death, becoming the second casualty, an accidental one. The cat that died, word was out, turned over on his fall partners years back. His family was going to miss him, but the game sure wasn't. Vietnam looked up at the sky, searching. He prayed to the thug god, making peace with him. The voice whispered in his ear all night long, that death was the only thing that was going to restore order.

Packing both candy sticks, he made his mind up to kill all that were involved. The unknown was how many he was going to be able to push to the next life before he succumbed to the lead death enforcers himself. There wasn't any doubt that his intended victims were strapped and ready to bang. The shooting didn't stir him. When he left the spot, all was well. Running into Karonda's mama at the seafood joint on Nicholson Drive was what brought him to the state of mind he was now in. Out of all the lowdown things she could accuse him of doing, with a look of disgust etched in her pretty brown face, she spat out, "Now ya shooting babies? You ain't gotta never worry 'bout seeing my baby ever again." Her words deeply penetrated his soul. Being dumbfounded quickly turned into anger. Mentally he lost control. The stick of genie he got from dude on Carolina Street that he smoked before he went to the seafood joint only aided in fueling his rage. Speechless, he left the place without the items he came for. Eating had left his mind. Killing was all he could think of. That night, he lay down early.

Sleepless, he questioned whether or not he was responsible for the little girl's shooting, along with everything that was taking place on West Roosevelt Street. Truth be told, it was his constant supply of drugs that brought out the dealers and hangers-on that were engaged in the ongoing battle. If the spot wasn't booming, no one would be there, he thought. In the end, he couldn't bring himself to taking responsibility for another man's action, but the next man's action was going to be the cause of him losing the only girl his age that paid any attention to him. Something that he wasn't going to allow to happen. A course of action had been chosen. With the voice assuring him that he had made the right decision, he now waited at the playground with two candy sticks on his lap, waiting to get the business cleared. It was time to regulate. A policeman had already circled the neighborhood, hidden behind one of the project buildings. He watched him circle the area, recircle, then dip out. If he guessed correctly, it would be another hour and a half before the next round was made, which was ample time to start the fireworks. Again, he lifted up his face to the heavens. This time he was staring hard, trying to look into the afterlife. "Live or die, either way, it's on," he whispered to the thug lord, then surprisingly, when he lowered his gaze, a calm like he never experienced before came over him. Ordinarily, when thoughts of murder were a blink of an eye away from becoming reality, his edginess level rose, but now that the possibility of his own demise had been thrown in the mix, strangely there wasn't an atom of anxiety floating around in his being.

Zeek and a female were one of the first to arrive on the set. She stayed back while he approached Vietnam. Zeek had been around for as long as he could remember. He was a good dude and a loyal cat to the game. In time, he had become one of the cats over there on the block he admired. Zeek was one way; that was what he liked about him. On a number of occasions, he was the only one with the heart to talk to him when he saw red, calming him by pointing out a more intriguing route to take. *Damn,* Vietnam thought. *I hate to do it, but if he come with that pussy-ass shit, tryna talk me out of it, he go get it too.*

"What up, baby?" Zeek asked. Vietnam nodded once, then averted his gaze. "Um, that's a lot of hardware you got there," Zeek stated nervously. "You 'spectn' trouble?" he asked.

Vietnam picked up both pistols, crossing his arms, resting on his lap. "Nah, no trouble. I jus' felt tha need to keep my regulators on hand," he replied dryly.

"I feel ya on that, nigga. Shit getting' too wild. That was fucked up what happened to that li'l girl out 'che yesterday," Zeek expressed.

Please don't get to sounding like a bitch, Vietnam thought.

"I see ya got death in ya eyes, but before you…"

Damn, Zeek, here ya go with that hoe shit, Vietnam thought. His body language and facial expression told Zeek, who threw up his hands.

"Nah, hold up, baby. All I'm saying is, we 'pose to be hold'n court on them cowboys that's shoot'n shit later on. Before you go busting at them niggaz on ya own, wait till after the meet and we all take care of bizness. You ain't tha onliest nigga out'che hustle'n ya dig," he said arrogantly. "You can tell us what ya think about how ya wanna handle shit," he added.

Vietnam never politicked with anyone before about what he had his mind set on doing, nor did he seek the approval of one other than himself to do what needed to be done. What Zeek said caught him off point. "Think," he said, the word coming out like he was confused.

"Yeah, think, my nigga. You do have a brain to think with, don't 'cha? I know them wet daddy's or genies—whatever ya call that shit ya blaze—haven't soaked ya shit yet. You jus' started," Zeek joked. "You got a lot of dips left in ya."

"Man, you ain't bullshitt'n me 'bout dis court shit, hah, Zeek?" Vietnam asked, eyeing him suspiciously. Smooth-talking was another attribute to add to his vibrant character.

"Straight low, souljah," he solemnly stated, his piercing gaze supporting his statement.

"When y'all planned that?" Vietnam asked.

"Last night, a few of us met up at Johnny's Liquor Store," he answered.

Who, what, when, and how didn't matter; Vietnam asked to stall time. He didn't want to seem too anxious to join them. Though curious however it went, he wasn't going to take orders and didn't plan on changing his plan. It wasn't going to hurt to see what the others had to say, he thought. "Fuck it, I'm with it," he said, placing the pistols behind him. Zeek nodded. "Where y'all getting together at?" Vietnam asked.

"Right here," Zeek responded quickly. "Um, you got work?" he questioned.

"It's good," Vietnam replied, neck swiveling, scanning the area.

"Peep this, let me buy a half-ounce. I got da money right 'che," he said, digging into his pockets, "and let ya big homie hold one till I get on today." He smiled. "Knowing, you at any given second, ya crazy ass might flip da fuck out, shooting everybody up. You'll be gone, an' I won't have nowhere to get dope from, so I wanna get all I can now. Ya feel me?"

Unmoved by his speech, Vietnam asked, all businesslike, "Brown or white?"

"Brown," he answered with less enthusiasm than before.

"You want individual packs or all in one?" he asked, testing him.

"Nigga, I ain't no junkie. I want mines all in one," Zeek retorted.

Drug users and new jacks to the game were the only ones that liked to be served prepackaged packs of heroin. Vietnam laughed. "Watch the bust," he said as he rushed off to his stash spot, hurrying. When he made it back, Zeek had one of his candy sticks in his hand.

"G, dis old bitch here look like them thangs them white folks carry," he stated matter-of-factly, turning the gun over, admiring it.

Stunned at the realism of his observation, Vietnam said, "I know, huh? Here's tha work, ah, zipper." He tossed the ounce of heroin on the slide next to his other candy stick.

Zeek's face lit up. "Square biz?" he asked.

"A-1," Vietnam replied, hoping that he put down the candy stick before he saw BRPD etched into the barrel.

Zeek lost all interest in the short gun; he dropped it on the slide, picking up the drugs in the same motion. "My nigga," he expressed joyously.

"My nigga, shit, where's my money for the half?" Vietnam asked with his hand out. There wasn't a need to peel back the bills in the roll Zeek put in his hand to make sure the count was good. Although he was a known schemer, when Zeek dealt with Vietnam, his business had always been square. That was the reason he laid the other half-ounce on him, on front. Back when they first started doing business, he never would have gotten a dime bag without payment for it on hand.

"You be easy," Zeek said with a smile.

"Yeah," Vietnam replied dryly.

"I mean it. Gangsta don't make no monkey moves. You gon' have ya time to lay the law down," he said frankly, with a hint of a promise in his statement.

"That's a bet, big homie. I'ma spare them busta's for now," Vietnam replied.

Zeek, without a word, spun, headed off to where he left the obedient woman standing. Placing the money in a discarded fast-food cup, Vietnam walked off to stash it. Five-o incorporated an old but new tactic of harassment. Whenever they harassed someone, they went in their pockets, confiscating their money. If they were free of warrants and clear, the officer would send the suspected dealer on his way with a "Thank you for your contribution to the Baton Rouge Little Leagues sports program." Out there, high-tripping and slipping, the Little Leagues got blessed twice in one day by him. Now, every time they spotted him, they hemmed him up, searching strictly for a stash of cash. Just as he was putting the flame to his second cigarette in ten minutes, it hit him, drawing out a chuckle from him. "That nigga Zeek slick as fish grease." He was now laughing at the thought. Without an obvious display of canniness, Zeek managed to delay the inevitable and roll out with an extra half-ounce of heroin. Word being bond, he had to sit on his word until after the powwowing session was concluded. With plenty of ticks to spare, he did something he hadn't done in a while. Expelling all the useless conception, he slipped his mind out of beast mode into grind mode, his original state of mind. For some people, when the money gets good, the passion for it starts to fade. Other things replace the desire, and getting back to the money mentality becomes a helluva task. Vietnam was somewhere in the ballpark of falling off if he didn't get it together soon. He knew it but couldn't figure out why. Kicking off his left shoe, he remembered a sliver of aluminum foil paper. Inside of it was a joint of marijuana laced with angel dust.

It was the levelheaded dealers out of the bunch that were in attendance, those who exercised their wit rather than picking up weapons to solve their differences. From the opening of the conversation, it seemed like everyone had gathered just to discuss the events that had been taking place and not to brainstorm up a suitable resolution to end them. In an orderly fashion, the paid elected politicians, of whom politics for a career would have been jealous, calmly took turns voicing their beef, feelings about the shootings, and predictions of the future outcome of the drug game across the track. Vietnam opted out when his turn came to speak, reserving his voice until the topic of who was going to murder who came up. Taking his quietness as an indication as bashfulness or whatever, one of the big homies expressed to him, "Peep this, li'l brother. Though you a child 'mongst men, you got as much say-so 'bout what go down 'round here as any'one of us. Yo livelihood on the line too. Ya feel me?" He was still silent, a series of nods his only response to his enlightenment.

Double D approached the group, dapping Vietnam off. "What up, nigga?" Vietnam happily asked. His absence had worried him. He'd been AWOL since the onset of the four-day shooting spree. No one knew what had become of him. Seeing him relieved Vietnam, but his presence seemed to disturb the rest of the guys. They fell hushed when he showed up.

"Ole junkie-ass nigga, we having a G meeting. What part of the game you representing?" a dealer spoke up, openly showing his scorn for Double D's interruption. "Move around, bum," he added.

Double D's face went slack. Lowering his head, he turned to push out. "Man, fuck all that! This myyy—he stretched the *i* sound in *my*—"muthafuck'n nigga. He ain't gotta bounce nowhere," Vietnam sternly spat out. "He represent'n what I'm rep'n, nigga. You tryna flash on my thug, nigga, you pump'n my work," he added.

"I know him," Zeek said, vouching for Double D, stepping in between him and the dealer. The big homie that had encouraged him was shaken by what he had betaken.

Vietnam's soft features could no longer hide his cruel heart. A nerve had been touched. He was sensitive about the treatment of those he deemed as friends. His face stoned, and his eyes grew as dark as a moonless night. All reason seemed to have left him. Frantically his hands groped at his waist, his body jerking and twisting, like he was doing a dance, as he frisked himself. Zeek, along with the rest of the big homies, cleared his path to the dealer when he transformed and started to reach for what could only be a gun concealed under his shirt. Due to ignorance, the dealer brushed Vietnam's behavior off as an act. So caught up in issuing a barrage of insults that no one was giving ear to, he failed to notice the shift in positions of the men standing around him. They all moved to one side, making a straight and clear line of fire to him. None of the men wanted to be an accidental casualty or be the dealer's savior by taking lead for him. Everyone present knew once Vietnam drew his candy stick, letting the hammer drop was absolute, there wasn't anything to impede his untimely destruction.

The group held their breath, anticipating the gunplay. The ants, birds, stray dogs, cats, and every living creature in the neighborhood, except the dealer himself, knew that he was seconds away from feeling the cold touch of death. The group let out a loud, audible deep breath when Vietnam's hand came from under his shirt empty. He had stashed the pistol before he joined the meeting. Mouth closed, the dealer glanced at the others they all had a mask of relief on their faces. He stood alone. With clear vision and mind, he let his gaze fall back on the young hustler in the group, who looked at him with loathing, but also mad confusion. Vietnam's mind had cleared slightly, and he realized that he and the dealer were facing each other in a standoff. As he stepped back, the lack of weight pulling at his side informed him that he wasn't clutching. *I know fucking well I didn't back myself into a corner without a rod,* he thought, letting his hand dangle in view. The predicament was evident, but he was struggling to remember what led to this point or what brought on the violent rage he lapsed into, preceding that.

"Let's get back to the biz-ness," the big homie demanded, breaking the ice. Calmly, as before Vietnam flipped out, the conversation continued politicking.

Vietnam remained quiet, trying to recover his composure while they discussed the obvious. The guys were reasonable to one another's opinion, until the question of how the beef started came up. That was when the conversation exploded into a heated argument. One dealer claimed that the three sisters that had recently moved into the projects were the cause of the cats trying to kill one another. The dealer that was sweet on one of them contested, saying that run-hards were the cause of them losing their mind. It had been several years since crack cocaine had first introduced itself to the scene. It was rooted in the neighborhood but was still getting the blame for the turning events and the unexplainable actions of people. The one that blamed the women for the deteriorating conditions of the game sold run-hards on the side also, and he defended the run-hard users and dealers, pressing aggressively that the broads brought evil to them. The dude couldn't stand the insults to the women he liked and her sisters. He got all in the crack seller's face, the rest of the big homies separating them. They embraced, apologized, dapped each other off, then resumed the powwow peacefully. All the thinkers agreed that death was the solution, but they wanted to stake a little more money before the bodies started to drop. No one volunteered to do the killing.

Wanting to secure plenty of funds before jumping into the ongoing conflict was a reasonable, lame excuse, if any. What Vietnam couldn't understand was how seconds before, when all agreed on a mass killing, they were insolent, but when the question of who all was going to participate in the act came, they all fell mute. Vietnam let his disdain show on his face and verbally expressed his contempt for those who talked the talk but didn't have the heart to put in work. His words must have made the men feel some type of way. Strained expressions landed on their mugs, followed by a chorus of unintelligible mumbling. After the mumble session ended, and disgusted, Vietnam yelled out, "Fuck it, I'll do it!" shaking his head in contempt at the dealers. Seeing visions of his free dope vanishing, Double D sighed loudly. Vietnam missed his exasperation. Excitement that they kept in check washed over their faces.

"You need a roscoe, or ya ah'ready tooled up?" the dealer sweet on one of the sisters asked concerningly.

"Need one," he replied, emotionless.

"Bet. I got'cha covered, big baby," he exclaimed.

"So…um, when ya gonna take care of that?" Zeek inquired. All the group's attention fell on Vietnam as he was asked the question zooming in him. They all waited quietly for his answer.

Vietnam scanned each of their faces, meeting everyone's eyes. "ASAP, my G," he replied. With a nod from them, approval of his response was shown. Also with the same gesture, a verbal contract had been signed. Vietnam now the hammer for the dealers, the meeting adjourned.

Strolling back to his spot, Double D on his trail, Vietnam flashed back, angered when he couldn't remember the keynotes of the conversation in its entirety. Only bits and pieces of it surfaced, with voids in between them. "Fuck!" he exclaimed. Double D mistakenly perceived his swearing as compliance toward the agreement he'd made.

"Too late for that," he blurted out.

Zoned out, Vietnam was startled by the sound of his voice. He gazed at him questioningly.

Monitoring the streets, without averting his glance, Double D voiced, "It ain't my business, but I wish you would'na took that mission."

Normally, Vietnam would have corrected him for not supporting his decision, but he detected the genuine concern in his shaky voice. "Why you say that, bro?" he asked instead of putting him in his place.

"Man, them ole scary-ass niggaz play'n on you, Vee. Neither one of 'em got the nuts to let shake the dust up off tha ground without them tearing down something, get'n out da way, pussy-ass niggaz," he said rapidly, breathing hard, the way he did when he got upset.

As Vietnam thought hard about what had just been said, the words sank in, but he allowed Double D a few ticks to catch his head before he probed into his accusations. Thoughts of someone trying to play on his mind never did set well with him. "What's dis shit 'bout them niggaz play'n on me?" he asked, fire in his voice.

"It's real," Double D said, bobbing his head, asserting his point. "They play'n ya like a game of tunk," he whispered. Vietnam was all ears, waiting for him to elaborate. "It's like dis, dog. You don't have nut'n to lose if them niggaz keep bang'n at each other, or nut'n to gain if you knock 'em off, but they do," he stressed, pointing in the direction of the diplomatic dealers. "Each and every one of 'em in that bunch gain. Playa been try'n get at the oldest of them three hoes that moved in da back. The other day, da same nigga that been slang'n that iron checked him, told him don't come back in da projects fuck'n with ole girl or nann other bitch in da Bricks. Then dude went in his pockets. Ya feel me?" he stated. Vietnam's high started to crash down, and his temper started to rise as the realization of what Double D was saying started to take shape inside his head. "Ole boy called himself pushing rocks on da cool. Damn near every nigga from da block got on his ass, 'bout get'n in their mix. I thought that nigga was gon' shit on himself when they jammed his coward ass up." He sighed. "An' Zeek scheming ass prolly got broke off jus' fo' get'n you to handle shit," he stated, disgustedly shaking his head.

"Muthafucka!" Vietnam shouted angrily. In a rage so violent that the sand under the slide started to tremble, he leaped up. "I'ma shoot tha fuck outa err'one of them bitch-ass niggaz!" he exclaimed.

"Not today, partner," a strange voice behind him replied.

Before Double D or he could turn to investigate the source of the third voice in the midst, the same person who had spoken now yelled, "Both of y'all put ya fucking hands up now!" Neither of them had to see with their eyes to visualize or understand who was talking and what was taking place. They both spun around simultaneously, with their hands held high, to face a flock of policemen with their service guns drawn. In the background, tires coming to a screeching halt could be heard, while several of the policemen darted past them. "Get down!" the cop commanded. Vietnam complied physically, but mentally his brain had ceased to operate. *How? What da fuck?* he kept repeating in his head, thus hindering any other thought from forming.

Outcries from the law-abiding citizens in the neighborhood were heard by someone with power down at city hall, complaining that with the increase of drug activities and shootings, they lived in constant terror. Thinking that they were going to be a victim of a stray bullet or mugging by an addict jonesing for a fix. Some said that they felt like they were being held as POWs in their own homes, while others claimed that they felt like they were residing in Cuba instead of South Baton Rouge, that the gangsters, hustlers, and street players were the ones dictating their movements. A criminal stronghold of a community wasn't something that civil servants took lightly. Giving ear to the people's voice, added with the fact that they viewed the unlawful atrocities taking place across the tracks as a direct challenge to administrative government policies, they launched Operation Levee Breach. The plan was to flood the neighborhood with policemen, strategically raiding every resident of informed lawbreakers, at the same time arresting anyone loitering on the streets that looked suspicious. Secretly, a command was issued to lock whoever up for whatever charges, squeeze some to flip, then turn them all over to the judicial system, letting it handle the rest. The order was followed. In a neighborhood of a 350 residents, a total of forty-one people got nabbed in the sweep. Thirty-four men, six women, and one juvenile were thrown into the cells of the Highland Road Precinct, waiting to get paraded in front of the media then onto the parish prison.

The chief of police, along with the mayor, was going through the department, congratulating their officers for the job well done. Once they finished shaking hands and back-slapping, they went to the holding tank area to peep out those unlucky forty their so-called courageous men and women in uniform snatched off the streets. In the crowd were some of the faces he prayed many nights to see behind bars. Walking up to the cell, the chief politely asked, smiling, "You in the red shirt with the fish on it, come here."

Double D, fighting through the crowded cell, then making it to the bars, wondered why he'd been singled out. Stammering, he asked, "Um, yeah, what's da haps?"

"Sir, your name wouldn't happen to be Mr. Winston Collins, would it?" he quizzed him.

"He 'bout to let you go!" someone in the packed cell voiced.

"Yeah, that's me," Double D excitedly replied.

Stiff-necked, Chief Likehis Mudpacked left the cellblock, returning moments later with the turnkey. "Winston Collins, step out!" he yelled. When the cell door was yanked back, a chorus of sighs, "Awe, mans," "Fuck, I wish dat was me," finished by "I told you they were 'bout to let you blow dis joint," accompanied him out of the cell. Being a juvenile, Vietnam couldn't be placed in a cell with the adults, so the bench was his designated area, one hand cuffed to the wall. Vietnam was uncomfortably lounging when Double D dipped down on him. The officer escorting him sat him next to Vietnam, cuffing him also to the wall.

"What up, G?" Vietnam asked.

"I don't know, dog. Them bitches just pulled me outa the tank," he replied, puzzled.

"Man, yo' name Winston Collins?" Vietnam blurted out. "Why da fuck they call you Double D if your name ain't got no *D* in it from da get-go?" he pressed.

"My name Winston. What about it?" Double D stated, not addressing the latter, getting straight to the point.

"Nut'n, jus' heard that dick sucka with all that shit on his shirt come out say'n sumthang 'bout Winston. If I'da known it was you, I'da ear-hustled a li'l more," Vietnam told him.

With all that said, Double D still wasn't any closer to knowing what was going on. He leaned back against the wall. Initially, he thought that his mind was deceiving him, then he realized every officer that passed mean-mugged or sneered at him. Already stressed from being held captive of the law, he could feel a sense of uneasiness fill him as well. Bowing his head, he prayed in a lowered voice, "My Lord and my God, O heavenly Father, I come to you as a humble servant. Lord, I ask you to forgive me of any wrongdoing, and, God, would you please, please, please, I beg you, rescue me out of this situation? I ask you this in the holy name of Jesus."

Vietnam was taken aback by the display. He didn't know what to think or what to say, so he stared at him, mute, lost. Double D didn't present himself as the praying type; neither hid he consider him to be one. Getting loaded on drugs, running game or suckers, cracking funnies, and facilitating him in evil deeds were the only things that he had been accredited for, nothing more, nothing less. The name tagged on him said it all. Swallowing hard, Vietnam nervously asked, "Um, you pray'n, my nigga?" Since a baby, he'd been hearing folks say, "When things get too tight to handle, turn to God." Double D pleading to the Creator put Vietnam on edge.

Without lifting his head, Double D sternly replied, "My advice to you, li'l brother, you need to do da same."

Vietnam felt his words. Until Double D was placed next to him, his mind was on how, when the day of retribution came, he was going to push Zeek and the rest of them to the next life and other things. Suddenly, his mental shifted. His present condition dawned on him. Scanning the room, feeling the cuffs, letting out a long loud, deep breath, he said to him, "Man, shit real." Once he grasped how serious the situation was, that it wasn't a doubt that he was going to take that ride, a part of him wanted to take up Double D on his advice about shooting up a quick prayer to the heavens. But after wrestling with the idea, he decided that prayer couldn't hurt. In his childish naivete, he thought, *If a raggedy-ass, dopehead ass nigga could pray to God, so can a gangsta-ass hustler.* Decision made, he sought for the words to say to God. But disappointedly, none came up. Giving up on his own prayer, he then thought about repeating Double D's prayer, but he couldn't remember the exact wordings of it. Highly discouraged, he gave up on the idea completely.

"Hold up a second, Sergeant, before you bring them out," the chief said, stopping in front of where Double D and Vietnam were manacled to a bench and the wall. In the distance, men could be heard griping and complaining. "Winston!" he barked out. When Double D raised his head, almost too quickly for the eye to see, Chief Likehis Mudpacked cocked back, then released at blinding speed a vicious slap that violently twisted Double D's body and head to the left when it landed. Vietnam cringed at the loud sound palm and face made when they met. The chief swung again. Anticipating the blow, Double D deflected it with his free arm abruptly. He relinquished from the slaps, then presumed another attack. He spit all over Double D until his mouth went dry. Vietnam didn't move or protest on behalf of his friend while he was undergoing a dehumanizing assault. He watched stupefied. *Wham!* "One to think about until I get back," Chief Likehis Mudpacked said, hammering Double D on the top of his head with a closed fist. Collecting himself, he brushed off invisible lint from his shirtsleeves, then turned to the officer holding the line of arrestees back. "Roll 'em," he commanded. He winked and nodded at Vietnam before he stomped out to the waiting news reporters.

"Fuck you," Vietnam mumbled behind him.

Double D lifted his head from its protected position. Four individual welts, extending from a misshapen circular one that ran in an angle toward his ear, protruded out at Vietnam. Chuckling, he said, "Damn, my nigga, I'm glad I didn't pray like you," cracking up at the pathetic sight sitting next to him. Double D had a stuck-on-stupid look on his ashamed, fear-ridden face, mouth agape. Globs of spit ranging from big drops to driblets peppered him, a hunk of spittle dripping down his cheek, forming a disgusting teardrop, swinging in the air several seconds before it finally let go, landing on his shirt. Shoulders slumped, aghast, he cried out meekly, "Why?" Pupils agleam with tears, he probed his little homie's face for an explanation. Vietnam tried to reply but couldn't stop giggling at his pitiful expression to let the words out. Embarrassed by the beating and destroyed by the lack of sympathy shown by Vietnam, he let a sob escape his lips before he examined the tile on the floor. Escorted by a pair of officers, single file, the prisoners marched out. Those that had seen Double D getting abused by Chief Likehis Mudpacked gave him the sympathy he was searching for from Vietnam. Vessel after vessel of doomed souls shuffled past them. None of the familiar faces seemed too thrilled about being herded out to a transportation bus, on-deck engine running, anxious to haul them off to East Baton Rouge Parish Prison. Majority of them were, in fact, guilty of some crime or another. Few were innocent men that got caught up in the law enforcement's rapture; they were the ones whose legs were rubbery, threatening to give out on them as the officers forcibly ushered them on out of the police station.

Vietnam lowered his head to avoid their gaze. He started to feel like a spectacle. Also, their pained features revealed the sadness that awaited him when his turn came to follow their footsteps. Flip-flops rhythmically clapping, along with the soft, feminine voices that replaced the low and deep-octave sounds of male voices, caused him to snap his head up. Planning to keep it down until he heard the last person pass, he was thankful that he didn't. It felt like the temperature dropped in the room. A cool breeze brushed across his skin. The sensual scent of the woman passing invaded his nostrils, accompanied by the sight of the lead woman wearing nothing but an oversize T-shirt falling an inch or two below her buttocks. The sight caused his sympathetic nervous system to kick in. "Goddamn," he expressed, eyes bulging out of his skull, watching the lady's butt cheeks jiggle out of control. Following behind her was a homely-looking woman wearing cutoff sweat pants and a wifebeater. Ms. C was in her late fifties. Out of shape with a bad leg, she limped badly when she walked. He stared at her flat buns as she moved on. She had her head held high, like she'd been down this path many times before. Next in the line of females was the eldest of the three sisters. If Vietnam had been an animated cartoon character, his tongue would have rolled out of his mouth down to the floor. She was so sexy and beautiful that if they weren't forbidden to, one of the gods would have come to earth, taken the form of man, and claimed her. He saw her occasionally from afar, but never this close. *I see why them niggaz tryna off each other,* he thought, gawking at the lovely creature standing handcuffed in front of him. The line halted, giving him a few more minutes to admire God's handiwork. All three of the women had bodies that women envied. Every ounce of fat they each carried was located in the right places. Their height was identical to one another's as well. Perfect specimen. They weren't too short for a tall man or too tall for a short man, but taller than the average woman. Only noticeable difference the sisters had besides their names and personalities was their skin. Though all of them had lovely skin covering their flesh, each of their complexions clashed with the other. The youngest resembled smooth dark chocolate, the middle one was caramel-toned, and the eldest of the sisters came out of her mother's womb the color of lemon drops. She even had the shine of the candy. She was wearing a pair of cotton short pants, blue in color, with a matching halter top that hugged her body, enhancing her curves. Color struck. A sucker for redbones, yellow bones, or caramel, Vietnam couldn't peel his glances off her; he hoped she'd look his way. For the time, the com-motion ahead of her had her attention.

"Sister, look at the boy staring at your booty, lusting!" the youngest yelled from the end of the line. While he was eyeing the big sister, she was on him. "I mean, girl, that nigga ain't batted his eyes," the middle sister voiced, giggling, drawing laughter from the line of women. The three sisters plus the lady separating the trio zeroed in on him. Vietnam peeked over at Double D to see if he was partaking in the eye cocaine standing in front of them. No longer misty, his eyes shone. He was fixated on the youngest sister. Double D liked his women either dark-skinned or white. Those sisters were undeniably some of the most gorgeous women alive. She glanced at Vietnam, then directed her attention back to whence it come. The line started to move again. She looked once more at him before she vanished. The youngest smiled, holding his gaze until she exited the station. Her big sister's face was stuck in his mind.

"Boy, them bitches fine as hell! I like that black one," Double D exclaimed. If he weren't being held hostage, he might have let fantasy override his thoughts. Faced with reality, he knew reality had to be dealt with.

Vietnam and Double D engaged in a bout of Q and A. The understanding both had and agreed to was that they both were going to take that ride. Vietnam leaned back, scanning the room. Nothing had changed but the calendar since the last time he was there. Double D started to comment again about the three sisters when he was interrupted.

"Uncuff that son of a bitch," Chief Likehis Mudpacked barked out as he approached them. Two officers the size of fullbacks walked up with him. One officer grabbed his arm, while the other one unlocked the cuff on his wrist, then he quickly grabbed his free arm, yanking him up to his feet. Before he caught his balance, they half-shoved and half-dragged him in the directions of the cellblock. Chief Likehis Mudpacked trailed them, shouting out profanities. Within seconds of the door closing behind them, sounds of a scuffle ensued, ringing out along with the eerie, agonizing screams coming from behind them.

"Look what the possum done dragged in," Detective Seymore Ballsaks said, looming over him, smiling. With Vietnam focused on Double D's dreadful shouts and screams, he had eased up on him, unnoticed by him. When Vietnam saw who was speaking, he sucked his teeth loudly, then frowned. Turning, he strained his ears, listening for a peep from his friend. Panic seized him when seconds of complete silence rolled on. The screams had stopped. Either the beating had been discontinued, death had rescued him, or he had fallen unconscious, he thought, hoping it was the former and not either of the latter. Detective Ballsaks looked puzzled, staring down at Vietnam.

"Man, what?" Vietnam asked menacingly.

The detective squinted, like one would when they were trying to identify a puzzling object or person. "Where's your cocky buddy?" he asked.

"I don't know," Vietnam replied. Mistakenly, which was good for him, he took his use of the word *cocky* as his way of describing a muscular guy.

"I thought ya'll were like peanut and butter, at least that's what the word was," he said, fishing.

Truth was, he didn't know where Li'l Who was; he hadn't seen him since the night he slayed Officer Dicken DaBeaudé. Neither did he give him any thought. Rumor among the kids was, he had moved to Houston or Atlanta. Some said he moved out west to Los Angeles. He bumped into his mama at the store. He wanted to question her about his whereabouts, but the look she gave him caused him to change his mind. He feebly nodded at her then darted out of her sight. Later on in life, Li'l Who would thank him for that dreadful night.

"Nuttin' like dat," he said, shaking his head.

"Oh well, gotta go," Detective Seymore Ballsaks said, clapping his hands together, hurrying away.

Vietnam didn't know it, but his real troubles were beginning. The minute the detective walked off, he headed straight to gather the files he had been sitting on the unsolved violent crimes that happened between Carolina Street and River Road, the ones in particular that had one thing in common, an unidentified short chubby black male who was reported to have been at or around the scene of the crime. As a seasoned detective, he came to believe that criminals commit crimes in areas they are familiar with and where they feel most comfortable at; although he matched the physical description of the person seen feet away from where Officer Dicken DaBeaudé lay riddled with lead, Vietnam was ruled out as a suspect by the detective. Northdale wasn't his turf. It wasn't his either, but when an officer of the law was murdered, it was everyone in law enforcement to help capture the perpetrator, or so it went. Detective Seymore Ballsaks was the type to chase a running man with baby steps. No matter how much distance the man put in between them or how far he might travel, he never wavered, trailing him every step until he finally caught up with the fleeing man. He was doggedly dedicated to apprehending those who had been accused of committing a crime. Whether their identity was known or not, he was going to close the case with an arrest, guaranteed.

Vietnam's heart bled for him, but he was glad to hear Double D's distressed screams continue. Amazingly, no one else inside the precinct exhibited any indication that they heard the boisterous sounds of a person suffering from extreme pain, clearly begging for mercy. "Dirty muthafuckas," Vietnam mumbled, watching the cops impassively carry on their duties while a man in the adjourning rom was being battered. The torture of Double D ended abruptly. Vietnam mean-mugged his friend's tormentors. Neither of them acknowledged his cold stare or the approving nods of their brothers and sisters in blue. They sauntered on, eyes forward, face glistening with sweat, breathless. The appearance of Chief Likehis Mudpacked and his two goon-cops would have been misleading to anyone that encountered them that wasn't present ticks before, when they were brutalizing one of their prisoners. In their condition, clothing in disarray, along with the congratulatory back slaps, one would've been unintentionally deceived into thinking that they had just concluded a fun, playful activity. Angered at their lawless act against his partner and their flaunting, celebrating conduct, Vietnam silently wished each of them a gruesome, slow, painful death. Double D had become the latest arrestee to sustain a beatdown at the Highland Road Police Station by the hand of John's law. The streets had dubbed the precinct the House of Horrors. Many had walked in only to leave lying on their back, with so-called self-inflicted injuries or by another arrestee waiting to get hauled off to the parish prison, "per the police report." All could change if one brave soul spoke out about the injustice, but those who had witnessed the action of the corrupt cops were bound by the code of the streets. To snitch on a cop was still snitching. For the victims that usually reported their incidents, in the end, the promise of a dismissal of charges, if applicable, or reduction of possible sentence seemed sweeter than pursuing their complaint against their abuser in uniform, which might have sent the shiesty cop to a penal institute. The game is cold on all levels.

Repeatedly, Vietnam yelled for someone to check on the welfare of Double D, but his yells went ignored for minutes. No one seemed to want to have anything to do with what had taken place on the other side of the door. Relentless, he cursed, swore, and bad-mouthed every person who wore a police uniform, past, present, and those who would in the future. "All right already!" a skinny pale woman, frustrated by his constant outburst, yelled. "Dammit, please stop! You're giving me a fucking headache!" she cried.

"Good," Vietnam retorted, then continued with his ranting.

The lady tried her best to shut Vietnam's voice out of her head, but every statement of insult he issued was delivered louder than the last one. His shouts were heard over any other noise in the building. He didn't pause with the disturbance. When his vocal cord became strained, he hammered and made silly sounds with his mouth. Once the burning in his throat eased, he continued. Agitated, the lady rocketed up from her desk, then bolted toward Vietnam, with her fist tightly balled up. Vietnam readied himself for the blow. "Look, you fat miserable black son of a bitch," she said through clenched teeth, waving her fist, "I'ma go check on your friend, and when I come back, if you breathe too loud, I'm going to ram my fist down your goddamn throat. You got that?" Vietnam gazed into her purple-red face, her body trembling as she fought to contain her rage. "Yes, ma'am," he replied, feigning fright.

Storming off, she swung open the door, then vanished behind it. The vision of her leaving was still fresh when she burst through the door, panting. She ran to the lady next to her. Vietnam couldn't hear her words, but he watched the color drain from the lady's face as she received the information. Their horrified stares attested to Double D's condition. He sighed. His suspicions were further confirmed when the lady who checked on him picked up the telephone. Looking at the clock, he realized a lot of time had elapsed since his torture ended. *If he wasn't already dead when the chief left him back there, surely he had to be dying or seriously damaged,* he thought.

Vietnam was raced out of the police station when the first responders arrived. He was in the back seat of a police unit, on his way to Ryan's Juvenile Detention Center.

His turn had come to "take that ride." Transitioning from being free to being a confined person isn't easily done for some. Like an animal captured after growing up in the wild rebels against its captor that attempts to domesticate it. Though eventually it settles down, its spirit to fight never dies. So it is with man. Incarceration starts in the booking department. During the processing phase, that feeling of being locked up is absent, but the numbness is present. Things start to move too fast for one's thoughts to produce an accurate feeling. As soon as one enters the center, the transporting officer removes the handcuffs, that act inducing a false sense of freedom. Reality being, the removal of the restraints symbolizes the conversion from a person being an arrestee to being a prisoner. Once the guard reviews the documents received from the officer, the guard then turns their attention to the prisoner. Now the false feeling gets chased away by distraction. The distraction comes by way of a series of questions. Name, date of birth, social security number, and sex—the five things found at the beginning of every job and school application are asked first. The inquirer wants to know the newly detained criminal's mother's and father's names, home address, telephone number, emergency contact name and number. Followed by questions pertaining to that person's current and past medical and mental health issues. Finally, to conclude the interview, the booking guard asks two of the most deep and personal questions. "What is your sexual preference?"

With much machismo, Vietnam replied, smiling, "I love bad bitches."

The guard stayed placid. "What's your religion?" he asked, moving to the next question.

"Huh?" Vietnam replied, revealing his confusion.

"Who is your God? Whom do you pray to, Mr. Franklin?" he rephrased his question, making it more elementary.

Confused at first, then awed by his redirect, Vietnam had to admit to himself he knew what the word *religion* meant; what he didn't know was that there were many denominations of it. Intelligent, though the guard's words were interrogative, they registered as declarative in Vietnam's mind. A seed of curiosity had been planted. He planned to investigate further into that matter. "Um, I pray to da almighty, one and the only thug god," he proudly stated. His response drew a puzzled look from the booking guard. He sighed, shook his head, then punched a key on the computer keypad. Phase 1 of the booking process was completed. Vietnam, just as the many boys and girls before him, was hurried to another office, where he was photographed and fingerprinted, thus ending phase 2 of the processing.

All the way, not a single thought had gained ground in his mind. It was his first time going through the procedure. In a strange way, he was fiercely anticipating the next move. Phase 3 was symbolic and very dehumanizing. Inside of a locker room, no different than that of a high school one, he was ordered to remove all articles of jewelry and every stitch of clothing. The shedding of any trance of freedom. Naked, he was then issued by the guard a bottle. He instructed him to rub the chemical-smelling solution over every area of his body that contained hair. The solvent killed any bedbugs or lice he might've been trying to smuggle into the detention center. Once the recommended time for the medicine to remain on his body was up, he was directed to a shower. Even the booking guard showed his discomfort. He fidgeted, avoided looking into Vietnam's direction. Both were relieved when he yelled, "Time's up!" Although the shower was steaming hot, standing under the scolding-hot water felt better than standing idly in the nude in front of another man.

Vietnam prolonged as long as he could. "Time's up!" the guard yelled. He still continued to let the water pressure massage his mind and body. "Time's up, goddammit!" the guard repeated, though with more aggression than before. The washing away of sins and worldly acts was completed. When he stepped out of the shower, a set of underclothing and an orange jumpsuit awaited him. Classification was the last aspect of phase 3 of booking. A phone call was part of classification. Vietnam opted out of his phone call; he didn't know a single telephone number by heart. The whole process was exhausting. He was already weary from being in the police precinct with all its excitement for hours, and now fatigue had commenced to sit in on him. When he was led to D-Unit, he was elated to fall on the plastic mattress awaiting him in cell number 3. In a matter of minutes, he was sound asleep.

The East Baton Rouge Detention Center housed fifty-two boys and girls held in one main cell divided equally on four different cellblocks, called units. The juvenile offenders' ages ranged from eleven to sixteen years of age. Louisiana was one of the nine states that considered a seventeen-year-old who committed a crime as an adult, but a person had to be eighteen years of age to have had developed enough mental capacity to cast their vote for a political candidate in an election, responsible as an adult would. Years away from the age of seventeen, he was in the clear from receiving the stiff, harsh penalties that an adult criminal would offer being convicted of a crime. Still, his life was in limbo, at the mercy of the juvenile courts. When worse came to worst, he could remain in the can until his twenty-first birthday. It's widely known that in the life and the game one has to pay to play. Vietnam was now being taxed in the worst way, joining the countless whose payment had been required of them. Incarceration was his total bill due.

When he awakened, it took a moment for his eyes to adjust to the brightness of the lights in his cell. Fully conscious of his predicament, when he woke up to new surroundings, he wasn't startled a bit, nor did the fact that he was confined fade him. En route to the detention center, he had accepted his fate, made peace, then planned to fall in, holding his own the way Gs were known to do. Emptying his bladder, which had threatened to relax on its own if it wasn't relieved, he surveyed his new home. A concrete slab resembling a tomb over a grave with a thing made out of the same material as body bags, green in color, stuffed with what one could only assume was cotton, sewn at both ends, was what he slept on and would have to sleep on until he was released. Flushing the toilet, he tried to catch the reflection of his face in the piece of eight-by-twelve-inch stainless steel screwed into the wall above the combination sink and toilet, but it was so scratched up to reflect a clear image. The doors to the cells weren't electronic or could be opened collectively. The turnkey had to unlock each individual cell door with a key. Once the cell doors were opened, all the offenders filed out one behind the other into the dayroom. There wasn't a set of eyes that didn't fall on him. Lips sealed, he returned their glances. No one said a word to him; they spoke hush-hush among themselves as they grabbed a chair from the stack in the corner. Vietnam followed suit. There were two tables in the dayroom. A group of kids sat at them, while others spread themselves out around the dayroom in small groups. Only one kid chose to sit directly in front of the television. Noting that he was alone, Vietnam thought better of placing his chair next to him. Another kid strolled out of the housing area late. He picked up the remaining chair, dragged it over next to the kid watching the news. He looked around and nodded at some, mean-mugged the rest that crumbled under his hard stare. Vietnam was still standing, holding his chair, looking dumb, trying to figure out where to post himself up at.

The kid sported a mini afro that desperately needed combing. His face was dotted with acne and black marks. Standing five feet, eight inches, muscles bulging against his orange jumpsuit, he looked like he belonged in the parish prison instead of the juvenile detention center. His gaze hit Vietnam, and he looked him up and down, waiting for a response from him. Vietnam knew what that look meant, but he didn't take the bait. The kid sucked on one of the gold crowns covering his rabbit teeth, turned, then planted himself in his chair. He and the guy dapped each other off, after which they fell into a quiet conversation. Other than the kid entertained by the television, not a soul in the dayroom missed the exchange between the afro boy and him. Some of their stares were still lingering on him when he positioned himself against the wall at the back of the dayroom. There wasn't any detectable hostility in the air, but every now and again, one group of boys would glance over at the other in a way that those forced to cohabitate peacefully would. While everyone else was either paired up in a group, Vietnam was by his lonesome. Waiting, watching, and listening for the sign. From all the penitentiary tales he heard, he knew what to expect. He was the new guy, and that meant he had to prove himself. How he dealt with conflict when it came his way determined whether he was going to have to sit down and piss the duration of his stay or piss standing up like a man. Straight from the shoulder, someone was going to get bloodied and swollen. No doubt his knuckle game was on expert level, he thought as he opened and closed his hands. Not having a home-made knife, if it came to that, was his only concern for the moment. *Shank or no shank,* he thought, flipping the switch on in his mind, *I'm gonna roll. Niggaz from across them tracks don't back down.* He smiled to himself.

On the way to breakfast and back, he was on the alarm. The entire time he was primed, ready to explode on anyone when they tested him. Back in the dayroom, the two television watchers were tuned into *Good Morning America*. Vietnam glanced at the screen. He wasn't sleepy, but his belly full of biscuits, eggs, grits, and slices of bacon had him sluggish. He rested his eyes during a commercial break, then the sound of a chair scratching across the tile floor caused him to open them. One of the boys pulled his chair next to him. Li'l One Gone was the runt of the unit. He was one of the ones that occupied the table. "What up, G? Where ya from?" he asked. Although no heads were turned in their direction, he sensed that all ears were listening for his reply.

"Where you from?" Vietnam responded with a question to toy with those who were ear-hustling.

"Shied, I'm from SOS," he replied proudly.

"O'yeah? Where that's at?" he said, pretending not to know. Li'l daddy looked at him like he was from another planet. Vietnam was enjoying himself.

278

"Straight Outta Scotland, that's where," li'l daddy spat out. Vietnam noticed that the body language of three at the table changed at the mention of Scotland. That was an indication that he had four sworn enemies and that in fact they were silently a part of his and li'l daddy's conversation.

May as well get the party started, he thought. "And what that do, nigga? I'm from Southside, 'cross da tracks, where them real gangsters roam," he retorted loud enough for everyone in the dayroom to hear. Setting the stage with his remark, he dissed every other neighborhood in Baton Rouge.

Once lunch was fed, the detention center went on lockdown for an hour. Those days and nights when he lay in the bed so bored, recovering from the gunshot wound and car accident, and placing voices with faces and identifying noise and sounds coming from outdoors became a game he played came in handy. Full, this time of fried catfish, baked potatoes, corn, and a hunk of bread pudding, he felt a nap seemed like the best thing to do. He was about to lie down until he heard mentioned, "Cell number 3." He listened closely. Though he hadn't been there long, still it didn't take long for him to place the voice. The dude hadn't shut up since the doors opened that morning. The responding voices were difficult to place, but he was pretty sure it had to be the two at the table with him. The decision had been made to check his temperature. When they came out, he couldn't hear which one planned on being his opponent, because the boy in the cell next to him flushed the toilet. When it quieted down, "You need to hold that fuck'n noise" echoed over the tier, followed by complete silence. No one had to tell him whom that voice belonged to. Meanwhile, Vietnam was racking his brain trying to figure out who was going to be the one that moved on him. *Fuck it. Why wait?* He decided that as soon as the cell door opened, he was going to get the business cleared himself. Sir Talk-a-Lot and the other Scotlandville representatives were already seated at the table when Vietnam mobbed into the open area.

The dayroom had a different vibe flowing through than it did before breakfast. One could smell the tension and taste the stale hostility that floated about. Those bodies that were lounging loosely and laxed in their chairs were now stone-stiff. No one murmured a word or uttered a sound. The room was graveyard quiet, which was a tell-tale sign that something was afoot. Grinning, he walked up to Sir Talk-a-Lot, stopping at a distance so he could watch his partners, and so when he started to unload, his punches wouldn't be smothered. First impulse was to get off on him without a word. Since he was under the spotlight, he decided to give the crowd a show to remember. "Say, my nigga, you wanted to do sumthang wit me?" he probed, getting straight to the point. Vietnam's brazen approach, along with his overly aggressive, accusatory tone of voice, stunned Sir Talk-a-Lot as well as the other juvenile delinquents. From the bit of conversation he overheard, they all had him pinned as a coward.

Sir Talk-a-Lot was now Sir Lost-for-Words. His mouth flopped open and shut several times, then he pursed his lips out like a tooth-less person trying to whistle before his tongue loosened up. "Um, what'cha mean?" he asked, mystified. When he glanced over at his crew, they conveyed a message of total disappointment at his response. Normally, when a semicowardly person knows that they have others backing up their play, the fact emboldens and empowers them. Before their shameful look inspired courage in him and the role of the aggressor got equally shared, to keep the starting role, Vietnam opened up the dance. "This what I mean, bitch-ass nigga," he spit out, decking Sir Talk-a-Lot. Vietnam couldn't tell whether it was his words or the sight of his meaty fist flying through the air toward him that made his eyes bug out of his skull. The first punch thrown was a straight right that landed on the bridge of his nose, which dazed him. Quickly, before Sir Talk-A-Lot could react, *ping, pow,* he two-pieced him. A sharp jab to his eye followed by a wicked overhand to the exact same spot the first blow landed closed the show. Sir Talk-a-Lot lost his will to perform, but his partners were full of fire. He sat palming his face, moaning in agony. His homeboys jumped out of their chairs to his rescue. He had been down this road plenty of times before, so his heart didn't flutter at all facing the odds. "C'mon, ole bitch-ass niggaz," he taunted them. "let's rock and roll!" He was egging them on. They observed the speed at which punches had been delivered. At his ferociousness, it was evident that it had an impact on their nerves. Sir Talk-a-Lot moaning didn't help their psyche much either. It seemed like that at the meeting, when it was decided who was going to be first to attack him, they all had fallen asleep. Each of them looked at one another confusedly. Tired of their hesitation, Vietnam made the decision for them; he brought the fight to them. At animal speed, stepping to the closest one to him, pouncing on him, with a crushing right hook to the jaw, he floored him.

The other two cowards had attacked him from behind, while he was beating their thug to a standstill. Blindly he threw a wild spinning backhand, and miraculously, it connected, struck his foe over the temple. The punch didn't do any noticeable damage, but it did enable him the opportunity to face and square up with his opponent. He and the chunky one stood toe to toe, swapping punches. Equal in size, he matched Vietnam's power but lacked the hand speed and stamina. Vietnam didn't have much wind himself. His lust for violence kept his fist pumping. The li'l daddy that he talked with earlier was the one giving him hell. The chunky guy was rapidly wearing down. He was backpedaling more, his blows starting to lose their sting and coming more slowly. Li'l daddy didn't engage straight up; he'd get off a few punches, then retreat out of Vietnam's arm's reach, then attack again from another angle, then step back in the opposite direction. Stick-and-move was his tactic. And it worked. Every time he punched Vietnam, despite the barrage of blows from the chunky guy, he felt his fist where chunky guy's punches had a numbing thump to them. Li'l daddy had a lasting sting that was painfully distracting. Desperately, he wanted to touch li'l daddy up, but he knew once he turned his attention off the chunky one, he might end up on his pockets. As long as he kept his hands in his face, he was going to have to stick with the punch-counterpunch routine.

Li'l daddy was all offense. He didn't have to worry about defense as long as his partner kept Vietnam in the blender. They paused only briefly to regroup, then went back at it. Chunky guy was almost out of gas. During a brief intermission, li'l daddy jumped in, and by a stroke of luck, Vietnam caught him flush in the mouth. The punch produced the intended effect, but he didn't have time to gloat. Just as he suspected, as soon as he turned to ward off li'l daddy's attack, the chunky one got a second wind. He rocked Vietnam with a slow two-piece, both of which checked his chin. He tried to strike back, but the effect of the punch had a momentary delayed reaction to sudden movement. It must have jarred his already-out-of-sync equilibrium, because as soon as he attempted to counterpunch, eyes on the target, the dude's chin was exposed, he thought. But instead of his body obeying the signal his brain sent to launch forward, it did the opposite; he fell backward. The one he initially got off on broke his fall. When he realized who it was that crashed down on him, he gave him that extra shove he needed to get to the floor. All four of them tried to stomp Vietnam into the afterlife. Paralysis or either gravity had a strong pull on him. His mind willed it. He couldn't lift himself off the floor. It felt like a pressurizing force field was all around. When he did gather the strength to rise an inch, he was knocked back down. Cognitively, he was still aware of everything, though slightly, his brain was processing information much slower. Although the boys were near, their words seemed to have traveled from afar. The first kick received was a gut shot. He curled into a fetal position, face cradled in his arms, protecting his face, chest, and stomach. Sadly, with his eyes squeezed shut, hands, feet, and eyes out of commission, his hearing was all that was left. With him balled up, a couple more well-placed kicks were planted, but unable to penetrate his protective posture. No damage was sustained to any vital part of him. *Go ahead, git yours,* he thought as the pairs of feet attempted to do him harm. *No mercy when my turn comes,* Vietnam silently promised. Abruptly the assault by foot ceased. With the wheels in his brain turning slow, it took a second to dawn on him what had happened and why. Clearly he heard someone yell, "Pussy-ass niggaz, let that man get up!" Here was where it got him. The information had been received in reverse. In his mind that attack stopped first, then he heard the words of the person coming to his rescue. His rescuer chose the perfect time. His arms and ribs had started to catch hell.

Vietnam peeked through his guard, and to his surprise, afro-boy was the one standing between him and his assailants. Having barked out the command to stop with so much authority, his voice didn't register with him. Why he intervened didn't either. A few minor scrapes and bumps were all he walked away from the skirmish with, with a little soreness here and there. More than anything, his ego was what was badly bruised.

Two nights had elapsed since the brawl. Vietnam was still heated from the ordeal. During rest period and lockdown, he replayed the entire incident in his mind, excoriating himself about not working off the jab, for being conservative with his power shots, and most of all, for turning his head away from the opponent directly in front of him. According to the spectators, he did exceptionally well going up against four adversaries singlehandedly. His business had been handled. Always his worst critic, he wasn't victorious; therefore, to him, he let himself and everything he represented down. On the third day of mind-wrestling with himself, convinced that he could take chunky boy down, he went with his move, but not before consulting with afro-boy. He promised Vietnam that he was going to make sure he got a fair shake, one-on-one. "Say, you put me down with a ole sucka-ass lick. Let's see, can ya fade da kid again?" he said, sternly addressing chunky boy.

Confidence sky-high, he accepted the challenge with a smile. "Shied, you ain't say'n nut'n, nigga," he replied, shooting up out of his seat to his feet. He charged at Vietnam like a raging bull, and like a matador, Vietnam sidestepped him, unloading a wicked check hook as he dodged his wild advance. Fight over, chunky-boy was out cold before his body reached the floor. Belly-flopping when he hit, lying out on the tile. Aside from his breathing causing his body to rise and fall, chunky-boy was motionless. A one hitter-quitter wasn't what he had expected, but he paraded around the day, putting on like he knew for certain the fight was going to end in a knockout. Up to that day, no one had ever got KO'd in that fashion in the detention center. Vietnam's name rang through the halls of the center. Offenders spread the word among themselves, and the guard that was on shift when it happened described the knockout to his coworkers as well as his friends and family. Redemption of his perceived defeat retrieved his agonizing thought. For the first time since he had been locked down, rest period was truly a period of rest.

That night, he didn't sleep well. His mind was burdened oppressively. Karonda was the source of the stress. To make matters worse, that dragon on his back he was in denial about had started to breathe on his neck, making its presence known. Seventy-two hours after an arrest, a bond hearing was supposed to be held for an accused criminal, and arraignment also when the accused was a juvenile. Vietnam entered the courtroom shackled and handcuffed. The bailiff directed him to his seat, his mama sitting directly behind him. The state-appointed attorney introduced herself, advising him to enter a plea of not guilty to all charges. Inside of the courtroom was his first time hearing what charges he was being held on. The officers had booked him on conspiracy charges ranging from murder to drugs. Truancy, shooting, hooky were the only charges the assistant district attorney chose to pursue; every other charge against him was nolle prosequi.

Following a lengthy speech about the severity of the alleged crimes against him and how lucky he was not to have to stand trial for them, the judge issued him a sign-out bond, then scheduled him a date to return for a status conference for the truancy charge, which was undisputable. He was, in fact, under the age of sixteen and arrested on the playground during school hours. When the court-appointed lawyer brought him papers to sign along with his subpoena, she ran down to him the conditions of his bond obligations. Also, she explained to him the charge he had to answer to, assuring him that jail time wasn't going to be the end result. Vietnam wanted to go back in front of the judge so that he could change his plea, so he wouldn't have to return on the later date. She went on to explain to him that there's a thing called due process; therefore, it would be ill-advised to plead guilty without all the facts of the case out in the open. The bright side was that in all probability, he was going to be released that day. She closed out by saying, whenever anyone returned from court, they had to be locked down in their cell for what was called a cooling period. One hour was the minimum time mandated. When his hour was over, he and afro-boy politicked. He had invited him to post up in front of the television with him, but Vietnam wisely chose to keep his back against the wall. They both leaned their chairs' back of two legs, rapping until his name was called to pack up and roll out. Afro-boy was from the Bottom. He and two other juveniles had been in the detention center for half a year for a caper; they had hit an armored truck. Though it was sloppily pulled off, they managed to make it off with a large sum of cash. Forty-eight hours later, they all were booked with attempted first-degree murder for shooting the guard and armed robbery. On the way out, stopping Vietnam at the door, he whispered an eyebrow-raising message in his ear to give to his big brother. He slipped a note into his hand also during their parting handshake. Vietnam gangster-mobbed the corridor in his orange jumpsuit a free man. Four days was the length of his stay.

Only the leeching-ass, smooching-ass cats were out. Other than them, across the tracks was dead. The white folks had devised and executed a plan that had successfully removed the movers and shakers, along with the gangsters, successfully from the neighborhood. Vietnam was awed by the desolate state of the streets. Walking them had a strange feel to it. It seemed to him like he was strolling through a foreign land. Fearful that he might get picked up again, hurriedly he went to his stash spot. To his amazement, the drugs and pistols he had stashed were still in place. Disappointedly, his money said, "Look for me." It didn't come by as a surprise when he couldn't find the cup he had hidden his fettiluchi in. Satisfied, he gave up the search for it, charging it to the game. It didn't make sense to make a stir behind it. Nor did he. Maybe a child picked the cup up to fill it with sand to build a sand castle and discovered the hidden treasure— at least that was the scenario he ran in his head to accept the minor loss he suffered. Uncomfortably, he posted up. Though vexed, he remained in his spot. Money was the furthest from his mind; hope in seeing Karonda pass by was what kept him stuck in place.

Gradually, days after his release, those who had bond money to bail out rolled back into the neighborhood, posting up exactly where they left at. Drug abusers don't stop getting high because suppliers get popped. Like a broad in heat, they're on to the next one. As a result of the mass arrest made, the constant flow of those seeking to cop a blow had dwindled drastically. The drug sales fell below what it had fallen to when the bullets had started to ricochet throughout the Bricks. Things had gotten so slow that the man came to check on him when his appointed time to score had come and gone. The man informed him that his visit was out of love, that it wasn't about the money. Leaving him with an invitation to visit him anytime he was in need. Vietnam wasn't in need for anything but to get high, and that was exactly what he did, stay zooted. Like a diamond mine that birthed its last stone, like a gold mine that panned out the last flake, the game had died out. The playground was a place where he once played at, where he made beaucoup cash at, but now it had become the place where he sat day in and day out, getting loaded, reminiscing and fantasizing about the future. The spot wasn't completely dead; the game had the potential to be revitalized. Vietnam didn't lack the hustle; he lacked the spirit to get the job done. Sadly, his time for the game began to burn out. He was too young for the streets to allow that to happen. Therefore, while he got shit-faced wasted, the streets summoned the game, the game summoned the life, and together in cahoots, they plotted a Vietnam resurrection and planned the triumphant resurrection of the drug-trafficking enterprise across the track. Incidentally, his unpleasant dilemma of not being able to spend time with Karonda or violating her mama's restraining order against him by visiting her was solved.

It had been two weeks to the day since his departure from the detention center. He patrolled the streets from the ante meridiem to deep off into the post meridiem. Not once, not even by chance, did he cross her line of vision. Up all night on all-night flight, smoking genies and sipping on cheap liquor, head spinning, he staggered home. Minutes after he settled in his bed, a recurring quaint notion growled at the back of his mind relentlessly. Unable to shake the thought, he surrendered to it. Rolling out of bed, he hit the door in a fog. One foot in front of the other, he floated toward the unknown. His mind said go, and tired of fighting it, he complied. At the end of the short journey, unexpectedly, someone was there, waiting. Her mama might have banned him from her house and forbidden her to visit him, but she couldn't stop them from meeting up at a public location. The bus stop was where his mind led him. Having dropped out of classes many moons ago, he had forgotten that school had existed. If he had remained consciously aware of the fact, their relationship wouldn't have been strained; he would've scheduled regular visits.

She excitedly ran up to him, the collision causing him to stagger backward a few feet. And as they held one another, the love and energy for her semisobered him up. All the frustration, aggression, and disappointment he harbored within dissipated as he peered into her eyes. Time slowed as their lips touched passionately, both of them cherishingly embracing the opportunity to once again be close to each other. Vietnam was enchanted by the moment. His smile seemed to have been a permanent fixture on his face. Though it was only mere seconds, it felt like minutes before they unclasped. During that short period of affection, amid his giggles and her sweet laughter, not a word had been said. Karonda spoke first. She didn't ask where he'd been or how he'd been doing. "I love you, bae" was what come out. "Real shit."

Pulling her back into him, looking around, peeping out the scene, he replied, "I love you too."

With her hands in his, they conversed, talking about some of the issues she had been dealing with. He told her sweet nothings. She promised him that she would always be his, and he promised her that he was going to do all he could to make her problems go away and make her life better. She smiled. He smiled back. She threw skinny arms over his shoulders, locking fingers behind his neck. He gripped the sides of her slim waist, and in that position for several ticks, they gazed into each other's faces. Behind the bloodshot, the love he felt for her was there in his eyes. The sparkle in hers framed the love in her eyes that she felt for him. Following a few more pecks on the lips and a tight hug, they small-talked to no purpose, their bodies transmitting all that needed to be said. It was really one of those times words wouldn't have adequately sufficed.

Vietnam's head was in the clouds. Karonda body was burning on fire, brushing up against his. Arousal ignited the flame. Both were so caught up in the love spell that they went deaf, dumb, mute, and blind. The bus had dipped down on them, the children had boarded it, and the driver was closing the doors, getting ready to push out, before either of them came to the realization of what was going on.

Lovestruck, warm, mind hazy, Vietnam didn't want to let her go. Like an overly emotional parent does their child on the first day of pre-K, he held her hand until her foot touched the first step on the bus before he released it. *I gotta make it happen,* he thought, watching the big yellow bus roll up West Roosevelt Street, until it vanished out of view. Tired from thugging and drugging and mentally distracted, he hurriedly stumbled home to rest. Though it had resonated to the back of his mind, when he lay down to sleep, money was on the forefront of it. Karonda saying "I love you, bae," followed by the touch of her body, was the last thought he had before he traveled into dreamland and was the first thing he thought of when he came out of it.

While he was brushing his teeth, the water in the pot on the stove started to boil. Before he had even begun his morning hygiene, he had dropped two ounces of cocaine in a Pyrex cup, sprinkling a little baking soda over it—not too much, just enough to cover up the product—then mixed it together. Half of the job was already complete; all that was left was to combine the two. Beforehand, he took a coffee mug, scoped out some of the hot water, poured it into the Pyrex jar, then placed the Pyrex jar inside the pot of boiling-hot water. He then let the product do what it did. Vietnam had never been in the lab without Double D's assistance before, nor did he drop more than a half-ounce. Run-hards weren't his thing, but the run-hards users had outpopulated the cocaine and heroin user. Like a boss, he made an executive decision and added crack to his bag. It went well. Like magic, a solid cookie appeared in the bottom of the Pyrex jar. On the triple beam, it tipped at fifty-four after it dried. That was damn good for a new jack to the cooking-run-hards game. Next thing in his agenda: flood the dope bags. Unlike cocaine, heroin had a tendency to lose its potency. The bundle he had been sitting on, no one complained about when they got their work from him. But when they returned, off the top, they wanted to negotiate the price of the package, which was a sure indication that the product was turning bunk. No matter the strength of the drug, be it dope fiend or hustler, more bang for their buck was always sweet as lemon meringue pie. In true entrepreneurial fashion, Vietnam dusted each gram of his fresh batch of heroin with 0.3 grams of the weakening stuff. Ten-gram packs to a bundle, once sold, that was an extra five hundred dollars in the pocket of the dealer. If not the maximum amount of five hundred dollars for the ones that had trouble flipping work, they had a margin for error. Everyone won.

Vietnam hit the block, putting out the word that it was customer appreciation week. Knowing that he was stringent in the game, smiling, they brushed him off, assuming that he was just high-talking. Because his statement was vague and he didn't elaborate his meaning, his words tumbled around inside one of the slow-witted smoocher's head until they severely vexed him. Irritated, he ran behind Vietnam, catching him before he made it to the basketball court, gasping for air. "Hold up, Vee!" he managed to force out in between huffs. "Customer 'preciate week, wat's dat?"

Vietnam studied him. "I'm show'n mad love to whoeva scoe from me," he explained in layman's term.

Comprehending now, he disappointingly asked, "So, um, ya gotta have ya bread right to git love?" seeing the hunger in his eyes. When he first entered the game, he had gotten burned for his cash, but his drugs were advertised and promoted. With that in mind, he said, "Yeah, for them," pointing to those on the block curiously watching their exchange. "But fo you, my nigga, bring me a sale and I gotcha," he finished, bouncing on, leaving the dude behind pondering his proposition. It didn't take long for the ball to start to roll. The sale the dude collared for Vietnam was a run-hard sale. He broke her off something proper. She couldn't believe the quantity of drugs he served her. After, he explained to her that the going was for one week and one week only, as a way of giving back. Distrusting his product more than his reason, she broke a piece of the run-hard, put it into the pipe she had, fashioned out of a car radio antenna, and took a long, hard drag, letting out the smoke slowly. With a nod, she floated away, staring into the clouds. He gave the dude the same amount he sold her for free. The next person the dude brought to Vietnam was one of his former customers who had drifted away because of the unsatisfactory quality of the dope he pushed.

Reluctant, he gave in to the "customer appreciation week" pitch Vietnam had thrown at him, along with a host of promised perks.

Although he had past dealings with the person he served the bundle of heroin to, Vietnam still passed the dude a gram of dope for reeling him back in his fold for him. When the dude broadcast his dealings with Vietnam, teasingly brandishing the product he had acquired as payment, the rest of the leechers and smoochers flocked to Vietnam to join the "getting it" team. Some came with their own money; others ran Murphys on dope fiends, pretending to have gotten the hookup for them on their muscle. Free drug week extended into the following week. Week 1, he retained the customers he lost, give or take a few new ones. Also, the following week, word had traveled afar. For every returning satisfied customer, three new ones arrived. Vietnam's devised strategy did wonders. Subsequently, the influx of people into the drug trade from one spectrum to the other was unprecedented. Sales dipped through one after another day and night. Run-hards were the hottest commodity. With all the currency flowing, smoochers no longer had the desire to smooch; they turned drug dealers.

Vietnam kept his distance from them and kept them at bay. The smoochers-turned-dealers knew how to make money, but they put bull crap in the game that he didn't want any part of. None of them knew the rules to the game; therefore, they didn't play by them. Though it was his responsibility and that of every other G that lived by the code to regulate when there was foul play in the game, he turned a blind eye to the offense and offenders. As long as the money kept rolling, they had a pass for their misconduct. Most of their deeds were minor ones shunned by hustlers that got checked. Vietnam wasn't much on chastisement of another man, anyway. Good for them no cardinal laws were being broken, for he would have had to lay the law down. All in all, things worked well under the "new deal." Although the first two weeks he showed love in order to pick his business back up out of the latrine, at the end of the month, not only did he come out clean, but he was also ahead, smelling fresh. His money had doubled.

The man congratulated him on his successful turnaround when he went to cop. The man smiled at him like a father watching his child get drafted into the pros would. "Vee, you accomplished something men twice, even three times, yo' age and experience in the game couldn't. You turned a dying, damn-near dead block into a boom'n hot spot. Here, roll up." He tossed him the usual fixing. "Boy, the gods really and truly smile on you!" he exclaimed. Vietnam was preoccupied with twisting up the killa to reply verbally; he smiled at the man, giving him a slight bow.

With the killa lit, he finally replied, "All I did was done what you told me to do," flattering the man.

"What's that?" he asked, already knowing the answer.

Every time Vietnam made a power move, purchasing more drugs than in his previous visit, the man always gave credit to the gods for his fortune. Vietnam's reply would be, "I just been good to the game." If not in those exact words, something to the nature of "Treat da game like it was my girlfriend." He shot out. The man, amused by his answer, erupted into laughter. His laughter made the wrinkles around his eyes more defined, revealing his aging in the game. Puffing on the chronic, Vietnam imagined himself in the man's position, lean, fit, youthful-looking, with the drug game under his thumb.

"There's one thing that concerns me," he let out, releasing a stream of weed smoke afterward. He gazed at him through the haze, his serious expression causing Vietnam to sit up erect. His wandering eyes were now unwavering, focused on him. "I see that you're getting more coke than usual and less dog food. You've been cooking it up?" he asked.

"Yeah," Vietnam replied.

"Vee, that crack game is a crazy game. It's not crazy as it's gonna get yet. I talk to my people in New York and out in Cali. They say that shit done turn da streets upside down, say dealers are killing anything that got in their way and the smokers are stealing anything they can carry," he told him. Shaking his head as if he pictured the images of the New York and Cali streets in his head. "It's gonna get da same way here also. I don't wanna lose you. Keep ya eyes peeled back. Trust no one or nothing. Ya feel me?"

Vietnam nodded.

"Real talk." His voice dropped and leveled out. "If shit gets too hectic on them streets, don't be ashamed to do the thangs normal teenagers do. I always told you how to make money. Now I'm telling you this: no amount of money is worth your breath, Vee," he seriously expressed.

There was only one time before in his short life that he had seriously thought about death, at which time he prepared himself for the possibility. All that day, the thought haunted him. He wasn't afraid to meet the grim reaper; he knew that nothing living or no one remained on earth forever. All must expire. He just didn't want to take that stroll into the afterlife before he had a chance to go inside of Karonda's body. To die a virgin was his only fear of death. He figured that the Gs that crossed over to the afterlife before him were going to drive him about not having sex the same way the ones living did. Eternity was way too long to spend with a steering wheel in your back, he reasoned.

For several mornings, Vietnam posted up on the bus, going over the lines he thought were going to get her out of her panties. When he saw her walking toward him, he'd lose all courage to even mention anything to her that would insinuate that he wanted to have sex with her. Each of those mornings, they publicly expressed their affection for each other by holding hands, embracing, and kissing. They laughed and talked, getting as many words in as they could in the small time before the bus pulled up. Then she'd hop on it, pushing out to school to get her needed education, and Vietnam would walk off to the playground to start his day, penis harder than Japanese arithmetic, wishing he had said something. That went on for quite a while, then he convinced her to come out a few minutes earlier than usual. "Why we going behind the da building?" Karonda asked curiously, mischief in her eyes, squeezing Vietnam's hand harder as he led the way. From the instant she walked out her yard, he'd been frisky with her, then he took a more serious approach, feeling all over her. His plan was to let his hands do the bidding for him. Right after he shut down the set for the night en route to his house, he detoured all through the Bricks. He crisscrossed the courtyards and breezeways until he found an empty unit he could utilize. "We not going behind no building. I got us an apartment to chill in," he replied, speeding up his pace, dragging her before she protested.

The door swung open at the slightest touch. Vietnam had kicked it loose from the structure's frame, and all gave under his running-flying jump kick. The smell of fresh paint attacked their nostrils when they entered the unit. "Sit down," he told her.

Karonda looked around for a suitable spot to place her bottom on. "I'm not sitting on that dirty floor," she cried.

A light mounted on the opposite building dimly lit the room. There was no way possible for her to actually see whether the floor was soiled or spotless. Vietnam scanned the floor also. "Man," he let out, then thought better of what he was about to say. He wanted to question her about her knowledge of the cleanliness of the unit. Like him, her anger rested on a hair-trigger; he was entirely too horny to blow his chance. An object in the corner of the room, under the window, grabbed his attention. He released her hand to investigate the object. Examining it with his feelers, he snatched it up quickly. "Here, sit on this, bae," he said in the sweetest Romeo voice, unrolling the bundle of painter's paper. Lying down next to her, he dry-humped on the side of her thigh, rubbing her stomach at the same time. She never resisted his touch or advance, nor did she assist him in unbuttoning her jeans. She lay back, returning his kiss, pulling his head, smashing his lips against hers. When he tugged at her jeans, she stopped him. "You first," she requested in an unfamiliar, husky voice. Vietnam hurriedly peeled off his jeans.

She reached out, rubbing her hand over his lap, brushing his manhood. Giggling, she snatched her hand back. Now throbbing, cheeks glued back, forming a smile, releasing his swollenness, he raised himself up, leaned over her, and commenced to pulling down her jeans. His exposed meat pistol touched her on her naked thigh right where it connected with the hipbone, causing her to flinch. Both of her hands shot up to her mouth. She tried to contain the laughter in her mouth, but it escaped through between her fingers. Scanning her body, one hand on his meat pistol, stroking it, watching her chest expand, rise, and fall, he thought, *Damn, I wish it had more light in here,* mind spinning from the excitement. He kissed her hungrily. His gentle touch became aggressive as his hand roamed her body. Karonda's body shivered at the feel of his touch. The heat from their bodies kept them warm in the chilly abandoned unit. As he climbed on top of her, his heart started to beat out of control. She stiffened underneath him, lying in between his knees. Through the predawn darkness, she stared into his face. Reaching up, she pulled him down on top of her. He stretched out on top of her, adjusting his meat pistol. It fell right in the center of her body. Through her panties he felt the heat generating from her private area. Holding her against him, engulfed in her love, he suddenly became afraid that he was going to smash her against the floor. He rose, but she held him there, preventing him from getting up. Their lips met in the empty space between them. Rolling over, he placed his hand on her vagina while he guided her hand to him. She gripped it, probed, slowly ran her hand down its length before she quickly retreated to stop his hands from venturing into her panties.

After the feeling-out process, Vietnam went with his move. Alert, he noticed how her body reacted to the different places he touched and the pressure he applied when he did so. When his hand rested on top of her female reproductive organ, she didn't remove it. As soon as he felt around, her body went rigid, then she placed her hands on his, hindering any further movement. Her legs never parted; they remained closed. The thrill of the moment started to fade, all hope of getting some slipping away. He tried everything to no avail. "Please," he whined when she stopped him in his attempt to ease her panties off. One hand on her mound, enjoying her warmth, masturbating, his head cradled in her arm, he remembered the words of his idol, Richard Pryor, striking him. His hand shot down to right where her thighs touched together an inch above her knees. Pecking on her stomach with his lips, he rubbed that spot in rapid circles. He got a reaction from her, though not the one he desired.

He kissed her stomach, and she pushed his head farther, past her belly button. The scent of her femininity got stronger and stronger as he inched his way down to where it originated from. Seriously unexplainable, her scent activated something in his brain. He became extremely excited and aroused. His mind was in a whirlwind. He lost control of himself. He didn't fight as she guided his head. Karonda had slid her panties down, stopping right below her clitoris. Down low, Vietnam continued to kiss her gently, chin resting on her panties. Giving up on rubbing her thighs, he stroke himself. The overwhelming scent of her privates, the feel of it against his lips, the way she squirmed and moaned every time his lips fell on her, the way she trembled, forcing his face into her when she did so—all this was too much for him to handle. Instincts overrode all reasons.

He knelt over her, the light of dawn filling the room, and gazed down at her slim golden-brown body, eyes roaming every inch. The moisture covering her private area glistened. Vietnam stared at her sideways-turned lips, jacking his meat pistol off like a maniac. The ordeal had beamed him to another world, where restraint was a deadly sin. Karonda watched, amazed at his self-pleasure performance. Not once did she take her lustful eyes off his hand shaking back and forward down the shaft of his meat pistol. Spaced out in another world, he squeezed and pulled until he ejaculated. His body jerked and shuddered as his bullets shot out. Never had he ever experienced such a powerful discharge before. Without any penetration, he and Karonda had made love for the first time. Vietnam took off his T-shirt, and with it he wiped himself off. Both of them were speechless. She giggled and smiled. He smiled and sighed, careful to avoid the wet, sticky spot on his T-shirt. She patted herself dry also before she got dressed. They sneaked out of the unit like two lovebirds, holding on tightly, their bodies swaying together in sync to the rhythm of beat only the two of them heard.

"I love you so much," Karonda confessed to him. The he released her grip. A car that matched the description of one filed away in his memory crept by. Vietnam focused in on it. "Bae, I said I love you!" she yelled, boarding her bus.

"I love you back!" he replied, distracted by the vehicle. Karonda's face had hardened at his dry-sounding reply. Noting it, he yelled at the top of his lungs, "I love you, Karonda!" blowing kisses at her. The bus tires hadn't made a full rotation before he turned, sprinting away toward his house. Safely behind the walls of his home, he still didn't feel comfortable until he had both his candy sticks in his mitts.

"I see ya ain't forgot nut'thang I taught ya!" a voice behind him exclaimed.

Startled, on the balls of the foot he had planted, pivoting, candy stick at the ready, he faced a bald-headed black man with a huge belly. Though his hair was gone and he had extra weight around his midsection, despite the fact that he'd been missing from the streets for many years, instantly Vietnam recognized the man that rescued him from the grips of starvation. "Monk!" he blurted out louder than he intended, unable to contain his excitement. Monk held his hand out to him. When Vietnam stuck his out to shake it, Monk pulled him in, grizzly-bear-hugging him. Vietnam was elated. He was happier that Monk was free than Monk was happy to be out. Looking down at his candy stick and bag in Vietnam's hand, Monk told him, "Go 'head an' git ya bidness right an' holla at me. I'll be over there." Nervously excited, he stashed his stuff, then rushed over to the spot where Monk was waiting. Like it was just yesterday, he sat in his favorite spot on the bench.

"Look at cha', boy. You done grow up. I damn near ain't recognize ya fat ass at first till ya mama told me you done packed on plenty of pounds," he joked. The car Vietnam thought, it was a Lincoln, same color. The tinted windows threw him off.

Glancing over at the parking lot, he realized there it was, clean and shiny, like he remembered it. "Shied, ya done put on some weight too. What happened to your hair?" Vietnam pried.

He rubbed his head. "Couldn't take care of it in the joint. I started to go bald, anyways, so I keep it clean-cut, baby," he replied by a pause. If he didn't know for certain, scoping him out—his skin complexion and his body structure resembled his—to an outsider they could pass for father and son without question.

"Seen ya da other morning. Ya was all lovey-dovey and whatnot. Dat's ya li'l girlfriend or 'nother one of ya many dames?" he asked.

"My girlfriend," Vietnam replied proudly.

Monk shook his head. "My li'l nigga," he expressed, "you done turn out all right. I was worried 'bout 'cha da whole time I was on tha walk. People coming off tha streets who knowed ya kept me up on ya. Ya mama used to shot me a kite er' now and then, telling me all tha ya been into. She worries 'bout 'cha too, son." Vietnam listened to his heartfelt revelation, astounded. Ever since he was a little boy, he knew that Monk cared about him; now he was finding out to what degree. No one ever told him the reason he had gone away. Monk ran it down to him about what caused his sudden departure. His take added sunlight to the tree of paranoia that grew in him. Monk had been released for a while; he had gotten pushed out of the brig the same day Operation Level Breach was launched. He said he had hit the tracks right when they were nabbing the cats posted up on the corner. They had stopped traffic from rolling through. He was in one of the cars in the line, awaiting instructions from the cops. When they gave him the signal to roll on, he said he hit the gas, thanking the Lord that they didn't make him pull over.

Vietnam conducted his business as usual. Under Monk's watchful eyes, he had swagger, moving with confidence as he served his customers. He and Monk hit a few blocks. Vietnam brought him up-to-date on the activities of the neighborhood. Monk congratulated him on his success in the game several times during the course of their conversations. Monk admired him the way an expensive clock builder admires his finished product. Vietnam was a product of his handiwork. Monk had landed him a gig. It didn't pay much, but he was content with it. Every evening he got off from work, he would stop by the playground and chill with Vietnam before he took it in. Just like in the old days, Vietnam would stalk the track, waiting for his car to cruise over it. He enjoyed his company, but he didn't allow himself to get attached to him. He had learned from the past that one day he might never show up. Monk was doing good, focused on doing the right thing. He was seriously taking the steps toward what they called rehabilitating himself. All that changed when the eldest of the three sisters got out of the parish prison, with jailhouse weight added to her thickness, and walked through the projects. Monk was a straight-up original gangster, but just like every other tender-dicked brother whose eyes had been treated so graciously by the sight of her, he wanted to get next to her. Peeping out how his expression changed as he watched her, Vietnam easily predicted his next move.

That night, he set aside a bundle of heroin and an ounce of coke for him. A man likes his wardrobe to be on point and his pockets fat when he's courting a woman. Monk started coming around dressed to kill instead of in his work clothes. Soon he and ole girl were inseparable; it didn't take long for him to smack her down, sewing her up tight. She started to hang out in the park with Vietnam and him. Whether or not she became dissatisfied with the money he earned on his job or he did—maybe it was that she got jealous because Vietnam was making money while Monk kept him company—no one knows. Whatever the case was, Monk came to Vietnam for some work. He popped him off with the issue he already had put to the side for him. It took a little longer than he expected, but his prediction was true. Vietnam sat on this, letting Monk pump the package he gave him. Initially, things were slow for him. It wasn't because the sales weren't coming through; he had stage fright, thinking that he was going to get busted for selling drugs. In time he got more relaxed, falling back into the groove of things. He reverted to the preincarceration Monk Vietnam had known. Things had the feel of the days in the past, but much better. Everyone was happy. Vietnam smiled more often, and not a single day passed that he loathed his existence in the game. Reason being, Monk and Karonda's mama were the best of friends. He talked her into letting Karonda come hang out with them. Although it wasn't necessary, he promised her that he wasn't going to let anything happen to her on his watch. Albeit that void in his heart had been filled by the current predicament. With the familiarity of the entire setup and electric atmosphere, some days he missed Wet Fish's and Double D's company the way he missed Monk's when he was absent. Double D was in the parish prison, housed in the infirmary, recovering from his numerous grave injuries. The chief and the other two cops really worked him over. When Vietnam inquired about his bond, he was told that he was being held without bond.

Monk turned chaos into order across the track. He structured the game to fit his calm demeanor. Karonda and Monk's woman got along like sisters. She instructed her in the ways of how a woman should treat a man, and they catered to Vietnam and Monk, keeping them fed and well hydrated while they were out making money. In a way, Karonda and Vietnam became their project. Monk had started coaching Vietnam on the finer points of pleasing a woman mentally. The couples did things that a family or couples would do. One week-end, unexpectedly, Monk instructed the crew to get in the car and relax. When the car came to its final stop, they were in the parking lot of a hotel room in Houston, Texas. That Saturday, they enjoyed the amusement park activities. Half of the day was spent at Six Flags, and the other half was spent at the museum. The museum in Houston, Texas, was one of the places Monk read about when he was in the brig. It had been on his mental for years to visit it. Sunday morning, they went to the stadium to watch the Oilers defeat the Redskins. On the way home, in the back seat, Karonda and Vietnam kissed so much that when they made it back to Baton Rouge, both of their lips were swollen from all the sucking.

Life couldn't get better for Vietnam. Things were lovely, he had his mentor back, the set was popping like bacon in a skillet, and most of all, Karonda had joined herself to his hip. The prince posted up in his slide, distributing narcotics with his princess next to him. The girls didn't carry out any business transactions, nor did they interact with the customers or other dealers, though they did protect their significant other by watching the streets, making sure five-o didn't leap down on them. Together, Monk and Vietnam converted a crim-inal enterprise into a crime family. Everyone played a role that was for the good of the others.

On top of Mount Sinai, the almighty, all-knowing Creator inscribed on two stone tablets a set of commandments that all of mankind should live by. "Thou shalt not covet" is the ninth com-mandment of the ten. *Covetousness* means to desire enviously what belongs to another. The Creator, being all-knowing, knew that once a man developed a longing in their heart for what another man pos-sesses, it opens up the door for evil to enter his heart. Once evil is summoned, the outcome is always detrimental to someone.

Christmas was truly a glorious event, one that Vietnam would always remember. Monk prepared a feast at his woman's residence, and he invited everyone to join them. All that came were greeted at the door by Monk wearing a Santa suit and his woman dressed like

Santa's naughty mistress. In their hands were some sort of gift to give to those who chose to spend the day of giving with them. Things couldn't get more perfect than it was. Although Karonda didn't stay long, she stayed long enough to nibble on a plate of food, dance with Vietnam, and wish everyone happy holidays. When she left, Vietnam didn't have time to miss her presence. After he walked her out, Monk's woman's youngest sister pulled him to the side before he made it back through the crowd to his seat.

Not much of a dancer, he rolled and ground with her as best as he could. The song ended, and she took him by the hand, pulling him toward a space on the sofa big enough for one person to sit. Pushing him down, she slapped her nice, firm round booty on his lap. She wiggled until she found a comfortable spot, which happened to be right on his erect meat pistol. Vietnam tried to converse, but she let it be known that she didn't want to steal him away from the party to chitchat. "Take ya pants off. Let me see dat dick," she commanded, jerking at his belt buckle. Vietnam couldn't believe what was happening. She had her hand on his meat pistol, pulling it out before he even pulled his pants off his waist. Releasing him, she started to undress. Staring at her chocolate body, breast spilling out of her brassiere, her flat belly, and a knot in her panties that looked like a wad of money, he forgot that caramel and lemon drop were his favorite flavors. "Come sit down on tha bed, baby," she barked. "Act'n all shy an' shit," she added. Vietnam happily complied. Unhooking her brassiere, cupping one of her breast, leaning over, she aimed it straight at his mouth. "Suck it," she said. Like an obedient child, he opened his mouth wide. "Do it soft," she purred. Vietnam was pulling on them like an infant trying to get milk out of it.

By the time she rotated, placing the other breast in his accepting mouth, he knew how to do it the way she liked. While he sucked her, she had placed his hand on her vagina. Unlike Karonda, she let him explore every inch of her treasure with his finger. In the room with her was one of the few times he completely zoned out. Though he was mesmerized past the point of being conscious, all his senses were tentatively aware of what was going on. Finger buried deep inside of her, he tried to visualize what his finger was feeling. The more he thought, the stiffer his meat pistol became. Taking her breast out of his mouth, she shoved him hard against the bed, her eyes falling on his manhood standing stiff and tall like the Washington Monument. He gasped when she untangled her pants from around her ankles and inched toward him. *Yes,* he thought. His meat pistol started to throb. Gripping it, he began to stroke and choke it. "Stop dat shit. Move. I got this!" she shouted, slapping his hand away. Taking over where he left off at, she asked, "Like dat?" gazing into his eyes. "Um-huh," he moaned, producing a chuckle from her. "Boy, ya know I been wantin' you," she confessed, stroking him harder and faster. "I like you."

"Shied, I like you too," Vietnam lied. Up until then, she had never crossed his mind. Now she was all he could think of. When she received him in her mouth, a surge of electricity raced through his body. *Unbelievable!* was the only thing that came to his mind.

"Do you really?" in between slurps and sucks, she asked.

"Yes, umm…I really do," Vietnam stammered out.

"Do you really, huh, boo, do you?" she repeated as she slowly slobbered on his barrel. It was the first time he had fellatio performed on him. It felt so wonderful that he wanted it to last forever, but his body said otherwise. "How much ya like me?" she asked, jerking him off. Overindulged in the moment, Vietnam didn't really reply. She placed her mouth over his penis until only a quarter of an inch of it remained visible. No longer able to hold back, he let go, ejaculating in her mouth.

The girl was destined to make a million with her mouth if she chose the other sister's profession. To his surprise, she didn't remove her mouth from his penis until the convulsions stopped. "I love you!" Vietnam solemnly expressed, paralyzed from the neck down.

Cracking up at his retort, she said, "Already? My head game must be fire. Wait till I give ya some of this good ol' pussy." She then put her clothes back on, shaking her head.

Downstairs, they carried on as before, but Vietnam's mind kept reverting to upstairs. The tingling in his privates acted as a remainder. Dizzy from the sexual experience and a combination of weed and wine, he stepped outside to get a breath of fresh air. Monk was on his trail. He exited the party. "How you like ya gift?" Monk asked,

"It's tight," Vietnam responded, rolling the rope chain draped around his neck between his finger. Vietnam had a four-finger gold ring with "Monk" spelled in it made; that was his gift to him for Christmas. Before he could ask how he liked his gift, Monk inquired with a sly grin, "How ya feel?"

Unconsciously, he cupped his johnson. "I'm good" he replied.

"Right, right," Monk repeated with a smile as they conversed, nodding.

Vietnam had a premonition that he was dancing around the intended subject. No way the host of the liveliest party of the year ducked off to rap about trivial things. He was right; Monk informed him that he planned on jumping into the run-hard game because the cocaine and heroin moved slower.

They had discussed it before, but he wasn't certain. He merely made a reference, hinting that he was interested in pushing rock cocaine. Vietnam tried to explain to him that dealing run-hards involved playing under a set of rules that he wasn't used to playing under. Stuck in his ways, neither was he going to be apt to following those guidelines. The smokers were super conniving, and the other dealers constantly wanted to gain new grounds in that game by any slimy or underhanded means. Both of which were the type of conducts he didn't have the temperament to tolerate. Vietnam painted all types of pictures, downsizing the run-hard cocaine game and showing him the perils of it. Adamant, he stuck to his decision to make the switch. "If you can do it, so can I," he stated, ending the conversation. The night was too lovely a night to be ruined. Vietnam pushed the conversation out of his head. He made it his duty to enjoy himself at the party to the full extent. Foresight, he knew that once the sun rose, happy days and nights were going to be galaxies away.

When the records stopped spinning and all the partygoers shook the spot, Vietnam still remained, sitting on the couch, exhausted, relishing the entire night. The chocolate girl joined him, and they fell asleep in each other's embrace. Monk had seniority of Vietnam in the game and in their loosely knit organization, but Vietnam had the connect on the raw, which Monk had to get from him to stay a factor on the set. And he had a flawless cook game.

Most dealers around the way weren't dropping their work in a jar; they were letting the smokers cook it up for them on big spoons, which was more time-consuming and drug-consuming. Also, doing it that way, there was little discreetness—the smell was so strong everyone who came to the spot knew that someone was in the kitchen, cooking cocaine. Learning how to turn coke into run-hard wasn't going to be a problem for Monk, Vietnam figured that much; finding some stuff as good as his was going to prove the problem for him. So he decided not to sell him any more crack cocaine. In his adolescent mind was the thought that was going to make Monk hopefully see it his way.

Vietnam had gotten used to having his once-father-figure back in his life. He enjoyed all the penitentiary stories he told when he went down memory lane. He never failed to put him on game about the things he missed or he did or said that weren't becoming of a G. Vietnam welcomed his correction; it was only going to make him better and a bigger name for himself. The growth in him was noticeable by everyone. Even the man, when he only saw him when it came time to re-up, mentioned the change that he was seeing in him. Vietnam loved him back then, and he loved him now. Like the man told him, he didn't want to lose him, so he figured, if he kept him away from the crazies, he could keep him free. Monk had a violent temper. He had a ten-below-zero tolerance for anything he deemed as disrespect to him or his hustle; therefore, Vietnam handled the run-hard smokers, the really strung out ones with ease. He found most of them amusing, reminding him of his buddy Double D.

No man can stop the real from doing what he wants or stop a true hustler for finding a way to hustle. Vietnam stalled Monk out so long that he made a move that, nearsighted or foresighted, he never would have seen coming. Monk made plans to meet with another connect that supplied cocaine already cooked up at a cheaper price, depending on the amount he copped. He wanted him with him when the deal went down. "Go with him," the voice whispered in his ear. He debated, feeling let down. "Nah!" Quickly changing his mind, he said, "Bet," agreeing to accompany him. Two hours before they were scheduled to meet up with the new connect, Karonda pestered him about purchasing her a Fila track outfit to match the one he had on. Finally, he gave in; he was going to get Monk's woman to run them to the shopping center on LSU Campus in his car so that he could get there and back in time to handle business. Karonda insisted on them walking. The walk was therapeutically relaxing. Karonda clung on to his arm. Every few steps, they stopped and lip-locked, swapping spit like madly in love couples do strolling through the park. Somewhere in the store or during the walk, he lost track of time. Noticing he was a few minutes late for the meeting, obligated and bonded to business, he broke out in a jog, urging Karonda along with him. He was on Wyoming Street when he glanced at his watch; therefore, it wouldn't take long for him to make it over the railroad tracks. It had been lined up to meet at G-work's house; his house was the first house on West Roosevelt Street coming over the railroad track.

Stopping in front of it, he told Karonda, "I gotta go in here right fast."

Blucka! A muffled shot rang out before she could reply. Wide-eyed, they looked at each other, then around. The shot was muffled, making it difficult to pin down its location. G-work's front door swung open. Monk came sprinting out of it. *Blucka blucka!* The man chasing him out of the house let off two more rounds. Vietnam pushed Karonda down, falling over her. They were directly in the line of fire. *Blucka!* The so-called connect, who in fact was a cat that robbed drug dealers, squeezed off another round. Warrior to the death, Monk managed to draw his candy stick, turning to face him. *Blucka blucka!* Two death enforcers struck him in the chest. The impact rocked him backward, and falling to the ground *boom, boom, boom!* His pocket cannon went loose, sending a lot of hot missiles into his killer's belly. Clutching his stomach, the jacker fled across the track, never to be seen again.

The paramedics did their best to prevent his untimely demise, but Monk was pronounced dead on the scene. Onlookers gathered on the street to get their last look at the fallen soldier outside a casket. Monk's woman went so hysterical when she saw him stretched out, face toward the heavens, eyes closed, covered in blood, that the medics had to sedate her. Tears from Karonda's eyes stained the front of Vietnam's T-shirt. Face buried in his chest, her body trembling as she let out heart-wrenching sobs. To lose someone to death is a painful experience; to watch that someone get murdered in the streets is devastating. Eyes blurry, Vietnam gazed into his mama's face over Karonda's head. She placed her arms around the both of them, one around Karonda, the other around him.

Sympathetic but always strong, not the one to show emotions, his mama whispered to him gently, "Don't cry, baby," affectionately rubbing her man-child's back.

The End

Epilogue

FOLLOWING THE DEATH of Monk, Vietnam started making irrational decisions like it was the proper thing to do. Shedding anything that resembled discipline, he started wilding out. Life or living carried a new meaning. "Make money, get high, and destroy other people's lives" became his motto. He tied up with a newly formed group in the neighborhood that called themselves the Spare None Committee. Causing havoc on the streets was their sole purpose for excitement. Vietnam shut down shop in the beloved playground, opening it up on the corner of West Roosevelt and Wyoming Street, where the clique hung out at. Magic was one of the cofounders. Plus, half of the members were distant cousins. So he fit right in. Worry-free, stress-free, and carefree, he ran the streets, doing whatever came to his mind. Not thinking was the reason troubles enemies wouldn't wish on enemies came his way. One of the homies had a caper he wanted to hit, but he didn't have a candy stick to pull it off with. The mission went south, and he got nabbed with the candy stick Vietnam lent him. The detective, with his relentless crusade for justice, pressured G-Child until he told him how he came in possession of a police-issued handgun. The fire was turned on. Detective Seymore Ballsaks didn't have probable cause to arrest Vietnam, but he sweated him every chance he got. It became a game to him and the rest of the young guns on the block to bail out when they spotted one time creeping up. Vietnam got sloppy. His attitude got the best of him. Blinded by rage, he stabbed a man twice in the chest for trying to run a Murphy on him for a few crumbs of run hard. Sergeant Lic Johnson was an eyewitness to the crime. He gave chase, but Vietnam got away after a short foot pursuit through shortcuts Sergeant Lic Johnson had no idea existed. Automatically, a warrant was issued for his arrest. Detective Seymore Ballsaks was elated, but he continued to build his case. A search warrant was issued for his residence. He was nowhere to be found, but the cops did come out with a .45-caliber handgun, which was the break the authorities had been seeking after so diligently.

An all-out manhunt ensued. Though he was still a juvenile, they plastered his face over all the news networks. With the heat on, he hid out in plain sight, regulating more so since he knew his days were numbered. Vietnam was on some real outlaw shit. Strangely, he took a liking to living on the run. But all good things must come to an end. Not that he gave a damn, Vietnam stayed too high off that genie to take in and analyze his surroundings while he was out. Thugging, making a name for himself among the legends of Baton Rouge. His mama was at home, searching for salvation. Though she was still pushing packages of cocaine and heroin, she was becoming closer to the Creator and steadily making preparations to walk away from the game. At night, when he was out doing God knows what under the cover of darkness, his mama was studying for her GED test. Praying and reading her Bible was her new way of life. Vietnam never noticed the change in her personality or her figure. His mama had conceived a set of twins. Vietnam was her only man-child and the love of her life, but she couldn't accept his evil ways. Selling drugs, getting high, and running the streets were understood; she had done the same in her youth and prime. But killing humans for no reason, she couldn't go for that. Vietnam never asked, nor did he hold it against her. His mama was his first love, but he often wondered, Was it her conscience bothering her when she accepted Jesus Christ as her Savior, or was it the thought of the cops killing him if they ran across him that made her set him up?

His mama got word to him that she really needed to see him. Like any other son, when his mama called, he came running. Hidden in the back room was Detective Seymore Ballsaks and a few more other officers, waiting to arrest him. Vietnam surrendered without a fight. He and his mama cried together. Vietnam was thirteen years of age at the time of his arrest. Louisiana legislators months prior, due to the increase of serious crimes being committed by juvenile offenders, passed a law that gave courts the right to try persons aged thirteen through sixteen who violated one or more selected list of the Louisiana revised statutes. First- and second-degree murder was one of the said offenses that could be tried and sentenced under the same guidelines as true adult offenders. Vietnam was arrested and charged with two counts of second-degree murder for the killing of Big Ed and the dude he stabbed, and one count of first-degree murder of a police officer, even though Officer Dicken DaBeaudé was off duty. Forensic evidence played an important role in obtaining a conviction for that charge; not to mention they retrieved the murder weapon of the officer along with the fallen officer's service weapon. A guilty verdict was read. For the stabbing death of the dude on the block, the testimony of Sergeant Lic Johnson was what nailed him to the cross, then put the nail in the coffin for that conviction. Not guilty was the verdict for the slaying of Big Ed due to the lack of evidence, which saved him from another murder conviction.

"The sentence I impose on you are in accordance with the laws of the state of Louisiana. By the power vested in me, Vietnam G. Franklin, as of count one, first-degree murder of a police officer, I sentence you to life in prison with the possibility of parole. Count two, second-degree murder, I sentence you to life in prison with the possibility of parole. Both sentences are to run concurrent with each other. Upon your twenty-first birthday, you will be eligible to go before the parole board. If you fail to meet the criteria of the parole board, thus getting denied parole, five years from the date of your appearance, you will be eligible to go before the board a second time. If then you also don't make parole, again five years from that day you will be eligible to go before the board a third time. If you so happen to get denied a third time, your next parole eligibility with be twenty-five years from that date," Judge Flip-One pronounced. With that said, Vietnam was shown out of the courtroom to begin his life sentence.

"Thug till I die!" he yelled on his way out.

Vietnam now resides at Louisiana State Penitentiary, in Angola, Louisiana, Camp D, Falcon Dorm. On any given day, you can find him on the big yard, pumping iron, trading war stories, but mostly he'll be out collecting his fettiluchi from the homosexuals that choose the pimple-faced killer for their pimp, and gathering the rest of his bread from the cats on the walk he got pushing packs for him. Like they say, "Da game doesn't stop 'cause a G got popped."

If you know deep down in your heart that the life or the game ain't for you, if you are already in it, get out while you can. If you are thinking about getting in it, don't. To the ones that are ten toes deep in the life or in the game, get money, my brothers and sisters. You'll figure out what to do when the time comes. Gs up, the fake I must respectfully demand that y'all please stand down. Much love from me to the real!

About the Author

CHARLIE T. SMITH is a native of Baton Rouge, Louisiana. Growing up, he was faced with the realities of the conditions and decisions those living in a hopeless environment—namely, the streets—have to make daily. Lured by the illusions of the street game and the limited option of the less fortunate, he chose to live the life of crime. Incarcerated at the age of fourteen, housed at the Swanson Correctional Center for the Youth in Monroe, Louisiana, known as the Baby Louisiana State Penitentiary, he returned to society at the age of twenty-one. As an adult faced with the same conditions and decisions to make in his youth, he chose the streets. After several more years of incarceration during the course of his adulthood, true to the street life, he decided to continue to live the street life through the vivid description of the lives of the characters of this novel and of those forthcoming.

CPSIA information can be obtained
at www.ICGtesting.com
Printed in the USA
LVHW041029171120
671900LV00003B/128